No Man's Chattel

An Arkansas Family's Struggle through Reconstruction

Written by

Patricia Clark Blake

SCOTCHWOOD HILL

Under Supervision of Scotchwood Hill Publishing Service

Published by: Patricia Clark Blake

supervised by Scotchwood Hill Publishing Service
3101 Scotchwood Drive
Jonesboro, Arkansas 72405

Original Cover Art: Sherrill Rodgers
Cover Design: Martha Rodriguez
IT Consultant: Noah Gregory

Scripture Quotations: KJV, copyright
1850.
1611 KJV.Com

Copyright: ©April 2024.

Printed in the United States of America.

No Man's Chattel: An Arkansas Family's
Struggle through Reconstruction

ISBN: 978-0-9998416-4-8
LCCN: 2024906813

Dedication

I dedicate this book to
Tara Katherine Gatewood
My beloved daughter…
The best gift I have given to the
world.

My endless gratitude goes to
God, Jesus, and the Holy Spirit
Whose gifts and grace
created whatever value
you find on these pages.

Acknowledgement

Writing historical fiction doesn't happen in a vacuum. Many people have helped me during the two years I have worked to finish No Man's Chattel. First and foremost is my family. I am blessed with an extraordinary daughter, a wonderful son-in-law, and three precious grandchildren, Kennedy, Noah, and Jake. And I hail from the Clark Clan. I couldn't have better support!

Writer's Ink of Northeast Arkansas, a group of serious writers, makes it a necessity to keep at the task of writing. I'd never have finished the book without their support.

I am grateful to the staff of the Butler Center of the Little Rock Public Library. Their conscientious efforts to preserve historical records for the state of Arkansas have resulted in an invaluable resource for anyone who researches the history of our state. My books are more accurate because I have had access to those records.

I owe a huge debt of gratitude to Sherrill Rodgers, my sister in Christ from First Methodist Church in Jonesboro, who created a beautiful oil painting of the opening scene of my novel. She was attentive to details and the atmosphere I wanted to create. As a result, No Man's Chattel has the most strikingly beautiful cover of all my books. I couldn't be more pleased with this visual portrayal of my words.

I also want to express my gratitude to Noah Gregory, the IT Tech, at First Church, who was able to convert the oil painting into a digital copy so that the artwork could become my cover. How blessed I am to know this wonderful young person with a heart for Christ and a brain for technology!

Last, but certainly not least, I need to acknowledge the excellent beta readers who pour over my manuscript and make suggestions to improve what I have written. I have been blessed because these ladies have been with me since I started writing in 2012. They are my beta angels.

Brenda Davis Thakkar , friends since high school, was the smartest person in our class then, and her intelligence and dedication to the task have benefited me as a writer more than she knows.

Beverly Thompson was my colleague at Westside High School. She taught English and history. My friend is an avid reader. I count on Beverly to be bluntly honest with me and point out weaknesses that I have overlooked. Her critiques have always made my books better.

Debbie Archer is one of my writer pals. Her unique talent as a beta reader is pointing out all those quirky sentences that writers think are so wonderful, but readers scratch their heads over. And she does it with so much humor that I don't even get my feelings hurt!

Martha Rodriguez is one of my two bff's. We talk the same language about our passion. She encourages me to write when I don't want to and puts me to shame when I compare my productivity to hers. I would have shelved No Man's Chattel months ago, but she wouldn't let me.

Finally, I owe a great deal to **Barbara Barbre** from my writer's group who gave my story it's final go over to give it the polish and accuracy it deserves. Barb is a wonderful friend and editor.

The Clan Kincaid

Parish of Campise, Stirlingshire, Scotland

Sean Hugh Kincaid & Mary Erin McRyan

b 1760 Scotland   b 1765 Scotland

Rory, Hugh, Ava, Maisie, Kell, Ryan, Grace

Rory Kincaid & Fiona Bruce

Sean, Ava, Maisie, Kell, Ryan, Grace

Hugh Kincaid & Patsy Ferguson

Scotland b 1791, d 1864   Virginia b 1794, d 1836

Naomi Kincaid

Naomi Kincaid & Benjamin Murphy

Arkansas b 1815   Maryland b 1810

Richard Hugh Murphy

b Maryland 1839

d Tennessee 1862

Benjamin (Sonny) Murphy

b Maryland 1849

Richard Murphy & Hannah Kennedy

b Maryland 1839   b Maryland 1843

d Tennessee 1862   m Maryland 1862

Benjamin (Sonny) Murphy & Molly Tangent

b Maryland 1849   b Arkansas 1851

m Arkansas 1867

Naomi (Nomie)

b Arkansas 1867

Benjamin Hugh (Benji)

b Arkansas 1868

Kell Kincaid &   Hannah Murphy

b Scotland 1837   b Maryland, 1843

m Arkansas 1869

The Kincaids
from the Quarters
St. Francis County, Arkansas

Rebecca [Mom Bec] & Gabriel Kincaid
d Arkansas 1848

Tobias, Hephzibah [Rose], Obediah,

Tabitha, ,Samson

Rose Kincaid & Thomas Kincaid
d 1860

Lucas, Elijah [Lijah], Patsy [Shataka],

Ezekiel [Zeke]

Lucas Kincaid & Gracie Kincaid
d 1865

Jonathan

David

Shataka & Marcus Kincaid
Abraham b 1861, d 1868

Glory b 1863

Moses Freeman b 1868

Elijah & Dorrie Kincaid
Samuel b 1859

Ruthie b 1868, d 1868

Chapter 1

*And Ruth said, "Entreat me not to leave thee or to turn from
following after thee: for whither thou goest, I will go, and where thou
lodgest, I will lodge, thy people shall be my people,
And thy God, my God:"*
Ruth 1:16

Hannah Ruth Murphy dropped to her knees to catch her mother-in-law as the older woman's strength failed her. Naomi Murphy gasped, and tears streamed down her ashen cheeks at the sight of her childhood home. The once graceful, safe refuge lay in ruins. Three years of neglect and the occupation of the house by both armies during the recently concluded rebellion had left the once elegant manor a mockery of the home the widow remembered.

"Hannah, we can't live here!" The slight woman dressed in widow's weed dropped to sit on what had once been the cobbled entryway to Sanctuary Hill. "It's impossible. We can't live in this hovel."

"We don't have a choice, Mother Naomi. It's all we have left."

"No. I won't stay here. I thought I was bringing you and Sonny to a better life, back to Sanctuary Hill. How could Papa have allowed our home to…." Sobs ended her tirade.

Hannah leaned over to help her mother-in-law to her feet and then laid her hand on the shoulder of the tall, quiet man-child with tears in his eyes. "It'll be okay, Sonny. Don't fret now. Pick up your mama's portmanteau, and let's go see if we can make us some kind of shelter before night falls."

"Hannah, why is my mama cryin'?" the lanky seventeen-year-old asked.

"She's sad to see her girlhood home in such a poor state, but she'll be all right once she has time to rest. Now come on and help me get her inside."

Hannah led them to the front porch. With her foot, she pushed her way through a tangle of wisteria vines, morning glories gone amok, and a variety of Arkansas weeds. Ivy ran up the eight pillars of the porch and hung from the eaves of the west side of the house. The dense foliage created an eerie grotto where rays of green light slanted through. A swing hung from one end. As the wind gusted, the low end scraped the floorboards below. The tired, younger woman, also dressed in black, shook her head in sheer defeat.

A heavy, gray cypress door barred her entry into the dilapidated structure she'd hoped to make a home. She pushed her shoulder against the door to no avail. "Sonny, please come over here and help me open this door." The rust broke loose, as the strong boy forced the door open. The wood creaked and the hinges moaned. The inside was no better than what they'd seen from the drive. Broken furniture was the least of the problems. Panes of glass from the many windows lay in shards on the floor, crunching underfoot as they entered the room. Dust covered the debris. What appeared to be smoke stains darkened the once beautiful wallpaper. Hannah cringed each time a string of cobwebs wrapped around her face, and they hung from every casement and opening they passed through. As bad as that was, the acrid bite of smoke and decay was worse. The foul stench brought on a racking coughing spell, and Naomi began to gasp, hardly able to catch a breath.

"Hannah, I can't breathe in here. Sonny, take me back outside."

2

"No, Mother Naomi. Please sit down and try to control yourself. We have to make this place a shelter for the time being. The downstairs seems to be intact. At least the walls are standing. I know it's not what you expected to find, but Sanctuary Hill belongs to you and Sonny." Naomi fell against Hannah again. "Sonny, get your mother that chair from near the fireplace, and let her sit down while I look upstairs."

Naomi screamed through her tears. "Hannah Ruth, I said I won't stay here."

Hannah knelt before her mother-in-law. "We have no other recourse. We have only this plantation, this farm, left. We will make do. I promised Father Murphy the day he died that I would bring you home to Arkansas, and I would make sure you and Sonny are safe. For now, sit and rest. Sonny will be at your side if you need anything. And Sonny, please open all the doors and whatever windows are left so the room can air out."

Hannah walked through the four rooms on the ground floor and found few things of use. In each room, she found once-fine furniture mutilated beyond use, smashed globes from once beautifully hand-painted porcelain lamps, and glass panes lying in shards on the floor.

Then she climbed to the second floor. The stairs were solid, and only three spindles had been broken from the banister. But when she reached the second-floor landing, she saw the azure Arkansas sky above scorched walls. Two rooms on the north end of the house were roofless. Somehow the rooms on the south wing of the house had not suffered the same fate. When she opened those doors, both bedrooms were sound, not a window glass was broken. Was this an omen? Could she care for her genteel fifty-five year old mother-in-law and the child-like seventeen-year-old brother of her late husband in this place?

The letter she'd stowed in her reticule had not led her to believe she would find Sanctuary Hill in this condition. When her mother-in-law showed it to her, they'd hoped the inheritance from Naomi's father would be the answer to their financial problems. After the estates of her late husband Richard and his father Benjamin, Sr. had been settled, so little remained that Hannah knew they could not stay in Washington where they had lived during the War Between the States. Lawyers in Washington sold both houses to pay debts from poor investments and Richard's gambling losses.

The remaining money barely covered the cost of train fares to Arkansas. They had left Washington just under a week ago with two golden eagles, sixty-six dollars, and three tickets to Madison, Arkansas. Since they'd arrived, Hannah had traded one of the golden eagles for the old nag of a horse that Sonny claimed as his own and a tiny wagon. She had purchased what food she knew they must have for a couple of weeks. When she'd counted her funds, she found she had $33.75 and one golden eagle left to live on until—she didn't know how long she would have to make do.

Regardless, she would know better next week when she met with Hugh Kincaid's attorney in Madison. Mr. Oldham, the local attorney, had written in his letter that he'd complete his disclosure of the late Hugh Kincaid's estate when they met in person. Hope was not dead. Some assets surely remained to provide for them. She couldn't think about that now. The sun would be setting, and she had yet to find anything to provide bedding for the night.

She pushed open the door farthest from the staircase. This room was a total loss. Entry into the second room was more of a problem as most of the roof had fallen into this bedroom. Hannah did find a small table and a crystal bedside lantern next to a burned-out mattress. She carried the lantern and table to the hall.

As she walked to the other side of the landing, she heard her mother-in-law crying, begging Sonny to take her back to their wagon.

Perhaps Naomi is right. I may be foolish to believe I can make this derelict into a livable place for us. Hannah shook her head, and she rubbed a tear from her face. *I must be mad to think I can take care of Naomi and Sonny. I don't even know if I can take care of myself.*

Nevertheless, she pushed on the first door on the west side of the landing. It wouldn't budge. The locked door demanded a key or Sonny's broad shoulder. In the final room, she found a bedstead, which someone mutilated with an ax, but among the broken remnants, she found a decent, if somewhat dirty mattress. Thankfully, Naomi wouldn't have to sleep on the floor that night. She also found a small chair that had once sat in front of a vanity in the room. Hannah glimpsed fragments of her disheveled appearance in mirror shards scattered across the floor. *That's how my whole world feels right now.*

She ran to the head of the landing and called down, "Please come up, Sonny, and help me bring down some things that I've found up here." As she waited for him to climb up to her, she pulled open the last door on that floor. This shallow room held the linen press for the house. The four bottom shelves were empty, but she found sheets, pillows, and even a few blankets on the two uppermost shelves. A closer look showed her they were the "old linens"—some needed hems repaired or a patch added. One of the pillows certainly needed more feathers. Hannah was delighted anyway.

"Whatcha want, Hannah?"

"Sonny, see if you can push open that door." She pointed to the one immediately at the head of the stairs. Sonny rammed his shoulder into it, and the door opened. This last room seemed to have missed the smoke damage the rest of the house had experienced. The ladylike bedroom was untouched except for a hint of soot next to the ceiling. A tall, carved mahogany, four-poster bed sat against the far wall between two windows still dressed with lace curtains. An embroidered coverlet

5

of pink roses and green vines covered the mattress and featherbed as if waiting for the lady of the house to come up for the night. Except for the topmost, the linens on the bed were clean and ready to use. Near one window, a small blue satin settee and a matching chair sat on either side of a small table holding a hand-painted porcelain lantern, half-filled with kerosene. The final piece of furniture was a vanity table with an attached mirror and a needlepoint-covered stool. Hannah thought how strange it was to find this one untouched room in the house.

"Hannah, what are you doin' up there?" Naomi's voice had taken on an unstable tone. "Come down here. I want to talk to you." Hannah knew her mother-in-law was about to have one of her spells.

"I'm coming, Mother Naomi." She motioned for Sonny to bring down the end table and some of the bedding she'd found. She picked up the two lanterns and returned to the room that would become their parlor in time. "Look, I've found lanterns, some bedding, a couple of mattresses, and a piece or two of furniture we can use. And there are two more rooms upstairs we can use now."

"Just leave that pitiful stuff. It's not enough to bother with. Surely, you don't think we can live here. It's impossible."

"You don't seem to understand, Mother Naomi. Father Murphy wanted you to come back to Arkansas, and I promised to bring you home. We don't have the means to go anywhere else." Hannah picked up her reticule and pulled out her money pouch. "This is all the funds we have left. Do you see? It amounts to about thirty-three dollars and some odd change."

Again, Naomi cried, "You're being unreasonable, Hannah. If you were going to be so mean-spirited, why did you come here?"

"I'm sorry you think I'm cruel. I am trying to do what I think is best for us. I don't want to argue with you."

"Sonny, take me to the wagon. We'll go back to Madison. Hannah can stay here if she wants. No lady can live in this filth!"

"No, Sonny, I need you to come with me. We have work to do." Hannah turned her back and left her mother-in-law standing in the middle of the front room. She knew Naomi would be all right when she began to argue back.

Outside, Sonny took the reins of the horse that remained hitched to the small wagon. The old horse they'd gotten for a pittance was well past his prime, as was the rickety wagon, but both had served them well. They walked together, Sonny leading the horse around the corner of the house. Then, she saw where the damage to the house had come from. The detached kitchen had burned to the ground, and only a large stone fireplace and chimney remained. A woodfire cookstove made of cast iron stood inside the fireplace. The stove had received only minor damage because it was located within the recess of the stonework. They would salvage the stove to prepare meals and heat the house when cold weather came.

Just as Hannah thought of the good luck they'd stumbled upon, Sonny broke her reverie. "Hannah, what are we gonna do? It's bad here at Grandpa's place. Mama always told me her papa had lots of money."

"Sonny, right now, no one has lots of money. The war took so much of what we all had. That terrible four-year struggle took our money, property, and even our menfolk. All our friends who were comfortable before the war are just like we are now. We are land poor, but at least we still have our land. We will learn to make a living on it somehow."

"Are we gonna be farmers?"

"Seems that we are. But we will be all right. We just need to get through each day as it comes. Today, we have shelter."

"But this house ain't no good, 'cause we ain't even got no beds."

"Well, we can make one for your mama, and we have blankets. That's enough for today."

A short distance from the burned-out kitchen, sitting near a neglected peach orchard, they came upon a shed with a lean-to. Stacked against the wall, they found half a rick of firewood. "Ya want me to grab some of this wood and kindlin' for a fire?" Hannah nodded.

"But first, Sonny, let's put the horse in the shed for tonight. He'll be safe there. Tomorrow, we'll find him someplace to graze. Do you think you can find him some water?"

"Yeah, I saw a well. Ya know, he's been a mighty good horse for us. I'm callin' him 'Pal.' Do ya think that's a good horse name?"

"Yes. It's a fine name for a horse. Walk him into the shed and take his harness off so he can rest. Let's push the wagon under the lean-to once we take our things inside. Hurry now because we have a lot of work to do before it gets too dark to see."

They returned to find Naomi asleep in the sole chair they'd found downstairs. With Sonny's help, Hannah disassembled the four-poster bed from upstairs and brought it and the bedding down to what had once been the informal parlor of the old manor house. This room would become Naomi's room. Another mattress laid at the foot of Naomi's bed provided a place for Sonny to sleep. By the time they had brought the vanity, mirror, and small bedside table down and made the bed with the freshly aired and beaten linens from the bed, the room looked almost pleasant. They carried the small settee and matching chair down to the front room. When they had time to wipe away the dirt and clear the cobwebs, they would have some semblance of a front parlor. For now, she would make herself a pallet in the front room near the fireplace, using a sole featherbed and a couple of worn blankets. She woke Naomi, and together with Sonny, Hannah prepared a simple supper of fruit, cheese, and bread. For that night,, they had a place to sleep. As she had told Sonny, they'd survived the first day, and they would deal with tomorrow when it came.

φ

Bone-weary, Hannah sank onto the featherbed pallet. She wanted to sleep into oblivion. Regardless of her fatigue and the number of weeks of uncertainty and disappointment, sleep evaded her. She had made those promises to her father-in-law the day he succumbed to pneumonia after receiving a chest wound at the battle near Petersburg. He'd been transported to Washington with other wounded union officers—brought home to die. After the death of her husband at the battle of Shiloh in April of 1862, her father-in-law turned to Hannah to see to the welfare of the family he'd moved to Washington to shelter from the war. That promise was the key factor that brought her to Arkansas in the spring of 1866. These memories denied her the rest she craved.

She beat against the wimpy pillow she'd brought from the linen press. The feather bed did little to soften the cypress floorboards beneath her. *Go to sleep, Hannah. You've got a thousand things to do tomorrow.* She closed her eyes once more, only to have a myriad of questions plague her. *Why didn't I remain in Washington? Couldn't I have found work there? What made me come to this place? Wasn't Maryland my home? Arkansas is a frontier compared to the place where I grew up. What horrible thing did I do in my life to deserve the life sentence I've been given?* She sat straight up and clenched her teeth. Under her breath, she spoke aloud, "Stop it! Deal with one day at a time. Stop feeling sorry for yourself and go to sleep. You're no worse off than hundreds of other women widowed by the war." Hannah once again pulled herself under her blanket and tried to sleep.

Sun shining through the broken window awakened her the following morning. She felt she'd just fallen asleep—perhaps she had. She pushed herself up, feeling sore and battered across the entire length of her body. She managed to get to her feet. She pulled on a simple calico skirt and white lawn blouse to replace the travel suit she'd worn the day before. The demands of this day would require the coolest, most serviceable clothes she owned. She also eliminated most of her socially expected undergarments. Corsets, crinolines, and hoops would not help her make this place a livable house. A simple chemise and her pantalets would serve. Naomi didn't need to know.

She went to the room that had once been Hugh Kincaid's study. Bookcases lined the back wall of the room, and the entire east wall was built of the same kind of stone as the fireplaces and chimneys. Every piece of furniture in the room lay in pieces. A large desk and two chairs with legs broken off lay in the corner beneath the bookshelves. The once beautiful leather upholstery had been slashed. Some barbarians had ripped covers from the books. Only those on the top two shelves remained. Places family portraits had once hung showed clearly on the smoked-stained walls. A single painting of a beautiful woman dressed in clothes from the early 1800s hung across from the bookcases. Hannah would ask Naomi who she was.

She pulled pieces from the debris pile and separated the few things she could salvage. When she'd made enough room, she and Sonny would carry the cast iron cookstove to this space next to the stone wall. They would concoct some kind of table and find three chairs. This room would be her priority for the day. Hannah knew she could make the family kitchen and dining room a reality before the day was over.

On day two, she'd clean first and create a way to prepare simple meals. Yes, she could do that.

With a broom she found near the back door, she returned to the front room to clear the area near the hearth. She built a small fire on the hearth and prepared a modest breakfast. She cut slices of bread they'd brought from Madison and toasted it in a cast-iron skillet. She slathered it with jelly from their meager supply box and stirred a pot of oatmeal. By the time Sonny and Naomi joined her, she was ready to make a table.

"Sonny, can you drag that old desk from the back corner so we can eat our breakfast? It doesn't have any legs. We'll sit on the floor."

Naomi began to cry again. She choked on her words as she complained. "Hannah, I thought after you'd slept, you see things more clearly. How can you think I could live like this? My father raised me to be a lady. He'd never want me to live in this squalor. Let's go see my father's attorney, get my inheritance, and go back to Washington or Maryland. Benjamin's family will take care of us."

"We will go on Monday. Mr. Oldham told us in his letter that he couldn't do anything for us until he settled the debts. We don't know if anything remains of the estate. Regardless, we only have five days until then, and for now, we have a roof over our heads."

Sonny dragged the desk near the fireplace. "Here it is, Hannah. This desk's got a nice top. I can make legs for it. Want me to try?"

"You don't know how to build tables."

"Sure, I do, Mama. I watched the men down at the furniture shop when we lived in Washington City."

"Yes, Sonny," Hannah said, "but first, I want you to help me clean up the room where the desk was. When we get the broken things out, we'll make a kitchen there."

The family ate in silence until Sonny scraped the empty tin cup where his oatmeal had been. "Hannah, can I have some more oatmeal?

I'm hungry this mornin'." Hannah hadn't made extra oatmeal, knowing how little food they'd bought in Madison.

"Yes, Sonny. You can have mine. I'm not hungry." She pushed the porcelain cup she'd used to him. She started to get up when Naomi grabbed her arm.

"Who's going to do all the chores around here?"

Hannah smiled at her mother-in-law. Naomi was not usually a needy person, but what they had found traumatized her more than Hannah realized. She patted her hand. "Mother Naomi, we are healthy, intelligent people. We can take care of ourselves for a few days."

Hannah picked up the broom and went to the new kitchen, brushing down the cobwebs as she went. As she carried her first load of debris outside, a rap on the door startled her, causing her to drop much of it. Sonny jumped up to greet their first visitor.

"Howdy." Sonny smiled broadly as he pushed open the door.

A tall bronze man, well over six feet tall, stood holding a Union military cap in his hand. "Mornin' to y'all. My name is Marcus Kincaid. Before the war, we was Mr. Hugh's people."

Hannah hadn't considered the possibility that people who once lived and worked at Sanctuary Hill would remain on the property. The Emancipation Proclamation in '63 broke legal ties to slavery. Yet, here at the back door stood a man who had more right to this land than she did. He had worked the land. She quickly walked to the door.

"Is there something you need?" Hannah wiped her face with her arm.

"Yes, ma'am. My wife and me, we seen y'all move in dis house yesterday. We think y'all be Mr. Hugh's kin. We wants to know do we gotta go now?" Marcus looked at the ground and shuffled his feet.

Naomi stepped up. "Where do you live now?"

"We live with our young'uns where we been all our days. Us and my wife's kin, we all got our place down in the quarters. One of her brothers, Lucas, lives with his two boys just down the road a piece."

"Well, I don't remember you. Just who's been takin' care of you since my father left Sanctuary Hill?"

"Why, Miss Naomi, we been takin' care of ourselves, just like we always do. I surely 'member you. We took care of the horses of your weddin' visitors. Lucas and me, just boys then."

"No, no. I don't know you. Go away."

Hannah interceded. "Mother Naomi, please calm down. I know you're still tired. Maybe you should go back to lie down for a while."

"I need to find…."

"No, let me take care of it. Go and read for a while. Your bed is comfortable." Naomi left the room, miffed at being dismissed.

"Tell me, Mr. Kincaid, have you lived at Sanctuary Hill long?"

"I ain't never lived nowhere else. I was born here. My mam and pap come here when Mr. Hugh bought this place."

"Didn't you and your family want to go North when President Lincoln said the Southern landowners couldn't own slaves anymore?"

Marcus looked directly into Hannah's face. "Where to should we goes? We don't know no other kind of life. Mr. Hugh treat us good. We never go hungry when he was here. He never beat us or treat us poorly. When he got sick and left Sanctuary Hill, he say we be free. He even hand us a little money, but we didn't know a better life was in the North, so we stay."

"Was ya scared when the soldiers came?" Sonny asked.

"No. We just stayed away from those soldiers in the gray suits. I fought with the Yanks for a time, but when my pap died, I had to come home to take care of my kin."

"How much family do you have, Marcus?"

13

"Just me and my wife, Shataka. We got us two chil'ren, our boy Abraham and our baby that we named Glory."

"You said ya have a brother. I had a brother, but he got killed in the war." Sonny continued to look at the stranger at the door.

"Lucas is Shataka's brother, son of Rose, and his two boys are David and Jonathan. My wife's grandmam is Mom Bec, probably named Rebecca, but no one knows. It's so long ago. Shataka's mam is Rose. Shataka's got a younger sister and brother. Ain't no more of Mr. Hugh's people."

"I'm glad you've been able to keep your family together." Hannah shook her head. The man in front of her wanted an answer. She didn't know enough about this new state or what provisions would come from Hugh Kincaid's will to give him an answer that he could rely on. She knew that she couldn't take on any further financial obligations. Yet these people had been resourceful and industrious enough to care for themselves for more than a year without any assistance from the owner of Sanctuary Hill.

He asked again, "Do we gotta go now?"

"I will be honest with you, Marcus. I don't know what lies ahead for us or this property. We will meet Mr. Kincaid's attorney in a couple of days. I see no reason for you to leave a place you've called home your entire life if you want to stay and can provide for yourself."

"We been doin' that all the time, ma'am. Thank ya. Will ya have work for us?" He looked up.

"There is certainly much to be done here, but right now, I don't know how much we will be able to pay. Again, we will know more in a few days."

"Well, to start we can help ya get this house cleaned up. Those soldiers that stayed here in '64 tore up Mr. Hugh's house right bad."

"Thank you, Marcus. I'll find some way to pay for your labor," Hannah said.

"I wanna help too, Hannah. Can I help him?"

Hannah smiled. "Yes, Sonny, but it may not be much fun."

Marcus turned to leave but stopped. "I'll get my family, and we'll start after we eat. What you want us to do first?

"Well, Marcus and Sonny, maybe we can make this room into a working kitchen."

And the work began. By nightfall, the large room was free of debris, clean, and set up as a kitchen with an eat-in dining area. Sonny had worked miracles. Much to her amazement, Hannah learned that her not-overly-bright brother-in-law was a natural woodworker. He had fashioned a table from the desktop and four pieces of lumber from the shed. Four chairs, mismatched and not much to look at, sat around the table, but they were sturdy enough to hold any adult who chose to sit down.

Marcus's mother-in-law kicked at the back door as Hannah's work crew was finishing the last chores of the day and preparing to leave for their cabins. With the infant Glory on her back in a sling, she held a large stew kettle with a heavy cloth. "Open the door before I spill the supper." Lucas pushed the door open, and she stepped in and plopped the pot on the cast iron stove, in which Shataka and Sonny had just built a fire.

"Mam, watcha mean bringin' Glory down here on your back?"

"Hesh yerself, Shataka. I done carried you like that 'til you could walk. Didn't hurt you none," Rose said.

"Hello. You must be Rose. Your family has been talking about you," Hannah said.

"I'm sure they have. Been wonderin' when the vittles would be fixed. I'm sure everyone's hungry and wanna good supper. This stew's fine. It's got some rabbit and a little smoked ham with lots of vegetables. Since ya got that oven a goin' now, I'll fix us a pone, and we'll all have a fine supper."

"Mam, we'd a been home in a while."

"Girl, you just hesh up. We gonna share this supper with Mr. Hugh's kin tonight. You know they ain't had time to lay back a larder."

Hannah's jaw dropped. This family had come this morning thinking she'd send them away from their home and now was offering to feed them.

"You want to share your supper with us?" Hannah asked just as Naomi entered the new kitchen. She stood looking at the conversion of her father's study into a kitchen/dining room.

"Hannah Ruth, this will never do. You know it's too dangerous to have a stove in the house—too much danger of the house catching fire."

"Hello, Miss Naomi," Rose spoke to her old playmate.

"Who are you? Oh, I know. You're Hephzibah, my mama's laundress."

"Yes, ma'am. When we grew up together, we had us some nice times then. I 'member days when we were little girls, playing down by the creek. We picked wildflowers to make posey crowns for our hair."

"I don't remember any such thing. Hephzibah, are you going to cook for us?"

"My name's Rose, now. Never did like that Bible name much. In the Bible, her son was a cruel king. When Mr. Lincoln freed us, I decided to be Rose because I couldn't think of a prettier sight. Now I am Rose Kincaid."

Sonny asked, "Did all of you change your names?"

"I did," Shataka said. "Mr. Hugh called me Patsy. I don't think that's a good name for a strong free woman like me. I read somewhere

16

that Shataka means free spirits that sting or charm. She knows what she wants and why she wants it. That's who I am."

Naomi looked at the younger woman. "Can you read?"

"'Course I can. All Mr. Hugh's people know how to read and write and do sums. He 'spected us to read the Good Book."

"Oh, my. Was my father breakin' the law?" Naomi grabbed the back of a chair. Hannah knew a fainting spell was in the making. "Hannah, send these people away. I must rest."

"No, Mother. These people have called this land home as long as your family has. They've brought us a hot meal tonight."

"Hannah! Have you forgotten who you are?" Naomi's cheeks blanched.

"No, ma'am. I have worked all day right alongside these people. They offered to feed us, and I'm hungry. I'm gonna eat with them."

Sonny added, "Me, too. I'm real hungry."

"Well, when they leave, I want to talk with you in my room." Naomi turned, hobbled across the hall, and slammed the door.

Within half an hour, Hannah sat with Sonny, Lucas, and his sons, Shataka and her entire family, Rose, and Mom Bec—all with steaming cups of stew before them. She cut the pone into wedges and was about to plunge her spoon into the savory dish.

"Miss Hannah, would ya let Lucas speak grace over our supper before we eat?" Shataka's voice trembled a bit as she asked.

"Surely. I forgot my manners." Truthfully, Hannah rarely took the time to speak grace over meals—not since her mother had passed away.

Lucas stood and bowed his head, "Dear Father. We thank ya for the blessin's of the day. You done gave us work again. You let us keep our home with Miss Hannah and Mister Sonny, and you provided a fillin' meal that's gonna taste mighty good. We are blessed. Amen."

Amens came from around the table.

When they finished, Hannah asked Sonny to take a bowl of stew and a wedge of cornbread to his mother. She thanked the Kincaids for the good day's work and asked them to return tomorrow. She didn't know how long she could pay for their help, but without them, she couldn't turn Sanctuary Hill into a farm that could sustain her family.

"Sonny, I am going to ride down the trail for a while before the sun sets. I want to see what I can find to help us rebuild this place. Will you stay nearby and look after your mother?"

"Sure can, Hannah. I think I'll work on another table 'cause I got plenty of wood."

Hannah walked to the shed and untied Pal, Sonny's horse. She put a rein and bit in place, tucked her skirt around her legs, and rode bareback toward the tree line at the creek. Her raven hair streamed behind her in the warm April breeze. For the first time since leaving Washington, she felt the heavy obligation of her widowhood lifted. Riding alone across the clover-filled pasture with a steady wind in her face, uncensored by the critical eyes of her mother-in-law, Hannah felt peace as she basked in the beauty of the countryside and an elusive sense of freedom. She urged Pal into a gallop for a short distance. *Can I just ride on?*

When she reached the tree line, she slid off the horse and skipped around the field of clover and wildflowers, dancing to a tune that only she could hear. Her arms swayed over her head, and her skirt swirled, exposing her calves. Hannah threw her head back and laughed and laughed and laughed. But shortly the laughter died, and she fell to the ground. She slumped, her face down into the clover where she had danced. She pounded her fists, and screams broke the silence of the evening. Pal flinched at her outburst, and birds took wing. The elusive freedom slipped away as quickly as it had come.

A hundred tasks wove themselves into a massive heap. Each responsibility demanded she deal with it. They were so entangled that she didn't know where to start. "I can't do this. My life isn't supposed to be like this. I don't want to live out my days trapped by a promise. I can't deal with this alone. No. I won't!" She screamed over and over until she exhausted her strength. She slumped onto the ground. Her hair flailed about her, carried by the wind. Hannah didn't know how long she cried out her frustration and fear. Then, she heard the cooing of a dove. She looked around and saw the gold-red of nightfall behind the tree line. She pushed herself up and wiped her face on her sleeve.

"Come on, Pal. Tomorrow is another day, and we have work to do then. Let's go back. I only have to live through one day at a time."

Hannah pulled herself onto Pal's broad back and reined him toward the house. She'd ridden only a few feet when the horse whinnied and stopped. Hannah looked up. Sitting on the far side of the creek, she saw a man astride a tall, light-colored horse. He was tall, like his horse. His hat covered his eyes and cast his face in darkness, but his posture told her he was watching her. She shivered and nudged Pal toward the cottage. The man didn't move. Hannah pushed her horse into a gallop and turned one last time to see if the stranger followed her. When she looked back, the tall man lifted his hat, turned, and rode toward the setting sun.

Chapter 2

And she said unto them, "Call me not Naomi, call me Mara:
for the Almighty dealt very bitterly with me."
Ruth 1:20

Monday afternoon, Hannah, Naomi, and Sonny returned to Madison to meet with Mortimer Oldham, attorney-at-law. He ushered them into his cramped, dark office and offered chairs to the ladies. Sonny was left standing behind his mother.

"Humph---humph. I hope you're settled and comfortable at Sanctuary Hill by now," the rotund, balding man said.

"We certainly are not!" Naomi stood with her hands on her hips, bending over the startled man. "How could you allow us to come here believing we could live in that wreck of a house?"

"I'm sure I don't know what you mean. Mr. Kincaid told me his home was in good order, and he planned to shut it up when he left."

Hannah interrupted, "Mr. Oldham, how long has Mr. Kincaid been away from Sanctuary Hill?"

Oldham took a step back from the older woman dressed in black. "He became quite ill in the winter of '64. His nephew arrived shortly after Christmas and took him to Marianna, where a doctor could look after him. I believe he passed away there the next February. Before leaving, he came to update his will, which I have."

"When did you last see our place?" Naomi asked.

"Mrs. Murphy, with the war, my clients, and my family, I've had no time to personally oversee the property left in the estate." Mr. Oldham tapped his pipe on a metal pipe stand near his desk as he looked at Naomi over the rims of his owlish glasses. "Won't you please be seated so we can get started?"

"You've not been there at all," Hannah said.

"No, madam. Not since before the war. Troops came through this area from time to time, but there was no battle near here." Mr. Oldham was interrupted once again by a knock on his door. "Excuse me." When he opened the door, a tall, well-dressed man entered the office. "Ah, Kincaid, I wondered if you'd make an appearance here today."

"Well, of course, I'd come. I hope I'm not too late." This vaguely familiar man had a brogue. He certainly had not grown up in the South.

"No, no. We've only started. Sorry, I have no chairs for you and the boy."

"No matter. I doubt this will take long."

Hannah knew this man from somewhere. Her gaze returned to him more than once over the next several minutes.

"As I was sayin', Mr. Kincaid charged me with the conveyance of his estate through this will, dated December 14, 1864. I was bound to find the heir of the property and notify the family, which I have now done." Oldham pulled a lengthy document from his desk drawer. "Before I read this will, I will tell you all debts have been satisfied, and the taxes were paid through 1865." He removed his glasses and looked directly at Naomi Murphy. "As I am obliged, I will ask again, have y'all any immediate needs I can attend to?"

Before her mother-in-law could launch another tirade with the lawyer, Hannah interceded. "Our furnishings and household items should arrive from Washington by the first week of May. We have a working kitchen and one furnished bedroom. We've met our neighbors, formerly Mr. Hugh's people, who are helping us. The roof is missing on the south side of the house—seems there was a fire at some time. No, I don't think we're settled, but we're making do."

"I could arrange boarding here in Madison until repairs are made."

Hannah looked over her shoulder at the tall man who'd interrupted their meeting. "Mr. Oldham, I'm not comfortable discussing my family's business in front of strangers."

"I'm sorry. I assumed you knew Mr. Kincaid."

"I'm your kinsman, Mrs. Murphy. Naomi is my cousin," the tall man said.

"How were we supposed to know that? Never seen you before," Naomi snapped back.

"Is this possible, Mother Naomi, that he's your kin?" Hannah tried to calm her agitated mother-in-law.

"Well, my maiden name is Kincaid, as you know. I know my father had family in Scotland. I suppose he could have contacted them at some time. I didn't know they'd send someone from the family to help." Naomi rose and walked over to the cousin she'd never met before. "You've the look of a Kincaid about you. All the men had sandy blond hair and eyes stormy blue, like a summer sky during a thunderstorm. Who might you be, cousin?"

"Kell Brody Kincaid, the second son of the Earl of Kincaid in County Sterling in Scotland. Father sent me here in the fall of '64 to care for his brother, Hugh. I was with him until he passed. Uncle Hugh asked me to take care of his little girl, Naomi. Your father prayed to see ya once again, but it was not to be."

"That's been more than a year and a half. Why is Sanctuary Hill in such poor repair?" Hannah asked.

Kell Kincaid turned and looked directly into Hannah's intense brown eyes. "I'm sure I don't know. And I also don't know who ya are to be askin' me such a question, lassie, but I've my own land to work. I had no hands to fight off the Yanks and Rebel troops who came through St. Francis County in the last months of the war. I did the best I could to keep the place in the condition it is now in."

"Humph...Humph. If it's all the same to you, I'd like to finish the readin' of the will." Mr. Oldham once again perched his spectacles on the end of his nose and began to drone on, spouting legal jargon for what seemed hours. Finally, he reached the dispensation of the property.

"I leave to my only male heir, Benjamin Kincaid Murphy, my lands, all buildings thereon, the mercantile store in Linden, all livestock, personal property, and securities. Benjamin Murphy will support my daughter, Naomi Kincaid Murphy, as long as she lives, and he will provide her a home at Sanctuary Hill. Until Benjamin Murphy reaches his majority at age twenty-one, I appoint Hannah Murphy his legal guardian. She will maintain all legal, financial, and contractual obligations."

"Mr. Oldham, I understand Sonny will receive ownership in three years, but what did my father leave us to live on now?" Naomi's cheeks were ashen gray, and her hands shook uncontrollably.

"Your son owns six hundred and forty acres of the best land in the delta, and three hundred acres are in virgin forests. That's more'n nine hundred acres. You have a house at Sanctuary Hill and whatever outbuildings escaped the war. If any livestock remains, they belong to Mr. Murphy. The store in Linden was once profitable. Mr. Kincaid also left me with about $50,000 of Confederate bonds and $50.00 in gold."

"Fifty dollars. Is that all that remains for us to live on?" Naomi sank to her chair, and loud sobs spoke of the depth of her fear.

Hannah moved to comfort her mother-in-law. "Please don't give in to this now. We will find a way."

Kell tapped Sonny's shoulder. "Excuse me, Mr. Murphy." Throughout the reading of the will, the younger man said nothing, and now his face showed concern for his sobbing mother.

Sonny didn't react. Again, Kell patted him on the back. "You talkin' to me, mister? I'm Sonny."

"All right, Sonny. I have something your grandfather wanted you to have." Kell pulled a gold watch connected by a chain to an ornate fob. On the face of the watchcase was the engraved coat of arms of the Kincaid clan. "Mr. Hugh asked me to tell you that we Kincaids are true to our kin. Our family motto is engraved here. It says, *'This I Will Defend.'* It's a valuable piece of family legacy from your grandfather."

Sonny looked at the embossed watch and ran his finger over the raised sword and castle

. "I like this. Is this our family castle?"

"Well, Sonny, the castle means home. For you and your mother, this is Sanctuary Hill. The sword is a weapon that may be needed to keep it safe."

"I ain't got no sword."

"We'll find ways to defend our home if we have to." Kell offered his hand to Sonny to seal their covenant. Sonny beamed. Kell was the first man who ever offered to shake his hand.

"Do you have any more questions for me, Mrs. Murphy?" Mr. Oldham rose from his chair to signal the meeting was over. Hannah shook her head and accepted the envelope containing the bonds and the gold from the lawyer. She lifted Naomi from her chair, sure that the older woman was near her breaking point.

Naomi whimpered, "Please take me home, Hannah."

"Will ya let me help ya get them back to Sanctuary Hill, Mrs. Murphy?" Kell asked.

"Thank you, no, Mr. Kincaid. I am more than able to drive us back to our house."

"What do ya intend to do?"

"Live one day at a time. I don't see I have any alternative right now."

"I will help ya anyway I can. That's what my father sent me here to do. I know the Lord will see y'all through these hard times if you keep your faith."

"Mr. Kincaid, I have an obligation, and I'll find some way to care for my family. I do thank you for being kind to Sonny. He's a gentle young man with a good heart, but he's just not too quick to understand some things. Good afternoon."

Hannah walked the three steps to the wagon and started to climb over the wheel. Kell was at her elbow.

"I'm pleased to know ya, Mrs. Murphy. I'll see ya soon."

Distraught from the news, Naomi took to her bed as soon as they returned to Sanctuary Hill. Hannah knew no way to lessen the disappointment her mother-in-law had experienced, so she decided to work off her frustration. A good two hours of sunlight remained that she and Sonny could use in the garden. Now more than ever, a good yield from all they could grow would be crucial to their survival. *But I can't do this alone.* Hannah shook off her negative thoughts. The young widow wanted to the depth of her being to keep her promise to Benjamin Murphy, but she doubted her knowledge and strength to provide for the household. *Hannah Ruth Kennedy, you grew beautiful roses and lilacs that were the envy of the county around Sharpsburg.* But roses aren't potatoes, and no lady in her family had ever toiled in the dirt to put food on the table. "Sonny, come with me to the shed. We need hoes and a shovel. We can't prepare a garden plot with our hands."

"Do you know how, Hannah?" Sonny scratched his head. "I don't think I do."

"No, but we will learn together."

"Maybe Marcus will show us what to do. He's been mighty helpful, ain't he?" He lifted his doe-shaped eyes to Hannah.

"He has, but we have to do this work, and we don't have the money to pay for help."

"Didn't that man we saw today say this farm is mine?"

"Yes, he did. When you are twenty-one, it is yours, outright." Hannah saw the puzzled look come over his face.

"I don't know nothin' about farmin'. Will I know then?"

"Sonny, in time, we will see." They went through the tools left in the shed, and most were broken or rusted. One hoe seemed usable, but the shovel had a broken handle. They did find a rusty spade in the back corner. "Well, it's not much, but maybe it will get us started."

"I'll fix this handle, Hannah. That'll be easy."

"Miss Hannah, Mr. Sonny. Where are y'all?" Lucas Kincaid walked around the corner from the quarters.

"We're in the shed. Is there a problem?" Hannah came to the door.

"No, Ma'am. Marcus say y'all be home now so he wants to know if ya need us to work tomorrow."

"Lucas, I want you and Marcus to help Sonny and me plow the garden plot. After that, I'll have no other funds to pay your wages. Can you do that for us?"

He nodded. "Walk over this way. I'll show y'all where the house garden always been planted." Lucas took them to an area not far from where the burned-out kitchen had stood. Three years of neglect allowed the good-sized plot to grow up with weeds, wildflowers, and even a few knee-high trees. Yet the soil had been cleared of rocks and roots of large brush, so tilling would be hard but not impossible. Lucas took the rusty spade and began to remove the small trees, and Sonny used his hoe to clear weeds. "Miss Hannah, tomorrow, I'll hitch our mule up to that plow back in the shed, and we'll whip this garden into shape."

"Can I plow with Pal?"

"Sure, ya can, Mr. Sonny. We got a plow down at our place."

Hannah smiled. Sonny would probably make a better farmer than she would. He loved his horse, so working with that gentle animal would make this work like play. Regardless, three and a half days of back-breaking labor was the price of preparing the site to grow the food their small family would need to see them through the winter. Hannah breathed a sigh of relief after dinner on that third day when they began to seed their first row. Before sunset that day, Sonny and she had laid out two rows of pole beans, two rows of corn, and the first row of potatoes. The next day with Shataka's help, they filled their remaining space with more potatoes, yams, some greens, pumpkins, squash, cucumbers, carrots, and turnips. All the seeds had come from the general store. Hannah was shocked to find so much had survived the looting of the troops who confiscated so much.

By Friday afternoon, the planting was complete, and a gentle rain began to fall about dusk. Hannah was relieved. Only yesterday, Mom Bec had bemoaned the back-breaking work of carrying water to the newly seeded garden plots. Hannah walked toward the shed to store the tools. Stepping back into the refreshing shower, she turned her palms skyward and lifted her face toward the clouds, and she smiled. The dirt from her hand and cheeks ran in streams. While she was bone-weary from the labor of the week, she felt hope. She'd not done it alone, but with the help of Sonny and one or another of the Kincaids from day to day, they had accomplished one critical task. They had planted a garden. Providence had provided the water. Hannah felt a vague sense of gratitude—not sure where or to whom she should direct it. Funny, she'd never given such a trivial event a thought before. That day she learned that spring rainfall was not trivial but vital to her welfare. What pleasure it brought her.

When she went in for supper, Hannah realized her dress was dripping water all over the floor.

"Why, Miss Hannah, shame on you for messin' up dis clean floor. Missus Murphy ain't gonna be happy with you."

"I'm sorry, Mom Bec. When we finished, the rain felt so wonderful, washing the soil off me, I didn't think. I'll clean it."

"No, ma'am. You got about half an hour 'til supper be done. Go on up and make yourself clean and ladylike."

"Mom Bec, I'm no lady. I'm a working person, just like you."

"Maybe so, but you have time to be a lady tonight. Go on and at least wash your face and hands. Put on a clean dress. Rest and enjoy dis evenin'. Gonna rain all night, so you can't work no more today."

"You are such a wise woman and dear. I believe I will."

When Hannah and her family finished the meal Mom Bec had prepared with the food from their meager pantry, she went to the front porch. The rain continued as Mom Bec had said it would. The sound of the patter on the trees, roof, and cobblestones was soothing. The porch was the most pleasant part of their home presently, as it had taken on part of its former glory. The Kincaid brothers and Sonny had removed the vines and weeds that encumbered two sides of it. They even took time to rehang the swing. If she could find money and time to whitewash the columns and paint the shutters, Hannah knew this house could be beautiful again. But she had learned what a large word IF is.

Sonny came out to join her. "Don't you feel good that we finished planting our garden?" she said.

"That was a lot of work. Pal sure is a good horse."

"Yes, he is. I gave the Kincaid's five dollars for helping us this week, but I can't continue to do that."

"Golly, I'd like to keep workin' with them. They help a lot."

"Would you mind if we offered a part of the land to Lucas and Marcus with their families if they are willing to stay here and help us work our land?" Hannah posed the question that she'd been mulling over since their meeting with the attorney.

"You mean we should give it to them?" He shook his head. "I wanna farm my land. My grandpa gave it to me."

"No, I mean sell them forty acres, and let them work off the cost. We must have some help."

"I can work hard, Hannah."

"Yes. I know you can, and you've been working hard every day. But one person can't work all this land by himself. Look how long it took you and me and at least one other person working every day to plant our garden."

"Is it a good thing to do? Do you think I need to ask my mama?"

"That's not what your grandfather said in his will. I am your guardian. The two of us will make the decisions together. The will said we have to take care of your mother, and you know she will be upset if we start talking about Sanctuary Hill."

"Well, maybe we need to talk to Lucas and Marcus. I like those fellows, don't you? Well, we made a good decision, Hannah. I gotta get to work makin' that shovel handle now. Good night."

Hannah tossed the entire night. The hard floor beneath the feather bed was not the sole reason. In restless dreams, she heard herself saying over and over to Sonny, "It'll be all right. We will be fine. Time will take care of things." Deep down, she doubted any of those things would be true. With the fifty dollars Hugh Kincaid had left them, she had little hope they could make it through the year, let alone for the rest of their lives. Fifty dollars wouldn't feed them, so making the essential repairs to the house was out of the question.

Perhaps she should use the money to purchase train tickets back to Maryland. She knew her family home had been destroyed during the battles at Antietam near Sharpsburg. Her father had written he had taken up residence in the overseer's house before he left to command his troop. That was the last letter she'd had from him. A Confederate sergeant wrote to tell her they had buried Joel Kennedy in the family cemetery near his wife on his plantation. She assumed she still owned the land, but the same problem existed there—too much land and no resources to hire people needed to raise crops. Hannah wasn't even sure the land hadn't been sold to satisfy tax claims. She knew no one had paid any taxes since her father died in 1863. Going home to Maryland was no solution to her current problems.

Returning to Washington was even more of an impossibility. The cost of living there was extravagant. Naomi would expect to return to the social realm she'd lived in before the end of the war. *Stop dwelling on all these things you can't change, Hannah Ruth. Let me help you. I'll listen.*

Where did that come from? She twisted to her side, threw off her cover, and pushed herself up. The room was warm, and heat lightning flashed across the western sky. She needed someone to talk to. She wanted someone to tell her about Arkansas…how things are done in the state with taxes, legal issues, legal authorities, and the name of the sheriff. Thunder exploded across the flatland of the Delta. The lightning forked and lit the sky day-bright for a split second. Hannah could see acres of rich delta cotton land laying bare. What did she know about growing cotton? Her father, Joel Kennedy, had successfully raised tobacco as his sole cash crop. Even so, Hannah knew little about the routine involved in growing tobacco. Ladies were not brought up to work in her world.

That stormy night, she felt more than useless. Her promise to Benjamin Murphy felt like her life sentence without parole, and she believed this to be an obligation for which she had no skills. The situation was doubly laden by the loathsome sense of being alone. Hannah couldn't bring herself to say she was lonely—she just felt isolated. She had no friend to talk with nor any social acquaintance to pass a pleasant minute in idle conversation. Her family would not understand if she tried to explain her concerns. *I need sleep. If I could just turn my mind off for a couple of hours, please!*

She returned to her pallet and beat her fists into her pillow. She clenched her eyes. Warm tears soaked her cheeks as she wept, making no sound. At some point, she slept. When she arose, she found Mom Bec in the kitchen putting together breakfast. Since the trip to Madison allowed them to buy a few staples, the family could have coffee, bread, and even a bit of sweetening. Hannah spent frugally, but they had to eat until they could get vegetables from the garden. Mom Bec had made a pan of biscuits and a skillet of gravy.

"Where did you get milk?" Hannah asked.

"We got a cow at the cabin. She's a pretty good milker, Miss Hannah. We got milk."

"Thank you for sharing it. Y'all have been very good to us."

"We's happy to help save our home. We gonna be all right. The good Lord, He's been watchin' over Sanctuary Hill. He's gonna keep on takin' care of us."

"I hope you're right, Mom Bec because I'm pretty concerned about all we have to do right now just to survive."

"Missy, don't ya be a frettin'. Folks around here be glad to help. Even if they don't, Mr. Hugh's family is right down that path. We ain't goin' no place.

"I can't believe how brave you are. You just face things and take care of what comes your way." Hannah shook her head and laughed. "I should be more like you."

"The Lord done tole all his chil'ren that he is our strength and our hope. That's all the brave I need. Don't you know the Lord, Miss Hannah?"

"I guess I don't know him the way you do. How long until those biscuits will be ready? I need to change for the day's work."

"Just a few minutes. You go on and make yourself ready. We'll talk about the Lord again."

Hannah wondered why Mom Bec had asked her such a personal question about her faith. The gentle, always happy old woman had caught her off guard. Hannah had thought little about religion since she'd become an adult. When she was a little girl in Maryland, she attended church with her mother. She understood little of the pomp and ceremony of the high Anglican church they'd attended. She liked the music but daydreamed her way through the sermons. Her father stopped taking her to church when she was about ten after her mother died. Surely, she'd have little time to spend in church here in Arkansas. There was too much work to be done.

Hannah returned to the kitchen with a pen, ink, and ledger book in hand. She took an end sheet from the book and began to write a list of things that had to be done immediately if they were to stay at Sanctuary Hill. If she couldn't get these things done, she knew she would have to return north.

Things I have to do....tend the garden, repair the roof, find some workers, replace glass in broken windows, lay in firewood for cooking and winter, find out about taxes, buy mules, get a few chickens, order supplies for the store, and reopen the mercantile. After reading her list, Hannah wanted to ask someone for help. She knew who she had to go to, and it was the last thing she wanted to do. "Mom Bec, do you know where Mr. Kell Kincaid's property is?"

"Surely do. Jist follow that path by the shed down to the creek. Cross over and after a spell, you'll see a grove of oak trees. His cabin is smack in the middle. Pretty place. Not like Sanctuary Hill used to be, but a pretty place. Probably ain't more'n two or three miles down there. But sit down and eat before ya start the day," Mom Bec ordered.

After consuming two large biscuits covered with gravy, Hannah went to the shed to saddle Pal. As she placed the bit between his teeth, she nearly convinced herself not to go. *You're being foolish. Like you have any alternative. Go on and get it over with.* She flapped the reins across his back and began the trip. She took a deep breath and relaxed her shoulders. *Kell was a relative, and he had offered to help.* How bad could it be? As she rode, Hannah's shoulders eased, and she found the beauty of the Arkansas springtime around every bend. Green in uncountable shades covered the landscape. The sunlight glanced off the rippling waters in the creek, and the bounty of wildflowers painted a scene no artist could reproduce on canvas. The trip across the open land erased much of the tension Hannah carried when she climbed onto Pal's back. If only every day could be so blissful and carefree!

Hannah easily found Kell's home nestled among large oak trees. The cottage was a single-story log building with a porch stretching across the front and side of the house. Blue shutters stood at either side of the four floor-to-ceiling-length windows. The front door was painted the same blue.

She tied Pal to the porch rail and climbed the steps to knock on the door. She waited and knocked a second time. No one came. From behind her, Hannah heard a large dog barking. She turned, somewhat frightened. She took a couple of steps back onto the porch at the sight of the large mutt that barreled toward her. He began licking her arms and hands.

"Heel, there, Scotty. I must be dreamin'. Mrs. Hannah Murphy wouldn't be a'knockin' at my door."

Hannah knew her decision to ask questions of Kell Kincaid was a mistake. His mocking, sarcastic greeting confirmed exactly what she'd feared since she left home. "I'm sorry I bothered you. I'll take up no more of your time." She stepped to the ground and began to untie Pal.

"Wait a minute, lass. I was only teasin'. I am certainly surprised to see ya, though. I was pretty sure you wanted to see no more of me and didn't like me at all," Kell said.

"I didn't want to bother you, Mr. Kincaid. I don't like to annoy anyone. That would take some depth of knowledge to know if you are likeable, and I don't know anything about you."

"Again, I sincerely apologize for my roguish Scottish humor."

"I did have a few questions that I need answers to. If we are going to stay at Sanctuary Hill, there are a few things I have to take care of as soon as I can arrange it."

"Tis no bother. I offered to help ya on Monday when we were in Madison. You made it verrra clear you wanted no help from me."

"I didn't need help getting Naomi and Sonny home. I do need some answers to questions if I am going to make a living here. If you answer a few questions, I'll be on my way." Hannah sat on the porch.

"I'll gladly try to answer your questions, but ya don't have to sit out here. You're welcome to come into my wee house."

"No, thank you. The porch will do fine. First, I made a list of things I need to do immediately, but you know from the settlement on Monday, we have little money to work with. I don't suppose you know anywhere I can cash in $50,000 worth of Confederate bonds?"

"I'm glad to see ya haven't lost your sense of humor. I'm afraid the best use for those bonds will be to start fires to keep ya warm this winter." Kell sat down beside Hannah. "What is the most pressing need on your list, lass?"

Hannah pulled the list from her skirt pocket. "First is growing food to feed us through the winter. We got a large garden planted earlier this week. Maybe one of the Kincaids can teach Sonny to hunt for game and to fish. But I'm afraid Sonny may be too soft-hearted to kill animals." Kell smiled at the comment.

"Then I must repair the roof. About half the south wing is open. Water will begin to weaken the walls and floors soon. I know fixing a roof that large will cost much more money than we have."

"Hannah, I think ya can get that done for nothin' and maybe even make a little profit." Kell's matter-of-fact tone told her he wasn't teasing.

"How can I do that?"

"Lease out a few of your forest acres to a lumber crew. Let them come in and harvest the mature trees for lumber. Take the lease cost out in lumber to replace the damaged part of the roof. You can also ask them to provide cedar shakes for the top layer and cut up the scrap wood for firewood. Timberland is at a premium now with all the construction after the war."

"Do you think I can do that?"

"I'll help ya. We'll barter for trusses, lumber, and shakes. People do it all the time. You will have to oversee the work to make sure they stay in the allotted acreage. Would you let me send a lumberman over to see you next week?"

"Yes, thank you. That's a big relief."

"What's number two?" Kell grinned as he saw Hannah relax a bit.

"I need to replace a lot of glass. Many of the downstairs windows are broken."

"That is a bigger problem. Ya will need to order glass from St. Louis. You can do that from the same people who supply the general store in Linden."

"I don't know much about that either. I've put that at the bottom of my list."

"We'll just board up the broken windows to keep out the rain and the cold. We may be able to find greased paper. It works all right, and it will let in some light."

"I guess it will do for now. I don't want to take up too much of your time."

"Ya didn't. I've enjoyed the short visit, but you didn't want to come here today at all, did ya?"

"Mr. Kincaid, thank you for helping me. I know some things I have to do now. It's not in my nature to ask for help from strangers. Since our meeting on Monday, I had some reservations about coming here, but you've been helpful, and I appreciate your advice."

"Why did ya fear to come ask for help, Hannah?"

"I answered that question."

"No. Ya didn't. You made an excuse."

"Just forget the whole thing. I don't want anything from you. I don't want to talk about this anymore. I won't bother you again." She folded her list and shoved it toward her pocket.

"Why do you dislike me, Hannah? Have I done something to offend you?" Kell looked directly into her face.

"You are very forward, Mr. Kincaid. Please excuse me". She jerked the reins free and mounted her horse.

"We could be friends if you'd knock down that wall you live behind, ya know."

Hannah pulled Pal in the direction of home.

"Please tell my cousin Naomi that I will visit her this evenin'. Good afternoon, Mrs. Murphy."

Ripe apples were no match for the color that rose in Hannah's neck and face. Her hands trembled as she tried to hold the horse to the path. "That man is incorrigible. How dare he say those things to me. I'll never go back to him for help."

Chapter 3

And Boaz answered and said unto her, "It hath fully been showed me all thou hast done unto thy mother-in-law since the death of thy husband: and how thou hast left thy father and thy mother and land of thou nativity, and art come unto a people which thou knowest not heretofore."
Ruth 2:11

The next morning Hannah flew through the morning routine of breakfast, assigning work to her small crew and cajoling Naomi to take up the task of repairing a few pieces of clothing, mostly to keep her occupied. She ran to the shed to get Pal, threw an old blanket across the back of the gentle old roan, and headed into Linden, less than two miles from Sanctuary Hill. She hoped to take inventory in the general store to see what could be salvaged to rebuild the house.

As Hannah rode into Linden, she noticed for the first time that little remained of the town after the war. Only three buildings showed any kind of activity—smoke drifted up from the forge in the livery stable, a few men loitered around the saloon door, and three women and a couple of small children had gathered in the churchyard of the small clapboard church. Other structures were dark, boarded up, or stood as burned-out skeletons. Linden had never been more than a small community, but she saw little indication of efforts toward reconstruction.

Hannah slid from Pal's back and stepped onto the wooden porch in front of Kincaid's Mercantile. She turned the key in the rusty lock, and the bolt slid open. She gazed across the general store that, except for the dust and a few empty shelves, appeared to have escaped the ravages other places nearby had met.

She walked down the three aisles, noticing that some shelves were bare. No food remained. Shelves labeled ammunition were empty. On the other hand, some sections displaying farm tools, books, and kitchen wares still had several items displayed. Mr. Hugh's array of fabric and ladies' notions seemed to be waiting for a customer. On the back wall, Hannah discovered several handmade quilts hung on rods. In a glass case, she found delicate needlework, like doilies and table scarves. She also found a few pairs of intricately embroidered pillowcases. These items seemed unusual in a country general store.

On the back wall, she found a door leading to a storage room. Leather goods, including two saddles and bridles, hung on the wall. Several large unopened wooden kegs lined the back wall. She remembered seeing kegs like these at bar-be-ques back in Maryland. Perhaps they held aged spirits. If so, that could be an immediate source of income. Hannah smiled. *Mother would be ashamed of me for thinking such a thing, but maybe this estate will provide our livelihood yet.*

After her walk through the building, Hannah was convinced that she had to work toward opening the mercantile as soon as she could get a cotton crop planted. Though frightened to use the last of their money, she would restock the store with staples that the people in the area needed. She would start with salt, coffee, tea, ammunition for hunting guns, and other items that were needed but not available. With the small amount of money she had, she knew she couldn't buy much, but this store could supply income to care for Naomi and Sonny.

A voice broke into her planning. "Top of the day. Is there anyone about?"

She dropped the bridle she'd picked up. She knew Kell Kincaid had arrived—uninvited. "What are you doing in here?" Hannah didn't hear a response as his smile melted her intended spiteful welcome. Kell stooped to pick up the bridle she'd dropped and hung it back on the peg.

"Ya are here, lass."

"How did you get in here?"

"I opened the door and walked in. Quite simple, really."

"How did you know I was here? Are you following me, Mr. Kincaid?" Hannah made no attempt to keep the edge from her voice.

"Actually, I was visitin' the preacher over at the church. We're pretty good friends. I saw your horse tied up out front. Why would you think I'd follow you? I got plenty to occupy my time." He took his hat off and leaned against the door jamb.

Hannah stepped back from him and smoothed her hands down the front of her skirt. Then she looked up, shoulders back and a slight smile on her lips and said, "Mr. Kincaid, is there something you need that I can help you with?"

That coy reply brought laughter from Naomi's kinsman. "Well, yes, now that I see you're in the mood to do business and have the mercantile open."

"Well, not really. I came today to look at the inventory. I didn't know if anything remained that would be of much use. I was hoping to bring back some good news. Naomi was devastated by the report we received from Mr. Oldham. She believed her father was a wealthy man."

"Lass, many men who were rich before the war found their fortunes to be a mere pittance after the defeat."

"And you, Mr. Kincaid, did you lose your shirt in the war, too?'

"No, I'm still wearin' my shirt. I even have a spare. I didn't come to America until late summer in '64. My father gave me a choice. I could come here with my portion—I know I told ya that I'm second born—and see to my uncle Hugh and his family, or I could join the service of the church or the military. My mother, God rest her soul, is a devout Catholic. She hoped I'd become a priest. Many second sons do. But in my roguish days, I had no faith. Those men take vows of poverty and obedience. Priesthood offered nothin' of the life I wanted. Besides, the lasses are an interest of mine."

Hannah stammered looking for a reply. Heat rose in her cheeks. "Oh, ah…I…."

"Forgive me, lass. I spoke too boldly. I beg your pardon if I offended ya."

"What is it that you need?"

"I'm needin' a new hammer. I was trying to repair the winch on my well and dropped mine to the bottom of the shaft."

"Perhaps there is one here. I've yet to find an inventory list."

"I see a hammer back there on the wall. That'll do. You've made your first sale."

They walked to the counter at the front of the store. Hannah searched for a ledger of some sort that may have a price list. After several minutes of sifting through the junk she found under the counter, she picked up a handful of papers and threw them across the room. "Tarnation!"

"What's got your ire up, now, lassie?" Kell asked.

"Where are the records? Surely, the storekeeper who worked for Mr. Hugh kept some kind of records."

"Of course, he did. Travis Hopkins was as good a manager as comes in these parts."

"Then where is he? He should be here trying to get this store restocked and opened again. Madison is too far for the local people to travel for common staples." Hannah began to pull open drawers and slam cabinet doors behind her.

"Calm yourself. Did ya forget we just ended a war? Travis was killed in a little skirmish near Leesburg. Left a wife and three young'uns."

"That was a foolish thing for me to say. I hoped to find the store records so I could make plans to reopen the mercantile. We need the income."

"If you'd heeded my words, I told ya I was with Uncle Hugh when he passed away. He left a box of papers for me to turn over to my cousin and her son. After meetin' Sonny, I'm not sure those documents will mean much to him."

"Well, you can give me those records now. I am Sonny's guardian. I will be from this time on."

"What happened to the lad?"

"Scarlet Fever when he was about ten years old. Doctors couldn't get his fever down for several days. When they finally got the fever to break, Sonny was…well…impaired. He can do whatever he's told, and he's good at doing things with his hands. He has problems making decisions, dealing with his emotions, and engaging in adult social life. His behavior is much what you'd expect in a ten-year-old."

"Is he not likely to grow beyond his present state?" Kell asked.

"We've not noticed any change in the seven years I've been a part of this family."

"Bless ya, lass. The Lord has given ya a challenge. Is my cousin much help?"

"She's a lady. Mr. Hugh raised her to be a Southern Belle, and he taught her well. She knows every social do and don't, every mannerism and rule of Southern culture. Unfortunately, the South lost the war."

"Do ya think you're gonna be able to provide for the three of you alone at Sanctuary Hill?"

Hannah recognized the compassion and concern in Kell's voice, but in her vulnerability, she moved to the defensive. "Mr. Kincaid, those things aren't your concern. I swore to my father-in-law on his deathbed that I would care for his family. I keep my promises."

"Excuse me, ma'am. The Kincaid family is indeed my concern. Did ya not hear me explain the family motto to Sonny? I did that more for Naomi and you than for the lad. *This I'll Defend*—those are more than words to our clan. My father sent me here to honor the Kincaid family pledge."

"My name is not Kincaid, Sir. My name is Hannah Ruth Kennedy. I can take care of my own."

"You were Richard Murphy's wife. Does that not make you Hannah Murphy?"

"Will you take that hammer and go?"

"You are the most stubborn woman I've ever known. Do ya have any idea of the obstacles you're gonna face tryin' to keep your promise alone?"

Hannah stomped her foot and jerked her shoulders back. "I suppose you're gonna tell me and then fix them for me."

"Well, as a matter of fact, I do have a couple of solutions to take care of some items on your list."

"How do you know what else is on my list? I only told you two things yesterday."

"Could be that I read it after finding it on my porch. I can help you with some of those things. This one about laborers for your farm, you're lucky there."

"I can't afford to pay laborers."

"No one around here can right now. I already said the plantation owners are land-poor just like you. Most of 'em lost their workers when emancipation came, but not all of Mr. Hugh's people left because he was good to them. So, some stayed to protect the land they called home. Did ya know they saved the big house from burning to the ground when the Yankees set fire to the kitchen? Lucas got some bad burns on his hands and arms that night."

"No, I didn't know. They told me they didn't want to leave, but I can't ask them to work for no wage."

"I'll bet they'd work for a plot of land for themselves."

"I've heard about tenant farmers. Sonny and I have spoken about asking them if they'd work to buy a parcel of land. We had a couple near our home in Maryland, but they were poor white immigrants. I might have asked you about the Arkansas law yesterday, but you are always so…so…oooh."

"Again, I ask ya to forgive my roguish wit. I fear it's the Scot in me. As for tenant farmers, I don't see that color matters if the people are loyal and hardworkin'. You can find those qualities in the Kincaids at Sanctuary Hill. They already call that place home. I think Congress has now ruled against preventing black ownership of land."

"I'll think about it. Now give me my list back."

"Whoa…what about this tax thing? You are right. Laws are different from state to state. And what will it take to get this mercantile up and going again? You don't know the people of this community. I know Uncle Hugh left you with little money to rebuild …Do you want me to go on?"

"Mr. Kincaid, I know all those things—every one of them. I also know now that for the first time in my life, I owe no man my obedience, my servitude, or my trust. I will never again put my fate in the hands of another person. I can take care of me and mine. I don't want your interference. I am going to rebuild Sanctuary Hill. No one will need to come to my rescue. I'm capable of doing what I must do."

"You seem mighty sure you can go it alone. I pray the Lord will smile on you as you try. But in any case, I won't be far should you need me." Kell laid two dollars on the counter and picked up his hammer. He started toward the door. As he put his hand out to open the door, he turned. "Oh, by the way, I enjoyed that lovely dance you performed the other evenin' out near the creek."

Ashen blotches appeared on her cheeks. She realized that Kell Kincaid had been the tall man who had witnessed her tirade.

"Lass, ya seemed so carefree and happy for a time, and then that scream came and set the birds to wing."

"I believe I said good day to you, Mr. Kincaid." She pushed the door closed behind him and locked it. She'd experienced enough unwelcome visitors for one day.

⨎

Hannah once again spent a sleepless night on the pallet in her room. The confrontation with Kell played over and over in her mind. *Why won't he just stay out of my life?* Yet, her lips curled in a smile when she remembered azure eyes when he laughed. But then he tried to take charge again. *All his suggestions! Who needs them?*

Throwing the sheet off, she rose and walked to the window. Hannah slumped into the one chair in her room. The moon-bright landscape of Sanctuary Hill rang with the song of cicadas, toads, and rustling leaves. The beauty of the Arkansas spring eased some of the fatigue she felt. A gentle breeze carried the scent of roses and the blossoms from the nearby peach orchard that had survived the devastation of the war. If only the daytime world could be so filled with such peace and pleasure.

She had to sleep. Every day demanded all the strength, patience, and ingenuity she could find. How was she going to find a work crew for this farm? How could she make a deal with a lumber crew? What would Naomi say and do when she suggested they offer part of the plantation to the Kincaids in return for their labor? After she'd explained they would not give all the land away, Sonny liked the idea, but if she did offer the land, Kell would think she chose to do it because he'd told her to. She didn't want to be obligated to anyone.

Hannah laid her head onto her arms propped on the windowsill. Through drowsy eyes, she caught a glimpse of three or four men on horseback stopped just on the grass near the cobbled drive. They talked among themselves, but she couldn't hear enough to understand. She lit the lantern and lifted the light to the window. At once, the men galloped down the drive toward the road. Another issue to deal with—Hannah pulled her nightdress over her head and changed to her work clothes. She would sleep no more this night. She went down to start her day's work.

At breakfast, Hannah asked, "Did either of you hear anything outside last night?"

"No, Hannah. I slept soundly until I heard you preparing breakfast this morning. Did you, Sonny?" Naomi asked.

"I thought I heard some horses runnin' around and men talkin', but I was dreamin' I guess. We only got one horse. We gonna eat soon?"

"Well, I know I heard some horses, too. After we eat, I'm going out to see if anything is out of place. And Mother Naomi and Sonny, I want to talk to you about something important when I get back. I'll meet ya in the parlor in about an hour."

"For Heaven's sake, Hannah, don't make everything so dramatic. We can talk over breakfast, can't we? I plan to make a social call on Mrs. Naylor at the parsonage before the day gets too warm."

"Very well. We need workers for Sanctuary Hill. We don't have money to pay for help right now. I think we should ask the Kincaids from the quarters to become tenant farmers here at Sanctuary Hill. In exchange for their labor, we'll sell them farms from our land."

"Hannah, where did you get such a ridiculous idea? My papa would never give his land away." Naomi paced the room. "How could you think of givin' away my papa's land?"

"Sonny didn't think it was a terrible idea when we talked about it. He likes working with Marcus and Lucas."

"Mama, I said it's okay. We got lots of land. Let's share it with our friends."

"Benjamin Kincaid Murphy, those people are not our friends. They are hired help." Naomi rarely called Sonny by his true name.

"Mother Naomi, I don't see that we have a choice. If we don't have a work crew, we can't grow a crop. No crops, and we have no money to pay taxes. If we can't pay the taxes, we will lose the land. This land is all we have left to provide a living for us." Rising to look into her mother-in-law's eyes, Hannah continued. "Do you understand what I am trying to tell you?"

Naomi crumpled back into the chair. Tears streamed down her face. Sonny pushed Hannah aside and pulled his mother into his arms. "Mama, we ain't gonna give all our land away, just a little bit. Hannah said it's gonna be all right. Okay?"

"Why bother asking me? I've no head for business. Do whatever you want, Hannah. You have since the day Richard brought you home as his bride."

"I'm sorry you're upset. I'm only trying to find a way for us to rebuild this place."

"Hannah, you've not been a proper daughter-in-law since the start. You know you never listened to my advice. You disliked the social life we had in Washington City. You were barely civil to my friends there. The one thing you could have done for me, you refused to do. You know how much I wanted grandchildren, yet you refused Richard your bed." Naomi bent over in deep sobs. "I should have sent you back to your family in Maryland when Richard died." Dabbing her eyes with her handkerchief, she rose and looked at Hannah, who made no reply to any of her hard words. The words left a statue in the place of the young woman. Hannah's face seemed etched in granite, hard as the cobblestones on the drive. Tears filled her eyes and fell from her lashes.

"Goodness me, no. What have I said?" Naomi tried to embrace her daughter-in-law. "Forgive my lashing out, Hannah. I've said too much. Please forgive me. You know I didn't mean all those things. I'm just so upset at the thought of losing my papa's land."

"Hannah, don't cry. I'll get you some water, okay? Will that make you feel better?" Sonny asked.

Hannah stepped away from Naomi and nodded to Sonny. "Excuse me. I have work waiting for me. I forgive you, Mother Naomi." Hannah sipped Sonny's water and left the house through the back door. Remembering the night riders, she pulled her apron up and wiped her wet face. Walking to the end of the yard, she found the hoof prints of horses on the lawn. She also found a cigar butt. She would need to talk to the local sheriff—if she could find out who that was. *Something else I don't know. I will not ask Kell Kincaid.*

Work waited. Maybe losing herself in physical labor would remove the anger and bitterness that plagued her at that moment. How could Naomi spit such venom at her? She'd tried all she knew to be good to the lady. At that moment, Hannah felt more alone and helpless than at any time in her life. And there had been so many lows.

Chapter 4

*Blessed is that servant whom his master when he cometh shall
find so doing. Verily I say unto you,
he shall make him ruler over all his goods."*
Matthew 24:46-47

Hannah gathered the Kincaid people on the front porch of
Sanctuary Hill. In the week since they'd met with Hugh Kincaid's
attorney, she decided the only real hope of saving something of the
estate would be to recruit the people who had always lived on the land
to become tenant farmers. Without money, she would offer them forty-
acre farms as payment for their labor on the land that Sonny owned.
Their work was already shown in the condition of the porch where she
now sat. Two days of constant work had removed the overabundance
of wisteria, morning glory vines, and weeds that had greeted them the
day they arrived. Cobwebs had been swept from every corner. Thanks
to Lucas's handiwork, the chain had been repaired, and the swing now
hung, ready to welcome any guest that may come to Sanctuary Hill.
The porch was a bright and sunny retreat, even if the rest of the house
was not.

The former slaves had yet to cease work even though gratitude
was the only payment Hannah had been able to give. She knew a time
would come when need would pull the Kincaid families from the land.
Alone, she couldn't raise enough cotton or even make a garden big
enough to feed Naomi, Sonny, and herself. She knew Sonny would

work hard, but her only true hope rested on the offer she was about to make.

Hoof beats pounded on the cobbled drive. "Mornin' lass. By glory, 'tis a beautiful spring day to see ya sittin' here on the porch. Are ya enjoyin' a quiet time before the day begins?"

"Mr. Kincaid, you are a bit early for a visit with my mother-in-law, aren't you?"

"Did I get the time wrong? Sonny told me you'd asked to see all the Kincaid family this mornin'." Kell removed his hat and smiled broadly.

"I didn't mean you." Hannah rose and walked to the front of the porch. "I plan to discuss a business arrangement with Mr. Hugh's people if it's any of your business."

"Yes, ma'am, I believe it is. And they aren't Mr. Hugh's people anymore." Sliding from the tall gray stallion's back, he seated himself on the porch near the swing.

"I know that...I just meant..."

Kell cut her short. "Don't be angry, Hannah Murphy. I've offered to help. You're not the only one with obligations to this family."

"Didn't I make it plain to you that I don't want your help? I know what I'm going to do. I don't need a man to do for me what I can do for myself." She turned toward the front door but stopped when Lucas and Shataka rounded the corner of the house with their babies in arm.

"Mornin', Miss Hannah," Shataka said. "We brought our chil'ren just as you said, the whole family. My mama and Mom Bec are right behind us. Lucas is haulin' 'em over in the wagon 'cause Mom Bec don't walk so fast no more."

"Good morning. I am glad to see y'all."

"Mornin', Mr. Kell. Mighty fine day here bouts."

"Certainly is, Marcus."

Within five minutes, the entire population of Sanctuary Hill minus one had gathered on the porch. Naomi refused to take part in the meeting. Truthfully, Hannah was relieved she wouldn't have to deal with her mother-in-law's intrusion as she laid out plans she'd designed to return Sanctuary Hill to a viable farm capable of supporting the surviving members of the Kincaid family.

"Thank you for meeting me here this morning. Because of your hard work, we have a pleasant place to talk about what we need to do here to keep our home."

Fanning her face with her apron, Shataka stood up and cried out, "Lordy Be, Miss Hannah. I was scared to death you and Mr. Sonny was gonna send us away. We hear the meetin' with the lawyer didn't go so good."

Marcus walked over and put his arm around his wife. "Ya know, she done tole us we can stay. Stop your frettin', woman." He turned back to Hannah. "It's good to have work to do again. The Lord didn't intend his chil'ren to be idle."

"I don't see that y'all have ever been idle. Even after the war, you pulled a living from the land for your family. My family is grateful to you for saving our home."

"We jist did what we had to do, like we always do," Shataka said.

"I know, Shataka, but y'all kept enough intact for us to live here now. This is what I think we need to do—what we should do—if you are willing." Hannah paused and looked toward Kell Kincaid. She was puzzled by his silence. "I have little money, so I can't hire y'all to work the land for me." She noticed complete silence, downcast eyes, frowns, and fear on the faces of the Kincaids.

"When Mr. Oldham read the will, Sonny inherited everything that had belonged to Mr. Hugh. The land is the biggest part of the estate, but he left little money. We may be able to survive here with your help until we can get the land back into production. If we can grow a crop, we should have enough money to pay the taxes and supply our need through the winter. There would be no money to pay wages."

"You want us to work your land for nothin'?" Rose asked.

"No, Rose. I want you to work OUR land. If your family decides to stay here, I'll deed parcels of land to each of your families, and you will pay me for that land with your work on all the land. Sonny will sell you each a forty-acre farm at half the present land value."

"You sayin' we can own our farm?" Lucas Kincaid's eyes were the size of marbles, and his jaw dropped after he spoke.

Hannah nodded. "Yes, Lucas. It's only fair if you work the land, you should own some of it."

Mom Bec stood up from the step and rubbed her hands together. "Ain't never heared of such thing. Since when is the master given way what's his?"

Kell took the old woman's gnarled hand. "Miss Hannah's no master here. She's a businesswoman askin' if ya want to work to buy a farm. She needs workers, and y'all need a home."

"Ya thinks we can grow a crop that will feed us and let us pay for the land?" Marcus asked.

"All I can say is we can try." Hannah returned to the swing.

"Say you'll do it, Marcus. I'd like to work here on our farm with you, growing cotton and stuff. Pal would help us, too. I think we can do fine 'cause we're good friends already." Sonny slapped him on the back. "Come on. Tell her yes."

The Kincaid family bunched together at the far end of the porch. Animated but muffled conversation continued for some time.

Kell walked to the swing. "May I join ya? Will some time before they thresh out this dream you've just dropped into their world."

"Yes, I'm sorry I don't have more chairs to offer visitors." As he sat down, Hannah moved to the far side of the swing.

"I promise not to take advantage of ya, lassie."

"Oh, it's not that."

"Hey, Hannah, why's your cheeks the same color as them morning glories by the porch?" Sonny plunked himself down on the step.

"Just too much sun yesterday. Go see if your mother is up, please." Hannah turned away from Kell, unsure of what to say.

"Ya did a fine thing this mornin', Mrs. Murphy. In this new world we live in, sharin' the land is the only reality big farmers have. We're all land-poor now. If we can't find a way to share what we have, we'll lose it all to taxes and greed."

"Seemed to be a solution. I didn't know what other options I had."

"The path you chose won't be an easy one. Last year, Arkansas law didn't allow the Black man to own property. Last year, President Johnson even tried to veto the Civil Right Code that promised some rights to the freed slaves. The Congress overrode his veto and then tried to impeach him."

"I know about the impeachment. Talk was raging all over Washington when we left. I thought the Northern states didn't like having a President from the South."

"Goes so much deeper than that. People around here won't take kindly to having neighbors who were slaves livin' next to them." Hannah looked across Kell's shoulders to look at the Kincaids.

"How else are the people who worked all this land going to make a living if they can't farm for themselves?"

"The old planters want them to become sharecroppers. They can control so much through contracts that way. If you decide to make the Kincaids tenant farmers, ya better keep the business end of your bargain to yourselves. Warn them not to go braggin' they got their own farms. Old ways die hard."

"I thought you came here to stop me this morning," Hannah said.

"You don't think much of me, do ya, lass?" Kell's brogue strengthened when he spoke of personal matters.

"I don't think of you at all. I don't even know you."

"Oh, it's that ya just don't like men in general?"

"You are the most exasperating human I've ever met. Why did you come over here today anyway?"

A grin grew across the width of Kell's face before a deep laugh broke the silence. "I came to invite my cousin, Sonny, and you to church on Sunday. We'll be having dinner on the grounds, singing in the afternoon, and our Bible class in the evenin'. I thought it would allow ya to get to know some folks before ya reopen the mercantile."

"I don't think--"

Kell broke in. "It's a small community church. It's all that's left since the war. Doesn't matter. The folks are good people, and we all pray to our same Lord. Will ya come?"

"I'll ask Mother Naomi if she wants to go. Thank you for the invitation."

"Well, I can see how pleased you are with my offer, but I do hope you'll decide to come. If you are gonna live and do business here, you need to know the people who call this county home."

Before Kell could take his leave, Marcus Kincaid interrupted his farewell. "Mr. Kell, Miss Hannah, 'cuse me. We don't 'xactly know how this will work, but we always trusted Mr. Hugh. We'll be takin' the deal 'cause we want to stay here at Sanctuary Hill. This be the Kincaid homeplace, and we sure is Kincaids."

"Marcus, thank you for your trust. We will make this legal so you can rest assured you'll own your farm."

Mom Bec, the matriarch of the Black Kincaids, stepped forward. Tears streamed down her lined face. "Miss Hannah, Lord bless ya for the angel ya be. I feared we'd have to go. I got only one dream left. I wanna rest by my man Gabe in our church yard." She wiped her face on her apron. "Never in my days did I dream I'd live on my own land."

"I'm afraid we'll have to work hard and long hours, but I think we can make a good home for all the Kincaids." Hannah laid her arm across the shoulders of the dear old woman who worked so hard to feed them all.

Lucas Kincaid spoke out. "We ain't afraid of hard work, Missus. And it's nigh time to get to those cotton fields if we're gettin' a crop in this year." Lucas slapped Marcus on the back, and they sprinted toward the shed. The others followed and for the first time, Hannah heard the family sing the words to an old spiritual.

"*Go down, Moses...way down to Egypt land...tell ole Pharoah 'Let my People go.'*"

"Lucas is right. If we're gonna have a crop this year, I'd better get to work," Hannah said.

"Ya aren't goin' to the fields, are ya?" Kell asked.

"I can't ask them to do anything I'm not willing to do. Sonny and I will help get the seeds in the ground. When that's done, I'll re-open the mercantile."

Kell took off his hat and stared at the woman before him. He shook his head. "As I was sayin', I hope you will come Sunday and meet the folks from around the county. You'll need to make friends if you want to live and do business hereabouts."

"I'll consider what you're saying. Good-bye, Mr. Kincaid."

"One more thing—don't make this plan you struck with the Kincaids too public. Don't use Mr. Hugh's lawyer or anyone else local. Just don't talk about it and warn the Kincaids. It's best for now."

Kell Kincaid mounted his tall gray horse and rode down the drive. Before he turned toward his farm, he lifted his hat in farewell.

℘

When Sunday came, Naomi, Sonny, and Hannah drove the short distance to the Linden Community Church with Kell riding aside in escort. Hannah had seen the small, clapboard building from a distance on her trip to the mercantile, but she was truly enthralled by the quaint, whitewashed structure with a steeple and gleaming brass bell as they drove into the churchyard. The church was set among beautiful trees surrounded by a groomed lawn. The yard blazed with a myriad of flowers, and greenery crept up the neat stone wall that separated the cemetery from the yard. Undoubtedly, this place was well-loved by its congregation.

Having arrived near time for the service, most of the people had gone inside to worship before Kell could make introductions. He opened the door and led the Murphys to an empty pew midway down the aisle. The first half-hour the congregation sang familiar hymns as the preacher led the singing. Linden Community Church had no musical instruments. Hannah wondered at the lack. She'd not attended church much since her marriage, but when she was younger all the churches she'd attended had a harpsichord or piano. She wondered if this congregation had lost its piano to the looting during the war. Even without accompaniment, the harmony of the voices rang out, full of praise and joy.

Following the singing, Brother Naylor, the preacher, spent several minutes announcing the news of the county. Mrs. Snyder had given birth to a son. The Jenkins family lost their cow on Friday. The sheriff was looking for the thief who took three chickens from the Arnold farm. Sonny took in every word. Finally, the ushers collected the offering. Hannah gave Sonny two coins to place in the brass plate.

Kell whispered to Hannah, "Ya didn't have to do that. Visitors aren't expected to give to our church."

"We pay our way, Mr. Kincaid."

The next forty minutes, Brother Naylor spoke about the nature of a man named Jesus. The beginning of the sermon usually provided Hannah with the opportunity to drift into her own world, but she found herself completely wrapped in the portrayal of this man whose name she knew, but whom she had never known. At her family's church in Sharpsburg, Maryland, where she had grown up, the service was formal, and the homily preached each Sunday morning did little to catch a young girl's attention. To hear the heart-felt, sincere words coming from a somewhat educated preacher touched her more than any sermon she'd ever been exposed to. Brother Naylor's testimony rang authentic and powerful, and he followed each example with a passage he read from the Bible. This church was not the kind of church that Hannah had known as a girl. When the sermon ended, her mind was filled with so many questions. She'd have to ponder them alone. She didn't know anyone she could ask about such things.

At the close of the sermon, Kell led them to the grove behind the tiny building. The arbor, surrounded on three sides by ancient evergreen trees, provided an ideal place to hold a dinner on the ground. Gentle breezes rustled through the branches and kept the hungry flies away from the abundance of food laid on plank tables. Ladies stood behind the tables, waiting to serve their menfolk and children, as they did the last Sunday of the month from March through October.

"Naomi, dear cousin, let me take you over and find you a place to sit among our ladies." Kell offered his arm.

"Kell, you should have told me we'd be having lunch. We could have brought our share." Naomi shook her finger at her much younger kinsman.

"Never mind that. There'll be food enough and more. Everyone will carry home supper. I want ya to meet your neighbors." They walked over to the ladies behind the table. Animated talk spilled out, and hugs came from right and left. Many of the women had been companions of Naomi in her youth.

Kell returned to Sonny and Hannah who were standing under a large maple tree. He pulled a barrel over for Hannah to sit on. "Do you want me to introduce ya to the younger matrons here today, Hannah?"

"I suppose. Neither Sonny nor I know a soul here, except you and Naomi."

"I'll go water Graystoke and Pal. Then I'll come back to join ya."

Kell's absence seemed an eternity to Hannah. She felt totally out of place sitting here under the huge maple tree with Sonny standing behind her, as if he feared being left alone. Brushing her palms down the front of her travel suit, she knew she was dressed entirely wrong for the day. She fidgeted with her hair, realizing no one else had taken the pains she had. Sonny paced a step or two, back and forth behind her, making her even more uncomfortable. Her observations of the people gathering in the arbor told her they were as leery of her as she felt toward them.

Sonny bent down and whispered in Hannah's ear. "Hannah, how long will my mama be gone?"

"Don't fret. She'll come back in a few minutes and bring you something to eat."

But Naomi didn't return. Even from a distance, Hannah saw her mother-in-law laughing and talking to a group of ladies who appeared to be about her age. When Brother Naylor called for quiet and blessed the food, she found a place to share the noon meal among her old friends. People formed lines down both sides of the plank tables. Hannah and Sonny continued to sit under the tree.

"Hannah, ain't we invited?" Sonny asked.

Kell approached them from behind the trees. "Everyone's invited. You know that. I was comin' to get y'all. Pal and Graystoke have been fed and watered, so let's go get ours. Mrs. Murphy, may I have your hand?"

Hannah rose and took Kell's arm. He led them to the table where he introduced them to the preacher.

"We're pleased to have Mr. Kincaid's family with us today. Are ya visitin' Linden?"

"No, Reverend. We have returned to my mother-in-law's home to live. We intend to remain at Sanctuary Hill."

"Oh, Mrs. Murphy, please don't call me reverend. My flock just calls me Brother Naylor or by my given name, Sam. We don't stand much on ceremony here. Can y'all live in that old cottage of Hugh's? That place took a beatin' toward the end of the war."

"Yes. We are making repairs as we are able," Hannah replied.

"Lord love ya. Perhaps our church can help. Don't hesitate to ask when we can do something to lift your load."

"That's very kind. I did enjoy your sermon today. I liked the way you wove the scripture into your storytelling. I found that very interesting. Not what I remember church being like back in Maryland." Hannah turned to leave, thinking she had said too much.

"Thank ya for your kind words, Mrs. Murphy. We hope you'll come again."

"Please call me Hannah. Naomi is Mrs. Murphy in our household."

The dinner on the grounds provided a more than filling meal. Hannah's dire need for a nap suggested it was overfilling. The peach cobbler spooned on her plate last was like manna from heaven, and she ate much more than she wanted. Following the meal, people broke

59

into cliques and began talking together. The groups were either all men or all women. In some places scattered across the churchyard, single mothers sitting on quilts covered their bodices with baby blankets and nursed small babies, rocking them to sleep. Groups of younger men moved toward the back of the church to smoke or have a chaw of their favorite tobacco. Sonny didn't join them. He decided to take a nap, too. Hannah returned to the upturned barrel to sit.

After a while, two women approached her. They introduced themselves and made small talk for a few minutes. Hannah tried to smile and respond, but she quickly found they had little in common. They were young mothers, married, and homemakers. When Hannah said she was widowed, they expressed their sympathy. Shortly, they returned to their friends. Mrs. Naylor walked over and brought her a glass of cool lemonade. Like her husband, she thanked her for visiting and asked Hannah to return. "You'd be mighty welcome here at Community Church, Mrs. Murphy. I know Ms. Naomi would feel like she's come back home, too."

Later, she stood up from her barrel seat, took a couple of steps, smoothed the front of her skirt for the twentieth time that day, and retied the bow on her mourning bonnet. She paced a bit. Her biggest desire at that moment was to go back to Sanctuary Hill. At least there, she could put her time to good use.

"Lass, would you like to walk with me for a spell?" Kell had walked up behind her again.

"Do you always have to do that? Where is my mother-in-law? We should start home."

"Ya don't wanna go now…We'll have singin' after a bit and then our evenin' service."

"I think I've had enough church for one day. Do you know where Naomi is, Mr. Kincaid?"

"She's having a grand visit with friends from the time she was the belle of St. Francis County."

"I suppose she's forgotten she didn't come here alone. Sonny and I don't know anyone here."

"Ya know me, and I just asked if ya wanna go for a walk." Kell once again offered his arm to Hannah.

She nodded and took a step ahead of him, ignoring his arm. "I'll walk. That barrel is about as comfortable as the cypress floor I sleep on."

They walked toward Taylor's Creek. Hannah's demeanor softened a bit—her shoulders not quite so square and her posture more natural. Around them, the sounds of the crickets, frogs, and other living things near the creek joined the rustling leaves, creating a symphony so calming and lovely. "Lass, no human orchestra can outperform God's handiwork. I do love the sound of nature in the spring."

Hannah giggled under her breath. She had been ready to give Kell a tongue-lashing because he had brought her to this country church where she felt so out of place. Refusing to give him the upper hand, she placed a scowl on her face.

"Now, Mrs. Murphy, will ya tell me why ya have a pout on that pretty face? It's a glorious day. How can ya not be filled with joy, just bein' outside in all this beauty? Did someone mistreat ya today?"

"No one acted badly toward me, Mr. Kincaid. A couple of ladies came and spoke to me, but we didn't seem to have much to talk about."

"Did ya try to have a conversation with them?" Kell swept his arm toward a fallen log to show Hannah a place to sit.

"We didn't know each other so I didn't know what to say to them. I've never been the social one in our family. My mother-in-law has all those talents. After all, I was a stranger. I thought they might…."

"They could have been strangers too for all you knew. Did ya try to be friendly?"

Hannah jumped up from the log she'd just sat down on. Kell Kincaid was baiting her.

"You...you..." She couldn't get words out to express her frustration.

"Calm yourself down, Mrs. Murphy. Those ladies were as intimidated by you as you were by them. Look at you in your fine city clothes, widow's weeds, at that! Your husband's been dead these three years. Why do you still wear that garb?"

Hannah turned her back. "I see nothing wrong with my clothes."

Kell reached across the short distance and took her arm. "Do you still mourn Richard Murphy, lass?"

"That is a personal question, sir, and frankly, I don't see what concern it is of yours." She began to walk back down the path to the church. Kell put his arms around her to stop her retreat. She froze in her tracks and then jerked away with all her strength.

"Don't touch me. Leave me be." Hannah tried to run. Kell planted his boot on the tail of her dress. Hannah fell backward and found herself sitting in a heap of crinoline and black serge.

Covering his face with his hand, Kell stifled a laugh. "I'm sorry, Mrs. Murphy. I didn't mean to cause a fall. Please let me help you up."

"I told you to leave me alone. I don't need your help, nor do I want it." The ice in Hannah's voice rang clear. She pushed herself to her feet, brushed her skirt, and walked back to the churchyard.

♬

Brother Naylor met Kell when he returned. "You've quite a scowl on your face, my friend. Are ya havin' a problem with your young lady?"

"Heaven forbid, Sam. She's no young lady of mine."

"She left in such a hurry. I thought surely you'd had a spat."

"Brother Naylor, Mrs. Murphy is Naomi Kincaid's daughter-in-law. She's a cousin of sorts. She's the most exasperating female I've ever met."

"So?"

"No, I'm tellin' ya truly. You know I came to Arkansas to see to the needs of my uncle. He asked me to care for his daughter and her kin because the war had left her a widow. My cousin Naomi is pleasant enough. She'd let me step in to help, but the daughter-in-law fights me at every turn."

"Perhaps time will help the situation, Kell."

"That's the problem. We don't have much time. My uncle Hugh left them land rich but with little else. My cousin knows how to care for a grand manor house and carry out every Southern tradition and custom, but practical things seem beyond her grasp. Hannah thinks she must make a go of the farm and the family alone. And for all that is holy, she seems to hate me."

"She is strong-willed."

"She's stubborn. I am at a loss of how I can help."

"Maybe a good talk with the Lord will help."

"At least, I know He will listen. Thanks, Sam."

"That He will. Let's go in for the singin'."

Chapter 5

He giveth power to the faint, and to them that have no might, he increases strength...Even youth shall faint and be weary, and young men shall utterly fall. But they that wait upon the Lord shall renew their strength. They shall mount up with wings as eagles; they shall run, and not be weary, and they shall walk and not faint
Isaiah 40:29-31

Naomi dominated the talk around the dinner table that night with an endless stream about her conversations at the dinner on the grounds that afternoon. She spoke the names of every friend who had welcomed her home and repeated endless bits of gossip that meant nothing to either Hannah or Sonny. After nearly an hour of the chatter, Hannah felt she was near a screaming tantrum, but she bit her tongue and continued to feign attention.

"Hannah, I am so glad we went to church with Kell this mornin'. You and Sonny surely must have enjoyed the fine meal we shared."

"I had me five pieces of fried chicken. That was real fine," Sonny said. Hannah nodded her agreement.

Naomi chattered on and on about her renewed friendships and being home in the center of the social life of St. Francis County. She never seemed to notice that neither her son nor daughter-in-law added one thing to the conversation. About the time Hannah believed her mother-in-law was ready to retire to her room, Naomi's conversation took on a new direction.

"Hannah, how soon do you think we can open Sanctuary Hill to visitors again?" The pewter cup Hannah was holding clattered on the floor.

"Mother Naomi, on Saturday at 3:00, we finished planting the garden we must have to feed us. We have yet to break an inch of soil to plant cotton. Our house has only half a roof. To tell you the truth, I've given no thought at all to making this place ready for visitors."

"Oh, those things will come about soon now that we have our people working for us again."

"They aren't working for us. We are working with the Kincaids who live here on Sanctuary Hill. We are hoping we can keep the land. We are trying to keep life and limb together. I have one priority right now. We must get a cotton crop planted to raise enough money to pay our taxes." Hannah pulled the dishes across the table and headed toward the dry sink at the window.

"Goodness me, that is no concern for a lady. Surely your dear mother raised you better than that. I think I will have a quilting bee with the ladies of the church as soon as our things arrive from Washington."

"And what will you serve them? We presently have no tea or real coffee. You could have Mom Bec brew you some chicory, I guess. Of course, there is no sugar, baking soda, or spices to bake with. I guess we could share that half a jar of honey we've been hoarding."

"Aren't you being silly? I'll have Lucas drive me over to Madison to buy the things I need." Naomi got up and began to survey the room. "When do you think we will get our things from the capital?"

Hannah sank to her chair, her head drooping into her hands. The day had been difficult from the time she arose that morning. She hadn't wanted to go to the Community Church because she hated being the stranger in the group. Kell had convinced her that it was a smart business move, so she went. She found no welcoming companion among the young wives and mothers there. They were polite, but she felt no sense of belonging. Then in the afternoon, her nice walk along the stream with Kell turned into a spat, and she'd embarrassed herself in front of Naomi's kinsman. Naomi's supper conversation guaranteed the day would end in disaster, as it had begun. Only the young preacher's sermon had shined a bright spot for Hannah.

"Hannah, I asked you a question." Naomi snapped at her.

"I am sorry. I'm tired. The station master said we could expect our furnishings at the first of the month, no later than the tenth of May."

"That's fine. That will give me enough time to plan a social by the end of the month. Sonny dear, you look tired. I think it's time for bed. You too, Hannah. Leave those dishes for Mom Bec." Naomi swept from the kitchen taking the best lantern with her.

"I'll help ya, Hannah. Want me to fetch some water?"

"Yes, please. And if you will, put that big kettle on the stove to heat some dishwater. I'll stoke the stove while you go to the well." Within the hour, they put the kitchen in order to prepare breakfast at sunrise. Both the Murphys knew they would spend the next six days plowing. Perhaps planting sixty acres of cotton would save Hugh Kincaid's legacy. But how long would it take to plow sixty acres with only two plows, one mule, and a fine old horse named Pal?

"Goodnight, Sonny. Thank you for helping me today. I will see you in the morning."

"Hannah, we're gonna be okay, I think. Don't you?"

"That's not like you, Sonny. Why did you ask me that? Are you worried about something?"

"You seem kinda sad today. I need you to be okay so I can be okay. Don't you fret. I'm gonna help you every day. I promise I will work hard."

Tears fell. She pulled her brother-in-law into a tight hug. He stood for a moment and then moved away. "Sonny, you are my helper every day. I'm okay because you are always here with me. You never complain and don't ask for things I can't give. I hope you sleep well tonight so we can get a lot of work done tomorrow."

Together they climbed to the second story. "Good night, Hannah."

"Good night, brother."

Hannah went to her room at the end of the hall. She'd endured as much as she could for one day. Sonny's sweet words as they parted ruptured the dam that had held back every ache, disappointment, regret, unfulfilled hope, and shattered dream she'd stored. The time in Arkansas had been the hardest, loneliest, most frightening period of her life. The long, drawn-out bantering of her mother-in-law nearly destroyed the wall of silence and tolerance she'd sworn to maintain where Richard's mother was concerned.

She sank into the small chintz chair she'd salvaged from one of the fire-damaged rooms. Hannah wrinkled her nose at the acrid smell of smoke still permeating the fabric. She looked around her private sanctuary–a pale blue room with smoke-stained lace curtains, her smelly chintz chair, and a pallet on the floor made of a feather bed, two blankets, a torn sheet, and one pillow. This was the totality of her domain, yet it was the only place she felt herself. Here, no one needed anything, and no one talked of things beyond reason. In this room, she answered only to herself.

Hannah pulled the hairpins from her not-so-neat chignon. Her tresses tumbled nearly to her waist. She dragged her fingers through her hair. *Too tired to brush this mane tonight.* She knew her mother would be disappointed with her. She removed the black traveling suit she'd worn to church that day and hung it on a peg. She let the white lawn nightdress slide down her tired frame. Her calloused and blistered hands snagged the delicate lace at the hem. *Where is the lady my mother wanted me to be? When did I lose that girl?* Hannah began to cry once again. She knew that loss started long before she came to Sanctuary Hill.

She lay on the pallet and pulled the sheet over her. Sleep didn't come quickly. Questions plagued her, one after another. Memories of things hoped for but never realized in her marriage pushed sleep farther away. The grief of losing her father and father-in-law in the war brought pain but also a real fear. How would she survive with the responsibilities of Naomi and Sonny without the resources she'd always known? That fear brought her close to despair. This was not the life she had been raised to live.

Hannah's gentle tears turned into racking sobs. She cried until she was spent. Finally, she stood, pulled her sleeve across her eyes, and scolded herself. "Stop this nonsense Hannah Ruth Kennedy! Who do you think is going to fix all the things that are wrong here? Get to work and find a way to survive. Your papa would be ashamed of you. Was it your pride telling Kell Kincaid that you needed no help this afternoon?

She remembered the list Kell had returned to her at the mercantile. *Why, I've already done two of those things. Sonny and I planted a large garden with the Kincaids' help, and I've made agreements with them to work in exchange for land. I can do this!*

She sat back in her chair and stared out the window. The cool breeze and the soft glow of the moonlight lifted her spirits. Then words from Brother Naylor's sermon came to mind. For some reason, Hannah liked the young pastor at the Community Church. He had said that when life's load gets too much to carry, give it to Jesus. Then he quoted the scripture, one she'd not remembered from her childhood.

He said, "Take my yoke upon you, and learn of me; for I am meek and lowly in heart: and ye shall find rest unto your soul. For my yoke is easy and my burden is light." The words brought the only peace she'd felt all day. She didn't understand how she was supposed to do it, but the remembering brought calm.

Hannah's inability to sleep was more than the day-to-day hardship and manual labor. She was soul weary. She had been for a very long time. She didn't know how to pray or to turn a load over to the man Brother Sam spoke of so tenderly.

She whispered, "I am tired. I wish I could rest." Almost at once, she yawned and stretched her arms. She walked across to her pallet one more time. She couldn't recall even laying her head on the pillow. For one night, Hannah slept the sleep of the innocents. When the rooster crowed the next morning, she awoke with a renewed energy. Not sure why, she knew she could face another week of hard work.

∮

With her strength back, Hannah approached the new day with the resolve to make a go of her lot in Arkansas. With the garden planted, she would put the negative thoughts away. She couldn't afford them anymore. The fastest way to lose Sanctuary Hill would be her failure to pay taxes. Copperheads and scalawags, derogatory names for Northerners and Southerners who had hidden their money away during the war, were buying up property for pennies per acre the minute the delinquent tax lists were posted in county courthouses. Arkansas, like all the Southern states, was strapped for funds. The state and the counties would not hesitate to sell their property due to delinquent taxes. They would not get Sanctuary Hill.

The day was beautiful. The sun was out, and tall, billowy clouds scooted across azure skies. In a nearby oak tree, two cardinals played chase, darting from limb to limb. Hannah heard the cooing of doves.

What a glorious day for a ride through the Arkansas countryside. Alas, that daydream belonged to the past.

Instead, Hannah and Sonny would join the Kincaids in clearing and plowing the four fifteen-acre fields. At a family meeting, they decided to plant just fifteen acres for each household this first year. If the price of cotton stayed fair, the amount grown should cover taxes and buy staples for the winter.

During those first weeks, Hannah worked harder than she'd ever worked. They used Pal and the one mule Lucas Kincaid had rescued from a slough to pull the plows—one old rusty plow from the shed and Lucas's plow. The small band plowed a ten-inch draw per row and set rows about a yard apart. Sonny took to farming as if he'd been born to till the land. He loved working with his horse and found easy company with the Kincaids.

Although she'd not been raised to the task, each day Hannah rose with the sun and worked the fields until sunset, just as did Shataka and Rose. She tied strips of cloth around her raw, bleeding hands so she could use the hoe to break clods of dirt and pull out well-rooted weeds. At sunset, she would walk back to Sanctuary Hill with Sonny. Often, she would fall into her pallet, too tired to do more than nibble at the supper Mom Bec always scraped up from somewhere.

A large thunderstorm blew across the county on Wednesday near the end of the workday. She didn't mind sending her crew home early that day. They'd made great progress. They had finished the plot for Sanctuary Hill, and if the weather stayed favorable, they could seed this field and move on to Mom Bec and Rose's field by Friday.

Despite the rain, Hannah was too tired to run. She trudged toward the shed to store the tools for the night. As she continued to drag herself toward the house, she smiled, remembering how much work they'd finished. She had not accomplished anything alone, but with the help of Sonny and the Kincaids, the promise of a crop seemed possible. The rain even took away the need to water their garden.

When Hannah entered the kitchen, she was soaked to the bone. "Mom Bec met her at the door. "Miss Hannah, ya put on a dry dress. Y'all is havin' company tonight. If ya hurry, ya can rest a few minutes so ya can enjoy the rest of the evenin'.""

"Since you are giving me permission, I'll take the rest of the night off. You're a dear, Mom Bec."

When Hannah returned to the kitchen, Naomi, Sonny, Kell, and Pastor Naylor and his wife were already seated at the makeshift table with a meal spread before them. Before Mom Bec left for her cabin, she had prepared a feast from the little they had in their larder. The table was laden with a platter of fried catfish, some pole beans, creamed corn, and pone. The meal was a feast for Hannah and Sonny who'd worked all day.

"Brother Naylor, I'm sorry we don't have anything special to offer you, but we have yet to fill our larder." Naomi waved her hand across the table to emphasize her plight. "I don't know when we'll get to Madison so we can buy supplies."

"Why my dear Mrs. Murphy, I love catfish fried up so golden. No one knows better how to do this than Mom Bec. I can't think of a meal I'd like more," the pastor answered.

Kell asked, "Miss Hannah, will you pass me the fish platter?" Hannah smiled, nodded, and picked up the pewter platter. "Thank ya. I know I'm hungry enough to eat anything, but this supper looks like a feast. I'll bet Sonny is hungry. He's worked awfully hard. Lucas said he'd never seen a straighter row plowed than Sonny and Pal's."

Naomi picked up her fork and began to distribute the fish. "May we bless this food before we eat it?" Kell asked.

Naomi nodded. "Brother Naylor, will you bless our meal?"

"Lord, thank you for this excellent meal and the company of this fine family on this rainy Wednesday night. We ask ya to bless those who worked to prepare this and all who will enjoy your gifts. Lord, we thank you for the rain. Brought us some nice cool air too. Father, we thank ya for our Lord Jesus. He is our constant blessing. In His name, Amen."

Over the clatter of dishes and Naomi's small talk, this meal lasted much longer than the food on the table. Naomi rose to bring a small blackberry cobbler that Mom Bec had left on the windowsill to cool. Just as she handed the Naylors and Sonny small dishes of cobbler, a stream of water dribbled across her forehead and down the front of her pink summer dress.

"Oh, good gracious. What has happened?" She looked up only to get a face full of water from the leak. "EEEEEK."

"It's all right, Mama."

"Sonny, grab that edge of the table, and let's move it over near the doorway, away from the leak." Everyone grabbed the chairs and barrels they were sitting on and moved across the room.

"What's to be done? How can we stay in this wreck of a house?" Hysterically, Naomi turned in circles, waved her arms, and paced back and forth.

"Mother Naomi, it's only a little rain. When it's over, we'll clean up the water in the kitchen. Please sit down and enjoy your cobbler. Mom Bec said these are the last of her canned berries until summer. We'll go with her when she gathers them and find some of our own." Hannah pulled out a chair for her mother-in-law and handed her a dish of dessert, but Naomi refused to stay in the kitchen. She took Brother Naylor and his wife into the parlor where she knew the roof was sound.

Sonny returned to his dessert, as did Kell. When Hannah was left alone with Kell, she got up to wash the supper dishes. "Why don't ya go in the parlor and help Mother Naomi entertain the pastor? I'll tend to this."

"Will ya let me help ya, lass? Ya must be tired after the long day you worked." Kell picked up two plates from the table. Then he picked up a bucket near the stove and put it under the leak.

"Kell, you are a guest here. I'll clean the dishes."

"Don't ya like my company?"

"I didn't say that. It's just not your place to do woman's work."

"Was it your place to work like a fieldhand in that cotton patch?"

Hannah picked up the remaining plates before she answered. "I have to do whatever it takes to keep a roof over our heads…."

They both broke into laughter. "Well, so much for that one," Hannah said. "I guess I'll have to try a little harder."

"You're an amazin' woman, Hannah Murphy. I suppose you already know that."

"Don't be ridiculous. If you want to eat, you grow food."

"That's not what I mean. How do you remain so composed—in control, as you did with Naomi tonight?"

"I'm sure I don't know what you are talking about."

"Hannah, just now you laughed at distress that should have brought you to tears."

"Would it have done any good to cry? I'd still have a house with half a roof. I guess I just make the best of what I have. We'll eat catfish instead of beef, and cobbler will do until we can have three-layer cake again. We can move a table to a dry spot if we need to."

Kell stared into her glistening brown eyes. "Do you have such a deep faith that ya can weather any storm, lass?"

"Faith? I'm not sure what that even means. I have to put one foot in front of the other and do what has to be done. My father was a stern man, and he taught me to face what life handed me. I will keep doing what is required. No Kennedy ever quit before the task was finished, nor did we ever break a promise. I will meet my responsibilities because I was raised that way."

"What about enjoying life, findin' beauty in the world around ya, carin' about the people, and lettin' them care about you?" Kell poured the heated water into the dishpan as Hannah placed the dishes into the soapy water.

"Kell, that water is too hot! The lye soap is bad enough…you don't have to scald me too."

"You always avoid answering questions about feelin', Hannah?"

"I'm not avoiding anything. That water is too hot."

"I can take care of that." He nudged her aside and plunged his arms into the hot soapy water. "Now, will ya answer my question?"

"I don't think about those things."

Naomi rushed through the kitchen door. "Come and say goodbye to the Naylors, Hannah and Kell. The rain seems a bit lighter, and they are headed home. I am so glad their buggy has a top, so they won't get drenched like I did tonight."

They made their way to the front room to wish the Naylors an easy trip home and then returned to the dishes.

They finished the task in silence until Kell took Hannah's arm and led her to the porch swing. The deep porch sheltered them from the continuing rainfall.

"Let's sit a while." Kell held the swing steady for Hannah to sit down.

"Maybe for a few minutes. I'm tired. This rain is wonderful, though, like a symphony as the raindrops strike different things."

"I love the sound of rain on the roof. If this gentle staccato continues, it'll be a great night for sleepin'," Kell said.

"If it doesn't tap on my head." Together, they laughed again.

Chapter 6

The heart of the prudent getteth knowledge,
and the ear of the wise seeketh knowledge.
Proverbs 18:15

Kell nudged Graystoke into a gallop as he left the porch at Sanctuary Hill. He turned his face skyward, aware of the full moon that had made its presence since the rain stopped. "Let's fly home, Gray. I do believe the lass is ready to let me inside that wall." Kell kicked his horse gently, urging him into a faster gallop.

For the first time since they'd met, Kell sensed that Hannah wanted to reach out to someone. She had talked more that night than at any time they'd been together. She'd not put up her defenses. Of course, there had been nothing special about their conversation. They'd talked about the chores, laughed about Naomi's face-washing in the kitchen, and talked about Sonny's affliction a bit. He could hardly believe that they spent the whole evening together, and Hannah had not lost her temper once. He believed she'd enjoyed their talk, perhaps even as much as he had.

Of course, he had steered clear of any topic that he feared was too personal or questions about her marriage. Those things always seemed to trigger Hannah's defenses. Kell had no idea how she felt about her dead husband. Once he'd suggested that Hannah didn't seem to mourn although she chose to wear clothes of grief. That statement had shut down communication entirely. As much as he wanted to talk with her about more than trivial things and work, he had learned his lesson. If he wanted to have a real conversation with Hannah, he'd bide his time.

And he did want to. Since he'd watched her dance in the clover-filled meadow the first time he saw her, she had been on his mind. That afternoon, she seemed so full of life and joy, and then her world crashed around her as she fell to the ground, screaming from her very soul. When Kell closed his eyes, he could still hear her scream echoing through his memory. He'd even relived the episode in his dreams. The powerful stallion had slowed to meandering in Kell's inattention. "Ya know, Gray, I do believe the Lord put me on the bank of that creek on that night. I'm not knowing yet why, but He intends me to do something to help that bonny lass."

Then he slipped off Graystoke's back and walked the few steps to the creek that separated his farm from Sanctuary Hill. He knelt in the quiet of the evening, only the babble of the stream catching his attention. He prayed as he often did when he needed direction.

"Father, I do thank ya for the very fine evenin'. The time I spent with my family provided a balm to my spirit…helped to erase some of the homesickness I've felt for Scotland of late. And then I had a while with Hannah, and we talked as friend to friend. I'm askin' ya to show me what you'd have me do, though. I know Hannah doesn't know ya, Lord. Bless her heart, she thinks she has to traverse this world all alone, carrying the weight of that family. As I am gettin' to know her, I think the lass has been alone nearly all her life.

"But what a woman she is, Lord. She's smart, sharp-witted, and strong. I've never seen such devotion to family in anyone so young…and they're not even blood. She'll keep that promise to my cousin's husband. I've naught a doubt. I've never known a woman to work as hard as she has these past weeks. Lord, please intervene. Help her find a better way in You. I'll ask this favor in the name of Your Son, Amen."

♫

After morning chores, checking on his small herd of cattle and the few horses he was raising to train and sell, Kell made a quick run into Linden. A swift morning ride on his beautiful gray horse was usually a treat, but this morning he was on a mission. He wanted to talk with Sam Naylor. With so much on his mind and a few local rumors that he'd heard, he had tossed and turned the entire night.

Kell galloped into the churchyard just as Sam pounded a nail into the handrail of the porch. "Morning, Kell. What brings you to town on this sunny Thursday morning?"

"Needed a friend to talk to. I got none better than you, Sam."

"I'll never turn down a chance to spend time with a brother. Come on down and sit with me in the grove. The sun's already makin' itself known today."

Kell wiped his brow with his kerchief. "Sounds good to me. Hadn't noticed how hot it was until I stopped." They walked a short distance to the grove that separated the church from the cemetery. A few carved benches were scattered among the trees.

"What's on your mind, brother?"

"Really, two things, Sam. One is a concern about my family."

"Is someone in the Kincaid family sick out there at Sanctuary Hill?"

"No, nothin' like that. I suppose you've heard that Hannah and Sonny have contracted with the Kincaids to work the land in exchange for a parcel of land."

"Truth be told, Kell, no one knows exactly what she'd done. We both know it was Hannah's doing and not Sonny's. People around town have speculated about everything from hiring them for wages,

77

takin' them on as sharecroppers, or offering to swap land for work. Just a lot of talk."

"Hannah did the right thing. She doesn't have money to hire help. Uncle Hugh did what every other planter in the delta did. He invested most of his money in Confederate bonds."

"That's a shame. Are they destitute, Kell?"

"Not yet. They have some food. They've made a garden. Right now, they are planting small plots of cotton to sell for taxes."

"Do they have enough workers to do that much?" Sam Naylor shook his head in disbelief.

"They have six adults and three children old enough to work cotton." Kell lifted his arm to the height of his waist to show the size of the children.

"I didn't realize that many of Mr. Hugh's people stayed at Sanctuary Hill."

"Marcus, Shataka, Mom Bec, Rose and her two other children, and Lucas with his two boys. They still live in their cabins in the quarters. Mom Bec is too old to work in the fields, but she is helping Naomi in the house."

"You said there were six adults. I only heard you call off four."

"Sonny and Hannah are working in the fields alongside the Kincaids."

Again, the preacher shook his head in disbelief. "Are you tellin' me that mite of a girl has been working as a field hand?"

"That's the Lord's truth. They work from sunup to sundown every day but Sunday."

"Lord help her! Wasn't she raised in a wealthy family in Maryland? Seem to remember Hugh Kincaid saying something about that "hothouse rose" that Richard had married."

"Hugh didn't know her if he thought she was a hothouse rose. She told me that she will do whatever it takes to make Sanctuary Hill prosper again. She swore it on her father-in-law's deathbed."

"This seems to have got you all bothered, brother. Why is this causing you to lose sleep?"

"Hang it all, Sam. I ain't got a clue. Ever since I saw her, she's been a fixture in my head."

"Are ya smitten?" A grin covered the largest part of the pastor's face.

"Wouldn't do me much good if I were. She has told me more than once that she wants no interference in her life. She doesn't seem to take to me much, truth be told."

"I know you, Kell Kincaid. You love the thrill of a chase. You'd not give her a second thought if she fell into your arms. You're up to the challenge."

"Sam, that's not what I want to ask ya. Ya see, Hannah believes she's alone. She doesn't feel a part of the family or the community…I'm not sure she ever has felt she belongs anywhere. She sees herself as obligated to earn a living for Naomi and Sonny by herself. She doesn't have the comfort and peace that comes from knowin' the Lord loves her."

"How do you know that's so?" Sam asked.

"She told me as much. I don't know what I can do to help. I thought maybe you could."

"I'd be glad to talk with her if she is interested. She hasn't shown much interest in church. She's been here only that one time."

"I've invited her every week, but I made her pretty angry that first day I brought her when we walked down by the creek."

"I'm startin' a Sunday afternoon Bible class here at the church. Maybe she'd like to join that group. Kell, you could ask her."

"I think the invitation would be better if you asked her, Sam. She did tell me she enjoyed the sermon you preached the day she visited."

"I'll ride out that way next week. Maybe the Lord will pique her interest—even if you can't." Sam Naylor slapped his friend on the back, and they laughed together.

"Have you heard of the night riders prowling this area of late?"

"Only rumors, but nothing I can say for a fact. Why are ya concerned?" Sam answered his friend.

"I'm hopin' those bullies don't get wind of the deal Sonny and Hannah made with the Kincaids. I told 'em not to talk about it. People hereabouts would let the Kincaids sharecrop, I think. But I got a feelin' in my gut that those vigilantes will cause problems if they know the Kincaids will own their farms in a few years. St. Francis County is Delta. Planters have been masters here for a long time. Some won't take to havin' Black neighbors."

"You're right, Kell. As much as I wish this war had truly freed our Black brother, many years will pass before the words written in our Declaration of Independence come to pass—that all men are created equal and treated equal...the way that God surely sees us all. We ain't there yet."

Chapter 7

Woe unto them that call evil good, that put darkness for light; that put bitter for sweet! Woe unto them that are wise in their own eyes, and prudent in their own sight.
Isaiah 5:20-21

Hannah awoke the following morning with a smile on her face. She stretched her arms widely and wrapped them around herself. She had slept the night through, even on the hard floor where her meager pallet lay. *Talking to Kell—one adult to another when I am not trying to appease or parent another person—is so freeing. He makes me laugh. I didn't think I'd ever laugh again.*

No sooner had the thoughts crossed her mind than Hannah shook herself and spoke aloud, "I'll never let any man become a serious part of my life." She threw off her coverlet. "I'll never let anyone order me around or tell me how to behave or what to think. I've had more than enough dictators in my life." Looking into a small mirror she'd hung on the wall above the chair, she jutted her chin out and scolded herself for her silly daydreams. *I am a free woman. No man's chattel. Hannah Ruth Kennedy Murphy will never again become the property of another man.* She pulled on her work clothes and jerked on her boots. Another day in the fields awaited.

Time blurred in the next weeks. Every day from sunrise to sunset, the small crew at Sanctuary Hill walked behind a plow, pulled a hoe to cover precious cotton seed, carried water to ensure the fertile ground had enough moisture to birth the tiny cotton plants, and pulled the intrusive weeds that seemed to grow up overnight. By Naomi's birthday on May 15th, they had plowed and planted all but one plot of the sixty acres of cotton they'd planned. Every night prayers went up from the tiny crew that the harvest would produce enough cotton to pay the taxes that would fall due at the end of the year.

One afternoon near the end of the day, Hannah found herself breaking clods in a field at Lucas Kincaid's farm. The men had gone earlier to plow the last three acres on the other side of the plot. A rare thing happened…Shataka asked Hannah straight out why she worked in the field alongside the Kincaids.

"Why shouldn't I work with y'all? Aren't we trying to do the same thing?"

"Well, yes, ma'am, we do be trying to earn some money for taxes. But I know you was raised up to be a lady, like Miss Naomi. She don't work the land."

"I know. She has had so many losses, and she is more delicate than I am. She has duties in the house, and Mom Bec works alongside her to keep us fed."

"Seem ya wasn't cut out for this life. I's amazed ya work so hard."

"Shataka, you've worked hard all your life. How have you been able to do all you've done?"

"Didn't know no other way to be. I's born a slave. We always taught to do the master's biddin' and don't cause no worry."

"But you don't seem angry or bitter that you had to live that way."

"Miss Hannah, you don't miss what ya never knew. I've had my share of blessin'. I tell ya truly that the Lord been mighty good to me."

"How can you say that, Shataka? You've worked your entire life for another's gain." Hannah slammed her hoe into a large clod of dirt that had defied her last blow.

"The Lord let us work for Mr. Hugh. He wasn't a mean master. He never used a whip on nary of his people. He fed us good and let us build solid cabins to live in. That's more blessin' than most of our people gits."

"Would you not have rather been born a free person of color?"

"Can't say yes or no. I got no way of knowin' how they live. We all happy that you 'llowed us to stay here and keep our homes. We got work, and we all talk about the dream comin' true for us. We thank the Lord every night that someday soon we'll own our farm."

"Shataka, would you be happier being somewhere else? Is this life one you like?"

"Every man got his thorn to bear. At night when I am wrapped in Marcus's arms in our cabin, he tell me I'm the only woman he ever love…that's my joy. I see my babies, growin' healthy and strong…that's my happiness. No, ma'am, I don't rightly see myself any wheres else."

"Sanctuary Hill is home to you, isn't it?"

"Yes, indeed. I's home because the man I love is here, and we are doin' the work to make us a real home. God's smilin' down on us each day when the sun comes up."

"That's a wonderful way to look at life, Shataka."

"I wished you had some of those things, Miss Hannah. The work don't seem nearly so burdensome when you have some of life's good things, too."

φ

Because every day's labor was the same, the passage of time didn't seem to matter. The next day was a repeat of the previous. Hours of toiling in the delta soil as the Arkansas sun beat down relentlessly on her shoulders had left its mark. Had not Rose given her a wide-brim straw hat she'd woven, her face would be the same golden color of her arms. She certainly didn't look the part of a Southern lady.

One Sunday morning, Naomi called up, "Hannah, Sonny, please get ready. Cousin Kell will be here in half an hour to drive us to church."

"Be down in a minute, mama. Gotta get this cowlick to lay down," Sonny shouted back. "We got anything for breakfast?"

Hannah pulled her limp pillow over her head. Every bone in her body ached, and she found it a chore to turn from her side to her back. No, she wasn't going to get up and dress to make an appearance at church that day. She intended this day to be her day of rest.

Sonny poked his head into her room. "Ain't ya gonna go to church with us today?"

"No, Sonny. Tell your mother I'm not well. I'll see y'all when you get home later this afternoon."

"Mama's gonna be mad at ya, Hannah."

"I'm sorry, but please, Sonny, just tell her what I said." Hannah heard Graystoke's shoes strike the cobbles near the porch. When she heard murmuring, she knew Naomi was making an excuse for her absence. She didn't care. Shortly, the wagon wheels indicated the trio had started on their trip to Linden. Hannah rolled over and went back to sleep at once.

About an hour later, she rose and breathed deeply the fresh spring air. The day was warm already but not unbearably hot. She finally had some time for herself. There was no work to be done, no family to answer to, and no excuses to make to anyone. For a few hours, she could do what she wanted to do. She took a towel and soap and walked to the creek. She craved a cool, leisurely bath. Sunday morning would allow her to pamper herself with a luxury that was rare most days. On workdays, too many people needed the creek, but today she could enjoy the beauty and peace of Mill Brook Creek. She spent more than an hour floating, splashing, and frolicking like a child in the blissful Eden before she got down to the serious business of bathing and washing her raven tresses. When she raised her head from the water after rinsing her hair, she startled. The birds, insects, and other living creatures around the creek had become deadly quiet. The scent of the air was different. Something was very wrong.

Hannah recognized the smell of smoke. The air was quickly filling with a stench of charred wood. She ran to the bank and gathered her clothes and boots. She pulled them on and began to run back toward the house. Before she got to the yard, she saw the reason for the smoke. The vacant cabin next door to Lucas Kincaid's cabin in the quarters was fully engaged in flame. Huge orange, black, and red tongues of fire pushed through the windows and lapped at the roof shingles. The porch had collapsed already.

No one was around to fight the fire. The Kincaids were all at the Black church more than three miles away. The congregation usually worshipped all day on Sunday, and they would not return until nightfall. The wind was calm, thankfully, and embers didn't seem to blow very far. Some of them did blow onto the grass between the cabins, and Hannah began to beat them out with her damp towel. She knew she would have to stand watch to ensure that the burning cabin didn't ignite the one shared by Lucas and his boys.

About noon, a breeze kicked up. The few grass fires that started from the embers began to spread. Hannah feared all the cabins in the quarter would be lost if she didn't keep the brush fires beat down. She ran back to the creek and soaked her towel and returned to beat the flames away from the other cabins. Her towel dried in the intense heat and caught fire. She threw it to the ground and stamped out the flame. What was left was too small to smother the growing grassfires. She pulled her skirt off and ran to the creek to soak the heavy chino. Once again, she returned to the endless slapping at the fire, pushing it back from Lucas's porch. She didn't know how long she stood between the flame and the houses of her tenant farmers.

Finally, the roof of the first cabin collapsed, and the flames died down. Her skirt was scorched beyond repair, so she threw it into the embers of the burned-out cabin. When the heat touched her skin, she realized her hands and arms had been burned, too. With the danger past, she dragged herself back to the house. About the time Hannah entered the back door, Kell arrived at the front porch with Sonny and Naomi. He ran ahead.

"Hannah, are ya here, lass? We smelled the smoke. Has something happened? Are ya all right?"

"Yes, Kell. I am all right. I lost my restful Sunday that I'd planned, but I'm all right."

He saw the red whelps on Hannah's hands and arms. "Have ya been fightin' a fire by yourself?"

Naomi waved her fan and gasped. "My dear gracious Lord. What have you done to yourself, Hannah?" The older woman bustled frantically from one person to the next in the room. "Kell, what's happened here? Sonny, get Hannah some water."

"Please calm down, Mother Naomi. One of the empty cabins in the quarter burned down this afternoon. I kept the fire from reaching any of the Kincaids' cabins. I seemed to have gotten a burn or two while I was putting out the grassfires that threatened the other cabins. I don't think we lost very much."

"Lass, do ya have an idea how the fire started?" Kell asked.

"I've no hint. No one lived there since we've been back at Sanctuary Hill. We've kept the empty cabins barred to prevent migrants and vandals from abusing the empty houses. There is no heat source there like a stove or fireplace."

"Well, Sonny and I will go down to have a look. Maybe we can find a reason for a cabin to catch fire all by itself. Come on, Sonny. Let's go make sure the embers are dyin' out so another fire doesn't start." He rushed out.

Hannah began to feel the pain of the deep burns. She went to the dry sink and plunged her arms up to the elbows into the bucket of water sitting there. The cool water took away the heat and alleviated some of the pain. She tried to remember what her mother had used to sooth burns so many years ago. The only thing that came to mind was the time her mother rubbed her hand with butter when she'd closed an ember in her palm. Of course, they had no butter because they had no cow. *Maybe lard will do as well.*

Hannah smeared both her arms and hands with the lard Mom Bec had rendered for cooking. After a short while, some of the pain eased. Hannah climbed to her room and dropped to her pallet. She slept.

ⱷ

Kell and Sonny scoured the area around the burnt-out cabin. Kell quickly found three sets of horseshoe prints that didn't belong to either Pal or Graystoke. In several places, the weeds around the unoccupied cabins had been crushed by heavy boots. "Sonny, this cabin didn't burn for any natural cause. Someone set it on fire. I have a suspicion that some of our local night riders set the blaze ...trying to scare off the tenant farmers," Kell said.

"They could have hurt Hannah bad!"

"They want to get y'all to leave the area. If ya were afraid, ya may decide to leave Arkansas." They continued to look around the grounds nearest the cabin.

Shortly, Sonny spotted a whisp of smoke behind a bunch of wild violets. "Look here, Kell. There's a cigar butt still burnin', right there in the grass."

"Crush it out but keep the butt. We need to talk to the local law about this. Arson is a crime. Let's go back and see if Hannah can remember anything else. I don't see any danger of this fire startin' back now."

A couple of hours later, Hannah awoke from her nap. She heard someone calling her name. She rose, put on a fresh dress, tied her hair in a queue, and went to the kitchen where she found her family and Kell sitting at the supper .

"Good evening, family. I feel better now. That lard has taken most of the sting out of these burns."

"Hannah, do ya know how the fire started?"

"I didn't see anyone when I came upon the fire."

"We found evidence, a lit cigar butt in the grass," Kell told her.

"Someone was probably playing a prank. No real harm was done."

"Some people here about won't like your arrangement with the Kincaids."

"Kell, whoever it was will probably stop now that they see there is nothing of value there. What can they want? We certainly have no valuables…no money."

"Lass, you are such an innocent. Some men in these parts want life back as it was before the war. They want this land. They don't want former slaves as neighbors."

"That may be. I can't change what's happened, and neither can they. I will continue doing what I've started. We have no other way to survive."

"I know you've told me you'll have no interference in how you lead this family. I have tried to respect that wish. I'm tellin' ya, I'm gonna watch over you, my cousin Naomi, and Sonny. You've got no say in the matter. You're one stubborn woman, Hannah Murphy. Like me or despise me, I'll keep the Kincaid family oath." Kell flung his arms wide. "This I'll defend, and all that belong here."

Kell walked to the front porch, grabbed Graystoke's reins, jumped into his saddle, and raced down the drive toward Madison. He called out… "I'll be back shortly."

Chapter 8

And I will cause showers to come down in his season, and there shall be showers of blessings. And the tree of the field shall yield her fruit and the earth shall yield her increase,
and they shall be safe in their land and they shall know I am the Lord.
Ezekiel 34:26B-27

Nothing changed, except it was a rare day that Kell not make his presence known at Sanctuary Hill. Almost daily, he sat at their table and rode around the grounds, always looking to the safety of the family. Hannah, Sonny, and the working members continued to toil in the sixty acres of cotton. Finally, on May 23rd, the last row was furrowed, and the last seed was sown and watered. Sprigs of new cotton plants pushed through the rich delta soil in the first fields they'd planted. As she walked home through that first field, Hannah sighed deeply, and a subtle smile emerged. She felt a tear trace its way down her cheek. *Maybe I can provide a living for us and our Kincaid family in the quarters here in Arkansas.*

Exhausted physically from the weeks of labor, she refused to let the aches and pains squelch the pride and hope welling up in her as she looked back over the newly planted field. Thoughts of gratitude filled her. She owed a well-done to Sonny and the Kincaids. All had worked day in and day out to plant this vital cash crop.

"Sonny, you have been the best worker on our farm. I couldn't do this work without you. Thank you for working so hard."

"Awww, Hannah, I didn't do nothin' more than anyone else."

"Anyway, I am very proud of you. And Marcus, Lucas, all of you with your hard work and cheerful attitudes, look at all we've done. You are earning your farm every day. We could never have gotten to this point without y'all. Thank you for your extremely hard work."

"Miss Hannah, we work because we know that you cares about us and Sanctuary Hill. You givin' us a home of our own, somethin' we ain't never had. Besides, we gotta work hard so you don't show us up." Marcus grinned and pulled his kerchief across his face. Laughter rippled across the field, and they began to walk home. Hannah had shown some of the gratitude she felt, but she knew that wasn't enough for some reason.

Sonny rushed through the back door calling out to his mother. When he told her the good news that the cotton was planted, the smile on his face told Hannah her brother-in-law had found his place on his grandfather's farm. She'd even noticed his interaction with the Kincaids and her had taken on a more "adult" manner than she'd ever seen in him. Perhaps his new role and the work he'd done was an answer to the curse the Scarlet Fever had inflicted on him nearly half his lifetime ago. For today, at least, Hannah had found life to be more than a struggle to get through another day.

"Mother Naomi, Sonny and I will take tomorrow as a day of much-needed rest. He has worked as hard as any of us. He's an excellent farmer. I'm just plain tired."

Naomi threw her arms around Sonny. "I'm so proud of you. I wish your papa could be here to see what a fine man you have grown to be. I know before any time at all, we will be able to restore our house into the grand manor where I grew up."

"I don't know about us living in a grand manor," Hannah said, "but the day after tomorrow, we will go to Madison to bring back all the things we shipped from Washington. Having some of our things around us will help us feel more at home," Hannah said.

"I'm sure it will, but what about the repairs? We can't stay here if we have no roof." Hannah's sense of accomplishment vanished. "Look at these boarded-up windows and the shabby wallpaper." Naomi's complaints hurt.

"If you will only be patient…we will get things done as we are able. The planting had to come first. Don't you understand?" Naomi sank into the settee in front of the cold fireplace. "Mother Naomi, I promise to have the roof repaired before cold weather sets in." Deflated with the evening's conversation, Hannah walked toward the stairs only to run into Kell.

"Are ye well, lass?"

"Not right now. I'm dead tired and dirty. I'm going to clean this dirt off and then I'm going to lie down. Good night, Kell."

"But Hannah…"

"Not tonight. I don't want to talk anymore." She pushed open the door and dropped onto her pallet. She made no thought to washing. Sleep came. Hannah dreamed of white cotton fields ready to harvest and her own four-poster bed that would soon sit in her room.

On Friday, the weather was fickle. For a moment, the sun would shine and then for several minutes, St. Francis County was peppered with drizzle. Such is Arkansas weather in the springtime. The rain was welcome because the sprouting cotton plants wouldn't need the meager force of Sanctuary Hill to carry water from the creek. Yet, the weather made the seven-mile trek to Madison a bit of drudge instead of a welcome day of change. Sonny had rigged a makeshift cover for the wagon and found a couple of well-worn oil cloths to cover the furniture they would bring home.

Shortly after sun-up, Sonny drove up to the porch in the small wagon and helped his mother into the seat under his not-very elegant canopy. Hannah pushed in beside her and Sonny took the reins and drove Pal toward the county seat. The trip would take a couple of hours, but if all went well, they should be back before dark.

"Hannah, do you think we can buy some coffee and sugar while we are in town? I have missed coffee." Naomi looked at Hannah with pleading eyes.

"Mother Naomi, you know that until the crop is in, we have about $40.00 to use to open the mercantile and to provide us with staples to see us through until the garden is ready to harvest."

"We haven't had coffee for so very long. I want so much to invite my friends over, but I can't serve them that chicory swill Mom Bec makes."

"I will give you two dollars to get what you want most. I'm going to place an order for the things we need at the store. Remember, only two dollars." Hannah reached into her reticule and pulled out her small wad of bills and handed two of them to her mother-in-law. "Please shop carefully. That little bit of money won't go far. Please buy things we can use to help Mom Bec feed us. Frankly, I don't know where she gets what we are eating now. She's been a blessing."

The family pulled the little wagon up to the porch of the train station. Hannah went in to ask about their shipment.

The station master peered over the top of his glasses. "Lady, 'bout time y'all come to claim those crates and all that furniture. I'd have to charge ya storage if you didn't get it before the end of the month. That stuff's been blocking the back porch since May 17th."

"I'm sorry it was a problem," Hannah apologized.

"Just so much of it. We don't usually have to look after so much stuff." The balding man came from behind his counter and showed Hannah to the back of the station where the numerous crates and pieces of their larger furniture were pushed under a large, roofed area. Hannah's mouth dropped when she saw the huge piles of things they had to move back to Sanctuary Hill.

"I didn't realize how many crates we'd shipped. I had never seen them all together before. Two households packed up. I should have realized. We've only a small wagon to take it home."

"Ya can make more than one trip. Ya still got three days before storage fees kick in."

"Is there anyone in town who delivers to Linden?"

"Well, sometimes we get a freighter between loads. You'd have to pay, 'course." The station master turned and started back to his cubicle.

"We'd expect that. Do you know where I might find one?" Hannah put herself directly in front of the door to get an answer to her question. "Will you please tell me? I need to get our things back home."

"Look, lady, that ain't my problem. I kept your stuff safe and dry as our contract requires. That's my duty. I got no freighter in my pocket. Go down to the saloon. If any are hangin' around waitin' for another load, that's where they'll be." The clerk opened his ledger as if to dismiss Hannah.

"We will remove all our things before the day's end."

"I got one boy here to help ya load. He'll work for two bits."

Hannah pushed the door open and motioned for Sonny to move the wagon to the back of the station where they loaded crates onto their tiny wagon. When they'd put as many as they dared, Sonny sat atop the last crate he'd loaded. "Hannah, we can't haul no more. Pal's an old horse. He works hard, but he can't haul all that stuff."

"Maybe we can come back again to get the rest of it."

"That's too much for Pal." Sonny's voice hinted at his taking command of the situation.

"You are right, Sonny. I'll walk down to the saloon and see if I can find some help. Take your mother down to the general store, and I'll look for you there in a while."

Hannah started down the main street of Madison. As she neared a two-story clapboard structure with bright red swinging doors, men sitting outside on the boardwalk whistled and made embarrassing comments directed at her. She averted her eyes and continued on her path to reach the doors.

A tall dirty man stepped in front of her and barred the doorway. "Now, look here. It's a pretty lady wantin' some company. Sweetie, ya don't wanna go in that place. You'd be better off stayin' out here with me and my friends. We're all gentlemen." Raucous laughter broke out all around her. "I know how to treat a lady."

Hannah took a step back so she could stare into the eyes of the lout who had stopped her. "Excuse me. I need a freighter. I'm not looking for a friend. Let me pass."

A man sitting on a barrel next to the hitching rail slapped his palm on his leg, producing a crack that startled two horses tied nearby. "Honey, Rusty ain't wantin' to be your friend." He reached out and grabbed Hannah's arm. As he tried to pull her into the middle of the group of men, a younger lanky man walked between them.

"Aaron, get outta my business," the dirty man shouted.

"Stop it, Rusty. We ain't here to cause no problems. The boss told us to stay outta trouble. This lady says she needs a freighter, not a lumberjack that ain't got the sense to know how to treat a lady."

Rusty swung at the younger man. Aaron dodged the blow, and Rusty's fist hit the doorjamb. Blood dripped from his knuckles, and he screamed. "Dagnabit, you done caused me to bust my hand. I'm gonna kill ya, you whelp of a kid."

"Rusty, just walk away before this fight gets any bigger." Aaron raised his arms, showing he had no intention of further conflict.

"Ain't gonna get no bigger. You just lost your job, boy. I'm gonna tell my brother how ya maimed me. We won't be needin' you to haul no more logs for us." The crew of men sauntered down the street toward the stable and the doctor's office.

Hannah approached the tall, lanky man who had taken on the role of her protector. "I'm sorry you lost your job, young man. I do appreciate your stopping to help me though. I don't know what I was thinking when I decided to come down here. I have no business going into a saloon alone."

"It's all good. I'm tired of haulin' logs day and night. I'll make my way. I got myself a good team of mules and my flatbed wagon. There is always a need for a freighter. About any job beats livin' in a lumber camp." Aaron smiled down at Hannah. "My name's Aaron Pierce. Pleased to make your acquaintance, ma'am. I heard ya say ya need a freighter. Will I do?"

Hannah looked at the boy who appeared to be no more than eighteen. "You're a freighter?"

"Yes, ma'am. Worked with my pa 'til he died. Then I took his rig and have been haulin' ever since. Work keeps food in my belly and a roof over my head." Aaron's grin was infectious, and Hannah found herself smiling with the good-natured boy she'd just met.

"Well, Aaron, I don't have a great deal of money, but I do have a large shipment of furniture and many crates that I need to be delivered to Sanctuary Hill near Linden."

"I gotta find work so I'll be glad to haul for ya. Maybe you'll feed me a good meal or two and give me a place to sleep for a couple of nights. We'll settle on a freight charge."

"Thank you, Aaron. You have turned out to be my blessing for the day. I've found several of those lately."

Hannah arranged for the wagons to be loaded, and she walked down to the general store to find Naomi and Sonny. Naomi greeted her as she entered and showed her the prized items she'd bought. She'd even saved fifty cents that she would use at another time. Hannah sent Sonny down to help with the loading, and she and Naomi spent the next half-hour learning how to order staples for their mercantile in Linden. Mr. Griner, the Madison merchant, was pleasant and more than willing to help Hannah get her first items ordered. "Mrs. Murphy, the warehouse in Memphis will make the run to Linden so you won't have to come here to Madison to tote your wares back every month," he told her.

By the time she and Naomi walked back to the railway station, the crew of three had loaded every crate and piece of furniture onto one of the wagons. After a simple, but filling lunch at the local café, the little caravan of two wagons left Madison, headed back to Sanctuary Hill. The sun pushed the rain away, and a gentle breeze made the ride home more pleasant than their early morning trip.

About the time the sun disappeared beneath the tree line to the west, the four travelers reached home. Road-weary and more than a little hungry, Sonny let out a yelp that the Kincaids probably heard in their cabins down in the quarters. Mom Bec opened the front door.

"I's wonderin' if dis family would be home for supper. Seems ya are. Come on in and eat while the food's still warm."

"Mom Bec, you shouldn't have stayed with us gone. It's late."

"I 'spect y'all be tired and hungry, Miss Naomi. Besides, I didn't do much a nothin'. Had me a nice restful day."

"Thank you for taking care of us. Sonny, if you and Aaron put those wagons under the lean-to by Pal's shed and stake out the horses, we'll call it a day. We'll worry about unloading everything tomorrow. Hurry back and we'll have our supper." Hannah laid her bonnet and reticule on the settee and followed Mom Bec into the kitchen. Naomi followed, carrying several small bundles.

"Mom Bec, we'll be very sparing with these things, but I bought two pounds of coffee, some sugar, a pound of salt, and even some tea. We'll be able to add a few special things to the good food you always seem to find for our table." Naomi handed the bundles over to the older woman. "You've been a blessing to us since we came home. Thank you."

"Well, set yerself down and when them boys get here, y'all eat up. I'm headed home to my family. A blessed night to ya." Mom Bec couldn't hide the smile on her face as she took her straw hat from the peg at the door.

"Mother Naomi, that is the first time I ever heard you give a compliment to Mom Bec. That was a kind thing to do."

"I'm trying to remember they aren't our people anymore. She works hard and feeds us well every day. I can at least be grateful."

When Aaron and Sonny sat down at the table, Hannah brought what seemed to be a large pie from the oven where Mom Bec had left it. The crust was flaky and golden brown. Hannah had no idea what their cook had prepared for their meal. She knew from the aroma it would be tasty, and they would not be hungry after eating. Mom Bec always made sure of that.

"By golly! I'm thinkin' that's a pot pie. That's what my ma always called it when she gathered all the spare stuff from our larder." Aaron rubbed his hands in anticipation. "Never was enough to make a whole supper, but when she mixed it all together, we ate real good."

"Well, Aaron, let's cut into this pie and see what Mom Bec found to piece together a meal." Hannah cut the pie into quarters and placed a piece on each of the four plates. She poured the chicory coffee into the pewter mugs and sat down to eat.

"Sonny, will you say grace for us?" his mother asked.

"You want me to do it? I ain't never done it before."

"Son, you are the man of our house. It is your task to ask the blessing."

Sonny looked around the table. Hannah nodded to him.

Aaron laid his arm across Sonny's shoulder. "Sonny, it's easy. Just ask the Lord to bless our food."

"I'll try. Lord, I don't know if I'm doin' this right, but will you bless this supper? It looks real good, so I'm saying thank you for the vittles and Mom Bec who cooks so fine. Amen."

"Man, ya did real good. Let's eat, okay?" Aaron filled his mouth with a large spoon of the stew-like filling and a piece of the golden crust. "Land a Goshen, I ain't never had a better taste of pot pie in my life."

For several minutes, the four tired travelers ate in silence. When they'd nearly finished, Hannah leaned back in her chair, realizing how tired she was. Naomi was nodding in her chair, sated with the good meal and the hard day's travel.

"Aaron, do you have to go back tomorrow?" Hannah asked.

"No, ma'am. I got no place to go right now until I find me another cargo to haul."

"Well, I intend to pay you for getting all our crates and furniture here. I was wondering if you might stay a couple of days and help with the unloading?"

"I'd like that. If y'all eat this good ever day, I might never want to leave. We ate swill at that lumber camp. That cook couldn't boil a tater and make it taste like human food."

"Tonight, all I can offer you is a pallet in Sonny's room. We will put together our beds tomorrow. That will be a treat for both Sonny and me. We will also be able to make a bed for you."

"Do you have work around here that I could stay on for?" Aaron looked up with hope-filled eyes.

"We are farming this land. I thought you wanted to work as a freighter," Hannah said.

"Don't really want to haul. Makes me feel like I got no roots. Traveling here and yon ain't much of a life—real lonely at times."

"Aaron, I don't care if you share my room upstairs. I got lots of space."

"Thanks, Sonny, but I gotta pull my own weight. I can't be a burden to your family."

"What do you think you'd like to do if you don't want to work as a freighter?" Hannah put the last bite of her pot pie into her mouth. She noticed that Naomi was now asleep, sitting at the supper table.

"Well, Mrs. Murphy, I see myself as a builder. When my pa didn't need me on a haul, my Uncle Henry taught me everything he knew about buildin' stuff."

"Did ya build big stuff, Aaron? I made this here table and patched up our chairs when we come here."

"Ya did good, Sonny. This is a fine, sturdy table." Sonny beamed at the compliment. "My uncle and me mostly built houses, barns, and farm sheds…stuff like that. He told me they'd be a lot of work for a good builder after the war."

"We could sure use a good builder here at Sanctuary Hill," Hannah said. "I just need to figure out how to pay for one."

"Do you really want me to stay for a spell?"

"Let me think through things and see if I can make it worth your while. Now, I think we need to go to bed. Mother Naomi has already gotten a head start."

"I'm ready, Hannah. Come with me, Aaron, and I'll show ya where we'll bunk down for the night."

Hannah helped Naomi to her bed and then went to her room. She took the feather bed from the floor and one of her blankets and carried them to Sonny's room. She lit a lamp on the crate next to Sonny's bed. She pushed her makeshift pallet against the wall opposite Sonny's mattress. "Goodnight, boys."

She carried her pillow and sole blanket down to the parlor and placed them on the settee. This would do for one night. She was about to undress when she heard boots on the front porch. She turned, looking for something to defend herself. Sonny's club stood in the corner. She ran to the door and pulled it open with the club on her shoulder, ready to strike.

"Whoa, lass. It's only your kinsman, doing one more check for the night. I haven't seen y'all today. Where have you been?"

"Have you been stalking around our house at all hours of the day and night, Kell Kincaid?"

"I told ya I'd not let danger harm my family. I've done it since those bullies burned the cabin in the quarters."

"I should have known, don't you think?"

"I don't need your permission to keep the family oath. There is nothing you can do to change my mind. Will ya tell me where the lot of ya went today?"

"I don't know that it's any of your business, but we went to Madison to bring home our furniture and personal belongings from Washington."

"And why didn't ya ask me to help ya with that task?"

"Because I can take care of this family. I did what I set out to do. I brought it all back. Have I not made it perfectly clear to you yet that I don't need a man to take care of me?"

"Ya surely have tried. I'll give ya that…and I'll give ya some space if it will make ya happy. Thank God that nothing happened to y'all on that long trip. I'll bid ya goodnight, lass."

Satisfied she'd gotten the upper hand, Hannah stepped inside the door and locked it. She returned to the settee and prepared to sleep. The next night she would sleep on her bed—the first time in more than two months. Before she fell asleep, Hannah felt the urge to express gratitude for the good fortune that had happened that day. She whispered, "Thank you, God, if that is where thanks are due. Many things just fell into place today that give me hope that things are going to work out for us here in Arkansas. I know I can't turn this place into a great plantation again, but I can make a living on a good farm. So, thank you, Amen."

She folded herself onto the tiny settee and promptly fell into a blissful sleep where once again she dreamed of snowy white cotton fields and herself standing hand-in-hand with a shadowy stranger amidst the white.

Chapter 9

*Ask, and it shall be given you; seek, and ye shall find; knock,
and it shall be opened unto you."*
Matthew 7:7

The next morning, Hannah, with the help of Sonny, Naomi, Aaron, and Mom Bec, began to pull items from the crates they'd shipped from Washington. Naomi touched each piece of crystal and china that she unpacked as if she were welcoming a long-lost friend home. Some of the fragile pieces lay in shards. Only Naomi seemed surprised. Crystal glasses lay in two pieces, snapped at the stems. Some of Naomi's beautiful hand-painted china was broken beyond any use. When she'd finished removing the last piece from the crate, seven plates, nine saucers, six cups, seven bowls, and several serving pieces remained undamaged. When she unwrapped her silver tea service, tears streamed down her cheeks. Hannah knew that Mr. Hugh had given that lavish gift to his daughter on her wedding day. *How useless that tea service is now. I wonder if selling that collection would bring the price of our taxes?* Hannah shook her head, not believing that ugly thought had crossed her mind.

Two large rugs would now cover Sanctuary Hill floors. They had been used to protect some of the furniture during transit. Hannah was beside herself when she recognized one of them was her rug. Her father had ordered it for her sixteenth birthday. With the rug slung over her shoulder, she pulled her way upstairs to spread it over her bedroom floor. They put furniture into place in all the rooms they could use. Both Hannah and Sonny now had real beds.

Sonny picked up a large, flat package wrapped in paper. "This is my papa's picture, ain't it, Mama?" Sonny snatched the paper away, revealing a large oil painting of Colonel Benjamin Murphy. "I wished my papa didn't go to that stupid war and get hurt. I miss him."

Naomi ran her finger down the cheek of the man in the portrait. "I do, too. Let's hang it over the fireplace in the parlor, Sonny. We'll always have him with us that way."

"Mother Naomi, you loved him very much, didn't you?" Hannah spoke hesitantly as if she'd doubted any affection between her husband's parents.

"I did come to love him, but not at first so much. We became devoted to each other as our life progressed. We loved our boys, of course. Life on our plantation in Maryland had been pleasant. His letters during the war kept me alive, but then you know how that feels, don't you Hannah? My Richard was a gentleman, and he was devoted to you."

"Yes, he was a gentleman." Hannah turned away. She had no desire to discuss her marriage to Richard with her mother-in-law. She'd not destroy his memory of her son. Hannah rushed back into the kitchen and slammed directly into Kell Kincaid, who was eating fried pie left over from lunch. She stumbled and he caught her just before her backside hit the floor.

"Careful, lass. You could break something with a nasty fall like that."

"What are you doing here again? I didn't hear anyone knock."

"Mom Bec was lugging a crate from the wagon, so I took it from her and carried it to the table. I didn't mean to intrude."

"Well, thank you for helping Mom Bec. She shouldn't be trying to carry those heavy crates."

"I agree. I'd be glad to help if you'd allow it. I've finished my chores for the day." Kell's grin annoyed Hannah.

"Suit yourself. You can do with your time as you please." Hannah returned to the crate she'd been emptying. She didn't speak to Kell the rest of the afternoon. *He is the most exasperating human that was ever born on this earth. How is it that he came to be in the only place I can live right now?* At sunset, the parlor had taken on more of the presence of a home. With the dirt scrubbed away, the wallpaper now displayed its color. The one intact window had been washed, and a lace curtain and damask drape hung at either side. The boarded-up windows were covered with matching damask drapes until they could be replaced. Small tables stood at either side of the settee and the two chairs salvaged from the unburned room upstairs. Silver candlesticks graced the mantle with six-inch beeswax tapers. Seeing her parlor complete, except for window glass, Naomi sat in the small chair and smiled. Hannah knew her mother-in-law felt some semblance of home.

When they'd finished work for the day, Hannah went to the porch to sit in the cool of the evening. She sighed, happy to have so many familiar things around her. While all the furniture had been placed, most of the rooms were still sparse. Nevertheless, with their household things around, Sanctuary Hill took on the semblance of home, as many of the objects brought memories of an easier life. She pushed the swing with her toe, a slight smile on her lips.

"Pardon…"

"Kell Kincaid, please don't intrude on my quiet time right now." Hannah turned to look and found a red-faced Aaron Pierce standing in the doorway. "I'm sorry. I thought that Kell was coming back to…to…well, never mind. Do you need me, Aaron?"

"Well, Mrs. Murphy, I didn't mean to bother ya. Mr. Kell left about an hour ago. Said he was goin' to Bible class at the church."

"On a Wednesday? Oh, never mind. What can I do for you?"

"Well, Mrs. Murphy, I thought you'd like to know about the damage to the roof from the fire."

"Yes, I would, but please don't call me Mrs. Murphy. That's my mother-in-law. You can call me Hannah, just as Sonny does."

"Yes, ma'am."

"Do you think you can repair the roof, or will we have to do an entirely new one?"

"Sonny and me went up there the other day. Ain't as bad as I thought at first. Good heavy cypress up there mostly. Some's charred, but not a loss. The roof of the bedroom over the kitchen will have to be rebuilt. Needs rafters, deckin', and cedar shakes. That was all burned to ashes, but that second room in the back, the rafters are okay. One or two may need to be replaced, but decking and shakes will fix that up."

"That's a relief. After we get a sound roof, we can work on the water damage."

"Yes, ma'am. I'd be glad to barter with ya to do the work, but I'll need at least two strong folks to help me."

"Well, Sonny's good with his hands. I'll ask one of the Kincaid brothers if they want to help.

"When can we get us some lumber? I'll start tomorrow."

"May have to wait a day or two. I'll try to find materials tomorrow."

♪

Now she'd done it. Hannah had no choice but to seek Kell Kincaid's help. She'd been such a shrew to him yesterday. Aaron Pierce had offered to repair the roof if she could supply the lumber.

But since giving Aaron five dollars to transport their belongings from Madison, she had less than thirty-five dollars. Nearly every penny of that money would be due when her order came from Memphis next week.

Kell had told her there was a solution. If she were going to make this happen, she would have to swallow her pride and ask him to help her, at least this one time. But that would be tomorrow. Tonight, she would sleep in a real bed. Sinking into the featherbed and laying her head on her own pillows was a luxury she'd all but forgotten. That night she slept again, after whispering a thank you to that unknown source that she knew was responsible for the good things that had been coming into her life. She wished she knew more about that feeling. Perhaps...no—this wasn't something to bring up with Kell.

Thankfully, Hannah didn't have to go to Kell in her widow's weeds. Trunks of her clothes now sat against the wall of her room waiting for her to retrieve the more climate-friendly clothing. She opened the lid and pulled out garment after garment. She twirled the lovely colors around the room, singing and dancing as she did as a sixteen-year-old preparing for a ball. A pink, sateen afternoon dress caught her eye. The puffy sleeves edged with lace and a green sash that tied into a large bow brought a smile to her face. She would dare Kell Kincaid to mock her appearance today. She pulled ringlets down the side of her face and put on a straw bonnet with white daisies on the brim. She could do this.

When she got to Kell's farm, she called out, but he didn't appear. She walked Pal to the back of the house toward the well so he could drink. She heard a noise from the barn. She walked the short distance and called out again. Hannah stepped inside just as a pitchfork of hay fell from the loft, covering her head and shoulders.

"EEE…. Do you greet all your guests like this, Mr. Kincaid?" Hannah flailed, flinging hay in every direction.

"Ah, lassie, I didn't know you were comin'. Sorry to have made such a mess."

"I don't suppose any real harm's been done. I've been dirtier."

"I'm surprised to see ya today. I decided you don't like me very much," Kell said.

"I never said that." Hannah removed her bonnet and shook the debris from it.

"Sometimes actions speak louder than any words, ya know. And you're pretty good with the words, too."

"Kell, I don't want us to be at odds with each other anymore. I was very rude to you yesterday and for no good reason. Please forgive me."

"And what brought ya to this realization, my dearest cousin?"

"After all, we are kin."

"I don't think that is anything new to the situation." Kell leaned against his pitchfork as he stared down at her.

"I've come to ask for your help…and please don't laugh at me. I need to know about something you mentioned to me the last time I came to call."

"Not exactly a social call then, is it, Mrs. Murphy? 'Tis a shame too. Dressed as ya are, lookin' like a proper lady, I could have offered ya a cup of tea." Kell finally climbed down the ladder to be on a level with Hannah.

"I might well enjoy a cup of tea if you've a mind to offer it. And thank you for the compliment. I do feel like a lady today. I haven't felt like this in a while."

"Well, let me get this right. You need me to help ya. That is what ya said, isn't it? Am I hearin' ya right?"

"Well, if you're going to be sarcastic and make a fool of me, I guess I misunderstood. I'm sorry I bothered you." Hannah pushed her bonnet back in place and turned to leave.

Kell caught the bustle on the back of her dress. "Whoa, lass, don't get your dander up. I didn't mean to be sarcastic. Come into the house with me. We'll have that cup of tea and then talk the matter out."

Hannah followed Kell into his kitchen where he pulled out a chair for her. Pushing a kettle over the fire, he turned to the table to sit across from his visitor. "Last evenin' I was sure that you'd marked me off your friend list altogether. What's changed?"

"Well, we've worked hard and gotten our crops all in. We planted only a small crop this year. Our kitchen garden is growing well, so we should have food for the winter. The day before yesterday, we drove to Madison to bring back our furniture and personal things from the train station. While we were there, we found a man to help repair the roof, if I can get some lumber."

"You got a new hand? Do you know anything about that man? Do you know you can trust him?"

"I know as much about him as I know about you. You've told me often enough that I can't do everything by myself, so I'm reaching out for help—a business arrangement."

"I see. You want everything to be business. Nothing can be done for you because of friendship or kinship."

"Yes. I think that it's the best way to deal with the problems that are ahead of me."

"Uh-huh. Yes, Mrs. Murphy, I can arrange for the lumber crew to come deal with you. Do you know the going prices for a board foot of lumber, how many boards you can expect from a tree, what kind of lumber you can barter, which trees are ready for harvest, or how to prepare a contract so you don't get cheated?" Kell took the whistling tea kettle from the fire and poured the hot water over the tea in the pot.

"Well, no. Perhaps you would be willing to teach me." Hannah looked up into the depths of Kell's stormy blue eyes.

"I'll see it done. Now, what's in it for me?"

"What?" Hannah sat, mouth gaped, and her eyes bored into Naomi's kinsman.

"Ya said everything is business. I was wondering what you'd be willing to give me in exchange for two or three days I'd have to take away from my farm?"

"You know I can't pay you right now. I need what little funds we have to buy staples for the mercantile. I can offer payment when the cotton is harvested."

"Lassie, we barter for our needs around here. I told ya that we're all land rich and cash poor. What can you trade for my time?"

"I have some jewelry, a few pieces of furniture that are mine…What do you want?"

"Certainly not some bauble that will lie in a drawer. I've all the furnishings I need here. Do ya have something more personal to offer?"

"I have no idea what you are suggesting, sir."

"Nothin' immoral or illegal, I assure ya, lass. I need a partner for the spring dance over in Linden next Saturday. Are ya willing to dance with me on Saturday night to get a roof over your head?"

Quiet followed. Hannah dropped a teacup she'd lifted to be filled, spilling the hot liquid across the table. Kell smiled at her. "That's all right. I didn't expect ya to say yes. I only thought it would be a nice way for ya to meet some of the neighbors and spend a pleasant evenin' listenin' to music after a long week of work. I suspect ya would find the company too uncomfortable. Never mind."

He won't get the upper hand on me. He thinks he knows me so well. "Yes, Mr. Kincaid, I'll gladly pay your wage. One evening of dancing will be a fair exchange if I can get a roof repaired at Sanctuary Hill."

⨎

When Hannah arrived at Sanctuary Hill, she found her mother-in-law and Sonny in the parlor talking with a man she'd not seen before. She called out, "Mother Naomi, I'm home now."

"Hannah, please come in here at once. Narvel, this is my son Richard's widow, Hannah. This is Mr. Narvel Tangent. Narvel has been a neighbor to my papa for many years."

"How do you do, young lady? I am sorry for your loss." He spoke as he rose from the blue chair across from the settee.

"Hannah, Mr. Tangent has come to make an offer on our land, but he doesn't want our house."

"Mrs. Murphy, let me explain. I know you have no menfolk around to deal with so much land. Without slaves to do our labor, we can't make our crops as we once did. I'm prepared to offer your mother-in-law $5,000 in gold for your acreage. Y'all can keep the house and the grounds around it, of course." He sat down in the chair. He smirked as he pulled a wad of money from his inner pocket.

"You seem to have survived the devastation of the war much better than most of the people in St. Francis County. Most of us hardly have money to buy food. Did you fight in the war, sir?" Hannah's direct question replaced his smirk with a scowl.

"I was the head of the local quartermaster's unit, ma'am. It was our duty to requisition supplies for the troops."

Naomi leaned over to whisper to Hannah. "That's a great deal of money. We could go back to Washington or Maryland where things may be better." Hannah shook her head and brushed Naomi aside. She stood up from the settee and walked near the chair where Narvel Tangent sat. "Mr. Tangent, you are mistaken. We have a man in our household. Sonny owns the entire sum of Hugh Kincaid's estate. He has told me that he wants to farm the land. We have no intention of giving it away."

"I assure you, young woman, my offer is very generous. Hugh was a cherished friend, and I'd never see harm come to his daughter. Land hereabouts is goin' for two or three dollars an acre. My offer of five is a gesture of friendship and Christian charity."

"I am sure that your offer is generous. But as I said, we are not going to sell this land." Hannah stepped toward the doorway.

Naomi stopped her. "Are you sure? We really need a way to leave here."

"Mother Naomi, if we sell this property, we will be destitute within two to three years. How do you think we can make a living in the city?"

"Mama, I don't wanna leave our farm. I like it here. I like workin' with my friends and Pal. I can grow cotton. Marcus and Lucas will help me, and I can help them." Sonny took his mother's hand, "Please Mama, don't make us sell our farm."

Tangent rose and took his hat from the table. "I didn't know you had some help here. Where did ya find help?"

"Mr. Tangent, we are taking care of our needs. That is all you need to know." He took Hannah's arm and turned her around to look at him.

"How can ya afford to pay for hired help? I know you ain't got money to hire."

"We make do. I don't see as this is your concern." She pulled away.

"Mrs. Murphy, you've got those ex-slaves working for ya. You know you can't use forced labor. A word to the right people …"

"And who would those right people be, Mr. Tangent? I've had little luck getting the sheriff to take any of my concerns very seriously."

Tangent pushed Hannah aside and walked up to Naomi. "Naomi, things could get very scary here. Why don't you take my offer and go back to your home in Maryland? I don't want anything to happen to you."

"Mr. Tangent, I am Sonny's guardian for the next three years. He doesn't want to leave Sanctuary Hill, and I don't intend to do anything against his wishes. Thank you for your offer, but we plan to stay. We believe we can earn a living on this land."

Tangent pulled his hat on his head and took a few steps toward the front door before he stopped. "Mrs. Murphy, I will let you think about my offer for a day or two. Perhaps you will see things differently when you've had a chance to consider all the problems that could arise. You know these parts aren't safe for a household without a man at its helm. We've been hearing reports of night riders in the area. You haven't been visited, have you?"

"I appreciate your concern for our well-being. I've told you my answer. Your offer cannot support a family of three for the rest of our lives. We will earn our living on the family lands."

"Well, I hope things go as you think they will. One bad crop year, and I'll get the place for the taxes. Save me a bundle of money, and you'll be out with nothin'—not even this wreck of a house."

"Good day, Mr. Tangent."

Hannah tossed and turned through the night. The visit from Tangent had ended with a veiled threat. She remembered the night when she saw the band of men at the drive to Sanctuary Hill and the fire at the quarters two weeks earlier. She had little doubt that the night riders participated in both events. Tangent had mentioned them to scare the Kincaid family, no doubt. Had he sent them to set the fire? One year of bad crops—that wasn't unique to Hannah and Sonny. Everyone who made their living from the land feared a poor crop. Everyone in the county would suffer, not just the Murphys.

At dawn, Hannah left her bed and pulled her work clothes on. She'd not even sat down in front of her oatmeal when Naomi brought up the sale of the land again. "Hannah, you can't make Sanctuary Hill what it was before the war. We need to return to the city where we belong."

"Sonny, please tell your mother what you want to do." The manchild looked at his mother and back at Hannah. His mouth quivered and tears formed in his eyes. Hannah walked over to him and held his shoulders, forcing him to look into her face. "Sonny, you are a man. Tell us what you want to do."

"I want my mama to be happy with me. She always took care of me."

"What did your grandfather ask you to do with his land?"

"He told me in the will to take care of my mother." He looked over his shoulder at his mother who was gently crying. "I like this farm. I am good at doin' the work here. Grandpapa gave it to me so I could take care of my mama. I want to stay."

Hannah went to Naomi and laid her hand on the older woman's bent head. "Naomi, I don't want to hurt your feelings or disrespect you, but I will not sell the land as long as I am Sonny's guardian. I may be wrong, but I believe it is the only way we have to secure a living."

"I see I have no voice in this matter. I will not bring it up again until my son reaches his majority. If we don't starve to death in these

114

next three years, we'll talk about it again." Naomi slammed her pewter cup down on the table and left the room.

"Golly, Hannah, my mama's really mad."

"She is, but you did the right thing. We can make a go of this place. You are turning out to be a very good farmer."

"Gee, ya think I am?" Sonny's smile erased much of the image of Naomi's scowl as she left the room. Hannah hoped her praise of Sonny would turn out to be true in the years to come.

Chapter 10

To everything there is a season, a time for every purpose under Heaven. A time to plant and a time to pluck up what has been planted. A time to weep and a time to laugh and a time to mourn and a time to dance...
Ecclesiastes 3:1, 2B, 4

Saturday morning arrived long before Hannah was ready to face the day. The week she'd just lived through had been long, physically draining, and lonely at times. She missed the fellowship with the Kincaids she'd had when she worked in the fields. With the garden growing nicely and the cotton sprouting, she'd turned the farm work over to Marcus Kincaid. She'd asked him to be the foreman of the work crew in exchange for five additional acres of land.

Without the daily worry about the crops, she had time to devote to preparing the mercantile to open. Each day, she and Sonny drove the two miles to Linden and worked to clean, inventory, and display what goods remained in the store. As they dug through the bins, cabinets, and storage room, they found useful items that could be sold.

Hannah put Sonny amid all she did. His recent performance in the fields held hope that he could become the public face of the store. Sonny's childlike demeanor attracted many people to him, as he was friendly, open, and cheerful all the time. Of course, his education was lacking, but he understood numbers and wrote a good hand so he copied information from one source to the other with ease. Hannah would teach him how to take payment for items and record the sale in the ledger. If the sale was complicated because the customer wanted to barter or use credit, Sonny would call her in to deal with it.

Pulling crates to unload and hauling heavy boxes to be stored filled the time from early morning until sunset every day. The back-breaking work never seemed to end. Standing on her feet twelve hours a day for the past week poisoned the idea of dancing for Hannah. Going to a country social was the last thing she wanted to do, but she'd promised.

Kell kept his part of the bargain. On Wednesday, he showed up at the mercantile with two burly, bearded giants. "Mornin' to ya, lass. I want ya to meet my friends, Zeb Obermire and his brother Sven. They own a sawmill over near Taylor's Circle. The mill was damaged during the skirmish there in '63, but they're back in business now and lookin' to secure forest land for cuttin' railroad ties. I told them about your trees."

"Howdy, ma'am," Sven said.

"Mornin' to ya." Zeb offered his hand to Hannah.

"Good morning. I'm happy to see you. We have some virgin timber land. We also need some lumber and cedar shakes for a new roof."

"Let's see if we can work out a deal then." Zeb smiled and the discussion began. Kell sat atop a cracker barrel nearby, watching the interaction between Hannah and the two men. Only twice did he interject a comment. Sonny also stood behind Hannah intent on every word. Before half an hour had passed, the deal was struck.

When the brothers departed, after buying a new mule harness, Kell turned to Hannah. "You're quite the businesswoman, Hannah Murphy. You got everything you needed and a bit of a payoff besides."

"You did good, Hannah. Are we gonna go mark fifty acres they can take the trees off?" Sonny had paid attention to the details.

"We will have to get it done some way."

"Now Aaron can start putting our roof on, can't he?"

"Yes, Sonny, as soon as we get the lumber. I guess we're beginning to get a few things accomplished around here."

"Well, I'll take my leave now. You handled yourself well. Ya didn't need me here at all," Kell said.

"Thank you for arranging the meeting. I'm sure your presence was part of the reason things went so smoothly," Hannah replied.

"I look forward to our dance this Saturday. I'll drive by to pick you up at 6:00. So long, Sonny. You are doin' fine work here at the mercantile. If you walk with me to the porch, I'll give ya the store ledgers that your grandpa Hugh left. They're in my saddlebags."

Ø

Six o'clock on Saturday evening, Kell drove an open buggy pulled by his freshly groomed stallion to the porch of Sanctuary Hill. Graystoke pawed the ground as Kell jumped to the floor to knock on the door.

Sonny pulled the great door open. "Howdy, Kell. Ya sure look different with your Scottish clothes on. I ain't never seen a fellow wear a skirt before."

Kell had considered and reconsidered wearing his formal family attire to this social. "Well, Sonny, me lad, this isn't a skirt. This is the family kilt. This green and black are the colors of the Kincaids, and this medallion has our family seal on it, just like on the watch your grandpa Hugh left you. You remember what it means?"

"I sure do. I don't forget important stuff. That seal means we fight to take care of our family."

"That's the pledge. I'd say you're a true Kincaid. Have ya been to a town social before?"

"Not me, but Mama said they always had 'em when she lived here with her papa."

"That's what they tell me. Before the war, it was a tradition in these parts. Is your mama dressed yet?"

"Oh yeah. She's been primpin' all day. Got out one of her fancy dresses from back home." Naomi appeared at the door.

"Cousin Kell, how fine you look this evenin'. Thank you for wearing our family's colors." She swept into the parlor wearing a violet silk dress with layers of crinoline beneath. Her hair was stacked atop her head in tiers of coils and loops. Golden earrings dropped to her chin. Her appearance was far from that of a destitute widow.

"How lovely you are, my dear cousin! I'm so glad the war didn't destroy all that was beautiful from your past. Tears would flow from your father's face to see you dressed so fine."

"Thank you, kind sir. Sonny, please call Hannah down. We don't wanna miss a minute of the party." Naomi perched on the very edge of the chair. "I am so lookin' forward to the social tonight. It's been ever so long since I've been to a real party."

"You'll have a grand evenin', Naomi. You'll be able to catch up with old friends."

Hannah strolled to the settee where Kell sat. "Good evening, Mr. Kincaid. I hope I didn't keep you waiting too long."

"Not at...." Kell swallowed and choked out, "not at all." The Hannah that stood before him was not one he'd ever imagined, and he had imagined this woman in many situations since the first day he'd seen her dance in the lea. Tonight she was a vision, dressed in sapphire blue organza, with a filmy blue shawl baring her neck and shoulders. The fitted bodice amplified her tiny waist and ample bustline. The skirt was not as full as most ladies wore. This filmy blue fabric traced its way down her body to reveal the tips of her matching shoes. Her raven hair fell to her waist and was held back from her face with two mother-of-pearl combs.

"Ya look fine for the town social, lass. Ya must be happy to have all your things here finally."

"Well, if I'd not gotten our freight, I could have worn the lovely black traveling suit that I wore to church that one time."

"This is much improved from those widow's weeds. Shall we go?"

Kell helped Hannah into the buggy. Tonight, Hannah seemed relaxed and didn't flinch when he touched her. Sonny seated his mother in the wagon. Kell had purposely planned with Sonny to take his mother in the wagon with the cakes, candy, and pies she'd made for the social. This one night he planned to spend some time with Hannah alone. Things had gone well the past couple of times they'd met. She'd greeted him warmly tonight. Perhaps she'd had a change of heart. "Lass, that blue is a wonderful color for you. You are beautiful tonight."

"Thank you, Kell. I am pleased that you approve of me."

"I didn't say I approved of ya. You do look beautiful dressed in your silks, but I wanted to warn ya, that both you and Naomi are far too finely clad for the company you'll keep tonight. Most of these ladies have little left of good quality. Some never had such finery."

"Why didn't you say something before we left? We could have changed to something more appropriate. We don't want to…"

"Don't want to what? Put your neighbors to shame? To make others think you are lording your wealth over them?" Kell flipped the reins across Graystoke's back.

"I didn't think. I should have been more thoughtful. Please take me home. We can go to the community dance some other time." Hannah laid her hand on Kell's arm. "Please, don't make a spectacle of me."

"I didn't make anything of ya, lass. I invited ya to the community dance. The dance is tonight. After watching ya make the deal with the lumbermen, I think you can win over this whole community, too. I'll enjoy watching ya do it."

"Please drive me home."

Sonny called back to them. "Hey, Kell. The church building's all lit up with candles and lanterns. Sure are lots of people here already. Bet tonight is gonna be a fine time." Sonny pulled his horse to the hitching post and helped his mother to the porch.

"All right, Kell Kincaid, I'll go play my part for you tonight. What do you want me to do?"

"Just have a good time. Enjoy your neighbors. Get to know some of the people. Be yourself. I'll ask ya to dance now and again. It's a party. You do know what a party is. Enjoy it."

As they walked through the door of the church, the church looked different than it had the one time she'd attended worship. The pews had been pushed against the walls to make an open area and bouquets of wildflowers were perched on nearly every flat surface that wasn't covered with food or several types of beverages. The candles and lanterns that Sonny had mentioned lit the darkened room just enough. A small group of musicians rambled around the raised platform that normally held the pulpit.

"Looks like we'll have some good music tonight." Kell pointed to a couple of guitars, a banjo, a washboard sitting atop an upturned galvanized wash tub, a long harmonica, and a violin.

121

"I love to hear the violin played well. Do you know who plays the violin, Kell?" Hannah asked.

A clean-shaven man with a string tie patted her shoulder. "Missy, that's a fiddle. No one around here abouts plays a violin." The people standing around laughed. Hannah laughed too.

"Well, Mrs. Murphy, seems like your little mistake got the night started off just fine. People laughing is a sign of a good party. You acted just fine. Your laughter will go a long way to gettin' these folks to accept ya."

As the musicians took a minute to warm up, Kell took Naomi's arm and led her to the matriarchs of the community who had chosen to sit near the open windows to the south. He then took Sonny to a group of young men who stood at the back of the church. "Sonny, these are the lads who come to the social without an escort. See, they hope to flirt with all the unattached young women here, not just one. They'll show ya how to get a girl to dance with ya. The reels are easy so everyone can do that. You'll like these fellows when ya get to know 'em 'cause they're just like you, all farmers."

"Mr. Kell, I don't know how to dance. I ain't never asked no girl to dance with me."

"Just watch the boys. They'll help ya get a partner. A good-lookin' lad like you ain't gonna have no trouble gettin' a girl to dance."

"All right. I'll try, Cousin Kell." He turned and began talking with the young men along the wall.

Kell returned to Hannah who had taken a seat in a pew near the back door. Sitting beside her, he asked, "Are ya gonna be a wallflower all night?"

"Need I remind you that I don't know anyone in this room."

"Indeed, ya do. There near the refreshment table is Mrs. Naylor. You met her at church that one Sunday. Your mother-in-law is talking with three ladies who live nearby—neighbors so to speak. All ya gotta do is go up and speak to anyone. They'll be glad to start up a conversation."

"I feel so out of place. I suppose you are right, but I am completely over-dressed for this occasion. I'm sorry that I came tonight."

"Ya won't feel like that when the evenin' is through. Come on, they're playin' the first reel. I wanna dance."

Kell pulled Hannah to her feet. Taking both her hands in his, he sashayed her to the head of the line. The lively music had strands of *Dixie* mingled with other familiar reels. The hands clapping and heels tapping on the floor provided a cadence that was exactly right for the lively reel. Kell pulled Hannah as he skipped his way to the middle of the line. He released her to take the hands of Mrs. Naylor when Reverend Naylor twirled Hannah around before he released her to return to Kell. They skipped back to the head of the line. All the couples met in the middle, stepped around each other, took hands, and sashayed to their position in the reel line. By this time, everyone was smiling and laughing—even Hannah. The first reel lasted for a good while, but when it ended, the couples clapped and called for more.

As the night continued, the dancing changed from reels to square dancing. The local blacksmith Reggie O'Neal was a gifted caller. He kept all the couples on their toes, but his calls were so clear that no one got lost in performing the complicated patterns of *allemande left*, or *do-si-do*, or *parade around*. Every square dance ended with *swing your honey round and round.*

Brother Naylor called guests to attention and announced the intermission. He said the ladies of the community had prepared a feast and it was time to eat. "But before we do, let's take a minute to give thanks to our Lord for this fine evenin' of fellowship and fun. Springtime in Arkansas don't allow us much time to kick up our heels just for the fun of it." He bowed his head. "Father, we are a blessed people. You've stood by us in the dry times and the rain. You saw us through when the war threatened but brought us back home. Now that most of us got our crops in the good delta dirt, you give us time to celebrate. You allowed our ladies to make us the best desserts to share. You are a good God. We thank ya for everything…mostly for just living inside us so we don't ever find ourselves alone. Amen." He looked up with a huge smile on his face. "Let's eat, my brothers and sisters."

With his plate piled high with cookies, pie, cake, and a daub of chocolate puddin', Sonny came to speak with Kell and Hannah. "This is the best night I ever had in my life. Those fellows treat me just like I am one of 'em. Hannah, look at all this good stuff. We ain't had many sweets since we left Washington."

"I'm glad you're having a good time, Sonny," Hannah answered.

"And you, Hannah…are you having a good time yet?" Kell picked up the conversation.

"As a matter of fact, I am. I haven't danced like this—well, I have never danced like this in my life. It's freeing and exciting."

One of the girls who had been in their square stopped by. "Hi, my name is Ellen Canton. I just want to tell you how nice you look tonight. Your dress is lovely."

"Thank you, Mrs. Canton."

"Oh, please call me Ellen. I don't think we've met before."

"I'm Hannah Murphy. I live at Sanctuary Hill with my mother-in-law and brother-in-law."

"Nice to know you. My husband David and I farm part of his family's plantation, not far from Sanctuary Hill. As a matter of fact, Mr. Kincaid bought part of our acreage and the overseer's house during the war. I guess we're all neighbors."

124

"That's nice to know. We've been working so much to make Sanctuary Hill livable again, we've not had time to get out and meet the neighbors," Hannah said.

"I need to get back to David. Our baby will need to be fed. Maybe we can visit soon. I hope you are having a good time tonight."

"I am. Thank you."

"Didn't I tell ya you'd make some friends among the folk if you'd just be yourself? Mrs. Canton is a nice lady, and she lives just a stone's throw from ya, lass." Kell and Hannah found a seat near an open window and began to eat their cake. After a while, the musicians began to warm up again, and the crowd began to partner up for the next round of dancing.

"Hannah Ruth…" Naomi bustled through the people to reach her. "Where is Sonny?"

"He was here a short time ago. He said he was having a fine time. I haven't seen him in a few minutes."

"Cousin Naomi, don't ya fret. He probably just went out to catch the breeze with some of the other lads. I'll go look for him." Kell walked outside to the hitching rail and spoke with the other young men that Sonny had been with earlier. They said they'd seen Sonny leave the church with Molly Tangent. Kell began to walk toward the creek. He saw a young couple wrapped in each other's arms, but he could tell from the slight build the boy was not Sonny. He walked further down the tree line and then walked a couple of yards toward the stream. This was the same place he'd made Hannah so angry the one Sunday he'd brought her to church. On that same fallen tree sat Sonny and Molly Tangent, having a quiet conversation that was not meant for his ears.

"Molly, we need to go back yet? Mama will be lookin' for me."

The girl wrapped her arms around Sonny and nuzzled his cheek. "Oh, Sonny, it's so hot in there. Look how pretty it is out here. See the moon shinin' on the water…look at those lightnin' bugs. They look like they're dancing as they flash on and off flyin' over us." She sighed.

"Yeah, it's nice. I guess we can stay a little while."

"Sonny. You are a man. You don't have to take orders from your mother. You have your own land. You're the boss at Sanctuary Hill. My daddy told me that's so."

"Molly, don't you do what your mama and papa tell you to do?"

"Well, I mostly do what I want to do, but I'm a girl and it's harder for me. We're supposed to do what our parents say until we get married. Then we obey our husbands."

"You thinkin' about getting' married already, Molly?"

"Of course, I am. I might even marry you." She kissed him on the mouth, and Sonny pushed himself back. Molly's laughter filled the night air. Frogs jumped from nearby logs, and the cricket whirring stopped momentarily. "Would you like to marry me, Sonny?"

Realizing Sonny was well beyond his comfort zone, Kell intervened. "Sonny, there you are. Your mother was asking if you would come and do her the honor of being her partner for the next dance."

Sonny jumped up and ran as if he were being chased by a demon. "I'm goin', Mr. Kell. Right now."

"May I see ya back to the social, Miss Tangent? I'm sure your father and mother want you to return safely."

"I'll go back, but I'm sure they haven't missed me. It's not time to go home yet." Molly picked up the bottom of her skirt and sauntered back toward the church.

Kell returned to claim Hannah from the small group of women she'd been talking with. They were excited when she told them Sonny and she would reopen the mercantile the following Monday. He stopped by her side, bowed slightly. "May I have this waltz, lass?"

In the center of the room, Kell put his hand on her back and drew her near. He took her other hand and coupled it with his much larger one. When the music began, they swayed together to the tempo of an intimate waltz. When Kell turned her, the small train of ruffles swung only to be pulled in the opposite direction a second later. For a moment, he looked into Hannah's deep brown eyes, and she returned his gaze. This one dance was payment in full for the bargain Kell had struck with Hannah. And the night was not over.

Some of the other men of the community asked to dance with the pretty lady with a winsome smile. Hannah curtsied and nodded at their requests. Kell knew she had done a great deal that evening to win over the members of the community. He claimed five waltzes that evening, including the final dance.

"Hannah, I hope you've had a good evening. I truly enjoyed your company. Thank you for tryin' so hard to please me all night. If ya don't mind, I'll claim the last dance."

As she nodded, he pulled her toward the floor one last time and placed his hand on the small of her back. He pulled her a bit closer than he'd dared before. As they waltzed their way through the couples on the floor, he held her gaze. With her lovely image in his mind, he silently prayed. *My dear Lord, how can I let this lass know how precious she is? Do I dare tell her how dear she is? Show me how to introduce her to you so that what I hope can be more than a daydream.*

The music stopped. He bowed and kissed her hand. "Thank ya, lass. I've had a beautiful evenin'."

♪

When Hannah let her lawn night dress slip down her body, memories of Kell's touch on her back came vividly alive. She had danced with men before and even danced with a few men that very night, but she'd never been moved as much as by that touch of Kell

Kincaid's hand on her back—almost as if it belonged there. Feelings of security, stability, and passion flooded her mind and evoked a night of dreams in which she relived her life with Richard.

Richard had never evoked those feelings in her—not that he'd ever tried. Of course, her father had guaranteed she'd have no opportunity to know how feelings evolved between a man and a woman. He forbade her beaus until he approved the match. That was how she came to be Richard Murphy's wife. The Murphy family was a well-to-do, socially established family in Maryland. Richard's mother came from the cotton aristocracy in the South. The family had the status Kennedy expected for his only child. She would marry well, and together she and her husband would take over the estate he'd built when the time came.

However, the war came first, claiming the life of Hannah's father. The war also destroyed all he'd built during his life, partly in the fighting and the rest claimed in debt and taxes. War took Richard Murphy. He too had left nothing to care for a widow, not even the fond memories of a happy marriage. Hannah found it impossible to mourn a man she hardly knew and who had never been a husband to her.

But in one night, her mother-in-law's kinsman left her with feelings she'd always hoped for, dreamed about, and even craved at times. She'd never allowed those feelings to surface since widowhood had given her freedom. How could this happen in a simple country social? When Kell bent to kiss her hand, she gasped. Reliving that moment woke her.

The evening had not gone as she'd intended. She meant to put Mr. Kincaid in his place—to tell him in no uncertain terms that she wanted him to stay out of her life. Hannah plopped into the chair near the window and covered her eyes with her hands. *How did I let this happen?* She had an oath to uphold. She promised herself that no other person would ever have sway over her life. If she let herself feel something, she put her independence at risk. This problem she didn't need. She'd met her obligation to Kell Kincaid.

Hannah pulled on her work clothes, preparing to work in the garden while her family returned to Linden for church. *No...that Saturday night social was simply what I promised, a debt paid.* Hannah determined to avoid any opportunity that would make them a couple again. She had no time to have a relationship with any man. She didn't want one, and she didn't need one. Richard Murphy had given her more than enough of married life. That is what she told herself that sunny morning in May

.

Chapter 11

And this is the condemnation, that the light is come into the world, and man loved the darkness rather than the light because their deeds were evil. For everyone that doeth evil hateth the light...
John 3:19-20

After washing the breakfast dishes, Hannah took her Bible out to the porch swing. The garden would be there after she spent a while reading. She knew Naomi and Sonny would not return until mid-afternoon, as Brother Naylor and his wife had invited them to share their noon meal.

Hannah's excuse of a bad headache was not a total lie. Her real reason for not going to church with the family was to avoid Kell Kincaid. She wanted time and space to put her resolve in order. Besides, she didn't need to go to church. She could read as well as anyone who sat in those pews that Sunday morning.

The beautiful tooled-leather Bible on her lap had been a Christmas present from her mother the year before she'd died. Lovely roses and ivy were embossed on the soft tan leather. Hannah prized the book because her mother had given it to her, but she'd never put it to much use. She remembered carrying it to church a few times that spring before her mother got sick. After her mother had died in childbirth three weeks before Hannah's tenth birthday, she stored the book carefully in a cedar chest. Her father rarely took her to church.

Brother Naylor's sermon about the man named Jesus had piqued her interest. She couldn't remember ever hearing those things spoken of during the formal church services she attended in Maryland. Of course, she never really listened to the minister as his booming voice rolled over the congregation. When she opened the book, though, she didn't know where to start looking to find the man Brother Naylor had described. She let the book fall open to the middle and found Psalms 109. When she read it, she found a man pleading for vengeance against people who were attacking him with lies and curses. In the end, the writer asked God to save him with his steadfast love, but this didn't seem to be the nature of the man that Brother Naylor described in his sermon.

Hannah flipped over several pages and found another book called Hosea. In the first chapter, God tells the man Hosea to go take himself a wife of whoredom and have children of whoredom for the land had turned from God. Again, she was not looking in the right chapter. Something seemed very different from the message she remembered. She laid the book face down on the swing and went in for a drink of cool water. The day was already too hot.

About the time Hannah reached the well for fresh water, Kell Kincaid rode up the front drive. He climbed the steps and noticed the open Bible lying on the swing. He picked it up and grinned when he saw what Hannah had been reading. He returned it to its place, not wanting Hannah to accuse him of interfering. He knocked on the door.

"Good day, lass. How are ya this beautiful afternoon?"

"I'm well, thank you. Can I help you with something? I am afraid that Naomi and Sonny aren't home yet."

"I knew they'd not be here. I saw them taking the noon meal with the Naylors. Naomi told me you felt poorly this mornin'. Just thought I'd check to see if you needed anything."

"No, but thank you for thinking of me."

"It would be quite neighborly if you'd ask me to sit a spell or offer me a cool drink, ya know." Kell smiled at Hannah the way he had last night when he held her in his arms.

"Yes, if you need a drink of water, I can give it to you."

"Need... no, Hannah, I don't need it." Kell stepped into the parlor and closed the door. "I was hopin' you'd come to church with your family this mornin'."

"I decided to stay home." She retreated to the kitchen and reached for a pewter cup. Kell followed her.

"Are ya upset with me for some reason, Hannah?"

"No."

"Well, you're actin' mighty strange. I thought ya had a good time at the social last night. Was I mistaken?"

"I had a nice time. The community provided lots of good things to eat, and the variety of music was excellent."

"Did ya not enjoy the dancin' and meetin' your neighbors?"

"Kell, I said I had a nice time. Our bargain has been met on both sides now. You helped me get wood to repair the roof, and I went to the social with you. The deal is complete, isn't it?"

"Is that all the evenin' meant to ya, lass?"

"What do you mean?"

"I had hoped that perhaps you'd let that wall crumble a bit and that you'd let me befriend ya. I believed you'd decided that I might be a good friend. I see you haven't let down that barricade yet."

"Kell Kincaid, I don't have the vaguest notion of what you are talking about. I always honor every debt that I incur. I want to be under obligation to no one."

"You are a cold woman, Hannah Ruth Kennedy. I'll mark your obligation to me paid in full. I will not be invitin' ya to join us anymore. Good day to ya." Kell stomped through the door into the parlor and picked up his hat from the settee. "By the way, ya left your scripture book open on the swing. If you're gonna start studyin' the Good Book, ya might start with the Gospels. That is the part marked New Testament. Maybe getting to know about Jesus will show you a world that is so much nicer when we let people love us." Kell slammed the front door and shortly Hannah heard Graystoke's hooves pounding the pavers on Sanctuary Hill's drive.

After a moment, Hannah ran to the door to call him back. The tall man on his horse had already reached the end of the cobbled drive. Hannah slammed the front door and walked to the armchair nearest the window, slumped down, and screamed. *Why don't I do anything civilly?* She truly hadn't intended to hurt Kell's feelings, which she clearly had. What were the words that would tell him she couldn't let herself become involved with him? She didn't know what to say to make him know that if she was dependent on him, she would be trapped again. *Lord, I am not mean-spirited, am I? Perhaps we could be friends.* No. Never again would she let herself fall into that trap.

♭

Monday at 7:00, Sonny and Hannah opened the Kincaid Mercantile for business in Linden. Many shelves were bare, but Hannah had used thirty dollars of their meager cash reserve to order some staples they must stock. The goods coming from Memphis, things like flour, sugar, baking powder, cartridges, and salt, would greatly restore the use of the mercantile to the community. Regardless, anything they sold in the meantime would be profit.

One of the first customers was Reverend Naylor, who didn't really want anything but had come to welcome them to the community. "Hannah and Sonny, gettin' this store back open will be a blessing to us all. I'm so happy you decided to go back into business."

"I hope it was the right thing. I also hope it will be a little bit profitable. We need some income to pay the taxes on our land in the fall," Hannah explained.

"Well, the Lord will see ya through. He is faithful. I hope you will come back to church this Sunday with Naomi and Sonny. Ya know, most of our community are members, so you could get to know your customers that way."

"I will try to get there. Seems like there is always just so much that needs to be done."

"Hannah, the Lord commanded us to remember the Sabbath and keep it holy. It's one of the Ten, ya know. There is time in the six days to work. We can give the Sundays to our Lord."

"Yes, Reverend, I will try."

"And I'd sure like for you to call me Brother Sam. We are simple folks. Besides, I'd like to think that we are family."

Later, several more community folks dropped by. One woman asked for baking soda, which Hannah didn't have. Mrs. Naylor came in and bought six yards of calico for a new Sunday dress. Hannah was so glad that several bolts of fabric had been shelved in the storeroom at the back. She and Sonny had set up a nice dry goods section near the front of the store. Sonny waited on a customer who wanted nails. He put a handful of nails on the scale and weighed them. He then took his pencil and figured out the cost of two pounds of nails. He took the carpenter's money and wrote the sale in the ledger as Hannah had taught him. At six o'clock, the end of their first day, they closed their door. Kincaid Mercantile had netted a handsome profit of $4.16, a rooster, and a pair of laying hens taken in barter.

"Did we do good today, Hannah?" Sonny held the small amount of money from the till in his hand.

"We did fine, Sonny. You were a very good storekeeper today. I can't believe you got two hens for that bridle Mr. O'Neal needed. Do you realize we can have fresh eggs now?"

"Ya think that was a good deal?" Sonny grinned.

"That was the best deal of the day. We can't eat that bridle, but those eggs are gonna taste wonderful." They locked the door, took the crated rooster and hens, and headed home. Good news awaited them there. Aaron Pierce and Lucas had begun reinforcing the partially burned rafters and hoped to begin rebuilding the rest of the roof structure the following day.

"Lucas, are you sure you can take time away from the cotton?"

"Yes, ma'am, Miss Hannah. We done started choppin' the weeds. Shataka and Rose been checkin' the fields. Now is the Good Lord's time to do his magic and grow those little seeds we planted into great big bustin' bolls of white. Just be patient."

"That's good to know. Sonny and I will help with the chopping and watering when we get home in the afternoon."

"No need right now. The Lord been givin' us plenty of rain to make a good crop. We been blessed, Miss Hannah. Surely blessed."

Hannah found Naomi in the parlor, cleaning the wallpaper between the boarded-up windows. She had used her time at home to unpack some of the items they'd shipped from Washington. She placed family keepsakes and pottery around the room. She'd filled a bookcase that Mom Bec had pulled from one of the partially burned rooms. After a good cleaning and a coat of beeswax, the bookcase was filled with books, some from Mr. Hugh's collection and some from their homes in the north. Mr. Hugh's portrait hung directly across from his son-in-law's. A smaller portrait of a dreamy-eyed lady that had once hung in the room being used as Sanctuary Hill's kitchen was next to Hugh Kincaid's likeness.

"Mother Naomi, who is that beautiful woman? Her picture was the only one not destroyed by the soldiers who quartered here?"

"That is my grandmother Kincaid. That is the only possession my father brought with him when he came to this country from his homeland. Papa called her his guardian angel. He told me he would have died in Scotland long before he reached his majority if she hadn't pushed him on the boat to the new world. Her name was Mary Erin McRyan."

"She must have loved her son very much."

"You will know that love one day, Hannah, when you hold your son in your arms. I know that love for Sonny now and will always carry the love for Richard in my heart."

"You have done wonders with this room. We have a parlor we will never be ashamed to invite guests into. And I promise to get you some glass for the windows as soon as we have the money."

"Yes, Hannah, I am pleased with this room, too. I'm reminded of the days of my girlhood." Naomi continued to move things around and add to her design, ignoring Hannah's presence.

So, Hannah went to the kitchen to see if she could help with supper. Mom Bec was ready to serve up a plate of catfish and golden pone. It would make a filling meal if not a well-rounded one. Their stock of vegetables had run out about a week earlier. Until the garden produced things ready to eat, they'd eat off the land. Fish and game would fill their bellies, even if the variety was limited.

That night Hannah went to bed soon after the sun set. She was exhausted. Standing on her feet all day at the mercantile was as tiring as plowing or weeding, just without the blisters. She tossed and turned for a long time. Her mistreatment of Kell came to mind over and over. She got up, lit a candle, and picked up her Bible. Perhaps she could read a while and then sleep would come. She drew her chair toward the open window. The hot breeze only added to the dampness on the back of her lawn nightdress. She found no respite from the heat or her nagging conscience.

Then she saw flashes of light across the yard. A line of six or seven horsemen, carrying tar brands rode toward the quarters where the Kincaid tenant farmers lived. Hannah pulled on her duster, slipped on her shoes, and ran across the hall to awaken Sonny and Aaron. They rushed toward the cabins. Before they arrived, Shataka screamed. The men were galloping at breakneck speed around the cabin, bellowing their rebel call, and cursing at the tops of their lungs at Marcus and Shataka crouching on the porch.

A tall, scrawny hooded figure flung his brand onto the porch at Marcus's feet. The burning stick ignited a fire on the wooden porch, which Marcus doused with water from the barrel nearby. The chaos continued to rage around the tenant family. The wide-eyed children gaped out of the window at the masked, robed men.

Hannah ran into the clearing in front of the cabin and climbed the steps to join her tenant farmers. The man who appeared to be the leader raised his hand, calling a halt to the band of vigilantes. "Madam, I don't know who you are, but we have no business with you. Leave us to our purpose."

"Y'all have no reason to be on this land. Who are you, and what are you doing disturbing the rest of hard-working people in the middle of the night?" Hannah walked to the front of the porch, hoping her voice sounded stronger than she felt.

"We came to warn ya. We don't intend to have Southern land turned over to slaves. Kincaid, best that you, your woman, and kids leave this county. We'll give ya a few days, but no more."

"These people are our workers. This land belongs to Benjamin Murphy, deeded to him by his grandfather. He's the person that decides who goes and stays at Sanctuary Hill," Hannah said.

"You're awful bossy for a female, ain't ya? I don't see no man here. Where is this property owner you are spoutin' off about?" a hooded man asked.

"I'm right here. Hannah told ya the truth. This is my land." Sonny walked to the front of the band of mounted men. Roaring laughter followed Sonny's declaration.

"Look at him—he's a kid. How old are you, boy?" the leader asked.

"Well, I'm old enough to own this farm. Y'all need to leave." Sonny pointed to the road. Again, laughter rolled.

A rotund, robed rider pushed at Sonny with his boot. "I'm so scared of this little boy, Captain. Ya think we should leave or maybe we should burn this eyesore of a cabin. Want me to start a blaze tonight, Captain?"

"No. I think we made our point. Kincaid, since there's no man here to protect this farm, you better leave. That way nothin' will happen to those pickaninnies over there. But if we come back and find ya here, remember you been duly warned." The leader of the ghostly band waved his hand as he turned to leave Sanctuary Hill. "Madam, we have no problem with a white woman, but you need to remember your place. I'd hate to see some harm come to a Southern belle."

The troop galloped toward the main road. As they did, one vigilante threw his lighted brand into the open window of the cabin. The last man arced his torch onto the roof. Then they both spurred their horses to catch up with the column of men ahead of them. Marcus ran into the cabin to extinguish any fire that may have started there while Sonny and Aaron climbed to the roof to retrieve the fire brand up there.

When Marcus returned to the yard, he pulled his shaking wife into his arms. "Shataka, it's all over now. Go on in and get those babies down for the night. They right scared so you'll have to sing 'em to sleep. I'll be in directly."

He walked to Sonny and Aaron and offered his hand to the two young men. Marcus then bowed his head to Hannah. "Folks, I can't thank ya enough for standing up against those devils tonight. They probably woulda burned us out and maybe gone on to my brother and Mom Bec and Rose. You saved our home."

"But Marcus, why are they mad at you?" Sonny asked.

"They ain't mad at me, Mr. Sonny. They's mad at the world. They done lost the war, and everything is changed here in the South."

"Do they think they can make it back like it was?"

"No, Sonny. They are just a bunch of hotheads that can't mind their own business," Aaron replied. "I saw 'em do some really bad things in other places—not those men, but some just like 'em. They try to scare folks into doin' what they want."

"Gee, Aaron. Are they all bad men?" Sonny almost whispered.

"Probably not most of 'em. Some of those vigilante groups are trying to keep the carpetbaggers and scallywags from stealing good people's land. But some of those gangs just haven't figured out how to live in the country now."

Hannah started down the steps. "Marcus, I will go to Madison tomorrow and report this to the sheriff. This kind of lawlessness can't be tolerated."

"That might not help none. Some people think they're doin' a good thing. That sheriff over in Madison is new here. For all we know, he could have been one of those hooded bullies."

"I hadn't thought of that. We may have to find another way to protect Sanctuary Hill."

"Miss Hannah, don't ya worry about us out here. We all be Kincaids. We always guard our home and our kin. That's what Mr. Hugh taught us." Marcus returned to his porch. "Go on. They won't come back tonight."

Chapter 12

He that soweth iniquity shall reap vanity: the rod of his anger
shall fail. Cast out the scorner and contention shall go out;
yea, strife and reproach shall cease.
Proverbs 22:8,10

The second Monday following the visit from the night riders, Sonny put up some argument about going to the store to work. He hinted all weekend that his place was at home with his mother and that he needed to work in the cotton fields. Hannah witnessed Sonny's restlessness at the mercantile. She had to make up tasks to keep him busy when there were no customers in the store.

That morning at breakfast, he had tried once again to convince her that he should stay home. He said, "Hannah, I don't know nothin' about workin' in a store. Let me stay here and put Pal to work breaking a couple more acres. We can plant us some corn."

"Sonny, you are the manager of the store. People expect to do business with a man. Maybe one day, I can hire someone to run the store for us, but right now we just have the two of us to run it."

"I can't be no manager. I don't even know what they do."

"Please look at me. Last week, you did a good job. You waited on customers, wrote sales in our ledger, and helped me restock. We are both learning. I'll show you what to do if something new comes up, and if you need me, I'll be right there."

"Okay. I don't wanna go, but I'll try. I'm worried about leavin' mama here since we had trouble with those bad men."

"Aaron is here to see after your mother. Sonny, for now you are the man who runs Kincaid's Mercantile."

Near 10:00, Brother Sam and his wife came into the store. Mrs. Naylor went directly to the yard goods section of the store and was delighted to find a spool of white thread. She put a dime in Sonny's hand when he told her that was the price. "Mrs. Murphy, are you about settled at Sanctuary Hill?" Brother Sam asked. "I wanted to offer the help of our church if you still need us to get your house in shape for the coming winter."

"Things are getting done a little at a time. We finally have the planking on the roof, but we still have no shingles. The lumber crew leader told me he'd have the shakes for us by the end of August. We may need some help getting those up."

"That's good news. Winter can be wet and cold here in the delta. We don't get a lot of snow, but the wind on those cold days can be brutal. Ya have ample firewood?"

"Yes. Thank you."

"We missed you at church again on Sunday. I hope when things get more settled, you'll join us."

"Brother Sam, I plan to come this Sunday. I enjoyed your sermon, and I do need to get to know the people who live here. I guess I can't argue with the Ten Commandments either, can I?"

Mrs. Naylor interrupted the conversation. "Sam,you need to invite Mrs. Murphy to our Sunday afternoon Bible class. She'd fit right in with the people there. They are all young people like she is."

"Mrs. Naylor, please call me Hannah. Mrs. Murphy is my mother-in-law."

"My given name is Mary Lee. Won't you come to join our class?"

"I don't know much about the Bible, I'm afraid."

Brother Sam grinned. "You'll fit right in. That is why we are studying together. We all learn from each other. I'm gonna expect ya this Sunday. Don't let me down."

The bell on the front door indicated another customer had entered the store. "Excuse me and thank you for the invitation." A rough-looking, dirty, unshaven man walked down the main aisle toward the counter where Hannah stood. With a voice as unpleasant as his appearance, he barked, "Where's the man who runs this store?"

"Good morning, sir. Is there something you need? I'd be glad to help you," Hannah said.

"I like to know who I'm doin' business with. I know old man Kincaid's dead."

"Yes, sir. We lost Mr. Kincaid more than a year ago. He left his store to his grandson, Benjamin Murphy."

"Where is he?"

"He's getting supplies from the storage room. I can get him for you. If you'll give me your name, I'll introduce you."

The dirty man looked Hannah up and down, and as if he disapproved of what he saw, he spat a wad of tobacco toward a spittoon near the counter. "I don't stand on no snobbish actin'. I can talk for myself, girl."

Hannah walked to the back of the room and called Sonny to the counter. She took her place directly behind him.

"You the owner of this here store, boy?"

"I guess I am. Can I get ya something?" Sonny imitated the behavior he'd seen Hannah do.

"I wanted to know who was gonna run this place. Hugh Kincaid and me was good friends. Don't want no riffraff movin' into his place."

143

"Well, I am a Kincaid, and this is my store. When I turn...." Hannah cut Sonny's comment short. She didn't want this man to think Sonny was not of legal age to conduct business.

"Excuse me, but we still don't know your name. If you'd tell us, we could check the books to see if Mr. Hugh left us some note about you. Perhaps he owed you something, or do you have an account you want to pay?"

"I wasn't talking to you, girl. What I want ain't none of your business."

"Pardon me. I didn't mean to offend you. I just wanted to know who I was speaking to." Hannah picked up a feather duster and began flicking it across the items on the shelf behind the counter.

"Boy, if you're gonna do business here, you need to teach your help some better manners." The man slapped his hat back on his head and made a beeline for the door.

"Why was he mad at me, Hannah?" The puzzled look on Sonny's face made Hannah laugh.

"Sonny, he's not mad at you. I'll bet he owed your grandfather some money and was afraid we'd ask him to pay up," Hannah told him.

"He sure wasn't very nice."

"No. He wasn't."

The rest of the week, several new customers made their way in to see the reopened mercantile. Most bought very little, for they too were in the same financial situation as Sonny and Hannah—all land-rich and cash-poor. Some of the local men began to loiter on the front porch, sitting on the benches and on empty barrels Sonny had removed from the store. They sat there for hours at a time, spinning yarns, chewing tobacco, and spitting streams of ugly tobacco juice on the ground. Brother Naylor had told Hannah and Sonny that some of these same

144

men had occupied their time in this manner before the war. Hannah didn't make a fuss about it because they didn't harass the people who came into the store. Most even tipped their hats and murmured something like, "Howdy," or "Mornin' ma'am" to the ladies who came in.

Finally, Friday came after a long, tiring week. Hannah decided this would be accounting day each week. She sat down with the sales ledger after noon. She found that in the two weeks they'd been open for business, Kincaid Mercantile had earned a profit of $14.58. That added with the two laying hens, the rambunctious rooster, three bales of hay, and a beautifully crocheted tablecloth was fair exchange for two weeks of her life, Hannah told herself. Pal could eat for a while this winter. Most importantly, she could put $14.00 away toward paying the tax bill for Sanctuary Hill.

That night at supper, Sonny told Hannah he couldn't work with her in the mercantile the next day. "I told Aaron I would help with that planking over our bedroom tomorrow. We're gonna have it done pretty soon and be ready to put up those shakes when they get here. I gotta help. Marcus is goin' to the field tomorrow to chop cotton."

Hannah didn't complain, partly because the roof had to be completed before winter. She knew she could handle the business in town for half a day.

"Let's ask Kell to go with you to the mercantile tomorrow," Naomi said. "I don't like the idea of you working alone. Naomi twisted her kerchief as if she believed Hannah was in mortal danger. "With those night riders causing problems and the sheriff all the way over in Madison, a lady can't be too careful."

"Mother Naomi, I ceased to be a lady in the winter of '64 when we lost your husband. I am more than capable of minding the store for four hours. I am closing the door at noon on Saturday, remember?

Besides, Kell hasn't been around in several days. He must be busy with his herds."

"Well, you do what you think best, but Kell is our kinsman. He wouldn't mind helping out."

"He has his own work to do. I'll be fine. I'm off to bed now. There is one more day to get through before we reach our day of rest." Hannah picked up a lantern and climbed to the solitude of her room. As she lay down for the night, she thought to herself that Kell wouldn't want to come anyway. Her conscience still nagged at her regarding their last meeting.

$$\phi$$

Hannah arose at the call of the rooster. She hated that bird at 5:00 in the morning. She pushed herself up and dressed for the day. At 7:00, she was greeted by a couple of idlers at the door of the mercantile. Most days they didn't come into the store, but that morning less than thirty minutes after she opened for business, a drenching rain began. Being Saturday, a few farm families came to town to do business and check their mail. The store was filled with people, some who wanted to shop and others trying to stay dry while they enjoyed their usual fellowship. The idlers sat on upturned kegs and crates or leaned against the counter. They began spinning their yarns, gossiping, and telling off-colored jokes. A time or two an offensive remark was directed toward Hannah in a hushed voice that she wasn't supposed to have been able to hear. She ignored much of it, not wanting to create a commotion in the store. A time or two she did ask a couple of the more boisterous men to speak more quietly.

Hannah tried to go about her work, waiting on legitimate customers who asked for something. One lady asked her to pull out three bolts of gingham for her to look at. "I am Ellenor Johnson, Mrs. Murphy. Mary Lee Naylor told me you had some lovely gingham. I was afraid I'd have to drive all the way to Madison to get fabric for my daughter's birthday dress. She will love this green. It will make a lovely summer dress."

"Yes, Mrs. Johnson. It is nice fabric."

"Please call me Ellen. I think I'll take five yards. Six would be better. But skirts are not as full now. What do you think?"

"Ellen, I'll take your word on fashion. I haven't seen a Goody's Style Book since I left Washington." Hannah slipped the shears down the length of the fabric.

Raucous laughter and shouts came from the back of the store. "Hey, clerk. I need some help here."

"Please let me finish here, and I'll be right with you," Hannah called back. Loud talking and more laughter followed. "Is there anything else you need, Ellen?"

Before the lady could answer, an order came from the back. "Hey, come over here and get me that can of axel grease from that shelf yonder." The man pointed to the topmost shelf in the store reached only with a ladder on wheels that moved along the wall. Hugh Kincaid had installed the contraption so he could take advantage of all the shelf space in the building. Hannah hated the rickety, moveable ladder.

"Sir, let me see if there is a can in the storeroom," she said.

"Nope. I want that can. It's the only kind I use at my gristmill. You go ahead and get me that can if you please." The store filled with laughter again.

"Hey, Tommy, what difference does a kind of grease make to that meal you grind? It's full of worms most of the time anyways." Another idler enjoyed his opportunity to get a laugh.

"Hank, you know that's the best brand for gristmills. Now you let this lady shopkeeper make some money. I need me that grease."

Tommy swiped his hat off, bowed, and cleared the way for Hannah to approach the ladder.

She pulled the ladder to the area directly beneath the can he'd pointed to. "Please don't move this ladder while I am climbing." Two ruffians moved to either side of the ladder. One pushed the ladder. The other pulled it. A third man fell into the bottom rung when Tommy pushed him.

"Please stop," Hannah screamed. "I don't want to fall."

Tommy reached up and grabbed Hannah's skirt. "I'll hold ya, darlin'. You're safe with me." Peals of laughter rang out. The men continued to jerk the ladder back and forth.

"Don't push the ladder. I'll lose my balance!"

Tommy stepped on the bottom rung of the ladder. "I gotcha storekeep." Hannah felt a hand on her thigh.

Hannah screamed. "Take your hand off..." Chaos and laughter filled the mercantile. Hannah fell backward. A man from the back of the crowd pushed forward to catch her. When Hannah was able to plant her feet on the floor, she turned and slapped the man with more force than she knew she was capable of. "How dare you take such liberties!"

Kell Kincaid drew his hand across his face. "You're welcome, Mrs. Murphy. I saw ya fallin' as I came in, so I thought I'd catch ya."

"Oh, you weren't the man...I thought...I'm so...I didn't...oh..." Hannah turned and ran to the storeroom and slammed the door. Again, a loud chorus of laughter filled the store.

She fell back against the door, gasping for breath. *How could I do such a stupid thing? And of all people, Kell Kincaid!* Hannah sat spraddle-legged, skirt around her knees for what seemed an eternity. When her composure returned to some measure, she stood, smoothed her clothes back into proper order, tucked a few strands of hair back into her bun, and returned to the store. She slammed the door for attention, marched over to the ladder, pulled it into place, climbed to the top, and retrieved the can of grease Tommy had asked for.

She returned to Tommy and handed him the can. "Is there anything else I can get for you Mr. Tommy whatever your last name is?"

"Well, I don't reckon."

"That will be two dollars." Hannah laid her open hand before him.

"Two dollars? That's might pricey grease." Tommy rubbed the scruff on his cheek.

"It's what you asked for. The kind in the storeroom is half the cost, but you said this is the only brand you use. That's two dollars."

The befuddled idler pulled out a handful of coins, counted out the price, and laid the money in Hannah's palm. He picked up his can and left the store.

"Gentlemen, y'all may remain here if you behave as gentlemen. If any of you decide to use me or Sonny for entertainment again, you'll be charged an entertainment fee...just as was your friend, Tommy."

Hannah returned to work with her customers, and the idlers slowly drifted out of the store. Kell had not been among those present when she returned. Promptly at noon, she turned the sign to read CLOSED and locked the door. She left through the storeroom to avoid any of the loiterers who remained on the porch. She wanted to get home, put one more week of work behind her, and spend the rest of the day working in the garden.

Chopped weeds and tied up vines helped sap the anger she brought home. When Mom Bec called everyone in for supper, Hannah was exhausted but could not forget the horrible day. She made several more sales that day, but she felt she'd failed. Without Sonny in the store, the men tried to run roughshod over her. They goaded her into making a fool of herself, and she'd slapped Kell Kincaid. Could the day have been any worse?

She sank into the ladder-back chair at the table. Pushing away the warmed-over greens and beans, she buried her face in her arms, wrapping one hand across her throbbing head. *I don't want to live the rest of my life like this…one endless dread after another.* Wet spots on her sleeves betrayed her hurt.

She was jarred by an echoing rap on the back door. Before Hannah could rise, she found Kell Kincaid standing over her.

"I'll have a word with ya, madam."

"Mr. Kincaid. I tried to apologize to you. I wanted to, but you were gone." He reached to take her arm, but she rose and stepped back to avoid his touch. "What more do you want? I can't undo what I did."

"I'll have ya walk with me in the sunset and speak your mind. I'll do the same." Kell's stature was ramrod stiff. His voice commanding.

"Not today. This day of all days, I want no walk, nor do I have anything else to say. I'm tired—beyond tired." She bent down to pick up her uneaten supper to return the food to the stove. Kell took the plate and dropped it in the dry sink.

"Ya owe me a slight concession, lass." Kell reached across the corner of the table and clasped Hannah's hand.

"I said no." She jerked hard, but Kell's grip held firm.

Just at that moment, Naomi opened the door from the parlor. "Why bless me, indeed. So nice to see you, Kell. How's my favorite cousin this evenin'?"

"Never better, Cousin Naomi. I've come to have a private word with Mrs. Murphy. We'll be walkin' down by the creek for a spell."

"I'd enjoy a visit when ya return, dear boy."

"I'd like that too. I always enjoy a conversation with my favorite cousin." Kell smiled.

Hannah was trapped. She could either walk with Kell or explain to her mother-in-law all that had happened that day. The least painful of the choices was walking with Naomi's kinsman.

"Let me get a bonnet. I won't be a minute." Hannah tried to move toward the parlor.

"Ya won't need it, lass. The sun's at the tree line. You'll put no more freckles on your nose today." He opened the door.

As soon as they were out of earshot of the house, Hannah tried to open the conversation. "All right, you won. Will you say your piece and let me go?"

"Nay...I'd like to collect my wits. Whenever I'm around ya, I always get tongue-tied. Let's just go on down to the creek. The sound of the water dancing across the stones and the rushing sound as it falls down that little stone levee...that's calmin' on hectic days. The wind over cool water may help make a man forget a stingin' cheek. Help to erase memories of ugly words. Don't ya find that peace in God's nature, Hannah?"

With her hand still captive, she continued to walk in silence with Kell. The wind blew through her hair, causing it to fall across her face. She tried to pull her hand loose to move it from her eyes, but Kell's grip never wavered. Hannah stopped, yet Kell pulled her on.

The sky began its evolution from summer blue to pink, gold, lavender, and gray. If Hannah had been aware of the glory around her, the scene may have dispelled some of the ugliness of the day. She failed to see one second of nature's beauty. "I'm not going one more step. Say your piece and let me return to my work."

"Hannah, look at all nature's handiwork around ya. If I tried to paint it, I could never capture the color and the light. Our Lord is a master artist. I never get tired of lookin' at the beauty I found here in Arkansas."

"What?" Hannah jerked free of Kell's grasp. "Did you drag me out here to talk about the sunset? Are you a lunatic?"

Kell reached out and rubbed her cheek with his thumb. "Why are ya so angry? You slapped me today, though it should have been me deliverin' the thrashin'."

"I am angry you drag me a mile from home and then gush on about a sunset. I told you I'm in no mood to walk." She turned to leave.

Kell pulled her back. "If you'd take a minute to look at it—the beauty and the peace of this place, you'd forget your frustration."

"Mr. Kincaid, you have been a briar in my flesh since day one. Why do you take it upon yourself to be the bane of my existence? What can you possibly gain from tormenting me at every turn?"

"Good. You are finally ready to talk." Kell walked to a fallen tree near the water's edge. "Want to sit a spell?"

"No. I want to go back to the house so I can work on the orders for the freighter next week."

"I've not said my piece yet. Come over and sit with me. I think I'm gonna enjoy that cool creek." Kell pulled off his boots and rolled up his pant legs. "Ahh, feels wonderful. Come enjoy what nature has for ya, lass."

"If I do this, will you tell me why you brought me out here? I have things I need to do at home."

"Is it home?" Kell looked into her eyes.

"What?"

"Do you consider Sanctuary Hill your home?"

"Mr. Kincaid, whether I do or don't makes little difference. This land is all that remains to provide for us. If I am going to keep a roof over our heads, I must do what I am doing."

"Do you have to do it alone?"

"What are you getting at, Kell Kincaid?"

"I need to get some answers from ya. I heard some gossip in Linden today that I hope is not true. A man at the livery stable told me that he heard about a night raid at Sanctuary Hill. Is it true, lass?"

"The night riders were back last night," she answered.

"What do you mean, back?" Kell asked.

"You knew about the burned cabin. Sonny said you found the second cigar butt still burning."

"We found one cigar."

"He told you about the first one, didn't he?" Hannah asked.

"No. Are you telling me they have been here twice already?" Kell rushed back to the bank where Hannah stood. He grabbed her shoulders. "And ya didn't think it warranted you tellin' me that they had come?"

Hannah lowered her eyes. "I told them Sonny owned the property. I'm pretty sure they were the ones who burned down the empty cabin back during planting season."

"And just like that, they said, 'Yes, ma'am. Enjoy the rest of the night.' Then they turned and rode off."

"Well, something like that. Anyway, they left."

"Why did ya not tell me, lass?"

"I thought I had taken care of the problem. I forgot I hadn't told you about the incident. I haven't seen you since you rode off to Madison to see the sheriff. Did you learn anything there?"

"Don't change the subject. Do ya think ya can deal with these attacks by yourself? Are ya so foolish? Hannah, be honest with me. Do you think you can fight off armed vigilantes by yourself?"

Hannah moved toward the creek, her arms flailing around her as her voice reached levels setting the birds to flight.

"Who is going to step in and take the obligation off my shoulders? Let me see...I have a dead husband who gambled away all our property before he died at Shiloh fighting the rebels. He preferred battle to his unsatisfactory wife. Maybe my father-in-law could help— no, the rebels killed him, too, but not before his partners had bankrupted the family business. Paying his debts cost Naomi her home in Washington. Oh, yes, there is Sonny. He owns all the land and the mercantile, but he wants to stay home with his horse rather than work at the store. Most ten-year-olds do like to play more than work. Naomi is my last hope. Maybe I can turn things over to her. She gives the most wonderful parties and balls. Did you know she writes lovely poetry and does needlepoint? She has a green thumb for roses, but she doesn't seem to know how to weed a garden. Yes, I guess I will do it alone."

Kell moved to gather Hannah in his arms. Hannah couldn't seem to stop flailing her arms and shaking her fists. He continued to hold her. When she stopped struggling, he lowered his lips to hers in a brief kiss.

"Why did you kiss me?" Hannah asked.

"Seemed to be the easiest way to calm the storm ya let yourself get lost in. Just because I asked a question didn't give ya rise to lose your temper. I only asked why ya carry this obligation alone."

Hannah pushed Kell away from her. After deeply sighing, she said, "I plant a garden so we can eat. I run the store to earn money to pay taxes. I work with my tenant farmers because I need laborers to keep this land. You know why I do the things I do."

"But you are angry at the responsibility. Why don't ya return to your family in Maryland and start a new life?" Kell returned to his seat on the log.

"Since it's none of your business, I should just leave it be, but I have no family left in Maryland. I cannot leave an obligation that I have made. Let me do what I have to do. Stop intruding into my life."

"I can't do that. I came to America to take care of my uncle. My father gave me my portion of the family estate so I could move to Arkansas to be near Uncle Hugh. My uncle needed me to care for his daughter's family. The Lord planned this for me. I've family here. I know a blessed future awaits, Hannah. The land here is fertile, and I believe life will be good."

"What does this have to do with me?"

Kell took Hannah's hand. "This isn't the ideal place or best time, but I'll speak my mind. When I went to Linden this mornin' to speak to Sam, I had only one thought on my mind. Then at the livery, I heard that gossip. All the way here, I've argued with myself to do it or not. Then we have a real spat, not just those icy words we seem to come by so easy. After everything, I believe my decision is the right one."

"Again, I ask you, what does all your ranting have to do with me?"

"I am going to court ya, lass. I won't stop until the Lord shows me I can't win your heart."

Hannah strangled as she tried to speak. She shook her head in disbelief. Then she burst into laughter. "For a minute, I thought you were serious. You're making a joke to take my mind off this horrendous day, aren't you?" She continued to laugh.

Kell pulled her to him and lifted her chin to look into her eyes. "Hannah Ruth, this is no joke. I meant every word as badly spoken as they may have been."

She stopped laughing and gasped, "You are a lunatic!" You want to be my beau? What makes you think I'd ever consider you a suitor?"

"Hannah, I'm certain it's God's will. He'll tell me when I've no claim to ya, lass."

"You can stop this nonsense right now. I will never allow any man to put me under subjugation again. I am my own person, finally. No one will control me ever again."

"I said nothing about control. Don't ya want someone to love ya, Hannah? Do you not think ya have the right for another to care for ya?"

She turned her back and bent to pick up her shoes. Kell stepped in front of her and clasped her shoulders again. "I'm not finished. You've spoken no words that will send me away. I've known since the first time I saw ya dancin' in the clover and dandelions down in the lea that the Lord had meant us to be together."

"Let me go. I don't know what you're babbling about."

Kell once again pulled Hannah into his arms. When he did, Hannah seemed to turn to granite. "Hannah, I only want ya to know I care. You are not alone. I'm here, and our Father in Heaven is here to help carry the burden." Still, Hannah failed to react.

"I'm sorry for the poor way I tried to tell ya of my intentions."

"Are we finished now?"

"Just one thing more. Hannah, you must promise me you won't go into another raid if that mob returns. I'll talk to the Kincaids, but you must not put yourself in harm's way again."

"I'll be more careful. Perhaps I was being foolish getting involved with that pack of bullies."

"Will ya talk with me again?" he asked.

"I don't see how I can stop you. We are neighbors, and you are Naomi's kinsman. I'm sure our paths will cross."

Kell walked Hannah back to Sanctuary Hill. The long silent walk was the final event of the most unbearable day of Hannah's life. She wanted solace. A long night's sleep in her bed may help…perhaps it would provide the peace she sought. Truthfully, she doubted it. Thankfully, the next day was Sunday, and she didn't have to face a day at the mercantile. Maybe she'd have a whole day without a new obligation, conflict, or failure

Chapter 13

Thus saith the lord God, Let it suffice you, O princes of Israel: remove violence and spoil, and execute judgment and justice. Stop dispossessing my people.
Ezekiel 45:9

Spring passed into summer. The delta heat was brutal. To make it worse, the humidity added to the oppressive climate. Hannah hadn't experienced this degree of summer heat before. Her home in Maryland had been near the river, and most days, a cool breeze tempered the hottest summers. Marcus Kincaid told her to be grateful for the hot and wet climate. The frequent rains kept their crops well-watered. Truly, only three times had they carried water from the creek to water their extensive garden.

The Kincaids assured Hannah their cotton crop should bring record yield that year. The plants were strong and healthy. The work of all the Kincaids and Hannah and Sonny had kept the weeds down, but Hannah hated the work of chopping cotton worse than anything she'd had to do so far. Between the heat, dirt, and blisters on her hands, Hannah came to despise the work and the need for her to do it.

The delivery of her orders from Memphis had brought more customers to the mercantile. She now had the staples they needed. Flour, baking soda, kerosene, coffee, and salt were sold almost before Hannah could get the lids off the barrels. With the sales, she was able to double the orders in those early weeks. The short delivery time of two weeks kept the shelves well-stocked. Even with her closing every day at three so she could help with the chopping, she felt a glimmer of hope. The endless work was beginning to put some money aside for taxes. And with Sonny in the store, she could do business without harassment.

Their family was eating better, too. The garden provided fresh vegetables and greens. Mom Bec had proved to be a gem. She worked tirelessly from sun-up to sundown every day to cook, preserve, and maintain Mr. Hugh's cottage, as she referred to the house. Even Naomi had taken an interest in cleaning, restoring, and creating a livable home for them. Hannah knew Mom Bec's influence had brought about that miracle, too. Hannah gave her a dollar every week to keep for her use. At first, she had argued that she couldn't take the extra money, but Hannah insisted. She could not overlook the sway this elderly angel had in their lives.

Life was looking up. Hannah should have taken pleasure in what she'd accomplished in the short time she'd lived in Arkansas. Because of her deal with the lumber crew and the chance meeting of Aaron Pierce, Sanctuary Hill now had a solid new roof. Aaron had also decided to stay and make his home as one of Hannah's tenant farmers. The deal with the lumber crew had benefited Sanctuary Hill in more ways than Hannah had dreamed it would. On the last day of cutting, the crew delivered three wagon loads of firewood. Much of it was small or gnarly, but the wood would keep them all warm during the upcoming winter. And even more, thirty-five dollars in cash had been laid away in an antique safe in the dining room.

If Hannah had taken stock of what she'd done since their arrival in April, she should have felt some degree of accomplishment—of satisfaction for so many jobs done well. Those were not the feelings that washed over her on that eighth day of July. Today, she turned twenty-five years old, and she was tired. More than that, she was frustrated, angry, and lonely. Every morning, she rose from her bed to face the same thing—another day of endless work. *Did life not hold more than this?*

Kell Kincaid was a frequent visitor at Sanctuary Hill. She often encountered him riding around the area of the manor and the quarters at Sanctuary Hill. He had dinner at their table at least once a week, and ofttimes he would spend the evening with Naomi and Sonny, sitting on the front porch. His demeanor toward Hannah hadn't changed at all, even though she spurned every attempt at courtship. Kell invited her to church every Sunday, asking her to join the afternoon Bible class. She was tempted because she loved books and learning, and she'd had little outlet for those things since she'd come to Arkansas. Yet, she couldn't figure out a way to go to the Bible class without Kell seeing it as an opportunity to court her.

Regardless, work called. Hannah rose and dressed for another day at the mercantile. She and Sonny opened the store at 7:00 as was their custom. Shortly after they opened the door, Mary Lee Naylor came in.

"Hannah, do you have any soft white fabric?"

"I'm sure we can find some, or if not, I will order what you want from Memphis. Are you making a new blouse or perhaps a night dress?"

"Oh, no, dear, I'm gonna make a christening gown and baby clothes."

"How wonderful! When is the little one going to be here?"

"In about two weeks. I am so excited." Mary Lee's smile radiated across Hannah's gloomy morning.

"But Mary Lee, you can't be about to have a…"

"Oh, no, Hannah. We are going to adopt a little boy who lost his parents in the influenza epidemic over in Crittenden County. He's a distant cousin to Sam." Mary Lee's laughter filled the room. "I shouldn't laugh. Those poor young people dyin' is a shame. But the Lord has taken a bad thing and worked it into a blessing for me. I always wanted to have children, but it wasn't to be. So, he found a way to make me a mother. Isn't God good?"

"I am happy for you. Do you see any fabric here, or do you want me to order something else?" Hannah didn't know why, but she felt even worse after Mary Lee left the store. The preacher's wife exuded joy and contentment every time Hannah met her. Having to live on a pastor's income, her lot in life wasn't so easy either. *What does she know that I don't?*

As the day continued, Hannah's mood continued to plummet. At 3:00, she told Sonny to ride Pal home and that she would come later. She planned to walk and spend some time alone.

"Hannah, mama ain't gonna be happy with me if I don't bring ya home."

"Sonny, I am fine now. No one will bother me out here in plain sight. I'll be home in a little bit." She had no intention of chopping cotton today, nor would she weed or gather food from the garden. This was her birthday. She deserved some time to call her own.

So, she walked down toward the stream in the shade of the trees. She pulled off her shoes and walked in the cool, flowing water. After a minute, Hannah pulled the pins from her hair and let it fall to her waist. The wind flicked it back and forth across her face. Pulling her skirt up to her knees, she kicked the water up into cool sprays that landed on her arms and face. How good that felt. She was tired. She climbed to the bank, and soft clover brushed her ankles. She sank under a full oak tree and lay in the green, white, and pink of the meadow. This bed of nature was a treat. Fatigue seeped from her body. Hannah slept.

About sunset, a blue and gold butterfly brushed Hannah's bare arm. Startled, she realized hours had passed. She picked up her shoes and began to run toward Sanctuary Hill. Just before reaching the yard, Hannah stopped to put on her shoes and pull her hair into some kind of bun before she entered the house.

"Surprise!" and "Happy Birthday, Hannah!" greeted her at the door. The house was full of neighbors, a few customers, and a few people she'd never seen before. Naomi, Sonny, and Kell stood at the fireplace together, one with a scowl, one with a questioning look of concern, and one with a tremendous smile.

"Hannah, you're so late. We were getting worried that something had happened to you."

"Please forgive me, Mother Naomi. I let time slip by me this afternoon."

"Well, you're here now, Hannah. Let's have a party!" Sonny took her by the arm and led her to a table filled with the small feast their meager pantry could provide. While not lavish by most standards, the table laid out by Mom Bec was filled with fresh fish, game, some vegetables, and a multi-tiered cake. The musicians had set up on the porch and begun to play a waltz. Several couples began to dance—some in the parlor, some on the porch, and a few on the lawn.

"May I have this dance, Hannah?" Kell bowed from the waist and offered his hand. She nodded. Kell led her to the porch away from Naomi.

"Why did y'all do this?"

"Lass, it's your birthday, and we're havin' a much-needed party."

"But I haven't been especially nice to you."

"Have ya not? I thought you were just trying to be honest with me. We need a party now and again. Your birthday seemed to be as good a reason as any."

"But these people here…I don't know any of them very well."

"Aye, but they know Naomi, and she's the one who invited them, ya see. Of course, you could get to know them if ya tried a bit."

"I still don't understand why…."

"Don't worry about the details. You're just supposed to relax and have fun. You work all the time. Not tonight. On this night, you're the belle of the ball."

Between musical sets, Hannah found herself engaged in conversation with the ladies who had come to her party. The neighbors from the next farm reminded her they'd met at the social. She was introduced to other young women who lived nearby. Rachel Miller seemed to be a natural belle, and she made everyone feel at ease. Hannah enjoyed the talks with the women her age and the conversations they shared about trying to make a living since the war. She found herself laughing and sharing tales with her new acquaintances.

Kell continued to dance with Hannah as often as he could. Other men did take her hand from time to time. Naomi had a wonderful time playing hostess at Sanctuary Hill again. Mom Bec's beautiful apple cake with caramel icing was a special dessert. Normally, Hannah would have scolded her about the excess because of the large amount of sugar, eggs, and even new apples that went into the delicious dessert. Perhaps for this one occasion, it could pass. All gathered declared the cake ambrosia.

At the last dance, Kell once again claimed Hannah. He pulled her close. "Lass, it is so good to see ya smilin'. You truly enjoyed the other ladies tonight. I don't think you know this, but when you allow yourself to have a good time, your eyes sparkle, even as dark as they are—a light glows through. Then you are truly a beauty."

"Thank you, Kell."

"If I could, I'd make it so this dance would never end. I'd keep ya in my arms like this 'til time stopped."

She met his gaze. "Kell, please don't spoil this night for me. I enjoyed the dancing and the attention. I just can't…"

"All right, Hannah. I've said enough. I will wish ya a good night now." Kell raised her hand to his lips and gently kissed it. "Sleep with the angels tonight."

Within the half-hour, Hannah, Naomi, and Sonny had said goodnight to all their guests. They made quick work of returning their home to its normal state. The plates, glasses, and flatware were quickly cleaned and stored. The night had been a success for all.

"Hannah, my dear, I wish I'd had the funds to get you a gift. I know I've been hard to deal with since we came home, but I'm not oblivious to the hard work you do for us."

"You gave me a fine party, Mother Naomi. This is a tremendous gift. Thank you for going to so much trouble for me."

"I had as much pleasure as you did from this evenin'. We had so many parties here when I was a girl. I hope we can get back to that time again."

"We'll see how things go. Perhaps someday we can."

Sonny handed her a roughly wrapped parcel. "Hannah, I made ya this for your birthday. I found the mirror at the mercantile, but I carved the frame just for you. You can see better to fix up your hair now."

"Oh, Sonny, what a fine gift! I'll always treasure it because you made it for me." Hannah picked up the lovely hand mirror that Sonny had painstakingly carved. Then she hugged his neck, knowing he'd be red-cheeked.

"Well, I think it's time for us all to go to bed. Tonight was a lovely party, but tomorrow is another workday. Saturdays are so busy trying to get ready for church." Naomi blew out the last lantern in the kitchen. "Good night, Sonny dear, and Hannah."

Φ

The Murphys slept well until midnight. Screams from the quarters brought Hannah to her feet. Scrambling to the window, she stumbled but managed to catch herself on her chair. Through the window, she saw twelve men carrying lit tar brands racing around Marcus and Shataka's cabin. Cursing and rebel screeches sounded above the thunder of the horse's hooves. The dozen glowing brands cast the area in an orange, gray light.

Hannah grabbed her wrapper and ran downstairs. Sonny and Aaron were already standing at the back door. "Aaron, run down and get Kell Kincaid. Tell him to come help us." He ran through the back door.

Hannah picked up a large knife from the kitchen, and Sonny carried his club over his shoulder. Sprinting as fast as they could, they reached the edge of the yard. Rebel calls and cursing mixed with Shataka's screams pierced the night. Within a minute, the man who seemed to be the leader stopped, and the other men gathered behind him. They waved their burning brands. Hannah believed they intended to torch the house.

Doubting she could stand, she walked with a trembling gait to the porch in front of the Kincaids. "Why have you come back to Sanctuary Hill?"

One man on a black horse let out the loudest rebel call Hannah had ever heard. She stepped back. Shataka pushed her children back into the cabin.

"We already warned y'all. In this state, we uphold the Black Codes. No slave's gonna own property in this county." The leader rode up to Hannah.

164

"No slave does," she said. "You need to take your leave. This property belongs to us."

"No silly woman owns property in Arkansas either," the ghoulish figure screamed back at her. For the second time, Hannah noticed the strange way the man pronounced the letter 's' that night. She had heard that before. She was sure. Then, three hooded men threw ropes around the porch supports and jerked them loose. The roof collapsed and fell on Marcus. Hannah was knocked to the ground.

Sonny had been standing behind the pack at the edge of the yard. He ran to the pile of rubble and pulled Marcus out. "Hey mister, this is my property. My granddaddy gave it to me in his will. You can't come here and hurt folks," Sonny yelled.

"You're just a dang kid. Get outta our business," another hooded rider yelled.

Hannah pulled herself to her feet. "We asked you to go. If you've said your piece, get off our land." Hannah didn't feel nearly as strong as the words she'd just spoken. "I'll be calling on the law to deal with this."

The pack started to laugh. "You think we're worried about the local sheriff? We ran the last one off. The new one is Southern, just like us." Again, Hannah noticed the strange 's' from the leader.

"Well, my uncle, the governor may not take such a light view of what you're doing here. Sonny, do you recognize any of these men?"

"I don't know about the men, but I sure know some of these horses. I think I can recognize 'em again."

Some of the riders pulled back, mumbling among themselves. The leader of the night riders turned to face his band. "Men, we've done what we came to do. Kincaid, if you got a brain in that frizzy head, you'll get. We won't be so merciful the next time." They flung their tar brands into the garden, toward the shed, and on the roof of the cabin. A robed man tossed a pail of melted tar toward Marcus. The hot mixture drenched Shataka's nightdress. Hannah pulled the cloth away from her trembling body as she screamed from the burns. Hannah jerked the garment off, and Marcus ran to cover his wife with his shirt. Aaron pounded out the small fires near the cabin while Sonny threw the blazing torches from the roof.

"Shataka, you be burned bad?" Marcus continued to hold his wife.

"I be all right. Just a little burned."

"Miss Hannah, thank ya. I know they'd a done more, but ya saved us dis night. Thank ya for keepin' my Shataka from bein' burned worse."

"Hannah, I didn't know the governor is your uncle," Sonny said. "Gee, that's good for us, ain't it?"

"Sonny, I am afraid that was a little white lie. We aren't kin to the governor that I know of. Who is he, anyway? I did hear the other day at the mercantile that the state assembly is talking about ways to stop the vigilantes that are terrorizing people across the state. I need to write a letter and tell them of our problems."

"I promise you, Hannah, but the next time I see 'em on our farm, I'm takin' my club to 'em. I carved it, and it's strong. I'll get me a night rider!" Sonny said.

Hannah shook her head. *Something else to worry about—Sonny going after armed night riders with a club!*

🙑

Within minutes, Kell and Aaron rode into the lane between the Kincaids' cabins. Aaron had found Kell near Lucas's cotton patch, just about half a mile west of the quarters.

"Sorry, I didn't get back sooner. Mr. Kell wasn't at his place."

"Hannah, are ya hurt, lass?" He saw her trembling. As he approached her, he saw the knife in her hand. "What were ya plannin' to do with that? Give one of them a scrape and make 'em mad enough to beat ya?"

"I was trying to defend our land."

"And Sonny, did ya not think of his welfare? With him carrying that club, they could've shot him and called it self-defense. Did ya not promise me you'd not get into the middle of such a fray again?" Kell yelled.

"I said I'd be more careful. I did send Aaron for help. Where were you anyway?"

"The same place I am many a night. Riding rounds, watchin' out for Sanctuary Hill. You are too naïve to be left unprotected here. Go back to the house. I'll see to the security of this farm from this point on."

"Wait a minute…"

"Go back to the house and go to bed. I'll see to Marcus and his family. I'll tell ya in the mornin' what I am gonna do." Kell turned his back and returned to check on Marcus's family.

Kell was true to his word. He appeared at the breakfast table with a plan to set up a night watch the following morning. Hannah hadn't quite come to grips with all he'd told her the previous night. She knew he intervened to protect them, but he had done it without her knowledge or consent. Sanctuary Hill wasn't his domain. *Am I trying to be too controlling? Am I just letting my pride overtake my good sense?*

"Hannah, this is what we are going to do. I am going to schedule a night watch of two men in three-hour shifts. We will ride around the quarters, the main house and alternate fields until the cotton is out and sold."

"Kell, our workers can't do that all night while we are still working the fields. When will they rest?" Hannah rose with her hands on her hips.

"That is why we'll do shifts. I know it will be a burden, but I obviously can't do it alone. I was no help last night."

"I didn't know you had been riding night watch. I appreciate your efforts, but you should have told me. Maybe my ploy about the governor was enough to keep them away. Some of them pulled back and seemed restless when I said that. They rode off before they burned the cabin."

"Reprieve only. And Shataka was burned pretty badly on her torso. Not a good thing with her expectin' this new baby."

Hannah continued to argue. "This will disrupt the whole routine here at Sanctuary Hill. Another way can surely be found."

"When ya find it let me know. As of today, we are going on watch at this plantation."

Chapter 14

Therefore, I say unto you, take no thought for your life, what ye shall eat, or what ye shall drink; nor yet for your body, what ye shall put on. Is not life more than meat? And the body than raiment? For Your heavenly Father knoweth that ye have need of all these things. But seek ye first the kingdom of God, and His righteousness; and all these things shall be added unto you.
Matthew 6: 25,32-33

Time seemed to ooze like molasses in January as Hannah waited for harvest time. Her hopes for sustaining their livelihood rested in that crop. Marcus had assured her the cotton was well on the way to producing a bumper crop. He reported that if the hot, humid weather continued, just three more weeks to mid-August, the Kincaids would be picking cotton at Sanctuary Hill and that it would be the best cotton in St. Francis County.

Hannah knew picking time would require every able person at Sanctuary Hill. She was concerned by the lack of rest all the men experienced because of the night watch. She planned to close the mercantile except on Wednesday and Saturday mornings. She'd never picked cotton, but then, before this year, she'd never chopped cotton or plowed a furrow or raised a potato. Now she knew how to do all those tasks.

She could be a pioneer woman with all her new-found knowledge, just like her beloved grandmother Lizbeth Campbell. She remembered the stories Gran had told her when she was a girl. Yes, Gran would be proud of her, but she knew her father would be appalled! But that would be nothing new. Because she hadn't been the heir he'd wanted and her mother had died, Hannah's memories of her father always were of his scoldings, chastising her for inappropriate behaviors, or punishment for infractions of his many rules. *I'm not going to think about that. Gran, I hope you are up there smiling down on me.*

That week, for some unknown reason, Hannah decided to return to church with her family. Reading the gospel of Matthew had left her with more questions than answers. Although Kell was near most days, she could not bring herself to ask him questions that plagued her. Brother Naylor had invited her to the Bible class, too, so there was no reason not to go. On Sunday, she arose and dressed in one of her modest cotton day dresses. She didn't intend to make the mistake of overdressing for the event again. This full-skirted dress of pink calico with small white daisies had a fitted bodice and short puffed sleeves. Both the neckline and sleeves were trimmed with lace, but it was not overly ornate or beyond what any of the other ladies could be wearing that day. After looking at her image in the mirror Sonny had made for her, she felt properly attired to attend the Community Church.

When the family arrived in Linden, Kell helped Naomi and Hannah from the wagon. Some of the ladies of the church came to greet them. Mary Lee Naylor took her arm and walked her into the church. This time, Hannah felt welcome there, not the tension of being the outsider. Shortly, Kell, Naomi, and Sonny joined her in the pew the family had adopted as their place.

"You look pretty today, Hannah," Sonny said. "Is it all right if I sit next to you?"

"I'd like that."

Sonny took her hand while she sat down, and he sat next to her. Kell smiled back at Sonny, winking as he seated Naomi next to Hannah. He took the aisle seat. Again, Hannah became almost at once immersed in Brother Naylor's sermon. She'd read that past week the text he used, and it had raised a question for her then. In the scripture from Matthew 6, Jesus told his followers not to worry about life's needs. Hannah had done nothing else for the past three years but worry about holding her household together. The passage said to stop worrying, but she didn't see how she was supposed to do that.

Brother Sam talked so plainly about faith and trust in Jesus. He spoke as if he knew the Lord on a personal level, almost as if He were living there within the preacher. At times, Hannah had sensed the same thing in Kell and Brother Sam's wife. She could not miss the conviction she saw and heard with each sermon he delivered. Why did this all seem so beyond her capability to grasp?

She looked down at Kell. Nodding his head, he seemed to take in every word as if he knew the message. Then he raised his hand toward the ceiling and said, "Amen, brother." Hannah dropped her gaze into her lap. *What are people going to think?* Then she stared at the roughly hewn cross that hung behind the pulpit, lost in thought until Sonny tugged at her dress sleeve. Brother Naylor had ended his sermon, and the congregation was beginning to sing, *Jesus, Lover of my Soul.* The words of the hymn echoed the message of the sermon.

"Well, Hannah, did ya like the good brother's sermon as well as the first one ya heard?" Kell asked.

"Yes, I did. He talks about things I don't quite understand, but I think you do. You seem to understand most everything because I saw you agree with so many points he made."

"'Tis true. Brother Sam and I see the basic principles of faith verra much alike. I guess that is why we enjoy scripture study together as much as we do. Are ya ready to have lunch, lass? I know Mom Bec fixed us a good picnic lunch yesterday. Been wonderin' all mornin' what we'd be havin'.'"

"Yes, I hope we can find some shade, though. It's hot today."

"Maybe we should go down to the creek and sit with our feet in the water again."

"I'm not sure that is a good idea. Seems I remember the last time I wound up falling on my backside when someone stepped on the tail of my skirt."

Kell laughed. "Lass, you've got a great wit. I so enjoy your tongue-lashings. You have a subtle way of puttin' me in my place."

Hannah found her place beneath a giant oak next to Naomi. Four families sat nearby, each pulling out a lunch they'd brought. Brother Naylor and Mary Lee joined them. "So glad you decided to stay for the Bible class this afternoon, Hannah. You'll enjoy this group, a couple of bachelors, hopin' to find a sweetheart more than learn the scripture, three or four young ladies, and three married couples. You'll fit right in."

"Thank you, Brother Sam. I want to understand some of the things I am reading. I have a lot of questions."

Before Hannah finished her talk with the preacher, Molly Tangent approached them. She scooted between Sonny and Kell on the bench. "Hi, Sonny. Do ya want to share lunch with me? My mama made me some sugar cookies."

"No, Molly, I better eat lunch with my mama. We got us a good dinner right here."

"Well, when you get finished, can we go for a walk? It's hot today so we can go wade in the stream."

"Well, maybe I can. I'll ask my mama, but we gotta eat first."

"All right, Sonny, but I'll be back in a few minutes. She jumped up and sauntered back to the porch where her parents were eating with two older couples.

"Mama, do ya think I can go walkin' with Molly after we eat?" Sonny asked.

"I don't mind if you don't come back late for Bible class. I may need you to help me look after the little ones while their parents study."

"Oh, Mama, do I have to?"

"You will have plenty of time to walk with Molly before then."

About that time, Kell arrived with a large basket that Mom Bec had prepared the day before. Sonny scarfed down his meal and jumped up.

"Wait, Sonny. Don't you think you would rather go play horseshoes with the other young men behind the church?" Hannah didn't like the idea of Sonny spending time alone with Molly Tangent.

"Naw. Molly always wants me to walk with her and sit by her at the creek. I never know what to say to her, but I listen while she tells me things."

"Hannah, Sonny can spend his Sunday afternoon with Molly if he likes," Naomi said. "They are just going to walk in the creek,"

Hannah watched as the young man walked toward the porch. Mr. Tangent came out to meet him and put his arm around Sonny's shoulder and gave him a strong handshake. Shortly, the young couple walked side by side down the path toward Wilson Creek.

"What's wrong, Hannah?" Kell asked.

"There is something not right with what I just saw. Molly is just a girl—too young to play the seductress for her father's greed."

Naomi choked on the sip of lemonade she'd just swallowed, showering all sitting near her. "Goodness gracious, Hannah! What a ridiculous thing to say. They are only children."

"Mother Naomi, I don't think this is the place to discuss our family business."

"Lass, enough for right now," Kell said. "Don't be sayin' things that'll only bring more problems to ya."

"But Kell, I know that."

He cut her short. "Ya think ya know, but for now, let's just keep it among the family. Please don't say anymore. I'll go check on the kids in a few minutes."

Hannah returned to the bench to sit beside her mother-in-law. She did stop talking, but the thoughts continued to run through her mind.

"Hannah, would ya honor me with your company for a short ride around Linden? Graystoke would like to stretch his legs."

"I'm not dressed to ride a horse, Kell."

"Sure, ya are. We'll be most discreet. I'll let ya sit side saddle, and no one passing by will question the ride, just two friends passing a lovely Sunday afternoon." Kell pulled himself to the back of the saddle and then lifted Hannah to sit sideways. He pulled the reins, and they trotted down the main road toward the center of town. They rode the loop around the few businesses still in Linden and stopped in front of the mercantile. The porch there offered them shade from the afternoon sun, and there was a soft breeze coming from the north. The benches would be a perfect place for a real conversation.

Kell slipped down and lifted Hannah to the porch. "Let's sit here for a spell. We still have nearly an hour before we need to get back. Tell me why seein' Sonny with that little slip of a girl has ya so agitated."

"The whole thing just seems wrong. Sonny has never paid any attention to girls before. But the worst thing, Kell, is that Mr. Tangent has ulterior motives. I'm sure of it. He came to the house one afternoon while we were in the field early on during the planting time. He offered Naomi five thousand dollars for Sanctuary Hill."

"Five thousand dollars is a reasonable price for the land, Hannah."

"That may be so, but it's not nearly enough for the three of us to live on for the rest of our days."

"That is true, but do ya think he may have been thinkin' it'd be a blessing to have the property off your hands?"

"No. Mr. Tangent will do whatever it takes to get our land."

"Do ya have any other reason to be suspicious of this man, Hannah?"

"Well, he threatened us when I told him we'd not take his offer and that we intended to stay on our land."

"What exactly did he say to ya?" Kell asked.

"He said that he'd buy the land for unpaid taxes because we'd never get a crop to harvest, and he had ways to get what he wanted."

"Not much to go on with that, lass."

"Kell, I am sure I recognized Tangent's voice the night of the last raid. You know he has that odd way of pronouncing the letter 's'. Sonny also thought it was Tangent."

"All of this is wrapped up with your feelings about Sonny and Molly," he said.

"Molly probably isn't a bad girl, but don't ya see, if she convinces Sonny to marry her, Tangent will get all of Sanctuary Hill as soon as Sonny turns twenty-one. I'll no longer be his guardian."

"Sonny has no intention of getting married. He's not like most other seventeen-year-old boys with the girls on his mind constantly. He hasn't spoken about her to you, has he?"

"Well, no, but she could connive her way to get him to think they should be married."

"Hannah, I don't…"

175

"Kell, I have no idea what Sonny does and doesn't know about...about..." Hannah stammered, trying to talk about a subject Southern ladies just don't talk about. "I don't know if Sonny knows how babies come about. With his father being gone before he ...." Again, she faltered. *I am making a blithering idiot of myself.* "I don't know if Sonny has reached manhood yet...I mean physically." Hannah stood and walked to the end of the porch unable to face Kell.

Kell walked down to meet her, turned her around, and pulled her into a comforting hug. "Bless ya for the angel ya are, lass. What courage it took for you to speak to me about this. Don't fret though, I'll step into Colonel Benjamin Murphy's place for a spell. Sonny's a good lad, and he'll do the right thing. I'll make sure he understands. We should go back now so I can check on Molly and Sonny because I promised I would."

$$\phi$$

When Kell found the two young people a half mile from the churchyard, they were in the creek. Molly had hitched her dress well above her knees and Sonny had rolled up his trouser legs. Kell sat on a stump where he could watch them for a few minutes. Not long after he sat down, he realized Hannah's suspicions were correct.

"Sonny, please let's take off these heavy clothes and swim in the creek for a while. We'll keep our underthings on. My papa said it's okay when it's hot like it is today."

"No, Molly, my mama wouldn't like it. She won't let girls come in my room when I got no clothes on...not Hannah, nor Mom Bec, not even her. She'd be madder than a hornet if I did that with you."

"Are you always gonna be a baby doin' what your mama says? I know some fun games that boys and girls can play together. They're lots of fun."

"Molly, we're having fun wadin' in the creek. Besides it's near time to go back."

"Well then, Sonny, I want you to be my beau. You are so nice and handsome. I'd have the best beau in the county. Would you at least do that for me?" Molly's protruding lip almost made Kell laugh aloud. He'd never seen such a fake pout.

"I guess I can do that, if it will make you happy, Molly, but now I want to go back to the church."

"Okay, I'll go back as soon as you kiss me. Beaus always kiss their sweethearts."

"If that's so, I'll have to think if I want to be your beau. I don't know much about kissin'. Right now, I want ya to put your shoes on."

Kell chuckled quietly. Sonny handled the situation very well. He needed no interference from him. Nevertheless, he knew that 'talk' with Sonny needed to happen sooner than later. He couldn't believe Tangent had intended his daughter to become the seductress to the man-child of Naomi Murphy. On the other hand, he wondered why Molly had been so forward. None of the Southern girls he'd met since he came to Arkansas had acted this wantonly.

Kell returned to the church so as not to be seen by Molly and Sonny. He was proud of the gentlemanly way the boy had ended the afternoon tryst with the young girl. He had taken command of an awkward situation and reacted as any other prudent young man would have. He silently offered a prayer of thanksgiving for the maturity he'd not known Sonny possessed.

A short time later, the afternoon Bible class began. Twelve people were present and sitting around a plank table in the arbor. Hannah sat across from Kell. Together the group read and discussed the scripture found in the book of Matthew. Kell had seen Hannah reading that passage last week. He watched her as best he could, without making her aware of his attention. He was curious about her reaction to each question and answer.

"Brother Sam, this whole region is a small area, isn't it?" Hannah asked after the preacher had shown them the location of Bethlehem, Nazareth, and Jerusalem on a map in a second Bible.

"Compared to our country, Hannah, indeed it is quite small. But how much impact this small part of the world and the life of this one man has made on the world."

Kell smiled as she answered a question about the East where the Magi had come from. She had studied that already and had found an old atlas on the top shelf of Hugh Kincaid's library. Then she asked about the prophets that had told of the Christ child's birth. When Brother Sam told the class about an Old Testament passage that spoke of Jesus's birth, she immediately turned to find it in her Bible.

Hannah smiled. "Thank you, Brother Sam. When you explain these things, I understand. I am so happy to know what the story means. I will try to be here every Sunday. I've got so much to learn."

"We all have to keep studying, Hannah. It is nice to have people to study with, though. That is the way we get to know the Lord, by reading His word and sharing His word with brothers and sisters. That is what He wants from us—all His children to know Him."

∮

Marcus had been right. By the first of August, the snowy rows of white cotton filled the sixty acres they'd planted. Every plant held boll after boll of their precious cash crop. If only that were the end of the process. Now lay the task of picking this fine lint and getting it ready for market. Of course, these were two more things that Hannah knew nothing about.

But on Monday, August 3, 1866, as the sun rose above the tree line, Hannah Murphy strapped a cotton sack across her shoulder and pulled her first handful of cotton. With her was the entire population of Sanctuary Hill, excluding Naomi, Mom Bec, and Glory, the toddler belonging to Marcus and Shataka. Even the boy Abraham, who was not quite seven years old, was in the field. The crew of ten started in the field belonging to Lucas Kincaid, the patch most ready to harvest.

Bending down to reach each boll, reaching inward to pull the lint from the boll, and dragging the increasingly heavy sack were acts of sheer drudgery. Hannah had never experienced labor like this in her life. Before the sun had reached the zenith, her hands bled from the cuts and gouges caused by her clumsy movements. Even with her best efforts, she lagged far behind the others, except little Abraham. She could keep up with the six-year-old. Even Shataka who was more than six months pregnant kept pace with the men.

When they took a water break, Hannah fell across her sack. Fatigue deadened every muscle in her body. *How can any human being live like this—days on end, working for the benefit of another man?* While she'd never really known much about a slave's life, the stories her father had told her must have been lies. No one could labor as she had without benefit and be content. She burst into tears.

Aaron Pierce came to her side, bringing a dipper of water from the pail. "Miss Hannah, are ya hurt?"

"No, Aaron. I'm sorry to make such a fuss. The heat and strain of the work just got the better of me. I'll be all right in a few minutes." Hannah drank the water in one long draught. "I thought I was made of sterner stuff. Thank you for the water."

The period until the noon meal seemed about three days long to Hannah, but she refused to quit. She found if she emptied her sack when it became too heavy to drag, she made better progress. Each trip to the wagon to empty her sack gave her a chance to stand up, straighten her back, and get a cup of water. She'd never appreciated how wonderful cool water tasted before.

At sunset, the crew called the first day over. The little crew had made some real progress on Lucas's field. As they trudged back toward the houses, Lucas announced, "We done picked more than five acres of my cotton today." He practically danced his way down the path. "First time in my life, all my hard work has given me something I can call my own. 'Course I know I didn't do it alone, but it feels mighty grand!"

"Brother, we got our long lives ahead to work for ourselves, 'cause Miss Hannah and Sonny give us this chance. We will always have to remember those that worked beside us. They's good people— not because they let us have our farm, but they care for us. Never knew a white man would be a friend." Marcus clapped Sonny on the back. "Ever night, I first thank my Lord for our farm, then I ask a blessing on those who shared what they had."

"I know we have been helped along the way, but I can't help but feel a swellin' of pride for this day. We done reaped the first of our labors," Lucas said.

The second time that day, Hannah felt tears on her face. She wiped them away quickly, not wanting attention again.

"Miss Hannah, whatcha want us to do with our day's pick? We ain't got no barn nor sheds at Sanctuary Hill to store it 'til we can take it to the gin." Lucas's question once again made her aware of how little she knew about being a cotton planter.

"I don't know…I guess what we have today can sit under the lean-to but that won't do for long." The others continued to stare at her for a solution to the problem. She had none. A blank stare was her only answer.

Sonny stepped up and said, "Hannah, I'll take this wagon to the lean-to. You go on and rest a spell."

"I'll go check on supper to see if Naomi and Mom Bec have enough food for this hungry group of field hands." Hannah had been surprised once again at Sonny's taking the reins of the task. Perhaps there was hope he would grow beyond the age that Scarlet Fever had dealt him almost a decade ago.

Naomi surprised Hannah, too. Before she entered the kitchen, the table had already been set up for the entire crew. A filling supper of fish, fresh vegetables, and warm cornpone was devoured within a breath after Sonny said the grace. Kell had joined them that evening. As a celebration, Mom Bec baked a peach cobbler from fresh fruit. As they finished, Naomi hurried her daughter-in-law out to the front porch to sit in the cool night breeze. "Hannah, you've done your share of work around here today. All of you have. Go enjoy the quiet of the evenin' for a while. I sent Mom Bec home, but I can clean up in here."

Sonny made a beeline to the shed to take care of Pal. Kell picked up his Bible and joined Hannah on the porch swing. "Today was a hard one for ya, lass. Oh, I don't mean just the pickin' cotton. This afternoon, something weighed heavy on your spirit."

"Do you always have to be in my business?" The question didn't bite as many of Hannah's comments to him did.

"Yes, I do, Hannah Ruth. I care about ya, and I know the life you're livin' isn't what you expected. I know you are alone too much."

"I don't understand you. How is a lady supposed to talk with a man about what she feels, thinks, or worries about?"

"Everyone needs a friend to share the low times. I hope ya had someone ya could talk to. Did ya not have a sweetheart?"

"No, not that it's any of your business. I don't know if I've ever had a confidant. I thought that was what a husband was supposed to be, but…."

"Well, none of that matters now. You are here, and I want to be your friend. You showed me a while back that you dare to share important matters. Now, I have started talking to Sonny about girls and their 'girlish ways.' He does like Molly, though, because she treats him like a young man and not a little boy."

"Thank you for that. I didn't know how I was going to talk with him about…."

"Will ya tell me why you were crying in the cotton field this mornin'?" Kell reached out to take her hand.

As quickly, she jerked it away. "Who told you I was crying?"

"Aaron mentioned it to me when I tied Gray down by the shed. He was concerned. I know you had to be tired, perhaps more than at any time in your life. I told him you were fine and that you wouldn't walk away from the work."

"Kell, for the first time I realized the kind of life our Kincaid families have led. All the effort, hurt, and sheer burden of the task that never ended—all for the benefit of Mr. Hugh and his family. I know that he was not a cruel master, but all their work was to enrich him. Nothing they did lifted them one degree above the level they were the year before. To see Lucas dancing in his tiredness because he finally worked for his own benefit—what shame that brings to us who never thought they had that dream or right."

"Walking in another's shoes can help us see things that are right in front of us, but we never saw before."

"I want to talk to Shataka and ask her how she feels about having a home. She told me some time ago that she felt blessed. She had food to eat, a roof over her head, and slept in the arms of the man who loved her."

"I suppose on the most basic level, that's what life is about, Hannah. What is it you want from life?"

Silence followed. Noises that had been pushed away from her awareness flooded in. Cicadas chirped from the hedge row, a dove cooed from far away, and a couple of mosquitoes whirred around. Even the creaking of the chain of the swing annoyed Hannah.

"Kell, how did you come to such wisdom about life? You seem to know how others feel about their sorrows and hardships."

"Where did that come from? I asked ya a question."

"I don't know. I suppose I'm curious how a person gains that depth of insight."

"I have lived such things."

"Kell, please tell me how you learned this. Is it in the Bible, and I am just too stupid to see?"

"Hannah, that's enough of that. You're far from stupid. For six months, you've kept Naomi and Sonny from starvation and ruin. That takes courage and intelligence. My story is a long, ugly tale, I'm afraid. I'm not sure it would help to tell ya."

"Please, Kell. I want to know."

"Will ya walk with me for a while?"

"Yes, of course." They stepped off the porch into the moonlit night.

"Hannah, when I was seventeen, my parents asked me to decide my future role in the family. My brother Sean was twenty-one and had already been named heir to our family lands. He would be the next Laird of Kincaid in County Sterling. My two sisters, just older than me, had made good marriages to other clans in the highlands. I had two choices. My mother wanted me to join the priesthood, and my father wanted me to join the military. Both professions were completely acceptable for a second son.

"Lass, I loved the land. Being out in God's creation in the highlands of Scotland is a spiritual experience. I couldn't join the priesthood. Several of my friends had already joined the church, but I never quite understood why we needed a pope. We can go directly to God without an intercessor. Anyway, I'd already fallen in love with a beautiful copper-headed girl, who was part of a neighboring clan. Claire sang like a nightingale. Her eyes were the green of the new clover, clear and bright. How I adored her.

"I asked her to be my wife. We'd spent many days together, playing at love. When she let me kiss her, I knew she was intended to be my mate. She agreed. I thought the fire in my heart would totally consume me.

"We agreed to tell our parents of our plans at the Christmas feast only a few weeks away. For that time, we talked, planned, and dreamed of what life would be together. Then came the Christmas feast. All the clans of the region were meeting at my parents' home that year. After the grand feast, my father rose, walked over to Claire's father, and they walked to the center of the hall. They called out the names of their children, Sean Kincaid and Claire Ferguson, to join them. Her father announced the betrothal of his daughter to the oldest son of the Laird of Kincaid.

"Sean knew that the marriage had been arranged for months. Claire was shocked, but being a woman, she had no say. On New Year's Eve, my brother married the girl of my heart."

"That is such a horrible thing to happen to you. I would think you would be angry with your brother and with God. He didn't take care of you at all."

"Well, there is more to the story. I spent a year livin' the wildest life you can imagine. I told my father I had no intention of joinin' the military or becomin' a priest. My father didn't mind I rejected the church because he was never much of one for religion—Catholic or Protestant. But he got very angry with me when I became the gossip of the whole county. He told me I drank too much, hung around with too many renegades, and he'd not hear of havin' grandchildren born on the wrong side of the blanket. He threatened to disinherit me if I didn't become a respectable young man. I dinna care. I told him his money meant nothin' to me. But my mother's tears nearly killed me, Hannah."

"Oh, Kell, how hurt you must have been. I am sorry that happened to you."

"Well, I finally told my parents about my love for Claire and our plans to marry. My father took me in his arms and begged me to forgive him. He said if he'd known, he would have arranged another marriage for Sean. I saw the hurt in his eyes. That day, I could not make myself say 'I forgive you'."

When I confronted Sean, he said nothing. He just smiled and said, "At least, Lady Claire is in the best family."

"I told him I hated him and would never forgive his cruelty to Claire and me. I turned my back to him and left the house."

"Well, you felt betrayed. I understand what you did."

"Anger makes hard words easy. I spoke many hard words that day. You've experienced that yourself. But Hannah, now I know better."

"Because your faith won't let you rest?"

"That's right. Anyway, I left home for six months. I roamed the length and width of Scotland. Even in the winter, the country is so beautiful. Yet, I felt like the most worthless, unwanted human on earth.

I canna count the sins I committed. One night, I picked up my Bible and truly began to study the scripture. The next Sunday mornin', I walked into a small Presbyterian church, and the preacher proclaimed in a loud strong voice that the hardest forgiveness we ever must make is to forgive ourselves. He read a scripture that I'd heard many times but had never thought of in that way. He said The Great Commandment requires that we extend love to three entities: God, our neighbor, and ourselves. That struck home with me. I'd always had issues with ME—never feelin' quite good enough, less of value than Sean, purposeless with no plans for a future. Even when I'd asked Claire to marry me, I hadn't thought what kind of life I could give her.

"That sermon struck me to the depths of my bein', Hannah. I fell on my knees and turned my will over to God that verra day. He's been with me every minute since." Kell came to the end of his story.

Hannah sat in silence for a few seconds. "Kell, I had no idea you had lived through such loss."

"Not all loss, Hannah. I went back home and asked my father to forgive my hurtful words. We became closer than we'd ever been. He even said his greatest regret was that he'd denied me the love of my life. He'd loved my mother all those years, and he wanted nothing less for his sons. Someday, I will ask my brother to forgive me, too."

"That's a perfect ending to your story. I'm glad you shared it."

"I am, too. Only true friends can share at this depth and not be embarrassed or ashamed. I hope someday you will share your story with me. Are ya ready to go back now, lass?"

"Yes. Kell." They walked back to the porch. "By the way, what did the sheriff say when you saw him in Madison?"

"When I got to town, I couldn't find him, but I did talk to a deputy. He said there had been no reports of nightriders in the county, but he'd pass the word on to the sheriff when he returned. Frankly, he didn't seem overly concerned. I haven't heard from him yet."

"I guess I'm not surprised. We don't have many people to enforce the law in this county, and we don't know which side of the issue they support. I should go in. I'll need all my rest if I'm gonna be of any help tomorrow. Good night, Kell."

He reached for her hand. "Don't run away from me, Hannah. I answered your question. Now I'd like you to answer mine. What is it you want from life, lass?"

As she sat back down, she said, "No one ever asked me that before. In my life, I've been raised to fill my role as a Southern lady, caring for my household, upholding social rituals and customs, and obeying my husband who in turn would make me happy and give me a secure life. None of that has happened. Now I only know obligation."

"But Hannah, life is so much more. Ya already learned some of the things that enrich life. You take special care of others. You do it so well. Look at the happiness you have given the Kincaids. That is God's love being shared through you."

"I don't think he knows me well enough to put me in charge of that. I certainly don't know enough to claim I do it for Him."

"You'll know in time, Hannah. I hope you sleep well. I've enjoyed our talk tonight, friend."

"Good night, Kell."

Chapter 15

Fret not thyself because of evil men, neither be thou envious at
the wicked; For there shall be no reward to the evil; the candle of the
wicked shall be put out.
Proverbs 24:19-20

By the third week of September, the weary crew at Sanctuary Hill had completed the first round of harvest. Hannah hadn't known until last week the back-breaking work was far from over. The fields would be picked twice more, once to pick the late growth and the other to remove the bolls that failed to open. She was also ignorant of the fact that farmers were responsible for the ginning and bailing of the cotton before the cotton broker would take it. She didn't know that the seeds were a valuable commodity nor how a farmer went about compressing nearly five hundred pounds of white lint into a bale.

In his role as foreman at Sanctuary Hill, Marcus's knowledge of cotton and experience with the land proved a Godsend to the Murphys. He had been right on the money when he predicted a bountiful crop. He told her and Sonny that by the third picking, their crop would top out over seventeen bales.

"But Miss Hannah, we got one big mountain I don't know how we gonna climb."

"What do you mean, Marcus?" Hannah asked.

"We gotta gin the cotton and stomp out those bales. The cotton factor gonna want the crop ready to ship to the mill. We ain't got no gin."

"Did we ever have one?" Sonny asked.

"Sure. We did. All the big plantations had gins. The Yankees burned ours when they tried to burn down the house."

"Well, I'll just have to look into it. Maybe a neighbor will still have a gin to share with us." Hannah started to walk away and then stopped. "Marcus, do you know how much money we can make if we have seventeen bales of cotton to sell?"

"Just depends...the cotton factors, they grade the crop sample over in Memphis."

"Are you telling me, we gotta haul all this cotton over to Memphis? We can't do that. We don't have enough wagons or draft animals to pull that load back to the river."

"Miss Hannah, it ain't like that. Ya just take 'em a box of loose cotton that we picked. They look it over, decide how good it is, and offer a price for each pound you can bring 'em." Marcus sat down on the porch, while Hannah paced back and forth.

"Isn't there any place closer to sell the cotton, maybe even take it as it is?" Hannah slumped into the swing. "We're all nearly exhausted now, and you say we have to pick the rows twice more and then gin this cotton."

"Hannah, don't get upset. We're doin' good now. We can handle this." Sonny plopped on the porch next to Marcus. "We can, can't we, Marcus?"

"Yes, Mr. Sonny. We will make our crop—and it'll be the best in the county. Too bad we don't have a county fair no more. We'd get that blue ribbon for sure! Best crop I ever seen at Sanctuary Hill. We should get top dollar for the crop."

Hannah stood and shook her head. She turned to push open the door and walked to the stairs. One step at a time, she pulled one foot after another, unsure if there remained the energy to climb the last steps to her bedroom. The image she held was of a warm bath, water dripping from a cloth across her face and bare body as the dirt and mire of the day's labor disappeared and then lay her head on a goose-down pillow on her four-poster, erasing the world she lived in for as many hours as she was allowed to sleep. *I don't know the name of a cotton broker. I don't know what to do with a cotton broker. I don't want to know…. I want to run away from it all.*

As she sank into her tepid bathwater, she spoke aloud, "Lord, if you are listening to me, I have too many things to carry alone. Kell said you will help me. I have worked to my limit this entire week, and none of my obligations have gone away. I want some rest."

She heard no words from heaven. She dressed for bed and lay on her pillow. "Even if you have no answers for me, I deserve a rest. Tomorrow is Sunday—I'd say I deserved a day off." With those words, she drifted into a deep sleep.

$$\oint$$

In the wee hours of the morning, the peace of Sanctuary Hill was shattered by a Rebel call, closely followed by Shataka's piercing screams from the quarters. "Stop! Leave my man be. He ain't never harmed nobody."

Hannah scrambled from her bed, falling because her entangled feet caught the hem of her nightdress. She pulled herself up by the bedpost, pulled on her duster, and ran down the staircase. Sonny had already reached the door, his club in his hand. Barefooted, they ran toward the towering flame in front of the cabins. "I'm coming, Shataka!"

She reached the yard near the porch in time to see Marcus pull his wife out of the path of the hooded night riders. Three hooded men drove a six-foot-tall cross made of railroad ties into the blazing pile of dead brush and broken tree limbs. The cross, which had been covered with tar and kerosene, exploded into flames—monstrous red, orange, yellow, and gray tongues twenty feet tall, reached into the night.

Two of the hooded night riders captured Marcus by his legs, pulled him down, and dragged him toward the flames. Shataka ran toward the man and grappled with him. He threw her to the ground, but not before she jerked off his hood and clawed his face with three long, jagged bloody gashes. She got to her knees and pleaded with the men. "Stop, please. Leave my man be. We ain't done y'all no wrong." Her pleas were nearly inaudible with the roar of the fire and the wailing of Abraham and Glory from the porch, who were witnessing their father's torture.

Hannah pushed her way in front of one of the men who was dragging Marcus. "What are you doing on this property again?" Hannah had to scream to be heard over the chaos.

"Get back to that derelict of a house on the hill. This ain't none of your business." A tall, hooded man approached Hannah but turned to face Sonny. "And git that half-witted boy and yourself back to where you come from."

"This is Kincaid land. You can't trespass here." Hannah stepped between Sonny and the nightrider.

A shorter, more rotund man stepped up. "You ain't no Kincaid, and even if ya was, ain't no woman owns no land in this state."

Hannah gasped. That voice, the same one again. Muffled somewhat by the hood, Tangent's voice wasn't hidden by the hideous cone-shaped mask. She'd heard him speak enough now that she was sure.

"Sonny owns this land."

"Look, lady, I already told ya to leave. Our business here tonight ain't got nothin' to do with you. We're just gonna help the Kincaids here remember they gotta keep the Black Code of this state. No black man is gonna own a farm in this county."

Another of the ghostly-dressed men joined the two holding Marcus. He began to tie his feet and wrists with pieces of barbed wire. Marcus cried out in pain. Shataka again tried to free her husband, but a man on a horse grabbed her hair and pulled her away from the center of the yard, dumping her in the middle of her garden. Sonny then raised his club to stop the attack on Marcus only to have another of the mounted riders bash him in the back of the head with a rifle stock.

"Sonny!" Hannah cried out.

The man who had hit Sonny pulled his horse between Sonny and her. "Look, woman, we didn't want to hurt ya, but y'all don't listen too good." The band of men laughed at the sarcastic .

"I'm telling you to let Marcus go. You know the Black code was abolished at the end of the war. Leave this place before I…"

"Before you what? Get out of our business. A little tar and feathers never kilt no one. Maybe you'd like a little taste of what I'm about to give ole Marcus here. If you feel the scorching of your lily-white skin right along with this Black man, maybe you'll be a bit more prone to move 'em out of the county like we told ya to do."

Hannah jerked away from the man who held her. She streaked across the yard toward the man she knew was Narvel Tangent. She grabbed at his cone-shaped mask, but he grabbed her wrist. "You better let me go. I will not let you harm him. I need all my help. Get your pack of vermin and get off Sanctuary Hill, Mr. Tangent."

Tangent sputtered back. "Don't know no Tangent, and I don't take orders from no woman neither." He backhanded Hannah, knocking her to the ground. He strutted across to the place where she had fallen, grabbed her hair, and attempted to pull her to her knees. "Come on, men. Let's start with the little lady. When we're done she won't be so high and mighty. Maybe a swipe across her pretty little face with this tar brand would be a good place to begin. Kincaid can enjoy the show until we have time to give him what he deserves."

"Hold up there, Captain. We ain't about harmin' no white woman. You said we'd teach some high and mighty Blacks their place. Pretty near sure they got the message. We ain't gonna do nothin' to this woman. You'd call the law down on us for sure." A tall, hooded figure pulled the brand from his leader's hand.

"Yeah, Captain. Ya know there's talk of the governor sendin' the militia into some counties already," another said. "We don't want 'em here. Didn't she already tell us that she was his cousin?"

Several of the riders who had not dismounted began to ride off in the direction of the main road. When Tangent and the two others who planned to cover Marcus with burning tar saw they were outnumbered by the black population and two white witnesses, they mounted and galloped after the rest of the band.

But Tangent screamed back. "Don't think you got the better of me. There are lots of ways to prove who holds sway in this county."

Shataka quickly removed the tangled barbwire from Marcus's wrists. He took her in his arms as she cried. The masked riders hadn't taken the fear with them.

"Marcus, what we gonna do? They could come back and hurt you or our babies."

"Shataka, that be enough now. We got scared kids in that house. I'll speak to Miss Hannah and Sonny. Then I'll be in to help ya put 'em to bed."

Hannah crouched over Sonny, trying to revive him. Lucas Kincaid came running up from his cabin and got water from a barrel at the end of the porch. "I needed to be here before now, Marcus. My boys was so scared, screamin' for me not to leave 'em alone down there. I'm sorry."

Hannah washed Sonny's face by dipping the bottom of her wrapper in the cool water. She tried to wash the blood from his mouth. Shortly, he came to.

"Ouch. My head hurts, Hannah. What happened to those night riders? Are ya hurt?" Sonny seemed aware of his circumstances.

"Don't try to get up too fast. You've got a bad bump on your head. Can you see all right?" she asked him.

"I'm all right. That rider on that black horse hit me, didn't he?" Sonny sat up.

"Did you notice anything else about him?"

"Not about those men. They all looked like devils in those robes and pointed caps. I did see just about all their horses, though."

"Did you notice the man who knocked me down?" Hannah wanted to confirm Narvel Tangent as the leader of the group.

"That was Mr. Tangent. He wasn't on his regular horse, that one with the white stockings, but everyone around here knows that funny way he says words with 's' in 'em."

"Where was the night watch? Who is riding tonight?" Hannah asked.

"Aaron is on the South side out by the farthest cotton patches. Mr. Kell hired three more men from the county to join the watch. I am not sure who was supposed to ride up here at the house and the quarters. I know Mr. Kell was trying to keep us from gettin' too worn out now that cotton pickin' is on us."

"I didn't know anything about the extra men. I'll speak to Kell about that. I am going to Madison tomorrow and report this to the sheriff," Hannah said.

"Miss Hannah, ya better be careful who ya tell about what happened tonight. Sometimes these night riders have members that ya wouldn't think. First, maybe we need to find out something about this new sheriff."

"Perhaps you're right. We may be better off if we handle things ourselves. Let's go home, Sonny. I'm sure your mother is scared."

𝛷

When Kell approached Sanctuary Hill the next morning, he smelled smoke. As he turned the bend in the road, he saw the glowing pile of embers with a partially burned cross fallen across the heap. "Marcus, Shataka," he called. No answer came. Fear pushed him to slap the reins hard onto Graystoke's backside, pushing the great stallion into a full-out gallop toward the house.

Gathered on the porch, all the Kincaids, Sonny, Aaron Pierce, Naomi, and Hannah stood together. Streaks of orange, red, and gray peaked above the horizon as the sun was about to breach the tree line. Those gathered spoke almost in whispers. Kell felt their fear. He saw strain, especially in the faces of the tenant farmers gathered behind his family. He jumped from his horse before Graystoke had come to a stop and approached Hannah.

"Hannah, what has happened to you, lass?" He tenderly moved his thumb down the left side of her face, which was now covered with a palm-sized black and purple bruise.

"Kell, one of those masked men hit me in the back of my head." Sonny bent to show Kell the open cut on his skull.

"Sonny, that's a bad gash. Ya need stitches. We gotta get you to the doctor. Marcus, did this happen down at your cabin?"

"Yes, sir. A big band of them hooded devils. They'd a killed me if Miss Hannah hadn't stopped 'em."

"Why was there no warnin'?" Kell asked.

"Mr. Kell, Aaron was out on the South side as you planned, but I never saw that other fella after the sun set."

"Was Roscoe here?"

"Yes, sir, early on, but I don't know where he went. Never showed up while the nightriders were here."

"Hannah, are you more hurt than I can see?"

"No. Tangent backhanded me when I walked between him and Marcus, but I'm only bruised. Kell, I didn't know you'd hired men to ride night watch."

"It's not important now. I'll take care of it." Kell walked over to Naomi. "Cousin, are you hurt?"

"No. I was in the house when they came back about an hour ago. I'm not hurt, but I am so frightened." Naomi began to cry.

"Cousin Naomi, don't fret. I am sorry this happened again. Just rest here for a few minutes." He led her to the swing.

"Now, Hannah, tell me the rest of the story. Why did you go back into the fray when I've asked ya not to." Kell knew his voice was too harsh and commanding, but his fear and anger at not being there to protect his family had taken the reins. "Land a Goshen, Hannah. I'm so angry with ya right now, I am afraid to speak…knowing I'd say something ya may not forgive later. You're lucky you didn't get killed last night or at the very least molested. Those men believe they are ordained by God to bring the South back to the way it was before the war."

"What else could I do? I wouldn't stand back and let them tar and feather Marcus—not in front of his children."

Hannah rose to her entire five foot, six inches to confront Kell. When she was in arms reach, he picked her up and carried her like a small child over to the swing where Naomi sat. "Excuse me, Cousin, I must have a word with this lass. I need to make her understand." Hannah squirmed and tried to get up. Kell only clamped his arms tighter. "You could have sent for me."

Naomi sat at the far side of the swing, nodding her head and dabbing her red-rimmed eyes with her knotted handkerchief.

"You've got to let others help you when you are in trouble. There is no weakness in allowing people to help you when things are too big to handle alone. Haven't ya learned that yet? Look at your crop. Did ya do that alone?"

"Kell, don't be so harsh with Hannah. She's had a difficult night."

"Naomi, I will handle this. Do you have a room for me? I'm comin' to stay as long as y'all are in danger."

"Well, all our rooms have a roof now, but the two on the end are not fit to live in yet." Naomi rose and walked to the door. "Perhaps I can make it livable."

"Wait a minute, Mother Murphy. Don't you think we need to talk about this before we move him into our house?" Hannah asked.

"Sorry, lass, you lost the time for talkin' when you refused to stay out of danger's way. The only way I can keep ya away from harm is to be here. I'm movin' in, even if I need to bunk in with Sonny and Aaron. We do have a lot to talk about, but none of it is about my movin' to Sanctuary Hill. That is not an option."

Kell walked over to the Kincaids who were still standing on the porch. "Marcus, I've heard that the violence only gets worse." His voice trailed off to almost inaudible. The tenant farm family nodded in approval several times. After several minutes, he walked over to

Aaron and spoke to him in that same hushed voice. He handed the younger man several dollar bills. Aaron, too, nodded.

"Come on, Sonny," he said. "Let's saddle Pal. Mr. Kincaid is gonna let me ride his horse. We'll go to Madison to see the doctor."

"No, Kell, I should go with Sonny. He'll need his mother."

"No, Cousin Naomi. They need to make a fast trip. I want them back before nightfall. Aaron will take good care of Sonny."

Hannah stood, watching Kell take charge as if he were the master of Sanctuary Hill. He sent the Kincaids home to rest for a while and then to take care of the chores. He asked Naomi to return to her bed to rest before she got up to dress for the day. She nodded and returned to her room.

"Well now, Hannah Murphy, you can say your piece. I know it's tearin' at ya something fierce." Kell leaned against the column.

"What good would it do? You've already made up your mind about what's to happen."

"Lass, I have one role here. That is to keep my family safe. You go right on and run this farm and operate the store. I'll not interfere— except when I must to prevent another event like that cross-burning last night. I thank the Lord ya weren't hurt any worse than ya were. Now go on up and rest for a spell. I'll be here until Aaron and Sonny return."

"Will you tell me about those men you hired? I don't like having people around that I don't know."

"I told ya that I'll take care of that. I will make a good team of men to be the night watch here. Go on up to bed. I'm on watch for now."

φ

Kell Kincaid became a routine part of life at Sanctuary Hill. He set himself up a bed in the room next to Sonny and Aaron's, even though it was far from habitable in Hannah's opinion. The roof had fallen into that space, and for more than two years, the walls and floor had been exposed to the elements. Aaron had replaced the rafters and the planking on the roof, but there were still no cedar shakes there to repel the rain. Kell didn't seem to notice, and he certainly didn't complain about it. Hannah noticed that he hardly spent any time in the room anyway.

He had moved his horses and cattle to pastures nearby so he could tend to them. He also housed four men in his cabin to supplement the night watch. Hannah couldn't believe he'd left his property. When she asked him about the risk, he said, "I am a Kincaid. The emblem on our family crest is an oath to us all. Family is our priority."

"But where does the obligation to family stop?" Hannah still didn't understand this kinsman Scot who had invaded her home.

"Hannah, an oath is a sacred promise before God. There is no limit to what I would do to keep that promise. The Lord has done far too much for me to neglect the slight things he asks from me."

Having arranged his place at Sanctuary Hill, Kell called Aaron, Marcus, and Sonny to the barn one afternoon. "I want y'all to go with me into Linden tomorrow afternoon. I need some witnesses."

"What ya gonna do, Kell?" Sonny asked.

"I'm gonna assure that our night watch will remain loyal to the job they promised. We've too much land and too many lives at stake here to do all the work by ourselves. We need some loyal hands to work with us, but they need to know we allow no slackin' when it comes to the job they're paid to do."

"How ya gonna do that, Mr. Kell?" Marcus asked.

"I'm plannin' a visit with Roscoe Smith."

The next day at two o'clock, Kell rode into Linden with Aaron, Marcus, and Sonny. The small band cantered down the main street, looking for Smith. He was not among the loiters at the mercantile, nor was he loafing at the livery stable. Kell turned Graystoke toward the saloon and spied the man sitting on a bench among a few other loiterers. Kell dismounted and tied his horse to the post in front of the group.

"I'll have a word with ya, Roscoe Smith."

"Well, come sit a spell. You're among friends," Smith said.

"I would have thought that until the night before last when ya shirked your duty and put my family in harm's way." Kell removed his hat and wiped his forehead with the back of his sleeve.

"What are you talkin' about, Kincaid."

"Why did ya fail to protect my kin when the night riders came to Sanctuary Hill the night before last?"

"I was on the job the whole time. I didn't see no problem. Ain't been no talk around town of nightriders." Smith stood and spat a stream of tobacco juice into the street.

"I hired you to ride watch around the house and the quarters and to warn me if you saw any hint of danger. The quarters were attacked. Both Mrs. Murphy and Sonny were hurt by the night riders. You were either not there, or you ran when you saw the danger. That makes you a liar or a coward or both."

"Wait a minute, Kincaid. I watched over that house, like I promised. That old woman never left the place. I'd of seen her."

"Did you ride the rounds I assigned to you?" Kell asked.

"I watched after the house, like I said."

Kell's scowl grew with each answer. "Why did you not go down to the quarters when you heard the commotion? Sonny and Hannah Murphy went down there. You didn't hear anything?"

"I did my job."

"You are a liar, sir. Ya put my family in danger," Kell shouted.

"Look, you foreigner. You don't pay me near enough for me to risk my life fightin' those vigilantes. Those Murphys know they ain't supposed to do business with the slaves. They've been warned."

"So, ya ran like the coward I said ya to be. You knew they were gonna attack the tenant farmers, and ya didn't warn me. You are the lowest of animals. You take my wage and put my kin in danger."

Roscoe Smith threw a punch and hit Kell squarely in the face. Kell caught himself on the hitching post and returned the blow. Smith fell to the ground. Then the man picked up a palm-sized rock and threw it. The rock struck Kell in the chest, knocking the breath from him momentarily. Kell then jumped from the porch in front of the saloon and straddled the disloyal employee. He began to pummel his face and upper torso.

"Get off me and let me be, you lousy traitor," Smith bellowed.

Kell's face was the color of blood, his temper so out of control. He put his hands around the neck of Roscoe Smith, choking him into spasms. "No man puts my family in harm's way. Not through cowardice or sloth. Ya stole from me wages ya dinna earn, you lied, and you let your cowardice prevent ya from doin' the job ya hired on to do. Ya don't deserve to live."

Kell continued choking the man until Aaron and Sonny grabbed his arms and pulled him away. "Stop it, Kell. If ya kill him, there'll be more trouble to deal with. He knows ya have seen his colors. Let him be," Aaron said.

Kell got up and realized what he'd done. "Lord, forgive me. I've once again let my temper trample on Your grace." He picked up her hat, mounted Graystoke and rode away.

Chapter 16

As the Father hath loved me, so have I loved you: continue ye in my love…This is my commandment, that ye love one another as I have loved you. Greater love hath no man than this, that a man lay down his life for his friends.
John 15:9, 12-13

With all that was within her, Hannah tried to maintain her routine as she had before the cross-burning. She would work in the fields, except on Wednesday and Saturday, when she opened the mercantile. She'd return home every evening, exhausted. And Kell was always around. He was at the table each morning and evening, and he drove her to the store on days when Sonny was working in the field. On the days when none of the males from Sanctuary Hill could accompany her to work in Linden, Kell stayed around the store, working with restocking, bringing items from the storage room, or shelving things that required the moving ladder. He never interfered with her interaction with customers or in any of the bartering conversations that went on nearly every day. Yet his presence was felt, but something had changed in Kell's demeanor.

One day, she was particularly stressed, and she asked him, "Kell, aren't you afraid something bad will happen back at home when you are here all day with me?"

"No."

"And why is that exactly?" Hannah was not satisfied with his curt reply.

"I've already worked it all out. I set up a twenty-four-hour, seven-day-a-week security watch, and we are constantly alert to signs that the band plans a return."

"Why didn't you tell me about this?"

"Why didn't you tell me you would continue to confront those night riders?"

"Kell, I told you I thought I had it all under control."

"Well, now things are under control."

Much to Hannah's surprise, other things about life at Sanctuary Hill changed for the better when Kell became a member of the family. Naomi took a new interest in becoming the lady of the house. She set the table each night for dinner as if guests were expected, using china and silverware instead of the pewter they'd used when they first arrived. Meals improved with the fresh vegetables coming from the garden and the newly picked berries. These were a blessing, indeed, for not only did they add to their meals at that time, but scores of jars were also being filled for their winter pantry. They looked forward to slaughter time in the fall when they could get a hog and beef for meat for the winter. Now, fish was the main source of meat for their table.

Kell asked that they share grace each time they met to eat. "It's a habit. The food always tastes just a bit better after I take a minute to thank the Lord. I am thankful to have food because some don't."

Naomi nodded. Kell and Sonny took turns asking a blessing over each meal.

Conversations at the day's end added an element that had been missing from the household mealtimes. The family of five now talked about the community happenings, concerns of their neighbors, and interesting incidents that Hannah had experienced at the mercantile. Kell initiated that routine from his first night at their table. Everyone enjoyed his stories about his life with the Kincaid clan in Scotland.

Hannah was especially intrigued, remembering her dreams as a girl when she wanted to travel to distant places. But Kell avoided personal discussions he'd always tried to start with Hannah. Perhaps this was better. Hannah's wall was not in danger of being breached if Kell stayed away from personal issues.

Naomi and Mom Bec took on the chore of cleaning the room that Kell had chosen. While they couldn't restore the damaged wallpaper and peeling paint on the door frames, they cleaned the room and furnished it with comfortable furniture. In the attic, Naomi found a framed family crest that she hung opposite Kell's bed. She replaced the tattered blanket with a quilt that she had made just before leaving Washington.

Whether or not she approved of the newest resident at Sanctuary Hill, Hannah was clearly outnumbered. She found no reason to oust him. He went out of his way to avoid interfering with any business decision or problem that arose on the farm. She could find no fault in his behavior. Her anxiety came from feeling her wall crumble a bit every day. No one could live so close to the charming Scot without falling victim to his wit and smile.

ꝗ

In those earliest days of Kell's residence at Sanctuary Hill, Hannah tried to maintain a cool indifference toward him. She hadn't invited his intrusion into their home. Yet, she couldn't deny that she felt safer knowing he was nearby. As much as she hated to admit it, she enjoyed dinner time so much more now that there was adult conversation around the table.

In their proximity, she learned many things she'd never suspected about Kell. The first night he was in residence, he reached to the top of the bookcase that held what was left of Hugh Kincaid's library and pulled down two volumes. "Praise the Lord, many of Uncle Hugh's excellent collection are still here. Look, Hannah, Thoreau's *Life in the Woods,* Lewis and Clark's *History of the Expedition,* two books by Hawthorne, and a history of Scottish Lords. He even has Whitman. I think I have died and gone to Heaven."

"I don't guess I knew you were so fond of reading."

"I've told ya before, lass, there are many things about me ya don't know." Hannah sat back down at the table and waited for Kell to make his selections before she blew out the lantern. She noticed that he picked the Whitman book and the Scottish history entitled *Origines Parochiales Scotiae.*

"I'll bid ya goodnight, Hannah. I am goin' up to read my Bible for a spell and then call it a night. I'm on patrol at midnight. Sleep well."

Kell's dedication to his faith became clearer to her also. Several times since the cross burning, Hannah had walked upon Kell, thinking he was asleep to find him deep in prayer. He wasn't on his knees, as Hannah thought a person was supposed to pray. Once, she found him sitting cross-legged on a bale of hay near the pasture where Pal and Graystoke were grazing. Another time Hannah had seen him sitting astride his horse with his head bowed. She knew he went to church but didn't realize he was so dedicated to Christian practices.

ʄ

One Saturday evening, Hannah sought some relief from the extreme heat of the house. As soon as she cleaned the kitchen, she went to the porch swing, her favorite refuge after a long hot day. She fanned herself with a small handkerchief and pushed the swing with her toe. The heat persisted, even though the sun had set behind the oak grove some time ago. She unbuttoned the top several buttons on her

lawn blouse and pushed up her sleeves. She pulled her long hair off her neck with her hand. Hopes for a gentle breeze seemed futile.

"You're lookin' mighty fetchin' this evenin', Mrs. Murphy. Do you mind if I join ya here on the porch for a spell?"

"You're welcome here, Kell. Would you like to share the swing, or do you prefer to sit on the porch?"

"I'll share the swing since ya offered. I came out to enjoy the stars before I go up to read a spell."

"The night is nice—hot but pleasant otherwise. The stars are bright, and the moon is full tonight."

"Yes, indeed. Beautiful night the Lord has provided. Don't ya think so, Hannah?"

"I think I just said it's nice tonight."

"I meant that the Lord has provided it for us."

"I don't know that I've ever given it any thought. You read your Bible all the time, I've noticed. Is that why you link nature to God?"

"Lass, I know that everything is connected to God. Yes, I do read my Bible, but since I was a young man of twenty-one years, I've known the Lord was God. He's my God, my Lord, livin' in me."

"But you told me once that you didn't want to join the church." Hannah turned to look at Kell.

"What I said I dinna want to become a priest, a part of the Catholic church. Those fellows take vows of poverty, self-denial, and celibacy. God bless 'em in their sacrifice, but that's not the life I want."

"Then I guess I don't understand. If religion is so important to you…"

"I care naught for religion, lass. The Lord wants every man to know Him as a brother—a friend. The church makes it easier to serve, that's all. My faith is my own. The Lord has been takin' care of me for many years. My walk with Him started in Scotland and will continue 'til the day I die. He gave me a new life, and I try each day to live it as a servant to Him."

"I truly don't understand all of this. Did you learn this from reading your Bible?" Hannah sat with pursed lips and slumped shoulders.

"Some of it. I also learned from watching other believers. My mother was a saintly woman. She tried from my boyhood to show me the love of the Lord and the benefit of the church. I had two friends in Scotland who helped lead me to the Lord. Then here, Brother Naylor is a dedicated disciple. I'm lucky to call him friend. We talk about the scripture often."

"Brother Naylor is kind. He's always been very welcoming to me. His wife is also friendly. I've enjoyed conversations with her."

"That's the way of God's children. We are charged to tell His story. His story is love. Anywhere you see love being shared, that's where God is." Kell smiled at Hannah and encircled her shoulders with his arm.

"Well, maybe that's why I've no understanding of God then. I'm not sure I know what love is. I've read stories that talk about it, but I think those are mostly fairy tales."

"Hannah, has life been so cruel to you? Sonny adores ya. I'm sure Naomi cares for you. Did ya not know love from your mother and your father?"

"I don't want to talk about personal things. Tell me more about reading the Bible. I like to read. I've always enjoyed studying things I don't know about. I tried to read some of the books, but it doesn't seem to mean anything to me."

Kell shook his head. Hannah stood up and started to walk away.

"It's all right. I don't need any judgment right now."

"Forgive me, lass. I want ya to know there is no judgment here. I'd be the last person to be passin' judgment. I've more failin's than I could ever tell ya about. If ya knew me, you'd never see me as a person fit to sit judgment."

"I apologize for jumping to conclusions. We do that to each other so often. Kell, is something bothering you? You have seemed…well, different these past few days. I don't know exactly what it is, but you seem to be present but withdrawn."

"I've had a thorn in my soul for a few days. I'm not verra proud of myself. Hannah, I came near to killin' Roscoe Smith last week when I went to see him in Linden. Did Sonny or Aaron tell ya what happened?"

"No. They said everything was worked out and that the night watch was set now."

"I believe it is, but I'm not verra happy with the way I handled Smith. He tried to pass it off as petty, and he lied to me. I told him he was a liar and a coward, and he put his fist into my face. I lost my temper."

"I wasn't aware you had a bad temper."

"Tis always been my bane. Part of my problem with my brother Sean and one of the reasons for my father's sendin' me to America. In a drunken brawl, I maimed a man from another clan. I wasn't totally to blame because he did strike me first, but I was the one who could not bring my temper back into control. I left him a cripple. I still feel that shame at times. I swore I'd never allow myself to get into that kind of brawl again. But I did. Had Sonny and Aaron not dragged me off that man, I'd have killed him last week."

"Is that what has been bothering you of late?"

"I have relived that afternoon in my mind so many times. Hannah, I canna blame the drink this time. I was seein' red. My temper destroyed all reason. I need to talk with Sam. I need to get this right with the Lord. He will help me lay it down. But my failin' has naught to do with you. I'll not stand in judgment. I want nothin' but the best for ya. If you are willin', I'll answer any questions ya have."

"I'm sorry I misunderstood. You have honored me by trusting me to share this burden. I think it is the first time these roles have been switched. What should I try to read first?"

"So ya want no farther explanation?"

"No. I just need to know where I need to read to find the Jesus you know."

"I feel better that I've told ya what I did. Helps me handle the shame of it. Studying scripture is always a balm for my bruised spirit. If ya want to meet the Savior, Hannah, read the four Gospels, starting with Matthew, and then read Mark, Luke, and John. Those four books tell you all the world knows about Jesus."

"All right. I can try to do that. Good night, Kell."

He bent and kissed her cheek. "Lass, a lot of people care about you. Sleep well."

Chapter 17

Wherefore, my beloved brethren, let every man be swift to hear,
slow to speak, slow to wrath: For the wrath of man worketh not the
righteousness of God.
James 1:19-20

A week after the cross burning at Sanctuary Hill, Narvel
Tangent came into the mercantile with his daughter, Molly. He spent
more than half an hour strolling through the aisles, picking up an item
here and there only to return it to its place. Hannah watched his
movements through the store. With the better selection of merchandise
that she'd been able to display since the deliveries from Memphis were
regular, she'd hoped for more business. Yet, she would gladly have
done without the trade of Tangent at the Kincaid mercantile.

At first, the unwanted customer seemed to ignore her presence.
Molly, too, walked directly in front of her to prance to the counter
where Sonny was measuring two pounds of flour for Rachel Miller.

"Do you need something, Mr. Tangent?" Hannah finally asked.

"I do. I wouldn't be here if I didn't, would I?" The smirk on his
face brought color to her cheeks.

"I'm surprised you have the nerve to come here after your visit to
Sanctuary Hill last Saturday night." Hannah squared her shoulders,
expecting some crude response from the man.

"I'm sure you're mistaken, ma'am. I've been to the state capitol
since a week ago Monday. My wife and I just arrived home last

evenin' about 6:00. Did somethin' bad happen at your place? I see ya have a bit of a bruise on your face."

"As well you know. What do you need, sir?"

"Well, my wife asked me to bring her a tin of cocoa powder, a half-pound of baking soda, two yards of white lawn material, and a matching spool of thread. Can you fill this small order, or do I need to drive over to Madison?" Hannah nearly lost her temper at the taunting of the smug man as he hitched his thumbs in his vest pockets and rocked on his heels.

"We have all you asked for. I'll cut the fabric for you while Sonny gathers the other things." As Hannah tried to walk past him to the wall of fabric, he grabbed her arm.

"No need to bother Sonny. He seems to be doin' a fine job entertainin' my little Molly. She told me Sonny is real sweet on her." Tangent smirked again.

"Mr. Tangent, Sonny hardly knows your daughter. He's not ready to begin courting yet."

"Just the same, I hope you've had a talk with him—about how to treat a young lady and how not to treat one, if you know what I mean."

Hannah hurriedly gathered all that Tangent had asked for. She didn't like one thing about his visit, even though he paid cash for his purchases. He took his saucy daughter by the arm and led her to the door.

"Just remember what I told ya. I think you are smart enough to know you can't go it alone here in this state. The offer stands." Tangent kicked the door open with his boot and pulled Molly out with him.

When they were outside, Hannah called Sonny to the back of the store. "What did Molly say to you, Sonny?"

"Oh, gee. She was just talkin' girl talk like she does every time I see her. She mostly talks about our Sunday walks and askin' me to hold her hand. I don't know why. We weren't anywhere that she would fall. She talked about gettin' married and leavin' home because of her papa. She wants to live in a big house with servants and lots of nice dresses."

"Sonny, does she talk about those things every week when you go for your walks?"

"Mostly."

"Do other young people go with you and Molly when you walk after church on Sunday?"

"Sometimes, but mostly not. Is it all right to walk with Molly after church?"

"Yes, I suppose so. I don't trust her father, though. I know he was one of those men who came to Sanctuary Hill last week and wanted to hurt Marcus. He said he wasn't, but I know I recognized his voice."

"I don't know, Hannah. After that man hit me, I don't remember much about anything else. I remember I was scared."

"I was too, Sonny. Let's finish our work here. Marcus says that we will be close to finishing Mom Bec's fields today. I'll be glad when harvest is over. Maybe we'll have time to work on other things when the cotton is in."

φ

Time crept as slowly as the harvest continued. Never-ending work-filled daylight hours six days a week. By the last week in September, though, the Kincaids had finished the first round of picking at Sanctuary Hill.

The night they finished the last field at Marcus and Shataka's farm, Marcus came to the door after supper with his hat in his hand.

"Miss Hannah, I don't like to bother ya at night 'cause I know how hard ya work, but I got a need to know how we're gonna get his cotton ginned and baled so it can get shipped off to the cotton brokers."

"Marcus, please come and sit here at the table with Kell and me. Do you want a cup of coffee? We have some real coffee now that I got my grocery order from Memphis. I always bring a little home."

"Yes, ma'am. Be right fine. Evenin', Mr. Kell."

"Do we have a place to gin cotton?" Kell asked.

"No, sir. The Yankees burned our gin the same day they tried to burn down the house. The rain helped save the house, but the gin was too far gone. We decided to try to save the house. I am sorry, Miss Hannah, that we couldn't get the fire out before the roof fell in upstairs."

"Marcus, we are so grateful that you saved what you did. We've made do with the house and have nearly finished the roof. But truthfully, I don't know anything about ginning cotton or making bales. I know it's a big job." She poured everyone more coffee.

"How much cotton goes into a bale, Marcus?" Kell asked.

"Oh, 'bout five hundred pounds. Cotton gets pressed into those big blocks. Then they's sold to the cotton brokers."

"Well, we'll have to talk to our neighbors. Someone surely has a gin. Maybe we can hire out the ginnin' for a share of the profit. I know that most of the landowners nearby didn't plant a crop this year. I'll ride about in the next day or two and find someone we can work with. The Millers are a nice young couple, and he's struggling to keep his land." Kell drained his cup and set it down.

"How do you know that, Kell?" Hannah asked.

"He asked me to pray for his two heifers to give birth to strong calves. He needs to sell them for tax money."

"Y'all talk about personal things among the church members?"

"Yes, Hannah, we do. We share each other's sorrows and joys. You would know that if you'd get out into the community." Hannah turned her back to Kell.

"Marcus, do you know who the cotton broker is?" she asked.

"No ma'am. Mr. Hugh sold our crop to someone in Memphis. He always made a trip ever fall. When he come back, we'd load up all our bales and take 'em over to the railroad.

"Kell, did Mr. Hugh leave anything about cotton sales with you?" Hannah asked.

"I gave y'all the records. Did ya look at 'em?"

"Only the ones about the store. I'll get into the papers again tomorrow. Thank you, Marcus, for bringing me up to date on our business venture. I don't know how we'd get along without you."

"Miss Hannah, I'm believin' it's gonna be a fine crop. Through this first pickin', I'd guess we got about nine bales. Weather holds we'll get another seven second time round. And the cotton is mighty white with long lint. We should get us top dollar for this crop."

"Let's hope we can, but first things first. Let's help Kell find us someone nearby with a gin that we can use."

"Well, goodnight to y'all. I'm glad tomorrow is the Sabbath. The Lord was mighty good to give us a day of rest. During pickin' season, we sure needs it." Marcus slapped Kell's back as he left the kitchen.

"Kell, did you know we still had to do all this before we could sell the cotton?" Hannah slumped into her chair.

"I knew it was a long, intense process. That is why the best fieldhands went for top dollar in the slave markets. Uncle Hugh didn't raise a crop that last year I was here. The few slaves that didn't run off stayed and grew gardens to supply themselves with food. Hugh had a few cattle, so we had meat. No. I don't know any more about cotton farmin' than you do, my dear Lass."

"Are you willing to learn alongside me? I'm sure I can't take this on by myself."

Silence followed. Hannah brushed her hair back and smoothed her skirt. She finally walked away and opened the parlor door.

"Wait, Hannah. Please don't go."

"It's all right, Kell. I understand why you don't want to do this. I have not treated you very well since we met back in April. I've no right to ask for help."

"Hannah, I'm not offended. You caught me off guard. I didn't want my reply to come across to you as sarcastic or prideful. I needed a minute to think."

"We don't usually have real conversations, do we?"

"They could have been friendlier at times. Yes, lass, I will try to learn about the cotton business right alongside ya. If I can help my family this way, I'll be meetin' my purpose."

"Thank you, Kell. I appreciate your willingness to help. I haven't told you this, but I'm glad you came here to Sanctuary Hill to live after the night riders' attack. I feel safer having you here."

"My pleasure. Shall we spend a while on the porch swing before the evenin's done?"

"That'd be a nice way to end the day."

∅

When Kell joined Hannah on the porch, he carried his violin. He propped it under his chin and played a soft melody that took him back to his home in County Sterling. The gentle tune drifted through the house that warm summer night. Naomi soon joined them to listen to the Scottish tune. "Kell Kincaid, how lovely you play the violin, my boy. I've tears in my eyes. You've brought home so many memories of times when my dear father played the old Scottish ballads for me on this very porch."

"You told me you played the fiddle. That was lovely." Hannah reached out and ran her finger across the side of the beautiful redwood instrument Kell held. "I didn't know you were such an accomplished violinist."

"Hannah, there's a lot of things about me ya don't know. If you recall, we've been on opposite sides of about every issue that's come up since we met. And this lovely old thing is a fiddle. I don't play anything fancy. My grandfather Kincaid handed it down to me. I don't know exactly how old it is, but it's one thing I do cherish."

Naomi asked, "My dear cousin, will you play more for me?"

"I'd like that. I'm in the mood for music tonight." Kell began to play a lively jig that always reminded him of holiday times at home, one where couples danced and swayed together or perhaps sneaked out to the garden for a quick kiss. When he finished, he sighed. "I guess I'm a bit homesick tonight."

"Play me a lullaby, Kell, and then I will call it a night. I need a good night's sleep. Mrs. Naylor has asked me to help serve communion in the morning. I can't oversleep."

"Just for you, cousin." Kell drew his bow across the strings of his violin and began to sing in his beautiful Scottish baritone brogue.

Seo chugainn an dràm-sa, A dh'fhàg an t-òr an àite, 'S e 'n t-òr a dh'fhàg an àite, 'S e 'n t-òr a dh'fhàg an àite, 'S e 'n t-òr a dh'fhàg an àite. Hùg air a' bhonaid mhor-bhuide, Hùg air a' bhonaid mhor-bhuide, Hùg air a' bhonaid mhor-bhuide, 'S tha 'n t-òr a dh'fhàg an àite.

Tears streamed down Naomi's face. A smile like Kell had never seen before came to her worn tired face.

He continued his song.

Can ye no hushe your weepin', all the wee lambs are sleepin'? Birdies are nestlin', nestlin' together. Dream Angus is hirpin' her heather. Dreams to sell, fine dreams to sell. Hush, my baby, and sleep without fear. Dream Angus has brought you a dream, my dearie.

Naomi pulled Kell to her and said, "God bless you, my dear cousin." She then walked to the door and called back, "Goodnight, children."

Smiling at Naomi's departure, they sat, certainly not feeling like children. "Hannah, I am surprised how much the music meant to Naomi. I hope it was a pleasant memory for her and not one to keep her up and frettin'."

"I know she loved it. When she can talk about it, I'm sure she will tell us Mr. Hugh sang the song to her. I know she was upset when she couldn't come home after learning her father was so ill. That was the same time that Benjamin Murphy had been sent home from the war. He was critically ill for those last few months."

"Hannah, I don't want to end the night on a melancholy note. I have one more air I'd like to play just for you if you'll allow me."

"Of course, I'd love to hear more."

Kell drew his bow across his violin, and a longing, hopeful note came forth. Then he sang,

Oh the Summer time is coming, and the trees are sweetly blooming
And the wild mountain thyme all around the blooming heather.
　　Will ye go Lassie go........
　　And we'll all go together to pull wild mountain thyme
　　From around the blooming heather
　　　　Will ye go Lassie go?
I will build my love a bower near yon pure crystal fountain
　　And on it I will pile all the flowers of the mountain
　　　　Will ye go Lassie go............

217

And we'll all go together To pull wild mountain thyme
From around the blooming heather.
Will ye go Lassie go?
If my true love she were gone, I will surely find no other
Where wild mountain thyme all around the blooming heather.
Will ye go Lassie go...........
And we'll all go together to pull wild mountain thyme
From around the blooming heather
Will ye go Lassie go?

Kell laid his violin aside. "Well, I'm a-thinkin' that's enough for one night, lass."

"I've never been serenaded like that before. Such a lovely, longing song. Almost as if someone is seeking something, afraid they will not find what they need."

"This is an old Scottish ballad. The words remind me of the Scotland I left behind when I came to America. The hills and vales of the highland were rife with heather and the thyme that grows wild there. The scent of that place, I can almost sense now. I play this tune when I get homesick."

"You aren't homesick enough to go home, are you?"

"Time will tell. I have a better opportunity here to make a good life. In Scotland, I can own no land. Since I've no trade, I'd be at the mercy of my family to provide a livin'." He moved to sit next to Hannah. "But most days, I feel that I've naught to keep me here. Naught except for my obligation to my Uncle Hugh's family and my oath to my father. I haven't figured out yet how that makes much of a future for me."

"Haven't you found things you like in Arkansas, Kell?"

"I have. I have bought myself land. There is an opportunity to prosper here. I know I can raise cattle and horses. I can never be my own master in Scotland. Being second-born would always put me under my brother's authority. Sean's a good man, but we rarely see things eye to eye."

"That's sad. I always wanted a brother or sister, but it wasn't to be. My mother died when I was nine, and my father didn't remarry. Besides the servants, there was just the two of us."

"How did you come to marry my cousin Naomi's son, Richard?"

"The Murphy family lived on the neighboring plantation. Richard was one of the few men my father allowed to call on me after my coming-of-age party."

"As pretty as you are, I'd thought you'd have lots of beaus," Kell said.

"Please don't flatter me, Kell. I am no belle. My father presented me with three options as a prospective mate. He wanted to make an advantageous social connection. Papa was a politician, you see. He planned to run for Congress after the South won the war."

"That's odd. I thought Cousin Naomi's husband was a colonel in the Union army."

"Oh, he was. My father didn't organize Kennedy's Rangers until the winter of '62. I had already married Richard that June."

Kell pounded his fist on his knees and bent over laughing. "I'll bet that about killed Colonel Benjamin Murphy. His daughter-in-law a belle of the South with a Rebel papa."

Hannah laughed with him. "Father Ben was the nicest person in this family except for Sonny. Naomi never quite approved of me."

"And Richard, did he treat ya well?"

Hannah's eyes dropped, and the smile Kell had been enjoying disappeared at once. With her hands in the lace at her collar, she stood up. "Kell, I've enjoyed our talk tonight. I think it's nice to have an adult to talk with, but I don't want to talk about Richard."

"I will respect your wishes. We had a lovely evening. I won't bring a cloud of gloom by meddlin'. With tomorrow bein' the Sabbath, I should go to bed. Sleep well, Hannah."

Chapter 18

What time I am afraid, I will trust in Thee.
In God, I will praise His words, in God, I will put my trust;
I will not fear what flesh can do unto me.
Psalm 56:3-4

On Monday morning, Hannah met Kell in the kitchen as he was about to leave. "I missed you yesterday afternoon after Bible class. Naomi told me on the way home that you said you had some business to attend to."

"Well, it is nice to be missed. I did," Kell said. "I spent the afternoon with Reuben and Rachel Miller at their place."

"They don't attend the Community Church?" Hannah asked.

"No. They are Catholic, like my mother. They go into Madison now and again for mass on Sunday. Reuben has a gin that needs a bit of work, but we decided if we can get the press to work, he will gin our cotton there. He said we'd need to supply a couple of people to work with him. If we send some workers, it'll take ya a little longer to get the crop out, but we gotta do somethin' because the barn is near full."

"Did he give you a price for the work?"

"We negotiated a price. He said he will take three cents a pound."

"Kell, is that a fair price?"

"I suppose so, Hannah. I know it's a lot of work. We have to get it ready to sell, and we don't have a gin to do the work. It's your call. You are the one who must make the decision."

"We need to do it. I hope repairing the gin isn't too costly and that it will not take too long."

"I'm a fair tinker. I'll go look at it myself. I will take Sonny with me. He seems good at restoring broken things."

"I appreciate your help, Kell."

"It's nice that you are finally willin' to let me help ya when I am able."

Hannah finished her coffee and headed for the fields at Lucas's farm. The second picking was every bit as hard work as the first, but this time it took longer to fill the empty sacks they dragged across the fields. The work crew of three women, five men, and three children toiled each day until dusk, only to be faced with another day of labor when the sun rose the next morning. Hannah had truly come to hate picking cotton. Even more, she felt shame for her feelings because she'd come to know and appreciate her crew, who had been forced to do this all their lives—for another man's gain. No, she wouldn't quit as long as there was work to be done.

By the end of September, the cotton crop at Sanctuary Hill had been harvested, except for pulling the boles. Even with Shataka and Rose working at the Miller farm to help gin and bale Sanctuary Hill's cotton, the rest of the crew had finished the last patch about noon on the last Friday of the month.

Marcus came to Hannah as they were about to take the last wagon to the barn. "Miss Hannah, our folks been workin' mighty hard, nearly ever day since April. Do ya think we can take one day off—just for the pleasure of it?"

"Marcus, that's the best idea you've had in a long while. Let's celebrate. We'll have a family cookout. We'll eat, get Mr. Kell to play his fiddle, and just enjoy a day of rest and fun."

"I'll tell my family. Where we gonna have this celebration?" Marcus's grin covered his face from ear to ear.

"Let's go down to the meadow near the creek. The kids may want to play in the water. I'll kill a couple of chickens so we can have a fine meal," Hannah said.

The following morning, all the Kincaid and Murphy families, along with Adam Pierce, made their way to the meadow where Kell had first seen Hannah. They quickly set up the feast on the tailgate of the wagon and strew quilts across the meadow to provide places to sit. The men set up the stakes for a horseshoe match. Sonny brought out several fishing poles, and he took Lucas's sons and Abraham down to the creek to catch some fish.

The adults sat and told stories about funny or strange things that had happened in the fields. They all laughed as Shataka told of teaching Hannah how to be a fieldhand. At noon, they ate as if they'd never seen food before. Every crumb of the fried chicken was gone, the cake Mom Bec had brought disappeared in a heartbeat, and the fresh vegetables from the garden were gobbled down just as quickly. Before long, Mom Bec and the babies curled up under a tree for a much-deserved nap.

Naomi organized a game for them to play. "This game is called the Gypsy Knot. We played this so often when I was a girl. Our crew works together so well that I know you can figure out the trick in no time." She pulled and prodded the entire crew into a circle, moving an individual or two when she didn't like who they were standing next to. Then she told them to join hands, skipping the person next to them, and not taking more than one hand from another person. When she was satisfied with the arrangement, she told them the object of the game was to figure out how to make one large circle where each person held the hand of the one next to them. "Now, my human knot family, get yourself out of the knot, but you can't let go of anyone's hand. Ready? Go." Naomi stood nearby, laughing and clapping her hands as if she were a young girl.

Chaos and noise filled the meadow for several minutes. Then laughter erupted from the group. No sooner would one person get untangled than someone would step over his arm to entangle him again. After a while, the entire huddle collapsed on the ground, laughing harder than ever.

"You musta got your crop out, Mrs. Murphy. I see ya got time to waste with your hired help." Narvel Tangent stopped his buggy near the group. Molly sat beside him.

Kell righted himself from the collapsed group. "Mr. Tangent, we weren't expectin' visitors today. We are celebratin' our fine harvest."

"Our? When did you become part of this...this family?"

"I was born into it. Ya know my name's Kincaid." Kell walked over and took hold of Tangent's horse.

"Molly wanted to invite Sonny to the box social at church next Wednesday night. I don't see the lad hereabouts."

"He's fishing," Kell said. "Is there anything else ya need here?"

"No. I don't think this is a place for my daughter or myself. Frankly, Mrs. Murphy, since you were raised by my dear friend Hugh Kincaid, I'm surprised to see ya out here socializing with your hired help. I'd think that would be a bit below the raising of a Southern lady."

Naomi's face flushed, and she grabbed Kell's arm for support.

Hannah walked to stand near Kell. "Mr. Tangent, we work side by side with this Kincaid family. We are enjoying a day of leisure and rest together. Do you see any harm in doing so?"

"To each his own, ma'am. Molly, I'm not sure this is a family I want you to associate with. Let's return home."

"But Papa, I wanna see Sonny." Molly stood up from her seat in the buggy.

Tangent jerked her down beside him. "Do as you're told, girl. Sit down and don't ya start cryin' on me." He pulled the reins of his horse and hurried back toward the road.

Kell lifted the wilting Naomi onto the wagon seat. "Hannah, I want a word with ya." He took her arm and walked several steps away from the group. "I understand your suspicions of Tangent now. He's 'Old South' to the core. He's not lookin' to build a better state, just a return to the old ways. He may be more of a concern than I thought. I am goin' to the sheriff over in Madison and tell him of what's happened."

"When I made that comment to the night riders on their first visit, they all laughed. I'm not sure the sheriff is the servant of all the people."

"The only way to find out is to talk to the man. I'll just go meet him and reach my own conclusion."

φ

The following Saturday, Hannah opened the mercantile. She allowed Sonny to drive her to the store and then return to the cotton field. To her surprise, she was busy with people streaming in the entire four hours she was open. Many of the people from the Community Church came in to pick up an item or two, but several people Hannah had never seen in Linden spent some time looking at the wares the

225

store had to offer. One man with a distinctly northern accent came in just before noon with a long list of things he wanted.

"I may not have everything on your list, but if you want me to, I can order it. It will be delivered here within two weeks. By the way, I am Hannah Murphy."

"Didn't expect to find a woman shopkeeper. I'm Matthew Garland. Just bought the plantation called Sweetwater. It's just a piece up the river."

"I see why you need so many things. I can give you most of these today, but some are specialty things that I don't keep in stock."

"Mrs. Murphy, who is in charge around here?" he asked.

"In charge? What exactly do you mean?"

"You know. Legal business, politics…those kinds of things?"

"This is just a small county. We have a county sheriff, and the courthouse is in Madison, about ten miles from here. I'm afraid I can't tell you much about the politics of this area. My family and I recently settled here from Washington City."

"I'll be going to Madison then. I need to register this deed for my land. The land agent, Mr. Tangent, told me that it was free and clear…sold for taxes, but I have to register my ownership."

"Who owned the property before?" Hannah asked.

"I wasn't given a name, just some Confederate who got killed at Leesburg, and then the family defaulted on the taxes three years running. Got me a good deal, too. Tangent sold me the land for fifteen dollars an acre, including the house and outbuildings. Never could have afforded a place like this in Indiana."

"Narvel Tangent?" Garland nodded. "Well, I have all these things in stock except the fabric for drapes. That is expensive fabric, and we don't get any call for damask around here. I will order it if you want it."

"Never mind. I will look for that drapery material when I get to Madison. How much do I owe you?"

Hannah totaled his bill, and he pulled out a wad of U.S. currency larger than Hannah had seen since before the war. Mr. Garland made the largest purchase at the mercantile since they'd opened.

"Thank you for your help, Mrs. Murphy. I'm sure we'll see each other often. You run a good store here. I'll bring my wife the next time I come."

When Garland left with his bundles, Hannah locked the door and put on her bonnet. She'd have to walk home the two miles since Sonny was still in the field. To her surprise, when she closed the back door, Kell waited for her in the buggy. "I thought ya might want a ride home."

"I'm glad you are here if that is a smile on your face instead of a smirk. I have something to talk to you about."

Kell grinned again. "Are we gonna have a real conversation again, or are we gonna talk business or solve a problem of some kind?"

"I see, it's a smirk." Hannah seated herself next to Kell. "Why are you always so sarcastic? I said I wanted to talk."

"You did. Let's drive for a piece." Kell drove in silence until he came to an old burned-out church set near an ancient cemetery. "I found this old cemetery a short while after I came to Arkansas. I walked through those crumblin' gravestones many times. See that one that looks like a log? Somebody spent hours carving that piece of art. It's a marker for a wee babe, hardly born before he left this world. See his name and dates carved here on the top. How much love is in that gravestone?"

"Such a loss. I can't imagine how that person felt."

"But it's a thing of beauty carved with love," he said. "We can appreciate it still today." Hannah walked to the grave marker and rubbed her hand down the intricately carved bark and flowers there.

Kell broke her reverie. "What did ya want to talk about, Hannah?"

"Today a man came into the store and bought a huge amount of supplies. He paid me in U.S. greenbacks that he peeled off a wad big enough to dam a river."

"That's a good thing, I'd think."

"Yes, the sale was good, but he told me he'd just moved to Sweetwater Plantation, which was sold to him by Narvel Tangent. He called him a land agent. Tangent charged him three times what he offered us for Sanctuary Hill. Garland thought it was a good price."

"Lass, it's happenin' all over the South. Carpetbaggers from up North and scallywags who hid their money durin' the war are buying up all the property bein' sold out for back taxes. Sometimes they pay a few hundred dollars, but then turn around and sell the land to Northerners who are looking for a better life than they had before the war." Kell slapped the reins across Graystoke's haunches and directed the buggy away from Sanctuary Hill.

"That is why he is trying to take Sanctuary Hill."

"Darlin', you're frettin' about something that's not gonna happen. You have made your crop this year. There will be ample money to pay the taxes and to finish repairs on the house."

"How can you be sure, Kell?"

"The Lord is takin' care of us at Sanctuary Hill. We worked hard and tried to keep his commandments. Lass, that is what faith is. If we believe our Father loves us enough to see our needs, we waste time and energy worryin'."

"I wish I knew what you know. Brother Sam and Mary Lee seem to know it too. Such a blind trust in the unknown." Hannah's tears flowed in streams down her face and into her lap.

"Believing in Jesus is no blind trust. You've been reading the gospels. Did those people who encountered Jesus have a blind trust? No, darlin'.

They were witnesses to miracles and resurrection. They experienced the gift of faith and love from our Father."

"I've read all that, and I've heard the people in our Bible class talk about it, but how did you come to know it was true—real?"

"That's the easiest part, Hannah. Just stop fightin' with the baggage the world has handed you. Throw it down. You don't need it. Surrender to Him. Faith grows, just like those seeds you planted in the cotton field. Doesn't that seem like a miracle to you? Our Father continues to show us his will, mercy, generosity, and love a hundred times every day. If we are aware, we'll see He is right in front of us."

Hannah sat for a while looking into Kell's stormy blue eyes. The warmth of his hand enclosing hers became a source of comfort. For a moment, she wanted to let the wall she'd put between them crumble, but just for a moment. Instead of laying her head on his shoulder as she wanted to do, she pulled her shoulders back and removed her hand to wipe away the wet tracks on her face.

Chapter 19

And when he came to himself, he said, hired servants of my father have bread enough and to spare and I perish with hunger. I will arise and go to my father and say unto him, Father, I have sinned against Heaven and thee. I am no more worthy to be called thy son: make me one thy hired servants.
Luke 15:17-19

The next day Hannah didn't go with her family to church. The family planned a long day, worship in the morning, dinner on the grounds, Bible class in mid-afternoon, and the monthly gospel singing that evening. For Hannah, the time provided an excellent opportunity to tackle the boxes of business records that Hugh Kincaid had stored in the attic.

She heard the clopping of horse hooves down the cobbled drive as she climbed the narrow, steep staircase to the attic. For the first time, she truly saw the damage the fire had caused. On the floor lay heaps of ashes, pieces of charred rafters, and parts of furniture that had been stored there. She saw fragments of a once beautiful buffet, but when she tried to pick up a newel from one of the posts, it crumbled in her hand. Overhead where partially burned joists remained, she saw the competent handiwork of Aaron Pierce. No partially burned joist remained unsupported. The new roof was sound. She needed to compliment him on his excellent work.

As she moved toward the side of the house that had been saved from the fire, she noted several items that would be useful as they continued to make Sanctuary Hill into the home it had once been. But all that was work for another day.

Hannah had one goal—to find the business papers Hugh Kincaid stored.

She hoped she would find the name of the cotton broker who had dealt with the Kincaid cotton crop. In a huge walnut cabinet, she found three boxes of ledgers, loose receipts, and letters from businessmen who had dealt with the crops at Sanctuary Hills in the past. Hannah drug each heavy box to the staircase, but she knew there was no way she would be able to carry them to the table where she had planned to work.

Loading her arms full, she made seven trips up and down the scary staircase before she retrieved all the records she found. On one final trip up, she threw the three crates down so she would have a place to sort what she found. By one o'clock, she was buried deep in her effort to find the broker's name. She started with the three large ledgers. She found lists of costs for various parts of the process. She found what looked like estimates of crop values for various years. She even found a list of clothing, shoes, and household goods that Hugh had provided to his people, but she found no names. She dropped the ledgers into the first box.

She picked up a second hand of old invoices as a loud clang outside the door brought her back to her surroundings. She gasped and dropped the papers across the kitchen floor. She was alone at Sanctuary Hill for the first time since she had moved here in April. She looked around for something to protect herself. *Where is Sonny's club?* Finding nothing, she moved toward the door. *Stop it, Hannah Ruth. Why are you so skittish? Night riders don't show up in the middle of the day!*

She opened the door. She found a very tall ebony-skinned man, a smaller woman, and a boy of about twelve or thirteen standing at the door. "Do you need something?"

"We lookin' for Mr. Hugh's family. I didn't mean to knock over that water bucket. I'll go fetch some mo' water."

"That's all right. I am Hannah Murphy. Mr. Kincaid was my mother-in-law's father. He passed away some time ago."

"We know Mr. Hugh gone. We's sad 'cause he was good to us. We was his people before the war," the man explained. "We just got back to Sanctuary Hill. We went to Cairo with some soldiers a while back. They tole us life be better in the North, but it ain't so good for us there. Work is hard to find, and it's so cold in the winter."

"I see. What do you want from us? As you can see things are not very good here. The house is hardly livable."

"Miss Hannah, we wanna come home and work here. Do ya think we can stay?"

"We can't afford wages yet. We are trying to get the crop out now, hoping to be able to meet the tax bill."

"Missus, we'd be satisfied with a roof over our heads and some vittles to eat. We don't ask much, just mostly to come home." With his words, the man removed his hat and lowered his eyes.

Hannah couldn't respond to his words at that moment. "Are you hungry?"

"Yes, ma'am. We ain't ate since yesterday midday. We jumped the train after we got across the Mississippi. Just kept comin' home."

"Well, come in and I'll get you some coffee and find something for you to eat." She made a simple meal of leftover pone, a few pieces of ham, a plate of scrambled eggs, and coffee. Not a crumb remained on the plates when they finished.

"Thank you, Miss Hannah. I didn't tell ya, but my name is 'Lijah Kincaid. This be my wife Dorrie, and our son, Samuel. We all willin' to work hard if y'all have us."

"Lijah, I guess that is short for Elijah, I can't answer you right now. I will have to speak to Marcus. He is the foreman at Sanctuary Hill."

"You mean Marcus Kincaid that marry Patsy, my sister?"

"Yes. Then you must be Rose's son." Hannah saw the family resemblance—the same ebony skin and high cheekbones that Rose had.

"No, 'em. My main name's Hepzibah. We all got Bible names, 'cept Patsy. She's named for Mr. Hugh's wife. She died the same year that Patsy was born. Her picture always hung right there over Mr. Hugh's desk."

"Well, Rose is the name I know. They can tell you about that when they get home. Y'all can go rest on the front porch until the family gets home. I have a lot of work to finish here this afternoon."

The afternoon went swiftly as Hannah poured through page after page. She found records of every sort, but nothing that told her who she might find to help her sell the abundant crop they'd raised that year. She tossed sheet after sheet into the second box. The next group of papers showed her the amount of previous years' property tax and the balances from sold crops.

She also found a few personal letters that she planned to give to Naomi when she returned from church. Finally, Hannah reached for the last heap of loose papers. The second paper in the stack was a receipt for the sale of 1863's cotton crop, Mr. Hugh's last harvest. The name on the bill of sale was Ira Levenstein, and it even included a street address for an office in Memphis, Tennessee. As Hannah dug deeper, she discovered other documents with Levenstein's name. She knew she'd found her answer.

When she put the last of the papers into the boxes, she looked out the window and noticed the sun was near the tree line to the west. She'd been so involved in her task that the entire afternoon had gone without notice. She stood up and stretched to get the tension out of her back. Then she heard noises outside the front door.

The sound of loud crying and riotous laughter made a strange combination. Hannah rushed to see what the commotion was. She found Mom Bec and Rose hugging and crying in the arms of Lijah Kincaid and his family. In her effort to find the broker's name, she'd all but forgotten the family she'd told to wait on the porch.

"My son, my son. I never 'spected I'd see ya again in this life." Rose moved to take her grandson in her arms. "Lookee here how big this boy has growed to be."

"Thank you, Lord!" Mom Bec's face ran with tears. "On this blessed Sabbath, He done helped this family heal. Only Rafe still out there somewhere."

"You must be plumb wore out—and starved to death, son," Rose said.

"No mam. Miss Hannah done gave us a good meal when we got here," Dorrie's soft, melodic voice sang Hannah's praises.

"She is a good lady. She's been mighty good to us." Rose turned and saw Hannah in the doorway. "Thank ya, Miss Hannah for feedin' my son and his family. We so glad they home now."

"Wait a minute, mam. We don't know if we gonna stay here. Miss Hannah tole me Marcus is the foreman. Me and Marcus had words when we left to go North."

"That don't matter now, son. For tonight, you will stay with Mama and me. We got our own cabin, and we got room." Rose answered her son.

About that time, Kell drove up to the porch with Naomi and Sonny. "Are ya havin' a party, and ya didn't invite some of your kin?"

"Part of Rose's family has returned. They've asked to stay. I told them that Marcus is our foreman, and we'd decide together," Hannah said.

"Sounds like a good plan. Sonny, do you wanna take Graystoke back to the corral and give him a handful of oats for me? "

"Sure thing, Kell. We gonna eat soon, Hannah? I'm hungry. It's been hours since we had lunch at church." Sonny led the gray stallion back to the shed.

"Well, Hannah, what did Marcus say?" Kell asked.

"I haven't seen him or Shataka today. I guess they returned home after church."

"Well, I guess tomorrow will be soon enough."

"What did you do all day after skippin' out of Bible class?" Naomi asked from her seat on the swing.

"Mother Naomi, I didn't just skip out. I had to go through all those documents to see if I could locate the name of the cotton broker." Hannah sat next to her mother-in-law. "And after hours, I found the name of the man that your father did business with—Ira Levenstein."

"That's great news, Hannah. Is he local?" Kell asked.

"The address I found is in Memphis, just as Marcus thought. I suppose we'll have to make a trip across the river soon."

"Who are we?" Naomi asked. "I'd love to go to Memphis again. Papa took me there many times when I was a girl."

"I was thinking that Sonny and I would go the week after next," Hannah answered. "The trip will be rushed, Mother. We have no money for shopping or long stays in a hotel. I'd like to spend only one night, but I'll definitely be home in two days."

"But there are so many wonderful things to do in Memphis."

"Maybe next year we'll be able to stay a few days there with a little money to spend."

A pout appeared on Naomi's face, but Hannah would not give in to her childish request. The money and the time did not permit her to make the trip anything more than the business trip it was.

"Well, don't bother about me, Hannah. I'll be fine. You just go and take care of the cotton sale. Surely life won't be so hard after that crop is sold." Naomi picked up her bonnet and reticule, went into the parlor, and slammed the door.

"She's in a snit. She'll get over it when she sees how short a time I am gone."

"Hannah, I'll be makin' that trip to Memphis with you and Sonny. Too much can go wrong to let the two of ya go on this trip alone."

"Do I have to remind you that I made the trip from Washington alone with Sonny and Naomi? Surely you have better things to do here."

"Don't argue with me, lass. I've made up my mind. Now, let's go in and get a bite of supper ready for our Sabbath meal." Kell took her elbow and helped Hannah to her feet.

φ

Almost before the sun rose, Marcus came to the house. Kell and Aaron sat at the table, eating biscuits and gravy. "Mr. Kell, is Miss Hannah still here? Do ya know if she tole Lijah he could stay here at Sanctuary Hill?" Marcus shuffled his feet, a rare reaction for this usually placid man.

"Yes, she's still here. Do you want a cup of coffee?"

"No, thank ya. Already ate. What are they doin' here?" Just as Marcus asked, Hannah came into the kitchen from the chicken house.

"Mornin', Miss Hannah. What's Lijah and his kin doin' here?" Marcus asked.

"They told me they wanted to come home. I told them I couldn't offer them a place here until we talked."

"What we gonna do with 'em now? The harvest 'bout done. They got no right to just squat here."

"Marcus, do you think your brother-in-law is a slacker?" Kell asked. "Won't he give a day's work like the rest of y'all."

"Mr. Kell, we had a mighty big squabble when they told us they was leavin' with the soldiers. Lijah took his family, and Rafe left with his wife. They followed some scallywags that promised a good life in the North. Didn't take long for them to see that lie, did it?"

"Marcus, will they be good workers if we take them back?" Hannah asked.

"They worked as much as the rest of us when Mr. Hugh was our master, but they run off with the Yankees when they tole all those lies. They forgot about family."

"Are you afraid they won't stay if we give them a chance to earn some land of their own?" Hannah asked.

"Ya can't do that upfront, Miss Hannah. We nearly got our crop out. Wintertime will be slow 'til spring planting time. No time for them to grow a garden for food this year. They gotta eat somehow."

"Let's ask if they want to work for a cabin and food to get through the winter, doing winter chores. If they work as hard as the rest of us, we can make them an offer of a farm site in April. That will be planning time for the year, just before we start a new growing season."

"All right, Miss Hannah, but don't 'spect me to cut 'em no slack. If they prove they're worth it, we'll do it your way." Marcus stood to leave. "I'm sendin' him and Sammy over to help Rose and Shataka with the ginnin' and balin'. Dorrie can fix up one of the empty cabins for their place, and then she can help Mom Bec with the laundry and cleaning the big house. Mom Bec tole me she's havin' a baby. Do ya care which cabin I put 'em in?"

"That is your decision, Marcus. You're the foreman. Whatever you think best will be fine with me." Hannah closed the door behind Marcus and returned to her now cold oatmeal and coffee.

"Lass, ya took care of that verra well. You're a good businesswoman, I must say."

"Thank you, Kell, but I've no more time for small talk. I've gotta get to the mercantile before seven."

"What about our trip to Memphis? When are we goin'?" Sonny asked.

"I guess in two weeks. Perhaps Thursday and Friday of that week. We should be able to do our business and spend one night and return the next day."

"I'd like to see some of the culture of Memphis with ya, lass," Kell said.

"We'll see. Remember what I told Naomi. Time and money are both in short supply. See you two at supper."

Chapter 20

Thou hast turned for me my mourning into dancing;
Thou hast put off my sackcloth and girded me with gladness.
To that end, my glory may sing praise to thee and not be silent.
Oh, Lord my God, I will give thanks to thee forever.
Psalm 30:11-12

The trip to Memphis was planned for the last week in October. After Hannah found the name of Ira Levenstein in Hugh Kincaid's papers and with the shortage of storage space at the gin, she needed to make a deal to sell the cotton as soon as she could. She had planned to take Sonny and Kell with her—well, Kell had refused to let them go alone—and she wanted to spend only one night away from Sanctuary Hill.

On Thursday afternoon, Hannah and Kell boarded the Memphis-Little Rock Train headed to Hopefield. Sonny had conveniently come down with a stomachache that morning. Hannah knew he feigned the pain, but clearly, he wanted no part of the business of selling cotton. At first, she almost insisted he come but stopped when she saw the fear in his eyes. In some ways, Sonny was growing up since taking on the role of farmer and landowner, yet his confidence in dealing with the adult business world was missing.

"Well, Hannah, we have a couple of hours to sit on these not-overly comfortable seats before we get to the end of the line. What are your plans?" Kell never intervened in her business. He'd made her that promise and would not go back on his word.

"I wish we'd had the morning train. We could have seen Mr. Levenstein and gotten back across the river by nightfall. We could have come home on the morning train."

"That would've been kinda miraculous, don't ya think?" Kell grinned at Hannah.

"I knew we couldn't do it, but staying overnight in a decent hotel costs a lot of money."

"And we will. We're staying in the best hotel in Memphis. I've stayed there a time or two. I'm gonna pay for our rooms because I want ya to enjoy a brief holiday away from work. The Gayoso is the place all travelers stay in Memphis, and they have a fine restaurant. I've found it's only a short walk to Mr. Levenstein's office. Some of the rooms overlook the Mississippi."

"Kell…"

"I'll brook no arguments from ya, lass. I can afford a couple of nice rooms and a good dinner for us."

Hannah shook her head in argument, but she knew it was useless. "I'll not argue."

"Good. Now let's talk about our adventure. I'd like to take ya dancin' after supper. Will ya honor me by acceptin' my invitation?"

"Dancing! How do you know there is a place to go dancing?"

"I think in a city the size of Memphis, there must be someplace we can go dancin'. Hannah, there are more than 30,000 people in Memphis." Hannah turned her face toward the window, trying to stop the conversation. "Don't ya like to dance?" Kell asked.

"I did when I was a girl. The only time I've danced since my coming-of-age party was at my wedding and the church social you took me to."

"Ya said ya had a good time that night. I'm thinkin' maybe ya need another."

"Yes, I think I'd enjoy an evening of music and dancing."

"Good. Hannah, ya work too hard. Ya forget that you are a young woman. The world has dealt ya a hard life. I admire your dedication to Naomi and Sonny, but you need to remember to be good to yourself."

"Please don't say nice things to me this morning. I don't want to cry in public."

"What did I say that should warrant tears?"

"I am strong enough to do what I must when I forget about myself. If I let myself go down that path, I'll get angry and frustrated that I've wound up here—caretaker to Naomi and Sonny. Then, I feel guilty when I think of them as an obligation. That's not the way you are supposed to feel about family."

"Hannah, you are so off-keel with your thinkin'. Love is much more than warm feelings and hugs. Love is an action you take every single day to keep that family safe and secure. Can't ya see how much love you pour out over your family every day?"

"Kell, please change the subject. I don't want to talk about life at Sanctuary Hill. What good will it do anyway? I can't change anything."

"No. I don't want to change the topic. What do you wanna change that is beyond your power?" Kell reached across the seat and took Hannah's hand.

She jerked her hand away and gestured wildly. "Everything—we wouldn't be so poor, Sonny would be a normal young man, and the Kincaids would be able to make their own living. There would be glass in our windows, and Naomi wouldn't be a widow, living in a derelict of her childhood home."

"What would you want for Hannah?" Kell tilted Hannah's head up to look into her eyes. "You've mentioned everyone but yourself."

"Kell, that's enough. This is too personal, and we are in public." Hannah moved as far from him as she could without leaving the seat.

"Hannah, there is one old man in the last seat, and he's asleep. Tell me what you want for Hannah."

"I want you to leave me alone. I wish we hadn't made this trip together. Please stop it."

"I told ya my entire miserable life story. Ya know about Claire and my brother Sean's betrayal of me. I told ya the ugly stories of my wasted years in Scotland. I want so verra much to know something of the real Hannah Kennedy. Why did ya marry Richard Murphy when ya dinna love him?"

Hannah brushed a tear from her lashes. "All I have ever wanted in my life is to belong—to feel a part of something, a family, a circle of friends, a person. That is what I wanted when I married Richard, even before in Maryland and in Washington."

"Do ya not belong in Naomi's family?"

"Naomi has never approved of me. No, not really. I'm the caretaker, meeting their needs and looking in from the outside."

"Have ya no sense of bein' loved by another, Hannah?"

"I did—a long time ago—my mother loved me. She made me feel that I belonged to her, but she died a very long time ago. My father wanted a son, and Mother died having that son."

"You've been alone for a long time, Hannah. I'm sorry for all those years you've been lonely."

"Well, now you know. Not one thing has changed. Is there not a more pleasant topic we can talk about?" Hannah dismissed Kell's interrogation with a flip of her bonnet ribbons and a smoothing of her skirt.

"Well, I think there may be one. Tonight, Mrs. Murphy, we are goin' to have an adventure in Memphis." Kell stood up and wildly gestured, resembling a tilting windmill. "When we get across on the ferry, we'll check into our fine hotel, and then we'll stroll along the beautiful bank of the Mississippi. The trees will be glorious by now. Then we'll sup in the elegant Gayoso dining room—then on to the ballroom to dance the night away—'til the wee hours of the mornin'."

"Kell, tomorrow, I have business to do."

"No respectable business opens before 9:00 a.m. We are goin' to enjoy this night, lass, or my name's not Kell Brody Kincaid." Hannah laughed at his antics.

℘

The trip to the hotel was short. The elegant portico of the building was easily seen from the river. Hannah was more than impressed when they arrived at the front door. A uniformed doorman opened the coach door and helped the ladies to the ground. He then collected the bags from the boot.

Kell slipped a coin in the hands of both the coachman and the doorman before he escorted Hannah into the grand entry hall. The hotel was as elegant as any Hannah had seen in Washington. With its plush seating and glittering chandeliers, the Gayoso was indeed a first-class hotel.

"Kell, this place will be very expensive. I think we should find a more moderate inn for tonight."

"I already told ya not to fret about the money. I am gonna take care of this. Ya need to enjoy a bit of the good things life has to offer to those who deserve them. You, my lady, work all the time. These few days, I expect ya to play as hard as ya work."

"But Kell…"

"I thought ya told me you'd not argue with me anymore. No more complaints today. Tomorrow at the cotton brokerage, ya can be in charge. Tonight, I am in charge. Now sit here on this lovely blue velvet settee. I'll get us rooms."

Hannah stopped arguing. She didn't know exactly why, but she did as Kell asked. She watched the smartly dressed people come and go through the beautifully decorated room. Even in October, beautiful flower arrangements graced the intricately carved tables. One impressive piece was made of cotton bolls and beautiful blue ribbons. The gilded framed artwork and the sconces along the wall gleamed in the gaslight.

After some time, Kell returned, followed by a liveried young man carrying their bags. "Are ya ready to go up and change, lass?"

"What are you planning for the evening? I am not sure I brought the right clothes."

"Ya can wear anything ya want, except those widow's weeds I saw ya stow in your bag. After supper, we're goin' to the theater. I wanted to go dancing, but that isn't until tomorrow."

"Tickets to the theater, Kell. That is too much."

"Not a problem. Our supper is part of our room cost. I can be the thrifty Scot when it's called for. See, ya worry for no reason."

When Kell opened the door to her room, she was almost speechless. A large glass door opened onto a wrought-iron balcony. From the vantage point, she could see the Mississippi flowing and lights from passing steamboats. The glinting light from the wharf cast waving orange ribbons on the water.

As she stood on the balcony looking out at the night scene, Kell walked up behind her and put his arms around her waist. "Isn't this a glorious night, Hannah? Hurry and change into the prettiest dress ya brought, and let's start our evenin'." Within fifteen minutes, Kell and

Hannah were descending the grand staircase and being seated in the elegant restaurant. The windows were opened to the gentle breeze that moved the brocade drapes in soft ripples. The chairs were upholstered in the same royal blue velvet that hung at the windows. Again, the gaslights on the walls flickered, creating a serene comforting atmosphere.

"What would ya like for supper, Hannah?"

"There is so much to choose from—things we haven't seen at Sanctuary Hill. I can't decide. What are you having, Kell?"

"I know what I'm not orderin'. Look at this entrée list. Calves' feet cooked in butter. Good grief! What kind of food is that?" Hannah shook her head and laughed at Kell once again. "Let me see…ah, there it is. I've been missin' it since I came from Scotland. I'm having roast mutton with boiled potatoes and carrots. My mother used to make such a feast on the Sabbath. No better meal for a Scottish family!"

"I've never eaten mutton, but I do love good roast beef. We've had so little beef since we got to Arkansas. I'll have that with mashed potatoes. And look, they have bread pudding for dessert. I want the bread pudding, please."

"And sir, make mine gooseberry pie."

Kell and Hannah spent nearly two hours eating the feast they'd ordered and talking about a world of nonsense. They avoided topics that could darken their mood. Hannah told Kell she hated the smell of buttermilk, and Kell admitted he couldn't stand to wear socks with holes in the toes.

At 9:00, they walked the two blocks to the theater. The minstrel show was lively, full of music, silly jokes, and antics. Hannah found herself laughing and laughing some more. When it ended, Kell took Hannah's arm and led her to the door.

"It's not so late, Hannah. Let's walk along the river."

"That would be a good way to end this fine evening. I don't remember when I've enjoyed an evening as much as this one."

They walked along the path near the river for some time. They didn't speak much. Kell held Hannah's elbow, and they strolled together. "Hannah, when ya laugh you're verra beautiful. I was watching ya tonight, at supper first and then at the minstrel show, and your face was aglow when ya were laughin'. I was enchanted."

"Was it? Tonight was certainly a new experience for me. When I was laughing and enjoying all the things we did, I forgot about everything. I was so caught up in the moment that I wasn't thinking about tomorrow or yesterday. I was just alive in the moment. I wish real life was like that."

"Ya have to let it be that way, Hannah."

"A person can't spend her life in a comedy show. You know that's not real. Tomorrow is business, and then we will travel back to the responsibilities and endless work. I don't want to think about it...just tonight. I'm going to pretend that laughter and a sense of well-being always fill my world."

♪

The next morning, Hannah took her sample box and met Kell for breakfast in the dining room, every bit as beautiful in the morning as it had been in the gaslight the night before. Yet for some reason the atmosphere she'd felt the previous night was missing. Regardless, the meal was every bit as filling as their supper the night before. Hannah especially enjoyed the ham, which she'd had rarely since she left Washington. Kell smacked his lips over the mulberry jelly he spooned onto his third biscuit. After their second cup of coffee, Kell rose, tipped the waiter, and led Hannah to the portico. of the Gayoso."Do ya wanna ride the three blocks and arrive in style, or should we walk the short distance? It's a bonny day outside, and the office is just around the corner, accordin' to the clerk."

"Let's walk."

"Ya look verra business-like today. I guess I'll put up with the widow's weeds for a while."

"Thank you. I do want to be taken seriously today."

"You will handle things in good order. I've got no doubt." Kell stopped at the two-story office building with the name Levenstein and Company etched on the door. He opened the door and allowed Hannah to take the lead from that point.

"Yes, ma'am. May I help you?" A squat, thin man with spectacles on the bridge of his nose greeted her.

"I am Hannah Murphy of Sanctuary Hill. I would like to speak with Mr. Ira Levenstein, please."

"May I ask your business with him?" the clerk asked.

"I want to show him a sample of our cotton that we can ship by the end of next month. He has represented Mr. Hugh Kincaid for many years. His grandson and I are farming the estate now."

"Yes, ma'am. Mr. Levenstein doesn't usually do business with women, but if you sit in the foyer, I will speak to him." The smartly dressed man rushed up the staircase to the second-floor office at the head of the steps.

Kell stood. "Well, Hannah, so far so good. Ya said something that struck home. That fella all but flew up those stairs."

Before Hannah had a chance to reply, Mr. Levenstein's office door upstairs flew open. A tall, bearded man in a beautifully tailored suit started down to greet Hannah.

"I am so happy to meet you, Mrs. Murphy. Every year I looked forward to brokering the crop from Sanctuary Hill. Hugh Kincaid and I were great friends. I certainly grieve his loss. But you can't be his daughter, Naomi. She must be at least….well, somewhat older than you are."

"I am Naomi Kincaid Murphy's daughter-in-law. I am the legal guardian of the estate owner, Benjamin, Jr. He is still a minor. Naomi's older son, Richard was my husband, and he died in the war."

"Please let me offer my condolences for your loss. How is Naomi? She was a beautiful child and a fetching young woman the last time I saw her."

"She is well. She is also widowed." Hannah wanted to cut short socializing and get to the business she'd come for. "I have brought you a sample of the crop that the foreman at the farm packed. He told me he always did it for Mr. Hugh."

"Well, I'd love to see what you've brought me, young woman." Hannah handed him the box.

"Your foreman did a fine job. This is exactly the way Hugh always presented his harvest. Let me take it upstairs where my partners and I can examine the lint. This will only take an hour or two. You and your friend may enjoy some shopping. You may find all kinds of goods you may not have back in St. Francis County."

"Do you think you will be finished before the train leaves going home this afternoon?" Hannah asked.

"My dear, I don't think there is a train goin' west today. You may check at the station." Mr. Levenstein returned to his office.

Hannah went back to the lobby of the office and found Kell sitting in a high-backed leather chair. He looked as if he belonged there, dressed as he was in his grey suit and blue cravat.

"Tell me, lass, why the frown? Did Levenstein give ya bad news?"

"No, Kell. He said he and his partners would examine the sample and have an answer in an hour or two."

248

"That gives us some time to go explorin' then." Kell picked up his hat and ushered Hannah to the door.

"Kell, we need to go to the train station to see if there is a train back home this afternoon. Mr. Levenstein said there's no westbound train on Friday. I didn't want to be away another day."

"Hannah, three days is not verra long. To set your mind at ease, we'll go ask." Levenstein was right. Hannah bought tickets for the next morning.

"I'm glad we have another night in Memphis. I'll bet we find something excitin' to fill our time. Let's see what's in all these shops here on this street." They spent more than two hours walking the length of the business district of Memphis. Hannah looked at many items but refused to buy any of the tempting things she found in the stores. What did she need with such finery in a country mercantile or in a cotton patch? Although Kell had saved her the cost of lodging, she couldn't let him do that a second night.

At 1:00, Kell and Hannah returned to Levenstein and Company. Hannah hoped the report would bring them a good price. Levenstein met them as they entered.

"Well, Mrs. Murphy, I see you are back. I don't believe I've met this gentleman."

He turned and offered his hand to Kell. "I'm Ira Levenstein, a long-time friend and business associate of Hugh Kincaid."

"How do you do, sir. I'm Kell Kincaid. Mr. Kincaid was my uncle. I am here as an escort to Mrs. Murphy."

"So nice to know both of you. Hugh was a fine man, and I counted myself lucky to be his friend. I am happy Mrs. Murphy has someone to protect her as she travels. Are you in the cotton trade, Mr. Kincaid?"

"No. I prefer raising cattle and horses to tillin' the soil, I'm afraid."

"Well, Mrs. Murphy, I want to tell you that your crop is fine indeed. The fiber is white, and the lint is long and strong. There will be no problem selling all ya have grown if it's all this quality."

"That is such welcome news, Mr. Levenstein. You see, Sanctuary Hill did not get through the war without considerable loss. This crop is important if we are to continue to live on the land."

"I feared as much. So many of my clients have lost nearly everything. Most have not produced a crop at all."

"That is certainly true. We have friends in St. Francis County that have not yet returned to their fields," Kell said.

"Mrs. Murphy, how much cotton can you bring me?" Mr. Levenstein asked.

"Marcus, the foreman, thinks we will have sixteen or seventeen bales when our second picking is finished. I am counting on fifteen."

"Not what I'm used to getting' from Sanctuary Hill, but I suppose it's a start. What kind of labor do you have?"

"We are using Mr. Hugh's former people. We have made tenant farm agreements with them," Hannah answered.

"Very sound business move, my dear. These people are a part of that land. It's home to them. They'll be loyal and will be good neighbors, too, I'll wager."

"I'm surprised to hear ya speak so well of former slaves, Mr. Levenstein," Kell said.

"Mr. Kincaid, I am a Jewish businessman. Jewish people are no strangers to slavery. Our history is a long treacherous path to independence. I'm blessed to be in this country where I can prosper by my own work."

"I understand. I have read of the struggles of the Israelites in the Old Testament. Thank you for settin' me straight." Kell offered his hand to the man.

"We Jews and you Christians have a common history. I'm glad to know you and call you friend, Kell Kincaid."

"Mr. Levenstein, can you tell me what the cotton will bring?" Hannah asked.

"Right now, the market is paying about sixteen cents a pound."

"Is that a fair price? I probably shouldn't tell you this, but I don't know what a fair market price is. This part of cotton growing is all new to me." Blushing, Hannah looked down into her gloved hands.

"Well, it's a fair price for good cotton, but I'm thinkin' your cotton is goin' for top price. I'll write a contract to buy all you've got for seventeen and a half cents a pound. I know my buyers in Liverpool will pay that price easily. We'll both make a good profit."

"Thank you, Mr. Levenstein. I am so pleased to do business with a good man." Hannah turned to Kell. "Did ya hear, Kell? We can surely cover the taxes and give the Kincaids some money for their share."

"Mr. Levenstein, we'll get our harvest here before the start of winter. We'll bring the bales to Hopefield. Your people can take it to your warehouses from there."

"Mr. Kincaid, cotton as fine as this will be sold long before it will need a warehouse to store it."

Hannah picked up her reticule and handed Kell his hat. "Thank you, again, Mr. Levenstein."

"I will have a contract ready for your signature later this afternoon. Why don't you and Kell come to my home tonight? My wife is throwing a sixteenth birthday party for our granddaughter. Won't be as grand as before the war, but we'll have good food, music, and dancing. Please come. I'll have the papers there for you."

Kell nodded toward Hannah. "We'll be there. Tell us where and when."

At 8:00, Kell and Hannah arrived at the impressive brick home of Ira Levenstein. The towering white pillars supported a second-story porch with elegant wrought iron railings. The house reminded Hannah of plantation mansions she'd seen in the countryside. Since the war, such houses were rare. The cotton brokerage business had made Mr. Levenstein a wealthy man, and he had not lost all his money in the war as so many Southern men had. Hannah was more than curious.

"Hannah, I'm glad ya changed from your widow's weeds back into your lovely blue dress. Ya look beautiful tonight. That smile makes up for the lack of jewelry that ladies usually wear."

"Thank you, kind sir." Hannah feigned a curtsy to Kell. "I'm afraid I left my precious jewels behind." She giggled at her silly remark. "I didn't have any except these gold earbobs my mother gave me and an engagement ring that I choose not to wear."

"I'm pleased to see ya so happy, lass. This is two days that I've been blessed with your smile."

"You've become a good friend, Kell. Better than I deserve as I've treated you as a cur much of our acquaintance. Thank you for making me come tonight."

Shortly after arriving, Kell and Hannah were introduced to Leah Levenstein, Ira's wife, and his granddaughter Esther. The event was Esther's first adult party, and she was giddy with the attention. The house was lit with candles and gas lights. Music filled every room. A huge dining table held all sorts of delicacies, many that Hannah had never tasted before. She bit into one flaky pastry and audibly reacted with 'Yummm.' Leah Levenstein was standing near and said, "Dear, those little crescents are called Rugelach. They are simply thin dough wrapped around something sweet, like jam or cinnamon and sugar. Esther has always loved them."

"I don't doubt that. They melt in your mouth. This is such a lovely party. Thank you for allowing us to share in the celebration."

"My dear, Mr. Hugh was a dear friend for all the years he lived in the Delta. We consider it an honor to do business with you and your family. You are always welcome in our home."

"You are so kind."

The conductor of the orchestra announced the beginning of the "Sweetheart Ball" where the honoree, Esther Levenstein, danced her first dance with her father, who in turn gave her hand to a young man of his choosing about halfway through the waltz. Her father then took his wife to the floor to finish the rest of the dance. Esther would then spend the rest of her evening dancing with all the eligible young men who were invited to her party. After the first dance, other couples joined her on the dance floor.

"When the next dance starts, will ya be my partner, Hannah Ruth?" She nodded.

The second song was 'The Jenny Lind Polka.' Hannah was familiar with this piece of music from her wedding. "Let's dance, lass." By the time the dance was finished, both Hannah and Kell were breathless and laughing. The next piece was 'The Prima Donna Waltz', a slow, sweet melody, that called for sweethearts to embrace each other. Hannah found herself relaxed and happy in Kell's arms. He guided her through the couples on the floor as if they'd danced together all their lives. Throughout the night, they danced the schottisches, polkas, and waltzes as they were played, only rarely taking the time to visit the dining table or to pick up a glass of punch.

At one point, the conductor announced the Jewish dance 'the Horah' would be performed. The people in the house who knew the folk dance took napkins and small scarves and formed a large circle. In the beginning, Esther was in the center of the circle, but after a time, her grandfather Ira pulled her into the ring and the dancing and shouting continued for some time. Hannah was enthralled in this celebration of joy she'd never witnessed before. Kell used the opportunity to get them a cup of punch. When the music stopped, a loud hoorah was heard across the room.

Then the last set for the evening began. "Put that cup down, Hannah. We've gotta join in this dance. It's the Royal Scot Quadrille. Back home we played it on the bagpipes, but this orchestra sounds mighty fine, too. Such a wonderful memory." Kell masterfully led her through the complicated steps of the dance from his homeland. "That makes this night almost perfect, lass." In the end, he picked Hannah up and twirled her around, leaving her breathless and laughing.

The conductor signaled the last dance. The music from the 'Cinderella Waltz' filled the room. Kell bowed to Hannah and pulled her close. They once again moved to the melody as if they were the only two people in the room. Hannah's awareness of Kell's firm touch on her waist increased as they danced. A sense of rightness and stability filled her. She wanted the music to go on. For this one night, her life seemed right. Things made sense for a time. She tilted her head up to look at Kell. When she caught his gaze, she trembled. *What is wrong with you, Hannah Ruth Kennedy? This is only a dance.*

The music stopped. Kell didn't release her. They stood face to face for what seemed an eternity. Then he took her hand and brought it to his lips. "I thank you, Lord, for this lovely night. And Hannah Ruth Kennedy, you are beautiful. This night has been the best of my life. Thank you for sharin' it with me."

Chapter 21

For the vile person will speak villainy, and in his heart work
iniquity...The instruments of the churl are evil; he deviseth wicked
devices to destroy the poor with lying words,
even when the needy speaketh right.
Isaiah 32:6A-7

Hannah found herself seated in the dining room of the Gayoso Hotel just as the clock in the foyer struck 8:00. She hadn't slept much—perhaps none would be closer to the truth. The weekend had been a whirlwind of wonderful happenings, but all the same, she felt unsettled. *How will I greet Kell when he comes in?* She hadn't intended to let her barriers down, but she had. She should have insisted that Sonny make the trip with them.

The immaculately clad waitress brought Hannah a cup of steaming coffee. As she picked up the spoon to stir in the cream, it slipped from her hand and flipped out of the coffee cup, splattering her pink and gray woolen bodice with brown stains. She pulled her napkin to blot the stain, and when she did, the fork and knife clattered to the floor.

"Ohhhh...." Frustration with her clumsy attempts to repair her clothes made her oblivious to what was going on around her.

"Mornin', lass. What's got ya so bothered on this fine fall mornin'?"

"Oh, nothing, except making a fool of myself."

"I don't see much permanent damage, Hannah. Just sit and let's eat a good breakfast before we go to the ferry."

"All right. I guess this coffee stain will fade some when it dries."

The waitress brought them hot biscuits, bacon and gravy, and scrambled eggs. When Hannah reached to get the butter, she found her hand on Kell's. The gentle touch again put Hannah on edge.

"Go ahead, Hannah. I'll wait."

"No. You have your knife ready. Take your butter and then I'll get some."

"Seems to be a lot of tension over a pat of butter, lass. Is something botherin' ya?" he asked her.

"Frankly, yes. I didn't sleep much last night. I didn't think I'd be—I'm not sure…Tarnation, Kell. What are we to make of last night?" Hannah knew her cheeks were the color of the morning glories at Sanctuary Hill's porch.

"I told ya. Yesterday was the best day of my life. I've had a wonderful three days here in this new place, makin' a new friend of Ira Levenstein and dancin' the night away with a beautiful woman. What do you make of it?"

Hannah laid her fork down on her plate. She stared at Kell across the table. "I don't know what to make of it. This was supposed to be a business trip."

"Ya did your business, and verra well, I might add. You assured all the Kincaids and Naomi and Sonny can keep their land. Ya more than covered the taxes."

"That's not what I mean. What happened between us?"

"Hannah, last night was two good friends enjoying each other's company. It doesn't have to mean anything more unless you want it to. We can go on bein' friends for a lifetime if that's what you decide."

"I'm glad you don't expect too much of me. I don't know what last night means to me. I did enjoy the evening—more than any time I can remember. Thank you for your thoughtfulness and care for me and my family."

"Hannah, they are my family, too. God tells us to wait expectantly when we don't know where our next turn will be. I'm a patient man. I wait upon the Lord. I pray someday you will find that peace, too. Now eat this fine breakfast. We've a ferry to catch."

By 10:00, they'd found their seat on the westbound Memphis-Little Rock railroad. In a little more than three hours, they'd be back in St. Francis County, back to the real life that awaited.

On the trip back, Kell and Hannah spent a good bit of time calculating what the crop would bring. Hannah had the signed contract securely packed away in her bag.

"Kell, help me do the math. What are we likely to have once everyone is paid?"

"Let me see. Marcus said we're gonna have seventeen bales of cotton ready to ship by the end of the month."

"He may have been a bit optimistic. Let's count on fifteen bales," Hannah replied.

"Have ya a scrap of paper in your reticule, ma'am?"

"I do. Here, and a pencil."

"Let's figure…fifteen bales times 500 pounds a bale. That's a lot of cotton." Kell scratched out the figures. Then he did it a second time. "Hannah Ruth, ya did well, lass! That's more'n $1,300.00."

"Well, let's not forget much of it is already spoken for. Reuben Wilson has earned his share. We'll owe him about 150.00 dollars. I still don't have a clear idea of how much taxes I will have to pay. I've seen past years, but some of those were war years. I need to go to Madison and find out how much the taxes are."

"There is nothin' to fear, lass. You know they aren't gonna be $1,000. I know you are going to be able to make the repairs on the house and have money to put in next year's crop."

"I am relieved, Kell. I can't wait to tell Sonny and Naomi about the crop getting top dollar. I guess all the hard work has paid off."

"Yes, ya worked verra hard. I am proud of your effort. But Hannah, ya don't need to forget what a blessin' came to ya from the Lord. Just the right amount of rain and sunshine. Rich soil that lay fallow for two years. The Kincaids stayed loyal to the land."

"Yes, Kell, you are right. Luck played no role in this harvest. We have been truly blessed."

♮

Before supper time, Hannah and Kell drove up to Sanctuary Hill. No one came to greet them when they called out from the drive.

"Where is everyone," Hannah asked. She went into the house and found the cookstove cold and no fires laid up in the fireplace to chase the chill of the October night. She returned to the buggy. They drove toward the quarters and found no one in any of the cabins, and when they passed the shed, Pal was missing, too.

"This is verra strange. Even if everyone was in the fields, Naomi or Mom Bec would be here gettin' supper ready."

"Kell, I'm frightened. Something has happened…something bad. I can feel it," Hannah said.

"Let's drive down the road toward my place. Maybe we'll meet someone who knows what is goin' on." Kell pulled the reigns to point Graystoke toward his farm. As they crossed the creek, they began to smell smoke. As they got past the thicket of brush surrounding the creek, they saw threads of smoke drifting toward the cloudy sky. Kell slapped the reins on Graystoke's back, hurrying his pace toward home.

As they turned the bend in the road, the burned-out rubble of what had been Kell's barn came into view.

"Oh, no! This can't be." Hannah jumped from the buggy and ran toward Sonny and the Kincaids, who were flapping wet burlap on small blazes that erupted here and there. "What happened, Marcus? Is anyone hurt?" Hannah cried out.

"It was the night riders, Miss Hannah. In the wee hours this mornin', Lijah found 'em. He was patrollin' like Mr. Kell told us. He saw a pack of eight or nine of those hooded riders fling torches into Mr. Kell's barn. Lijah, he hid under the porch 'til they rode off."

"Is he all right, Marcus?" Kell asked.

"Got burned some. He ran into that burnin' barn to save some of the cotton. He pulled out three full cotton sacks, but the fire got too hot. He got his hands and arms burnt bad."

"Marcus, do you know for sure it was the night riders?" Hannah asked.

"No doubt, Miss Hannah. The same ugly robes and hoods, a couple of those same horses we saw that night they came for me. We found an almost burned-out cigar butt, too, just like y'all found when the cabin got burnt."

Hannah dropped to the ground. Sobs racked her body at the loss. Kell bent to pick her up, but he found trying to pick her up in her hysterical state to be nearly impossible. "Hannah, stop. You're makin' things no better." She didn't respond to his soothing.

Sonny walked up, clutching his mother. "Mr. Kell, make Hannah stop. She's scarin' my mama."

"Sonny, take your mother back to the house. She looks near exhaustion. I'll take care of Hannah. We will be home later. Can you do that?"

"Yes, I can. I'll do it right now. Come on with me, Mama."

Instead of trying to stop Hannah's breakdown, he picked her up and carried her to the buggy. "Hannah…Hannah Ruth, listen to me! You stay right here. I'm gonna check on the Kincaids and post some security. Then I'll take ya home. Do you hear me?" He got no response, but she did what he said. Kell then posted Samuel at the barn to put down any more blazes that sprang up. He sent Lucas and his oldest son to the Miller's farm to protect the already baled cotton, praying the night riders hadn't already gotten to it. "Lucas, come by the big house and get my rifle. The baled cotton needs to be secured if it is still safe."

"Yes, sir." Lucas and David began to run toward the house.

"Lijah, you come down to the house and let me treat those burns." Kell motioned toward the back of the buggy.

"I'm sorry I couldn't save the cotton, Mr. Kell. I wish I coulda got a few more sacks."

"Lijah, you did the best ya were able. That's all anyone could ask. Ya did us a great service here last night. Thank you."

"Marcus, will you and Abraham stand watch until midnight? I'll come then and take over for ya. I need to see to Miss Hannah."

"We will, Mr. Kell. But no sense watching over the barn. Ain't nothing left except that two hundred pounds that Lijah drug out in those sacks."

"How much do ya figure we lost, Marcus?" Kell asked.

"Was at least three or four bales in the barn. We took all we could haul to the gin on Friday, but we still had quite a lot in there."

"That's a serious loss. Do ya know if the cotton at the gin is safe?"

"Shataka was there this mornin'. Nothin' out of sorts then. We been real hushed about our deal with the Wilson folks."

"I want Lucas to stay there tonight. I'm sendin' a rifle with him. Our main task now is to keep that crop safe." Kell patted Marcus on the back. "Thank ya for takin' charge here today, Marcus. You did a fine job."

"I try to take care of our land, Mr. Kell."

Kell found Hannah calm by the time he returned to the buggy. "I'll drive us home now, lass. Are ya all right?"

"Yes." This was the most lifeless word Kell had ever heard from Hannah.

"All's not lost. Most of the crop is still safe. It's mostly baled and stored at the gin."

"Whatever. It's more of the same."

"Hannah, ya frighten me with your tone. Sanctuary Hill is safe. God will see us through this loss."

"I don't want to hear any more of your optimistic dribble. I've labored like a field hand for seven months. What will there be to show for it—nothing. Just another major disappointment, like every other part of my life."

"Hannah, you'll feel better in the mornin'. After some rest, you'll see that things are gonna work out."

"I should have known better—spending three days living a fairy tale with you in Memphis had to end in a nightmare. And it has. Please just get me back to the house so I can think. Somehow, I must get things back under my control. I can't live like this expecting help from the outside, only to be beaten down again."

"Hannah, everyone has bad times, but we can bear it because we know the Comforter is with us every step of the way." Kell pleaded with Hannah, hoping she would listen.

"I don't want to be preached to anymore. All I want is a soft bed and a pillow."

When Kell stopped at the porch, Hannah hurriedly stepped down and ran inside without another word. For the first time since he'd known her, Kell was afraid for Hannah. That fighting spirit he'd sensed at the first sight of her had gone. Perhaps she felt so defeated that she would give in and sell Sanctuary Hill so they could return to the city. He didn't want her to go.

ᴓ

The following morning, Hannah feigned sleep when Sonny knocked at her bedroom door. "Hannah, are ya ready to leave for church? Mama said don't let's be late."

She didn't answer. When he peeked in from the doorway, Hannah appeared to be asleep—her eyes still shut. He pulled the door almost closed, trying not to awaken her.

When he returned to the kitchen, Naomi stood next to Kell. "Did Hannah say she'd be down soon?"

No, Mama. She's still asleep. I don't think she's goin' with us today."

"Why, of course, she is. Go up and wake her."

Kell put his arm out to stop Sonny's return upstairs. "No, Cousin Naomi. It's best to let her sleep. She is tryin' to deal with the loss. She'll be all right once we put it all down on paper, and she can see that we've cleared the debts. When she knows Sanctuary Hill is safe, she will return to herself. Are ya ready to leave now?"

"Yes, we are. Sonny has the wagon hitched, and I've got our lunch basket. I've made plenty for you too, Kell," Naomi added.

"You're always thinkin' of others, dear cousin, but I'm gonna stay around close. With all the Kincaids off for the Sabbath, except Lucas, I don't feel good about leavin' the place unprotected. Tell Brother Sam. He'll understand. Tell him about the night riders burnin' my barn, too."

"Kell, you hate to miss worship," Naomi replied.

"I can worship right here in the beauty of the Delta. Don't fret about me—I'll spend some time with the Lord today."

Hannah didn't make an appearance until noon had come and gone. She'd gotten up shortly after Sonny made his morning visit, but she couldn't bring herself to get dressed for the day. She sat at the small table near her window and spent more than two hours trying to make sense of her financial plans that were now lost because of the arson attack by the unholy mob.

No matter how much she rearranged and changed the amount that the Kincaids deserved, the sale of the thirteen bales of cotton would not provide enough money to do the things that she'd planned to do. The purchase of extra mules and plows was a necessity if they were to increase their production. With their present equipment, they would have to farm the same sixty acres again. They had to replace the windows before the worst part of winter reached them.

Perhaps she could forget the Kincaids' payment on the land this year and give them a percentage of what was left after the taxes. That would let them buy things they'd need for the coming winter. Something had to be left over to pay Sonny and Aaron. She feared another year of a scarce diet and no new shoes or clothing, except for Sonny who had outgrown his work boots before the harvest was over. He didn't seem to mind going barefooted, but the owner of the land shouldn't have to go without shoes.

Hannah went back to her bed and pulled the blankets around her. She felt warm tracks down her face. As much as she'd sworn that she wouldn't give in to this brutal act, she felt defeated. The hurt was so much worse because she'd come home only yesterday with the vivid fairy tale memories of Memphis and an evening with Kell—feelings so deep. *What am I feeling? It doesn't matter. The reality is that all the hard work was for nothing. I am no more secure today than I was in April when I first came to this wreck of a house.*

Three loud raps on the door broke her thinking. "Hannah, I know you're not asleep at this late hour. I want ya to come downstairs and eat dinner with me. I'll give ya ten minutes to dress. If ya don't come, I'll be back." Kell's gruff voice told her she had no choice in the matter.

Hannah pulled her day wrapper over her nightgown, pulled her unbrushed hair into a long queue with a ribbon, and shuffled her slipper-clad feet down the stairs. With about a minute to spare, she appeared in the kitchen.

"Don't ya look lovely, lass?" Sarcasm dripped from his words.

"You didn't say I had to dress for company. I'm here." Hannah sat in her usual place at the table. "What's for dinner?"

"Not much. Mom Bec didn't leave many leftovers. Probably forgot in all the confusion yesterday. I've got a bit of cheese and some canned berries. There is part of a loaf of good bread and a couple of pieces of ham. It'll do until suppertime."

"I'm not hungry anyway," she said. "Maybe I could drink a cup of coffee,"

"Hannah, we need to talk through this thing. It's not the end of the world. First, we will report this to the law. Arson is a crime. That barn belonged to me."

"Well, I think you should report it, for all the good it will do," Hannah sighed.

"If the county sheriff won't do his job, I think we need to go to the governor. If that pack of hoodlums knows we've contacted him, they'll not be so brazen." Kell continued, "The Arkansas State Assembly has been gettin' serious complaints about the vigilante activity in this area of the state. The governor has been pushin' local law to clamp down, using threats of martial law. I don't know if the local bullies are under suspicion, but they're doin' some of the same kinds of damage."

"Even if we go to the governor, how does that help our situation? I've gone over and over the figures. When it's all done, we'll be in the same place we were when we started last April."

"That's not so, Hannah. Think of all the blessings that have come to you this year."

"Let me see. I learned to wrap my palms in rags to prevent blisters when I chop cotton. I now can pick cotton as well as any five-year-old. Oh, and best of all, I have learned to scold down a troop of hooded, masked reprobates who gave me a black eye. I have certainly had a banner year."

Kell took Hannah by her shoulders and shook her. "Stop it, Hannah. Just yesterday on the train, you said you'd been blessed by the Lord with a fine crop and a signed contract for more than most." He let her go and tilted her chin up so he could see her eyes. "I'm not believin' ya, lass. You're actin' so defeated. This is not the girl I saw screamin' and fightin' against all odds that first day I saw ya on the lea."

"I'm afraid that silly girl has grown up now. That Hannah believed she could change the world around her and make a decent life. Maybe even find some good for herself. She knows better now."

"Listen to yourself, Hannah. You are not a quitter."

"Kell, it doesn't make any difference now. I'm no better off than I was when I left Washington to come here. Sanctuary Hill—that name seems ridiculous today. I don't feel safe. I can't. It's all a lie."

"You are so wrong. If you take a few days to get past the shock of yesterday, you'll see the cup is not half-empty but half-full. God will take care of us. He always does if we let him. Don't ya see the promise?"

"I know you believe He takes care of you. I'm pretty sure that I'm the unknown stepchild. I worked so hard to make things better for Sonny

265

and Naomi. I inherited the Kincaids when I came here. No matter what I do…. never mind. Yesterday was another loss. Frankly, I'm not sure I can deal with another."

"Let me help ya, lass? You've worked yourself into my heart."

"No, I didn't. You don't know me at all. Please just let me be. I've all I can deal with right now. I can't be responsible for you, too."

Hannah fled from the kitchen and returned to her room. She sought solace in sleep. She didn't care that the sun had yet to reach the western horizon. She wouldn't make her way back downstairs until the morning when she had to go to the mercantile for work.

Chapter 22

Ye are not in the flesh, but in the Spirit, if so that the Spirit of God dwell in you. Now if any man have not the Spirit of Christ, he is none of His. And if Christ is in you, the body is dead because of sin, but the spirit liveth because of righteousness.
Romans 8:9-10

Hannah had barely opened the mercantile before Mary Lee Naylor walked through the door. She carried her newly adopted son, wrapped snuggly against the nip in the early fall air. "Hannah, sweet friend, I am so sad about what happened at Sanctuary Hill. You must be devastated with all the labor you put into that crop."

"I appreciate your concern, Mary Lee."

"Did the sheriff say anything about how the fire started?

"We are going to Madison this afternoon to file a complaint. With yesterday being Sunday, we doubted we would be able to see him."

"Bless your heart. You are being so brave." Before Mary Lee got out her words, Rachel Miller, the wife of the man who was ginning the cotton, rushed through the door. She didn't say a word before she threw her arms around Hannah.

"Goodness gracious, Hannah. I am surprised to see you at work today. That attack on your crop was a low deed. Are you and your folks all right?" Rachel finally took a deep breath. "Ahhh, me. You are so brave to deal with all this."

"We are all right. One of the Kincaid family was burned badly on his hands and arms. Lijah pulled about three sacks full of cotton out of the barn before the flames got so bad that he couldn't go in again. He probably saved more than two hundred pounds of cotton from the fire."

"Well, you can rest assured that the rest of your crop is safe. Reuben has set watch at the gin. We will do our part in keeping the crop safe for you."

"Rachel, it was kind of you to come here to bring me word. Kell and Aaron will work with your husband until we can ship it to market."

"Well, Reuben says that can probably happen within two weeks. With the added help we've had from Lijah and his son, the ginnin' and balin' is all but done. Thank the Lord, more damage wasn't done."

"Thank you, Rachel."

The door opened again and two more ladies from the church came over to tell Hannah of their concern. Throughout the morning, a steady stream of townsmen and Community Church members appeared. Some did buy an item or two, but clearly, their main purpose was to show Hannah that she didn't stand without support in the community.

About noon, Kell arrived as he'd told her. Instead of taking Hannah to the sheriff, he'd brought a deputy sheriff to Linden, making it unnecessary for her to close the store. "Hannah, this is Henry Chandler. He's the deputy sheriff assigned to this part of St. Francis County. I ran into him this mornin' on his way to look into our arson problem."

"Afternoon, ma'am. Are you the legal owner of Sanctuary Hill?" the deputy asked.

"Mr. Chandler, you know good and well that no woman legally owns property in Arkansas," Hannah answered.

"Well, Mr. Kincaid, why in Sam hill did ya bring me over here? I've got enough to keep me busy without wasting my time talkin' to a woman."

"Mr. Deputy Sheriff, the arson was on my land. My barn was burned to ashes. But this is just the last of several attacks on Mrs. Murphy and her family at Sanctuary Hill," Kell answered.

"Why didn't anyone report the problems over this way?" The deputy looked around the store, spotted a barrel of crackers, and picked up a couple. He walked over to the stove and sat on an upturned barrel.

"We left a message for the sheriff before. We're reporting the arson now. To tell you the truth, on one of the last visits I had from the night riders, their leader laughed at me when I told him that I'd go to the sheriff. He said, 'See if that will do any good.' Was he suggesting that you wouldn't protect us?"

"Who said that?" Cracker bits flew from his mouth. "I do my job to take care of all the people of St. Francis County."

Hannah put her hands on her hips. She took a couple of steps toward the man. "The night riders all laughed."

The deputy stood and jutted his chin out. "Well, it's no laughin' matter to me. Why are you making this complaint if you don't own the land?"

"I am the legal guardian of Benjamin Murphy, the owner of Sanctuary Hill. He is a minor."

"A minor, ya say. Does he know about these attacks?"

"He's seen every one of them. Sonny recognized the horses the men rode. He also identified Narvel Tangent as the leader of the gang," Hannah said.

"Now wait a minute, Mrs. Murphy. You got any proof? Mr. Tangent is a well-respected man in this part of the county."

The sheriff stood to confront Hannah. Kell stepped between them. "Deputy, Hannah was struck in the face by the leader of that pack of hoodlums. He spoke to her, and she knew his voice."

"Well, I'll file the report and do some investigatin' to see if I can find any support for your accusation."

"We expect you to do that, Deputy. You might start by looking for a man who smokes cigars. We've found tossed-out butts at two different fires, one at the cabin and a second one last Saturday at the site where Kell's barn was destroyed, along with at least three bales of harvested cotton."

"Mrs. Murphy, why are ya linkin' the two fires together? Coulda been caused by lightning or a lamp someone left burnin'," the deputy said.

"Kell's barn was full of cotton from Sanctuary Hill. Narvel Tangent doesn't want us to make a profit this year. He's already told us he wants the land. One of the tenant farmers saw the band of eight to ten masked, robed riders throw torches into the barn."

"Is this tenant a white man? I need to talk to him."

"Does it matter? An eyewitness is an eyewitness. He'll be available when you come to see the damage. I'll be glad to take ya to my place now if you're ready to go," Kell offered.

"I will get back to it in a couple of days. I've got a more pressing task to do today." The deputy couldn't get out of the mercantile fast enough.

Hannah stood at the door when he reached to open it. "Deputy Chandler, I don't get the sense that you are overly concerned about this arson. A citizen lost his barn. We lost a sizeable amount of Sanctuary Hill's harvest. If you don't follow through with this matter, I will go to the governor and seek his help."

"Now wait a minute, ma'am. I said I'd look into this problem. I will. The last thing any of our citizens need right now is to be put under martial law. We don't want that here. Give me a couple of days. I will get back to ya."

"I'll be patient for about a week. I expect to hear from you before the end of that time. I would like to see Little Rock. I've not had the opportunity to go there." Hannah opened the door and the man rushed through. She had no doubt he was headed to Madison to seek the help of the sheriff.

Before the man was out of earshot, peals of laughter rang across the mercantile. Kell and Brother Sam, who had come in the back door, were wiping tears from their faces from the fit of laughter they were unable to control.

"Lass, I was so worried about ya on Saturday and then that talk we had yesterday afternoon. I hardly slept thinkin' that unholy mob had broken your spirit. Now I see ya just needed a wee bit of time to gather that endless strength ya have hidden in that wee frame of yours."

"Yes, indeed Hannah. I see the strength of David in you. You stand for what is right. Thank the Lord for His care." Sam Naylor added.

"Oh, hush, you two. I don't have a clue what either of you is babbling about. If I had any real strength or authority, I wouldn't let so many vile things happen to me."

Brother Naylor pulled the young woman near. "Dearest Hannah, don't ya know that terrible things happen to all of us? We're not to blame, but it's how we deal with those disasters that we have to account for. Look at what happened to little Sam's parents, both taken by the influenza. He didn't deserve to lose them, but Mary Lee and I have been blessed to step in and make a good life for the boy.

Something good will come from this loss too, Hannah. God always takes care of those who believe in Him. I know you have been reading the scripture. Spend a little time in the eighth chapter of Romans. When ya get to the 28th verse, read it more than once. This verse has carried me over many trials in my days." He turned toward the counter. "I've gotta get home. Mary Lee told me she forgot to get the gingham she ordered to make the baby's quilt."

"Hannah, I'm so proud of ya. Ya dinna quit," Kell said. "You just pushed that deputy into doin' his job. I believe he will now."

"I guess I did. I'll get you that fabric, Sam."

"By the way, we missed ya at church yesterday. Considerin' what happened, you needed some rest. Is there anything the church can do for you?"

"Not right now, Brother Sam. For the time being, we will just finish the ginning and get what's left of the harvest to market."

"Kell, I've talked to the elders of the church. As soon as you can get the lumber you need, we'll have a barn-raisin' at your place. You're gonna need a barn before winter."

"Thanks. I hadn't thought that far ahead, but you're right. I'll have animals to care for through the worst part of the winter."

"I'll see you two next Sunday. Hannah, we'll talk about that Romans passage at Bible study."

"Afternoon, Sam." Kell closed the door behind his friend and turned the sign to read CLOSED. "Let's head home, Hannah. Ya must be tired." Kell picked up the till of cash from the counter, and he and Hannah walked to the buggy he'd brought.

Leaves had turned. The trees dripped with red, orange, brown, and deeper green. Hannah rested her head against the back of the seat as Kell turned Graystoke toward Sanctuary Hill. "Can't you take the long way home, please? I want to talk a while." Hannah reached out and laid her hand on Kell's.

"If that's what ya want. Won't ya be too cold?"

"No. I've some things that I need to say to you."

At the crossroad, Kell took the left turn, which led to the Miller's land, instead of continuing toward Sanctuary Hill. "Ya never cease to amaze me, lass. I'd decided you'd said your piece to me last evenin' before supper."

"That's the first thing, Kell. Please forgive me. I said some hurtful things to you. You have never done anything to earn my wrath. I should never have struck out at you as I did."

"It's all well, Hannah. I know you're disappointed with the loss. Seeing so much work lost because of another man's greed—how can you not feel defeated?"

"Losing the money is hard. I had such grand plans for that money…more mules, plows, restoring the house, get back into full production to secure an income. I suppose I was dreaming too big."

"Lass, it doesn't have to come all at once. I know ya told me not to preach to ya, but I want ya to know that the Lord is gonna take care of his own ."

"You say that like I know what that means."

"I wish ya did, darlin'. I wish ya did. Just the knowing would bring you so much peace until you can get the land back to the prosperous state it was in before the war."

"Kell, why did all the people from the church come to the store today? Some of them bought a few things, but most of them just came and talked to me—asked me if I was all right. They had to know we weren't even home when the fire started."

"That is just the way of a church family. They wanted ya to know they care about what has happened to ya. You are part of that body, whether you know it or not."

"I didn't even go to church yesterday. I was sulking in my room all day. I guess I was angry with God because he had not kept all my efforts from harm. I don't belong to the church."

"In their minds, ya do. They care about ya."

"This morning surprised me. I don't think I've ever been treated that way before."

"I am happy that it happened then. Is there more ya have on your mind?" Kell gently flapped the reins against the tall gray horse. As they turned the bend, they saw the Miller's barn and behind it the gin. "Let's stop and look at the progress we've got here." He pulled up to the door and tied the horse to the handle. "Hey, Reuben, ya around?"

Lucas Kincaid came around the corner of the gin. "Afternoon, Mr. Kell, Miss Hannah. Come to see the work we doin'?"

"Yes we are, Lucas, and to have a word with Reuben. Is he around?"

"Mr. Miller is by the press. We nearly finished all our cotton. Maybe got three more bales. Probably ready by Thursday."

"That is wonderful news, Lucas." Hannah broke into the first smile she'd had since seeing the burned-out barn.

"Let me help ya down, Hannah, and ya can watch Reuben bale cotton." Kell and Hannah walked to the back of the gin, where they found a large wood structure with a huge screw mounted in the center of the roof. A heavy metal plate was attached to the bottom. An assortment of various-sized cogs was attached to the screw, and a long rail was attached to a mule that walked in circles around the wooden structure. The plate compressed the clean, white lint into a large rectangle.

Lucas said, "We keep doing this over and over 'til the bale measures 'bout fifty-five inches bulging of about thirty-three inches. Then that bale weighs 'bout five hundred pounds."

"Lucas, what is bulging?" Hannah found the entire process fascinating, never having seen a bale of cotton produced before.

"Why, it's where the cotton puffs out from the twine. This is mighty fine cotton, Miss Hannah. I hope ya got a fair price for it."

A shadow passed over Hannah's face, and her smile disappeared.

"Are you all right, Hannah?" Reuben Miller asked.

"Yes, I am fine. I think we got a good price for the crop. We sold the lot for top market price this year."

"That is fine news. From what I've heard among the few planters here that have already sold their crops many of them got less than about ten cents a pound due to poor quality."

"But Reuben, ya know we had another visit from the night riders on Saturday. They burned my barn with about three bales of cotton we had ready to bale. Total loss. Lijah brought you the last two hundred pounds this mornin'."

"I know, Kell. When he told Rachel and me this mornin', she couldn't wait to get to town to see about Hannah."

"Yes, she did come early this morning. I appreciate her caring. That was a bit of a trip for her."

"Yeah, but she felt better when she got home, and besides she did get that half pound of sugar she'd been needin' for a few days." Kell and Reuben laughed. "Leave it to my practical wife. Don't know what I'd do without her."

"Where are the bales ready to ship, Reuben?' Kell asked.

"I put 'em in the barn and piled up hay to hide them. I already had all my winter feed put up, so it was an easy task. I'm glad we don't have many more to hide, though. The loft's about full."

I'll be sending over some guards to help, Reuben. They'll be a couple of extra guns around until we are ready to ship. I don't want you to lose your barn as I did. Hannah will be able to make do with the rest. I'm sorry your portion will be smaller than I'd told ya. You've been a true friend to us in this time of need. I won't be forgettin'."

"I am pleased to have the income. Since I didn't grow a crop, I didn't know where the money would come from to pay my taxes. Now I can do that and still have a bit left over to plant a crop next year. If you can grow cotton at Sanctuary Hill, I imagine I can do it here. You've got a good plan in place. Think I'll copy it."

"Thank you, Reuben. We will get this cotton off your hands next week." Hannah brushed his cheek with a kiss. "Please tell Rachel what her visit meant to me. I'll not forget her friendship."

As Hannah stepped into the buggy, Kell called back to Reuben, "So long, friend. See ya later tonight."

"Kell, we are secure here if ya want the night off."

"No. I'll be back. Sleeping on those bales ain't so bad." He stepped into the rig and pulled Graystoke back toward Sanctuary Hill. "Did our little excursion help reassure ya, lass?"

"I believed you when you told me, but it was nice to see all those bales waiting for us to ship them off."

"Hannah, we can ship them by train, but the shipping cost would cut into your profit. Besides, protecting the bales will be difficult since we wouldn't be with the cotton. I think we should borrow another wagon and some mules. I know some of the churchmen will help me drive the crop to Hopefield to Mr. Levenstein's warehouse. We could make the trip in three or four days."

"Do you think the night riders would attack the train?"

"Hannah, all I'm sayin' is that I think goin' over land is best. You are the one in charge at Sanctuary Hill, though, so the decision is yours."

"I want the crop delivered safely. If you think overland is best, I agree." Hannah pulled her shawl closer around her neck and face. As the sun approached the horizon, the night air caused her to shiver.

"I was afraid you'd get cold. May I put my arm around ya, just to help block the wind."

"Yes, dear Kinsman, you may put your arm around me, though I hardly know why you would."

"I already told ya. I'll not be askin' again until I know ya want to hear it."

"That's the last thing I wanted to say to you, Kell. I am ashamed of the way I pushed away yesterday. The three days we spent together in Memphis were the best days of my life. I felt so alive, seeing interesting places, being treated as a grown woman at that lovely hotel, and getting the respect of the brokers who worked with Mr. Levenstein.

"You were a competent businesswoman during all your dealings at the hotel and the brokerage. No one would ever know you'd never handled a business transaction before. I was verra proud to be your escort."

"Thank you, dear friend. You were so much more. Being with you helped me remain confident that I could do what I needed to do. You have always tried to encourage me, and yet I continued to bark at you instead of letting you know that I needed someone to believe in me. I am always so unsure of my decisions."

"No reason for that, Hannah. You've a good head for business, and you make good decisions for Sonny and Naomi, even though they fight you when they disagree. You always stand your ground because you know you have to."

"But Kell, I feel like everything is so out of my control."

"You are just too young to know it. Life is always that way, lass. We have no say of how we were born into it, whether we'd live with want or plenty, or what wrongs of others we will have to endure."

"But you don't let the crises take you down. On Saturday night, I felt my world had come to an end. I wanted to give up. I am so tired of endless obligations. So much so that when a friend wants to share in some support, I crawl into my dark cave where I know I am safe."

"Are ya safe in there alone, Hannah?"

"I don't know. It's familiar, and I've hidden there so much that I seem to fall back into the pit whenever my life doesn't go as I wish."

Graystoke trotted on for some time. Shortly, they reached the crossroad when Kell turned toward Sanctuary Hill. Hannah shivered even more as they rode facing the wind. Kell pulled her into his arms and held her close.

"Don't you have anything to say about what I just told you, Kell?"

"I would love to tell ya several things, but ya have forbidden me to preach to ya. I've already told ya that you've won my heart. Hannah Ruth, I know I love ya. I want for ya the thing I have that makes me whole. I canna be a man without the spirit I've been given. I don't even want to try. Love is the essence of God, and He lets us live in that love if we will let Him."

"I wish I knew what you are talking about." These words came almost as a plea—soft and muzzled by the warmth of Kell's coat.

"What did ya say?"

"Nothing, Kell. I am afraid to feel close to anyone. All my life, those who were supposed to care for me didn't want to or didn't know how. Not since my mother died have I felt a sense of belonging. I know it's me.

I'm the broken one. I don't think I deserve to feel that I am cherished or accepted beyond what I can do for others. Thank you for caring enough to try to reach me."

"I'll not stop until the Lord shows me I've failed. You are precious, lass. A good woman is more precious than jewels. That is in the book of Proverbs if you're still trying to study the word."

Chapter 23

*Every man also to whom God hath given riches and wealth, and
hath given him power to eat thereof, and to take his portions, and to
rejoice in his labors; this is a gift of God.*
Ecclesiastes 5:19

October slowly melded into November, and the weather became
much colder. The boarded-up windows and the three oiled paper
windows in the kitchen did little to buffer the cold. Yet Hannah didn't
let the problems push her back into the fretful, agitated state she'd felt
following the fire. Kell gradually became Hannah's confidant and
advisor concerning decisions she had to make for the farm. After he
returned from Hopefield with a check for the cotton crop, Hannah
found herself asking him something every day to provide some
solution for a member of the Sanctuary Hill family.

The check from Levenstein's Brokerage totaled $1,137.50. They
had sold thirteen bales of first-grade cotton. Hannah decided to forget
the plans she'd made when she'd thought the crop would yield more
than $1400. The first money went to Reuben Miller. The fee of
$135.00 seemed a small payment for the work it took to gin and bale
the harvest. Hannah and Kell then went to Madison to pay the taxes.

The tax collector scoured the books looking for overdue taxes.
Finally, he concluded that Sanctuary Hill had no outstanding taxes, a
rarity for people in the county. "Mrs. Murphy, I was sure that you

owed back taxes. There's been a couple of men here asking if the property was up for sale on the delinquent tax list."

"Mr. Hugh Kincaid paid the taxes before his death. His will shows that he had cleared all taxes. We have the paperwork if you need it." Hannah was determined that no additional charges would be added to their bill.

"No need, ma'am. We got a record here that the taxes are up to date. This year's tax bill is $160.18."

"Are you sure you have calculated the tax correctly? Most of that land isn't even in production."

"Mrs. Murphy, don't get upset. Maybe I can do business with your husband there."

"Mr. Curtis, Mr. Kincaid isn't my husband. I am the guardian of the owner of this land. You can deal with me."

"Ma'am, please. See here is how it breaks down. Your cotton land is taxed at .149 per acre for a total of $95.40. The forest land adds another $49.78, and you have claimed one mule. That totals to $160.18. I know the tax bill is high, but with the cost of the war still bein' settled, the county and the state need money."

"And you think taking it from the people who are having trouble keeping food on the table for their families is the way to pay the debt?" Hannah said.

"You don't have to pay the taxes. The property probably won't go on the delinquent list for six months. 'Course then anyone could buy the whole place for the overdue taxes."

"Never mind." Hannah shoved the money across the counter. "Write me a receipt."

On the first day of November, Hannah called the tenants to gather in the parlor of Sanctuary Hill. She'd asked Mom Bec to bake a special dessert and prepare enough coffee for them to celebrate the end of a long harvest season.

"Our hard labor has been blessed, folks. We got top dollar for our crop. I am going to give you your share of our earnings. Then you can decide if you want to continue our arrangement for the next year. Marcus, you have been an excellent overseer for us. You know how to grow cotton, and you worked as hard as anyone else in the field besides. Because of your extra responsibilities, you deserve more pay. I wish it was more, but perhaps next year we'll have a bigger crop." Hannah handed Marcus $185.00. She then handed $160.40 to Mom Bec and Rose, Lucas, Aaron, and Sonny.

"Lijah, you and your family came to us when most of our work was finished for the year. But since you came, you have worked hard and even saved us about two hundred pounds of cotton that would have burned with the barn. We are glad you decided to come back home to Sanctuary Hill. You have earned your wages." Hannah handed him $30.00. "If you and your family want to stay on, I will work with you as I have with Lucas, Marcus, Mom Bec, Rose, and Aaron. We all work together, plant together, and share the profit. In return, I will give you forty acres and a cabin that you can buy with your earnings."

"Hannah, that didn't leave none for you and Kell," Sonny said.

"Sonny, we have the farm share, and you have your portion. The tenant farmers will be able to pay their first year's land payment. With that, you will be able to take care of your mama and me."

"Will that be enough, Miss Hannah? I mean, can y'all make do with only that little money?" Lucas asked.

"I believe we can do quite well. Of course, the first thing is your decision of whether to stay or go out and look for a better life."

Lijah Kincaid was the first to answer. "Miss Hannah, I already seen they ain't no better life up North. If'n ya let me buy my own place here, I be proud to stay."

"Ya know I ain't goin' nowhere," Mom Bec said. "Sanctuary Hill been my home for more'n fifty years. How much money do ya need us to pay for our farm?"

"You're priceless. If you give Sonny $10.00 each year, in six years you will own your farm."

"In six years, we be owners!" Shataka began to dance around and raised her hands. "I never dreamed I could have my own land—even before my babies are growed. Thank ya, Mr. Sonny, Miss Naomi, and Miss Hannah! Thank ya, Jesus." Everyone in the room laughed and clapped their hands at Shataka's prancing and praising.

"Okay, everyone, before we celebrate the good things that happened this year. I want all of you tenants to sit down with Marcus, the foreman, and Sonny, the owner of Sanctuary Hill, and decide how much money you want to set aside to make next year's crop."

Kell spoke up before the group broke up. "Folks, remember, we don't talk about our business arrangement with Miss Hannah and Mr. Sonny outside the family. We don't want any more trouble with the night riders."

"Yes, sir, we all know, and we don't talk to folks about our good fortune. We know we have been blessed." Marcus assured Kell that the agreement was safe within the Kincaid family.

A serious discussion among the tenants began. Kell and Hannah left the group and found a quiet place on the porch swing. The November day with its westerly wind was warm enough to be comfortable

283

"Hannah, ya never cease to amaze me, lass," Kell said. "Ya split the crop money evenly. Don't ya know that's not the way planters share their profit?"

"Look, my friend, these people are not sharecroppers. They are tenant farmers. Their work is their payment to this farm. Sonny has his portion that came from our fifteen acres. I saved one portion for things that I know will come up. With Sonny's share, we will make do here until there is another crop."

"Will ya have enough to finish the repairs on the house and replace the windows? The cold will be so much worse in January and February than it is now."

"I know. I am ordering glass on Monday. In two weeks, I'll have Aaron begin replacing all the broken windows. You told me yourself that things would be all right if I'd just have a little faith. I am trying to learn what that means."

"I am relieved to hear that. What about heat?"

"Well, there are fireplaces in two rooms downstairs and two upstairs. We get good heat from the cookstove. I guess we will just have to keep it going all the time. I was hoping that Aaron, Sonny, and you would look at the fireplaces and make sure that they will allow us to build fires for the night times."

"Pardon, Miss Hannah. This is what we decided to do." Marcus spoke as the foreman of Sanctuary Hill. "Each family agreed to put back $25 into next year's crop. With that money, maybe we can find a couple of mules and maybe another plow. If we can do that, we 'spect we can grow twenty acres of cotton on the farms next year, and maybe even fifty here on Mr. Sonny's land. That gives us more money for the next year's crop." Marcus shuffled from foot to foot during his entire report, and his smile stretched from ear to ear. "Ain't this a fine plan, Miss Hannah?" The words tumbled out of his mouth.

"If the tenants agree, it's a wonderful plan. Do you agree, Sonny?" Hannah waited for his reply.

"I think Marcus made us a good plan. We can grow more cotton next year because we have more help. That's what we're gonna do." Hannah smiled at her brother-in-law, who seemed more adult every day.

"Yes, sir, Sonny. The land belongs to you," Hannah said. "We will try. Well, everyone, now that the business is done, let's go eat that excellent blackberry cobbler Mom Bec has made for us. I know the coffee will be good and hot."

ϕ

The Kincaids returned to the quarters about suppertime. Mom Bec had already helped Naomi prepare a filling meal for her family. Shortly after stuffing themselves on the excellent fried rabbit, stewed potatoes, string beans, and cornbread, Naomi said good night and Aaron and Sonny disappeared out the back door with plans to check on the livestock in Kell's pasture. With the setting of the sun, the evening was too cold to return to the swing, but Kell didn't want the almost perfect day to end. "Come over here and sit with me on the sofa, Hannah. This fire feels real fine tonight."

"Yes, it is nice."

"Ya have no idea what this day means to the Kincaids, do ya, lass?" Kell asked.

"They must be pleased to have some profit to show for all the work. They seemed quite happy."

"Oh, so much more than that. I'd wager none of them ever had more than a dollar to call their own. You handed each family a fortune and even more, you gave them the right to decide how to use that money."

"Kell, it's only a part of what they earned. I wish it could have been more."

"Did ya not see the pride on Marcus's face when he handed over that money to you to keep for next year's crop? Never before have these people had a choice, and they made a good decision."

"I believe they did."

"I'm so proud of you, lass. You do a fine job managing this farm and the store. I've no worry about ya being capable of caring for my kinsmen. Uncle Hugh made a good call namin' ya Sonny's guardian."

"I don't know that I'm so proud of myself. That two weeks after the fire, I let everyone down. Sonny was sick about me, and Naomi thought I was going to leave them behind and run back to Maryland. I truly felt defeated. I knew I'd let everyone down. I nearly quit."

"Ya thought about it, but I knew you wouldn't. The loss was a terrible shock. I saw how hard ya worked and overcame stumbling blocks time and again. That barn fire was nearly too much. I knew ya would not quit. It's not in your nature."

"I railed against God at first. I was so angry that all my efforts had been for nothing. My plans all fell apart. I asked myself why he'd let such a useless tragedy fall on me."

"Do ya still feel that way?"

"No. After a couple of weeks when some of the shock faded, I saw that God hadn't caused the loss. Evil people do terrible things. I know that. One night I read in Romans that God works toward the good in all things for those who love Him. I know I've done very little in my life to show that I love Him. Until I came here and met you and Sam Naylor, I didn't know anything about Him."

"Hannah, many people in the world are just like that. When someone has no understandin' of the scripture or have never been under the teachin' of a Godly preacher, like Brother Sam, they've not had the chance to know about the blessings of his ways."

"I still don't know much. I want to continue to learn. Even in those two dark weeks, I didn't quit reading my Bible, but so much of it didn't mean anything to me. But I have learned one thing. Our living for the next year is secure. I know that miracle has more to do with God's work than anything I have done."

"Don't be sellin' yourself short, Hannah. I'd say what ya did today was very much you bein' an instrument for God's will. Reading your Bible is a good step forward, and you are grateful for His blessin'."

"Yes, I am grateful. I've often thought I needed to offer my gratitude for things that have happened to me, but I never knew where to direct the thanks. For now, I'm going to offer them to the Lord. I am pretty sure that is where it belongs."

"So wise and so beautiful, my dearest Hannah."

"Thank you, Kell. I am happy here in Arkansas finally. It took some time for me to see but this place is home."

"After so short a time? Ya lived in Maryland nearly all your life."

"I lived under my father's shadow. I never made decisions about anything important. I never made a difference when I lived at Green Meadow. Papa was the master. Even my marriage to Richard he orchestrated. Yes, I like being my own person. Things I do here are important, and I make a difference."

"That ya do Lass. Ya certainly made a huge difference today. Ya worked verra hard. I'm glad we're goin' to take off Saturday and Sunday this week. I'm happy ya allowed me to take ya to the Harvest Festival at the Community Church. I can hardly wait for the dance."

"I'm happy, too. But now we need to get down to our Bible study for the night."

Hannah looked forward to the community festival on Saturday. Since she'd met most of the people around Linden, either at the Community Church or doing business in the mercantile, she'd gradually begun to belong. Spending an evening dancing with Kell would also be a welcome diversion from her daily routine at the store. She'd not forgotten the wonderful evening they'd danced away at the Levensteins' home in Memphis.

She took special care to arrange her hair in loose curls, tumbling down her back. Mom Bec had helped her use a hot iron to make several ringlets that framed her face. She tied her mane with a midnight blue ribbon, nearly the same color as her winter ballgown that she planned to wear. This dress was less ornate and lacy than the one she wore to the first community dance, but it was her favorite, because the cut of the gown accentuated her shape so well.

When Kell called for her at 6:00, he'd already placed hot bricks on the floor of the buggy and had brought a thick quilt to stave off the autumn cold. Once again, he'd made sure that Naomi would make her way to the church with Sonny earlier. This was an easy task this time because Naomi was the chairman of the festival committee. The time alone with Hannah was the thing that Kell looked forward to the most. They lived under the same roof, but they had so little time alone together.

"Ya look beautiful, lass. You will be the belle of the ball."

"I didn't overdress again, did I?"

"Not a bit. Ya look like the prosperous businesswoman that ya are!" Kell drawled.

"Don't be ridiculous. I've hardly a cent to my name."

"Ya have treasures more than you'll ever know."

"Kell, do you think the night riders will take advantage of our being away tonight?"

"Don't ya fret one minute. We are still watchin'. Even with the crops no longer in danger, our people are on the alert."

"You have done so well defending our home. I hope you realize how much happier Naomi, Sonny, and I are now that you are with us. We are safe now."

"And next week, we'll all be warmer since Aaron can begin replacin' all those missin' window panes!"

Hannah pushed her elbow into Kell's ribs. "You make a joke about everything. I was trying to say thank you."

"Lass, I'm not jokin'. It'll be fine not needin' to go to bed to get warm enough to feel my toes."

"I guess that's true. All the upstairs windows are intact. And we do have two fireplaces upstairs."

"And heat rises...Thank the Lord!" They laughed for the first time that night.

Hannah pointed toward the sky. "Look, Kell, it's a harvest moon. How beautiful this night is. I think that from now on this will be my favorite part of the year. The labor of the summer is over, the worries are temporarily set aside, and nature is so beautiful as the leaves turn to red, orange, gold, and brown."

"Tis a beautiful site I see." Kell was looking only at Hannah. "This time of year Arkansas reminds me of Scotland."

"Are you homesick, Kell?"

"At times. I'd like to know how fares my parents and my three brothers—yes, even Sean. I wonder if all is well at home."

"Do you want to go back to Scotland?"

"Not to stay. I'd love to visit again someday. Maybe take my bairns back to meet my clan."

"Bairns? Kell, I am afraid my Gaelic's not good enough to know what you mean." Hannah laughed.

"My offspring. I aim to have several."

"Perhaps you should start by finding yourself a wife, don't you think?" Hannah teased.

"My plans are already in the makin', lass. The Lord's workin' everything out to His purpose. I'm a patient man."

When they arrived at the Community Church, music already drifted outside. The lights glowed in every window. Laughter told them the evening was off to a fine start.

"Let's go have another memorable evenin', Hannah." He lifted her to the ground and led the way to the front door. They no sooner walked inside when Sam Naylor pulled them into a square. He took their coats, and they skipped in time to the music and the calls for the first square dance.

By the time the dance ended, everyone was laughing and out of breath. Reuben Wilson had moved in the wrong direction, and their square found itself at a total loss of how to get back in step with the caller.

"I'm sorry, folks, but I've never been able to tell my right from my left," Reuben said. "Maybe I'd better stick to waltzing."

Kell slapped him on the back. "What? And let us all miss the fun of laughin' at ya, man? There's no fun in ya quittin', my friend."

The next dance was a reel. Nearly every person in the church building paired up to participate in the lively dance. Sonny had taken Molly as his partner. His smile and shining eyes told all his mood.

"You know, Kell, I don't think Sonny has ever danced before. He'd never had the nerve to ask a girl to dance with him," Hannah whispered.

"He's grown up a lot this year since y'all came to Arkansas. He works like an adult, and he does some tasks better than anyone else. He's even made some minor decisions with Marcus's approval."

"That's wonderful. Maybe he will overcome some of his…problem—in time." Hannah said.

"Don't mistake me, Hannah. I respect and love Naomi verra much, but I believe part of Sonny's problem is Naomi's constant motherin'. He acts more grown up when he's away from her."

"Kell, Sonny nearly died from the Scarlet Fever when he was ten."

"But don't ya see, that's all the more excuse for Naomi to wrap him in a mother's love to keep the world out."

"I've never thought about that."

"Well, I don't want ya thinkin' about it tonight. I want ya to relax, eat, dance, laugh, and enjoy the company and the evenin'." Kell took Hannah's hands and sashayed her to the end of the lane and back home again.

At the end of the reel, the little band took a short break. Everyone congregated around the tables to pick up any variety of homemade sweets, or to fill a cup with warm apple cider. When the music resumed, the tempo changed. The waltzes and polkas called for partners to dance together. Kell claimed Hannah for the first waltz.

She was happy to be in Kell's arms again. He had a way of holding her, and she never doubted what the next step would be. The firm touch of his hand on her waist felt natural as if it had always belonged there. And as he'd done in Memphis, he held her gaze with his deep blue eyes—almost as if some force melded them together. Hannah loved dancing with Kell.

Several men from the community asked Hannah to dance. She always agreed because that was the purpose of a community dance, to mingle and socialize with everyone. After all, she saw Kell every day since they lived under the same roof. Nevertheless, after three or four dances, Kell always reclaimed Hannah for a dance before he'd relinquished her to another set of men.

At the intermission, Naomi approached Kell and Hannah. She was concerned, bordering on frantic. "Kell, Hannah, have either of you seen Sonny in the last hour? I've looked around and checked the porch, but he's not to be found."

"Mother Naomi, I'm sure he's just outside with some of the young men," Hannah replied. "You know they don't like to talk with the "old folks.""

"But Sonny doesn't have his coat. It's still on the peg where I hung it." Naomi pointed to the back wall.

"All right, cousin. You go and get a cup of cider. I'll go find Sonny. I'm sure he's not far."

"Thank you, Kell. I'm relieved having you to find my boy." She walked toward the table in the back of the room.

"Wanna take a brief walk outside with me, Hannah?" Kell asked.

"I'd enjoy a walk in the fresh air. Let me get my coat."

They walked arm and arm down the steps and toward the tree line where other young men stood chewing a bit of tobacco. "Any of you lads seen Sonny Murphy around here?" Kell asked.

"About ten minutes ago, he was walking with Molly down toward the grove where the preacher put those benches." One boy answered. "Three or four other love birds went down that way, too." The boys in the stag line laughed.

"Kell, do you think Sonny would take Molly down to the grove to…to…well, would he?"

"He's a young man, Hannah. I had that talk with him. I'm pretty sure that he understands how to treat a young lady. When I explained how people have children, he said he kinda already knew. He told me he'd never do that with any girl unless they were married."

"Thank goodness, he understands."

"But he is curious about girls, and he asked me if kissin' is bad."

"For goodness sake, Kell, what did you tell him?"

"Hannah, some things Sonny and I just need to keep between us. I can assure ya, though, that Sonny knows that any more than kissin' is wrong. He will keep his word. That's the kind of person Sonny is."

"I'll take your word on that. Thank you for stepping in where Sonny's father couldn't. Where do you think he is?"

"Since he's not down here in the kissin' grove, I'd suppose he's returned to the church to get some more of those sweets and hot cider. It is a wee bit cold out here. Are you ready to go back?"

"No. We can walk a bit more if you want. The band is just now tuning up for the last set."

"Are ya sure ya aren't chilled, Hannah?"

"Maybe a touch, but I like the night. The sky is so clear. The moon is like a beacon, and I could never count all the stars."

Kell put his arms around Hannah. "Lass, you're a romantic at heart. Ya praise the night while you shiver to death." He pulled her even nearer as they walked to the edge of the churchyard. The owls in a nearby tree hooted their goodnight, and the rustling of the leaves made a melody, though unseen in the ebony night. The grove was empty when they reached Brother Sam's bench. The lovebirds had already returned to the dance. Kell and Hannah sat on the carved bench.

"Are ya havin' a good time, lass?"

"I am. Since I've gotten to know these people, I feel more at home here. I've found that I truly enjoy dancing with you. You are an excellent partner, Kell Kincaid."

"Thank ya for those kind words. The credit goes to my mother. She insisted that all her sons knew how to dance with a lady. It's easy when the lady is someone ya want to hold anyway."

"I'll take that as a compliment."

"You've no sense of how beautiful you are tonight, have ya?"

"I don't think much about it, but it's nice to hear you say it." Hannah was glad for the night. Kell could not see the blush in her cheeks.

"Since our trip to Memphis, Hannah, I've thought of little else. I think about how fine, strong, and capable you are, yet so beautiful and kind. I've never known any woman like you."

"Thank you. To be honest, I took special pains with my hair and dress tonight. I hoped we might enjoy another evening together like we did in Memphis."

Kell pulled Hannah close. "Your words have given me a wellspring of hope, Hannah Ruth." He looked into her eyes, and he saw the moonlight reflected there. Hannah did not avert her gaze. The strength in his arms as he held her brought the same intense pleasure she felt when they waltzed together. Suddenly Kell stood and drew Hannah next to him. He lowered his lips to meet hers. Hannah clung to him, as she returned the passion of his embrace.

When he stepped back, Kell placed his arm around Hannah's' waist, and they began to walk back toward the church. Neither seemed to have words at that moment. Just before they stepped into the light, Kell stopped, tilted Hannah's face toward him, and kissed her once again. Slowly, tenderly—almost reverently. "Hannah, save my salvation, ya've given me the greatest gift of my life."

She looked into his beautiful eyes. "I wish I had the words to tell you what I feel—perhaps in a day or two. I believe this night will be a memory far greater than our Memphis adventure."

Chapter 24

*Verily, verily I say unto you, he that receiveth whomsoever I
send, receiveth me; and he that receiveth me,
receiveth Him that sent me.*
John 13:20

Hannah and Kell's change in behavior didn't go unnoticed at home or in the community. Not that they announced their truce, but the little things that happened daily could not be overlooked. However, neither of them purposefully did anything to suggest that they had moved beyond the friendly antagonism they displayed since April.

Kell made sure he did not step over the line that Hannah had laid out. He knew she would continue in her role as guardian to his kinsman. He also did not press the romance he wanted to blossom. He knew that slow and steady was the only way he could hope to win Hannah's acceptance of his suit.

The last Friday afternoon in November, about two weeks following the Harvest Festival, Sam Naylor met Kell as he was leaving the local blacksmith's shop. "Hey there, Kell. Got time to come by the house for a cup of coffee? Seems like ages since we've had any time to talk." Sam matched his stride to Kell's, and they walked the short distance toward the parsonage. "Mary Lee has gone to the church to the quilting bee this afternoon. They're making a quilt for the new family that moved over to the west of your place."

"That's a great gesture. Those folks are from Indiana, I think. I met Matthew Garland in the mercantile one afternoon. Seems to be a nice fella."

"Yes, they are from the North. I've invited them to church."

"Sam, ya didn't ask me over here to talk about the quilting bee. What did ya want to talk to me about?" Kell asked. "Can't be that ya just missed me. We were at Bible class just last Sunday."

"I know that, and you did a fine job leadin' that class too."

"Thanks. I enjoy the study time."

"You seem to be enjoyin' it a lot more since Hannah has become so active. She's a good student."

"She's studied the gospel already. We have finished all four of those books and now she is reading Romans."

"That's not an easy book to discern for one not well-versed in the Bible."

"I know that, but she is eager to learn. We read and study together almost every evenin' after supper. Great way to pass the time since it is too cold to do much outside." Kell took the cup of coffee offered to him. "Thanks. This hot coffee will be good on this cold day."

"What were ya doin' at the blacksmith's shop?"

"Graystoke had a loose shoe. Thought I'd take care of it before time to drive Hannah home after she closes the mercantile at five."

"You two seem to have buried the hatchet. Am I imaginin' that?" Sam asked.

"There never was a hatchet, Sam. Hannah has had some bad times in her life. She's very cautious about lettin' people get close. Right now, we're gettin' along verra well. We had some time to get to know each other lately. Our trip to Memphis opened the way for us to talk. Ya shoulda seen the way she handled those cotton brokers. She's a born businesswoman."

"I wasn't aware you were looking for a business partner."

"Hush up, brother. The whole family had a couple of bad weeks right after the barn burnin'. Hannah took that especially hard."

"I still can't believe that bunch of hoodlums made such a vicious attack on two widowed women. Her hopes had to be dashed for a spell."

"I was worried for the first couple of weeks. I feared she might quit and sell the farmland and return to Maryland. But Hannah is a sensible woman. After she took some time to consider and evaluate what she had left to work with, she accepted the loss and began to make plans for the next growin' season."

"Thank the Lord."

"Sam, did ya know that she divided the profit from the cotton sales in equal parts to all who worked to make the crop? She even let them decide how much to put toward next season's crop."

"You're not serious! Doesn't she know that she's supposed to keep the owner's share before she splits the remaining money? She'll never return Sanctuary Hill to its former state like that."

"She has no plans to become a plantation mistress. She gave Sonny his portion from the cotton grown on what will remain Sanctuary Hill. She told him it was his job to take care of his mother and her." Kell's smile spoke of his admiration for Hannah's wisdom.

"It's done a world of good for all the Kincaid people, and Sonny most of all."

"Lord bless her. I pray things work out well."

"I'm sure of it. Hannah has been asking questions about my faith and why I believe so strongly. We talk about church quite a bit."

"Do you talk about anything else?"

"Of course, we do. We talk about work, family, our pasts—we've gotten to be good friends, finally." Kell looked down at the toe of his boot and bent to wipe the dust from it.

"To tell you the truth, my friend, the people of our community are abuzz about the new couple in town. I'm beginning to think there is more there than gossip." Sam laughed at the pink in Kell's cheeks.

"Don't ya get carried away. I will tell ya confidentially—I would take Hannah to wife in a heartbeat, but she's not ready for that. She's all I've ever wanted in a woman to complete me. She's clever, kind, educated, bonnie, self-sufficient—maybe too much so."

"Seems like she'd make a great wife for you, Kell Kincaid."

"That would be a dream come true when she comes to terms with her stand with the Lord. I think she wants to believe, but she's strugglin'. Her past life has left scars that make trust and surrender very difficult for her. I'm prayin' about it."

"If you'll allow, I will too," Sam said.

"Sam, please keep our talk between the two of us. Too many good Samaritans could only drive a wedge between us."

"I understand."

"I've gotta run. It's near five now. Hannah will need a ride home from work. We didn't have enough money from the harvest to buy another horse. Thankfully, we did get a good deal on a mule for next season's plowing. We only spent $60.00."

"If the weather holds, next week the churchmen are gonna start buildin' that new barn at your place. We think that with a whole crew working, we can make the barn up weather-tight in three days."

"What a blessing to have a church family. How do people live without one?" Kell tipped his hat as he left his friend's home.

He drove the buggy across the street from the blacksmith's shop to the mercantile. Hannah was just putting the closed sign in the window and locking the door. "Good evenin', lass. Ya ready to head home?"

"Hello, Kell. I am more than ready. I guess it's because the Christmas holidays are not far away, people have come in all day, ordering items. That's good because I'll only have two more deliveries before Christmas. Tonight, I am worn to a frazzle. What kept you occupied all day?"

"Well, this mornin' I had lumber delivered for the new barn. Sam has arranged a barn raising for next week. I talked with Sonny. He's worried about Pal. He told me that the horse is too old to work so hard. I told him about the new mule you bargained to get. He was relieved. Then I brought Graystoke to town for a shoe repair. And I had a verra nice visit with Sam. Been a good day."

"Seems so, and you've been busy."

"Yes, but the best part of it just started. I get to help ya into this rig and now we'll talk all the way home." Kell took one of Hannah's hands. "Where are your gloves, lass?"

"I loaned my mittens to Naomi. She told me that Sonny was driving her over to the Garland place for tea. She doesn't do well with the cold."

They were quiet for the better part of the way home. Kell sighed. "Kell, are you sleeping well?"

"Yes, lass. That sigh was just the sound of complete contentment—our being together. I don't feel cold or hunger, just contentment."

"Oh, you." At the crossroads, Hannah asked, "What did you and Sam talk about today?"

"Not much. Just friends passin' a time. He did tell me he liked the Bible lesson I taught Sunday afternoon. I told him we are trying to read Romans."

"I agree. You are a good teacher. I learn a lot from you."

"Good to know."

"Did ya know Naomi is planning a Christmas social at Sanctuary Hill?"

Kell shook his head. "She's not said a word to me."

"Since Aaron now has all the windows replaced, and we are doing a fairly good job of heating, she wants to go back to the old traditions of Sanctuary Hill. In his day, her papa gave a lavish party every year and the following week, he hosted a special party for his people."

"Bless her heart. I'm glad she has decided to revive some of the family celebrations. She has the lower level of the house lookin' verra nice. Hannah, you will have to keep a rein on her though. Even though y'all have lived through a lean year, I fear my cousin still doesn't know the value of a dollar."

"I don't look forward to that job. Overseeing the cost will have to take priority over her need to have an extravagant party. She has already asked to make one change. She wants the back corner room that we've used to store things redone into a formal dining room. Sonny says he can make a large table, but he doesn't know about making eight chairs from scratch. That may be a problem."

"If that's the only problem we have to face, so be it!" Laughter drifted through the air as they turned into the drive home.

$$\phi$$

Preparing for the upcoming Christmas celebration took the forefront of all activities at Sanctuary Hill. Naomi worked endless hours, trying to put her childhood home back as she remembered it. Some scars of the occupation by the Confederate and Union troops couldn't be covered up, but she seemed to work miracles, regardless. A cedar wreath with a red bow covered a hole knocked in the wall near the kitchen window. The replacement of portraits of her mother and father covered areas above the buffet in the dining room that had been ruined with some kind of black tar-like substance. She rearranged furniture and mended, washed and rehung drapes, some from her Washington home and some she'd found in trunks in the attic. The front parlor and the new dining room were hardly recognizable.

"Mother Naomi, you've worked miracles in your house. How did you manage such a change?" Hannah ran her fingers across a gleaming lamp globe near the window.

"Mom Bec and I just went up to the attic and went through all the old crates and trunks stored up there. So many nice things Papa had bought over the years, stored away. Some had never been used at all."

"Everything looks lovely and new. I know we didn't have enough money to buy all these things."

"I guess I needed to learn a lesson about money. I never thought about it much before the war. With lots of cleaning, polishing, and mending we were able to bring parts of our house back to the way it was before the war happened. I think Sanctuary Hill will be ready to receive our visitors on December 18. Papa always held his Christmas party on the Friday before Christmas. On that day, we will renew the Sanctuary Hill tradition of Christmas hospitality."

"What do you need me to do to help get ready?"

"Yes, Hannah. I need you to order oranges, apples, and peppermint candy to make our gift baskets for our people. Papa always had Christmas gifts for them—much more than that, but we could still get fresh fruit and candy and nuts. We always gave them those things."

"I'll get those things ordered this week."

At supper, Kell and Sonny sat and listened to all that Naomi and Hannah had planned. "Golly, Mama. We're gonna have a real party right here in our house. Are we gonna invite everyone to come?"

"Of course, we'll invite all the best families from around the county. We always did."

"Well, does that include our church family?" Kell inquired.

"Certainly, most of them will come…the Naylors, and my friends from before I left St. Francis County."

A frown replaced the usual pleasant demeanor on Kell's face. "Naomi, we need to invite all the church folks. Times have changed since the war—not much of a planter culture here anymore. Most of us are more yeoman than master. We're all farmers trying to make a livin'…even us."

"You're right, Kell. The church has been very good to us. This week they have nearly finished the barn, so we have a place to shelter our animals. Let's invite the entire church, and the Millers and the Garlands," Hannah said.

"But Hannah, those Garland people are Northerners. They don't know our ways."

"Seems to be the perfect reason to have them here. They will be able to learn about Southern hospitality and the life we live in the South. They are nice people, and we do business with them at the mercantile," Hannah answered.

"I suppose the more people we have, the more we'll enjoy the evening. Do you think we will have enough room?" Naomi twisted the handkerchief she held.

"Cousin, has this lovely old house shrunk since ya left it?" Kell's teasing lightened her mood.

"I'm being silly. I know it. I am just trying to be the mistress of this house, but right now, I'm tired. I'm afraid it's going to be a very cold night." Naomi walked to her bedroom and called back. "Hannah, you will see about the fire in the kitchen stove, won't you? It does provide us with the best heat."

"I'll do it Hannah," Sonny said. "I'm gonna go out to the shed to work on Mama's chairs. That table was easy to build, but those chairs are takin' some real figurin'. I think I can do it though."

Hannah and Kell remained alone at the kitchen table. The quiet was comfortable. Kell reached across the corner of the table and took Hannah's hand. "What would ya like for Christmas, Hannah Ruth Murphy?"

"I've not even thought about Christmas gifts. I guess I should. We have less than a month now."

"I know the date, lassie. What I don't know is do ya have a dream you'd like to come true?"

"Kell, I haven't dreamed about anything except keeping this family together in a long time."

"And ya have done that. Things are secure and in place for another year. It's time for ya to decide what it is that you want in this life."

"What do I want? No one has ever asked me that before. My father told me what I was to do. He chose my school. He picked any companions I ever had—mostly governesses who were supposed to take the place of my mother. When I was old enough to enter the adult world, he selected the three men he deemed eligible for his daughter's hand. I didn't know any of them.

"You know more about me than Richard ever did. After we were married, Richard took my father's place. He told me what he liked me to wear, who we would socialize with, and what social circles we would be a part of. We'd been married less than nine months when he joined the cavalry. He died at Shiloh in Tennessee."

"I'm sorry no one has ever asked you about your dreams. Every one of God's children deserves a dream and the chance to have it come true."

"Truthfully, I've always wanted to feel I belong somewhere—that I am a part of something worthwhile. I think I've felt that more here in Arkansas than anywhere I've ever lived."

"Why is that, Hannah?"

"I know if I work hard enough, I can make life possible for Sonny and Naomi. That gives me a purpose, I suppose. I know they need me, so I am worthwhile for them—here and now."

"That is why you fight so hard to do things by yourself."

"I suppose that's true. If I can take care of things by myself, I don't have to depend on anyone else—I don't run the risk of being disappointed or hurt."

"Are ya not setting yourself up for a life of loneliness if you never let anyone help ya carry the load? And what about those tragedies that take everything out of your control?"

"Kell, this talk is getting far too serious, and I don't want to delve into all the things of my past. I don't know why I've told you all I have. Talk doesn't change circumstances."

"Talk does help lift the weight off your shoulders, doesn't it?" Kell looked Hannah squarely in the face. She turned her head, feeling uncomfortable for the first time since they'd sat down. She didn't speak for a time, but she could feel that Kell was still looking at her.

"Yes." She lifted her face to meet Kell's gaze. "I like talking with you. You are the only person I've ever said these things to. Thanks for listening."

"I'll always listen, lass."

"I never feel like you're judging me or suggesting I was a terrible daughter to my father. I always thought he was disappointed with me. You never make me feel as if I were a bad wife. I know I was. Richard found me to be nothing he wanted. I don't know why he asked me to marry him."

"Lass, you don't have to tell me anything ya don't want to tell."

"Richard never kissed me the way you did at the Harvest Festival. In public, he would place a chaste kiss on my cheek or brush my lips if he thought someone may notice." Kell continued to hold Hannah's hand. He didn't comment on anything she said. "On the few occasions when Richard felt obligated to make love, he was brutal. I always felt he was angry with me, but I didn't know why. I could count those horrible occasions on one hand. He knew his mother wanted grandchildren. I was glad when he enlisted because he was gone from Maryland. I saw him only once after Father Ben moved us to Washington."

"Again, lass, I am sorry for what ya have lived through."

"The worst part was that he told his mother I refused him our bed, and that was why I had no child. That was not true, Kell. I hated Richard's brutal love-making, but I thought that was just the way of things. I never refused him his right as my husband. Naomi does blame me that Richard has no heir."

"I doubt it, Hannah. She loves ya, lass. She may have spoken in anger to ya, but she knows you are her kin—ready to do whatever it takes to care for her and her son."

"Whatever she believes, I cannot tell her my story. She loves her son, and I'll not tarnish his memory for her. For myself, I carry no good memories of my time as Richard Murphy's wife."

"Not all marriages are like that, ya know."

"How would you know that? I don't believe you've ever been wed."

Kell laughed at her comment. "You are a saucy lass when you want to be, Hannah."

"And why should I not be—I've told you the whole ugly story of my life. No reason to be sweet and demure with you now."

The door sprang open, and Sonny rushed in. "I think I figured it out. I'm gonna make those chairs for my table!"

"Great news, Sonny," Kell said.

"But I'm beat now. Too much thinkin'." Sonny dashed upstairs.

"Well, lass, I suppose we should call it a night, too. Tomorrow is another workday."

"You're right about that. And I am exhausted."

"Baring your soul takes a lot out of ya." Kell pulled Hannah into his arms. "I want ya to know how much I appreciate your willingness to share so much with me. Thank you for your trust." He tilted her head up and kissed her tenderly. Hannah fully returned his embrace. In his arms, she felt warmth and security—the feeling she'd longed for all her life. Kell's presence had come to mean that to her. "Ya can go on up to bed while I stoke up the stove one last time. We can't have Naomi catchin' a cold."

The last two weeks leading up to Christmas were the happiest days Hannah had ever experienced. Business was good at the mercantile, and Sonny was coming to the store nearly every day. He'd learned to do business nearly as well as Hannah. More and more, he was losing the ten-year-old demeanor she'd always known in him. She knew in some ways he'd never gain the maturity that most men did, but in many ways, he was growing up. Kell had told her that much of Sonny's maturity had been done outside his mother's shadow. Hannah thought perhaps he was right.

The Kincaids had taken over all the winter chores at Sanctuary Hill. Their efforts had freed up much of Hannah's after-work time. The new baby had been born to Lijah and his wife, Dorrie. They asked to name her after Hannah because she'd let them come home. The little girl would be called Ruthie.

Kell and Hannah planned holiday gift baskets for their church family. The present wasn't lavish by any means, but between the two of them, they provided fruit, candy, and nuts they had been able to order from the wholesaler in Memphis. Sonny had included a lovely carved cross that he'd made in his shop. They felt it was a small way to show their gratitude for the new barn.

The night of the Christmas party, Sanctuary Hill was filled with people from across the county. For some old friends of Hugh Kincaid, this was the first time they'd returned to the estate since the outbreak of the war. Naomi filled her role as mistress of the house with all the grace and hospitality they'd remembered from the past. The newcomers, like the Garners, fit in as if they'd always been a part of St. Francis's social life. They didn't even mind the teasing about their strange pronunciation of the English language.

Hannah had a wonderful evening. She was among friends and family. She realized she no longer wanted to sit on the sidelines and watch other people enjoy life. Kell took every opportunity to make sure she was at the center of conversations, dancing, and playing her role as a member of the hosting family. She danced nearly every dance the small musical group played that evening, many times with Kell.

Life seemed so much better than she'd thought it could be. Her despair concerning the fire was all but forgotten. Hannah knew that the hard work would continue, but she didn't see that as an obstacle. She'd done it one year. She knew she could do it another. She felt a purpose she'd yearned for most of her life. Hannah was happy.

"Lass, are ya all right?" Kell asked. "The look on your face just now tells me you're far from these festivities."

"I was for a minute. Isn't this a lovely party—such a beautiful way to begin the celebration of Christmas?"

"I agree with ya. Naomi will be verra happy. I'll wager my dear cousin will be walkin' on clouds for weeks after the success of this evenin'."

"I almost wish it didn't have to end. Everything seems so right tonight."

"This is the first of many fine memories we are gonna make together, Hannah. And we have a couple more before the end of the year. The candlelight service on Christmas Eve is one of my favorite times of the year. The people light their candles, and we all sing *Silent Night.* While we're singin', the children bring in the figures of Mary and Joseph. Next, they place the three magi on the altar and add sheep and a camel or two. The last child brings in the Christ child and puts Him on a bed of hay. Then we all sing *Joy to the World.*"

"That sounds like a wonderful way to spend Christmas Eve. I've never been to a service like that."

"Well, you'll be there this year. I can't wait to take ya, lass. Then the next day, we'll share our Christmas dinner. I know that will be special this year. Aaron and Sonny have been watching the creeks and rivers. They've seen geese. Roast goose and Hot Cross buns. Hmmm. My mouth is waterin' already. Then we'll spend the rest of the day with family, tellin' stories about favorite Christmases past."

A frown darkened Hannah's face for a minute. "I know which Christmas I'll talk about."

"Come on, lass. I wanna dance again—not that I like dancin' all that much, but it's a fine excuse to have ya in my arms for a while."

They danced until the last note faded away. The song had been the Sweetheart Waltz, the last dance of the evening. Together with Naomi and Sonny, they began to gather coats and scarves and wish good night to their visitors. It was still a bit early, not yet ten o'clock, but some of the families had a good distance to travel. Naomi and Sonny retired soon after their final guest had left.

Kell took Hannah's hand and drew her to the blue velvet sofa. They sat together, hand in hand, for some time in front of the fire. They didn't talk. They felt no need to. Being together was enough—more than Hannah had ever expected to know. The clock on the mantle steadily marked the minutes. At midnight, Hannah broke the silence. "I suppose I should go upstairs. Tomorrow, I have to go to the mercantile. I'll be busy with the holiday being so close."

"I guess we should call it a night." Neither made a move to rise from the sofa. Instead, Kell put his arm behind Hannah and drew her head to his shoulder. She rested in this tender embrace, feeling that was where she was meant to be. Hannah trembled.

"Are ya cold, lass?"

"No, Kell. I'm happy. This night has been a blessing in so many ways. To know happiness is a gift. Will you kiss me goodnight?"

Kell stood, brought Hannah into his arms, and bent to meet her waiting lips. His arms pulled her even closer. "Hannah, you're a blessing. I thank God for our meetin' every day. Now ya need to go to bed. I need to go out and get water for Mom Bec to use when she cooks breakfast in the mornin'. The cold air will feel good after the close quarters we've had all night. Goodnight, Hannah Ruth."

He kissed her once more and walked her to the stairs.

"Thank you, Kell, for the wonderful memory. Good night."

Chapter 25

And the angel said unto them, Fear not for, behold, I bring you good tidings of great joy, which shall be to all the people. For onto you is born this day in the city of David, a Savior, which is Christ the Lord. And suddenly there was with the angel, a multitude of Heavenly host praising God and saying, Glory to God in the highest and on earth peace, goodwill toward men.
Luke 2:10-11,13-14

Hannah experienced Christmas as she never had before. After the successful Christmas party at Sanctuary Hill, other ladies in the community planned smaller gatherings which Hannah attended when work would allow. She found Mary Lee Naylor and Rachel Miller shared common interests, and while they were both married with children, Hannah had come to regard them as close friends.

When Naomi and Sonny asked Hannah to help prepare Christmas baskets for the Kincaids and the people at the Community Church, she found a new kind of joy in the holiday. The three of them worked every evening of a week to make enough that everyone would receive a gift. The baskets held simple gifts, apples, nuts, and candy, but preparing them made the Sanctuary Hill family feel grateful to have these people in their lives. Kell had remarked that this was a tiny way to repay these people for helping them rebuild the barn. The new structure again was larger by half the size of the burned barn.

On Tuesday, Christmas Eve, Kell drove the family to the Community Church. Each had brought a candle to light during the service. Hannah's excitement made her giggly. Kell had told her this was his favorite part of Christmas. She wanted to experience the event simply because it meant so much to him. On the short drive to Linden, Mother Nature scattered lacy snowflakes the size of bantam eggs across their path. Hannah reached out her gloved hand to catch the miniature works of art, but to no avail. No sooner than landing on her palm did they turn to water, providing more reason to laugh.

Brother Naylor prepared a special sermon for Christmas Eve. As he read from the gospels of Luke and Matthew and the prophets Isaiah, and Micah, the children of the congregation brought beautiful carved figures to represent the events he spoke of. At the end of the sermon, the altar was filled with wise men, shepherds, Mary, Joseph, sheep, cows, and camels. The tallest boy carried the Star of Bethlehem and held it high above the scene. Two children, who looked to be about four, brought in a carved manger and the Christ child. The nativity picture was complete. Brother Sam lit his candle and began to spread the light across the room. When the last candle was aglow, the congregation began to sing *Silent Night* while Kell played the gentle melody on his violin. Hannah felt the tears on her cheeks. She didn't realize she'd been crying. At the fading words of *Silent Night*, all the people lifted their candles toward the ceiling.

"You are God's chosen people. Share His light with all the world." Brother Sam then pointed to Kell who broke into a robust introduction of *Joy to the World*. The service closed with hugs and wishes for a wonderful Christmas. Again, Hannah found her cheeks wet with joy. As they stepped outside the Community Church, the congregation saw they'd been blessed with a white Christmas.

"Oh, Kell, this is so beautiful! This Christmas has already been more than wonderful. I've never had such a lovely time at church in my life."

"Tis no doubt our God is good," he answered.

"I liked the wooden people the kids brought in," Sonny said. "I'd like to make some for home—maybe not so big."

"Sonny, that is a great idea. You are so good with woodworkin'. You could even make sets to sell at the store. I know people would want them because you made them." Kell smiled at his younger cousin. You've grown into a verra capable young man."

"Awww, Kell." Sonny's cheeks were pink and his smile huge.

"Did you enjoy yourself, Mother Naomi?" Hannah asked.

"I did, but I guess I'm a bit sad too. Benjamin and I were wed on Christmas Eve so very many years ago. I miss him, especially at this time of year. He did love Christmas so."

"What do ya have planned for dinner tomorrow, Cousin Naomi?"

"Kell, you know very well. Sonny and Lucas got us three geese from the pond near your place. We'll have one of them, and our tenants will dine on the others."

"Yeah, and Kell, Mama has baked pies and a cake. For breakfast, we're havin' hot cross buns, just like you asked."

At that remark, Kell leaned over toward Hannah and whispered to her, "I'll have feast enough just to sit beside ya and see you smilin' tomorrow. You are so beautiful when ya smile."

"Shhh…" Hannah put her finger to his lips. Kell broke into a chorus of *Joy to the World* again, and the family sang the rest of the way home.

⨍

The next morning the house was abuzz with activity. Hannah and Naomi bustled around the kitchen preparing a huge Christmas breakfast. Hannah made hot chocolate, which she'd not had in more than a year. Mom Bec told Naomi she would come and cook for the family, but Naomi politely refused her offer. "Mom Bec, if any one of the Kincaids deserves a day off, it is you. Stay home and enjoy your family."

Hannah helped her mother-in-law lay out bread hot from the oven, eggs scrambled with pieces of ham, a plate of crisp bacon, and even a pitcher of freshly squeezed orange juice from a few oranges left over from the gift baskets. Hannah placed a pot of blackberry jelly and a jar of honey with melted butter on Sonny's beautiful dining room table. He'd only finished three of the eight chairs he planned to make, but it was good to celebrate the day in the almost finished dining room, even with the piecemeal chairs from the kitchen. Naomi created an aromatic centerpiece with some cedar boughs and holly, some snippets of red ribbon, and three long tapers, which she chose not to light.

Finally, Kell, Sonny, and Aaron finished morning chores and came to the dining room. Sonny stood tall at the head of the table and offered grace for the morning meal. "Happy Birthday, Jesus. We sure had a good time at your party last night. We hope you are havin' a fine Christmas, too. Please tell my papa and my brother Richard 'Merry Christmas' for us. Now, we ask you to bless this meal, and thank you that we have so much good stuff to eat." Amens echoed around the room.

"Fine prayer, Sonny," Aaron said. "Now, let's eat. I'm hungry as a skinny boy can be."

"Dig in, Kell, but not too fast 'cause we got lots to eat. We're gonna open presents after this." Everyone laughed at Sonny's assessment of the meal in front of him.

Within the hour, the five members of the Sanctuary Hill family were gathered in the parlor in front of a roaring fire. A heap was growing near the sofa where the family had placed gifts. Kell was the last to bring his, which he had wrapped beautifully with pretty paper and bright ribbons.

"Goodness, I didn't expect y'all to bring gifts," Naomi said. "I know the money is about gone."

"Mother Naomi, I'm afraid all my gifts are homemade." Hannah laid her bundles in the pile. "I wanted to save our money. I'm still nervous that some needs may arise that I haven't budgeted for during the winter. But we still need Christmas presents."

"Yes, Mama. The baby Jesus's ma and pa were real poor. They had to live in a shed, but what great stuff he got."

"Sonny, you are right. Everyone needs a Christmas gift. So, you all can open mine." She had made special gifts for her family. She knitted scarves for Kell, Sonny, and Aaron. They were made from old woolen shawls she had found in the attic. They were beautiful—gray woolen yarn, perfect for the men she honored. She gifted Hannah with two gold combs for her hair. They were inlaid with mother-of-pearl. Hannah remembered Naomi had worn them at her wedding to Richard. On that occasion, Hannah commented on how lovely they looked in her hair.

"Oh, Mother Naomi, are you sure you want me to have these? I remember how beautifully you wore them."

"That was before my hair was gray. But Hannah, my ringlet days are well gone. They will be perfect in your raven tresses."

"I will treasure them always." Hannah clutched the small box tightly to her chest.

"Me next!" Sonny jumped up to hand out the gifts he had wrapped in odds and ends of paper he'd found at the mercantile. His bows were made of twine and one sprig of holly. For Hannah, he had made a set of three pegs on a carved foundation that she could use to hang her shawls, bonnets, and reticule. "Hannah, I'll hang that in your room this afternoon," he told her.

For Kell and Aaron, Sonny had copied a picture from a catalog and made carved, stained bootjacks with their names etched on the handle. "I noticed Aaron tuggin' and tuggin' tryin' to get his boots off. I knew he could use this. I hope it's good for you too, Kell."

"Mighty fine gift, Sonny. I had one of these back home in Scotland, but not since I've been in Arkansas. So proud to have it, lad."

"Mama, I couldn't figure out how to wrap your present. It's too big. I left it on the back porch. Let me get it." Sonny returned with a huge grin on his face. He was carrying a large mirror with a carved wooden frame. "It's for your bedroom, Mama. Now you can see all of yourself when you get dressed."

Tears ran down Naomi's cheeks. "My dear boy, you have made me a wonderful present. Mostly just because you made it, but look at the carving—this ivy vine and the butterflies. There is even a little squirrel like the one I pointed out to you the other morning. Hannah, look, it's even holding an acorn."

"Merry Christmas, Mama."

Aaron's gifts were small sachet bags filled with dried wildflowers. "Tain't much, but I remember my ma always like to tuck these little bags in with her fresh washed clothes. She's the one that taught me how to make 'em."

"Why, Aaron! This is so thoughtful. You must have been saving these flowers ever since you came to Sanctuary Hill."

"I did, Miss Hannah. You gotta get the ones that smell best when they bloom," Aaron explained.

"I love this gift, Aaron. Thank you."

"Well, I guess it's my turn." Hannah reached into the much smaller pile and retrieved her homemade gifts. She'd used her downtime at the store to do most of the sewing. For Naomi, she'd made a cream-colored, long-sleeved flannel night dress. She knew her mother-in-law had trouble staying warm at times. She'd salvaged some delicate lace to decorate the collar and the sleeves. For Sonny and Aaron, she'd sewn dark blue damask vests to wear to dances or even to church. She'd used old curtains from the attic for the fabric. They did look quite nice on the young men as they tried them on over their white Sunday shirts. For Kell, Hannah had splurged and ordered the best shirt linen she could get from Memphis. She'd sneaked into his room one day to take one of his other shirts to make sure the size was right. She made the full-pleated sleeves that she liked to see Kell wear. She'd made the tiny pockets to slip stays in the collar. Those collars always looked so crisp and masculine.

"I canna believe ya made this, lass. It's the finest shirt I've ever owned. No tailor could have made a better one."

"I am glad you're pleased with it. I think you will look very handsome in this new shirt when you wear it to church next Sunday."

"I'll do it with so much pride, I may bust the buttons loose. Now it's my turn to share my gratitude and thanks to my family." Sonny and Aaron received identical boxes. Kell had bought them pocketknives with ivory handles.

"Wow! These are great, Kell."

"Sonny, these are Celtic folding knives. They come in very handy for all kinds of things."

"Thank you, Mr. Kell. This is one fine knife. Never had one so fine." Aaron beamed as he ran his hand over the ivory handle.

"Aaron, we are proud to have ya as a part of this clan. And now, my dear cousin Naomi, I bring ya gift from all your Kincaid kinsmen in Scotland. My mother gave them to me when I left for America. I've no use for 'em myself, but you might."

Naomi opened the small box and found a pair of gold drop earrings. A small ball was made to sit on the earlobe. The ball was brushed gold. Attached was a small charm displaying the Kincaid family crest.

Again, tears streamed down Naomi's face. "Too, too beautiful, and they mean so much to me. Thank you, my dear cousin. I will cherish them always. And someday, I will leave them in my will to your daughter."

"I am pleased ya like them. That leaves me with one wee gift. Who can that be for? Oh, I've overlooked Hannah. If it's all right, lass. I'd like to give it to you later." Hannah reached for the small box which Kell pulled back. She looked up into his stormy blue eyes with questions in hers. "I won't forget. I'll give it to ya in a while."

The family scurried around the room, picking up the shreds of paper they'd removed from the gifts. They made great flames shoot up as they tossed the discarded wrapping into the fireplace. The members of the family began to find reasons to leave the parlor. Aaron had to go to visit his girl, who lived in Linden. Sonny declared he'd eaten too much, and he needed to get outside for a while. Everyone knew he would head to the barn to share Christmas goodies with Pal. Naomi declared it was time for her nap. Within ten minutes, the room was quiet. Only Hannah and Kell remained seated in front of the roaring fire.

"Hannah, will ya walk with me in this beautiful snowfall?"

"Kell, it's cold outside."

"We won't be gone verra long. I'm longin' to walk through this beautiful morn with a beautiful woman on my arm."

Lacy, nugget-sized snowflakes drifted across the lawn of Sanctuary Hill. They were slowly finding their way into soft mounds or onto the stark, bare limbs of the trees surrounding the house. The sunlight scattered glittering diamonds across the landscape.

"I am so glad you made me come out here, Kell. This place is as beautiful as I ever dreamed it could be. The wounds from the war are disappearing, and the snow is covering so many of the scars that remain. I wouldn't have wanted to miss this." Hannah's bliss was reflected in her sigh.

Kell took one of her mittened hands in his and placed a small gift wrapped in red paper with a green ribbon bow. "Merry Christmas, lass."

Hannah carefully unwrapped the gift, not wanting to tear the paper. She would tuck it inside her journal. When she opened the box, she found a beautiful gold rosary with a pendant etched with the face of a saintly lady. "Kell, this gift is very extravagant."

"Not so, my dearest Hannah. It's a gift from my mother to you. I know you aren't Catholic, but this rosary is special. The image is that of Mary Magdalene, the patron saint of women. She was one of Jesus's most loyal followers. Some say they loved each other. I am sure they did, but maybe not in a romantic way. The Bible doesn't speak to that. My mother used these prayer beads until my father gave her another at Sean's birth. Mother gave me this rosary to give to the woman who embodied all I wanted and needed for a wife." Kell stopped. He looked into Hannah's eyes. He brought her mittened hand to his lips and kissed it tenderly. "Lass, I know you aren't ready to make a commitment. Nevertheless, you are the only woman I want to have my mother's rosary. She loved that pendant. She gave it to me to give to you."

Only the breeze through the trees broke the silence for a time. Hannah continued to look in awe into Kell's face. She brushed a snowflake from his eyelash. "Kell... Kell, you have left me speechless. I have never had a more sincere, heartfelt compliment in my life. You have become my dearest friend. I have shared more of my life with you than any other. I know I have feelings for you, but I am not sure I can ever marry again. I don't believe I have the courage."

"Ya have forgotten, Hannah Ruth, I am a patient man. I'll not stop caring—ever. But, lass, I will cease the chase of ya when the Lord tells me I can't win ya over."

"I love your Christmas gift. I will keep it with me always because you gave it to me and because it belonged to your mother. Thank you." A smile broke across Hannah's face.

"That's the best thank you I ever got. Will ya let me kiss ya for Christmas, Hannah?"

"You can kiss me on any holiday, Kell. Those are little gifts to me whenever they come." Kell pulled Hannah into his coat and wrapped his arms around them both. The kiss—sweet and tender—was shared.

"We need to get back." Kell began to run back down the path they'd made on their walk, pulling Hannah along. The joy of the day was an added gift to them both.

ϕ

After enjoying their Christmas feast that afternoon, the family lounged around the table, savoring the last of the coffee. They had just begun to share stories of favorite Christmas memories. Before Aaron could finish a funny tale of his brother and him opening the wrong gifts, an unexpected visitor pounded his fists on the front door.

"Who would come on such a snowy Christmas evenin'?" Naomi's concern was evident on her face. "Something bad must have happened."

"Don't fret, Cousin Naomi. Maybe someone has just lost his way. I'll go to the door." Kell hurried to the front of the house and opened the door.

"Mr. Tangent, this seems a strange time for a visit. Please come in out of the cold." Kell stepped aside to let the man enter. Tangent took off his hat and shook the snow to the floor.

"I want to see Naomi Murphy and that half-wit boy of hers."

"Mr. Tangent, I see no need for insults or anger. I invited ya in out of the cold. If there is a problem, I'm sure we can work it out." Kell's effort to placate the man had little effect.

"Are they here?" Tangent's voice echoed through the house. "If so, I demand to see them now."

"My family is all here. We're just finishin' our Christmas dinner. I'm surprised you aren't home doin' the same thing."

"Kell, what is it that Mr. Tangent wants?" Naomi stepped in from the kitchen.

"Mrs. Murphy, I want to talk to you and that…that…that boy of yours—in private." Tangent turned his back to dismiss Kell. "We don't need an audience for what I have to say. It's…well…personal."

Hannah intervened in the conversation, having overheard Tangent's rant in the dining room. "Mr. Tangent, I am Sonny's guardian. Anything you say to him, you will say in front of me."

"Mr. Tangent, is Molly sick or hurt?" Sonny asked. Tangent walked across the room and took Sonny's collar in his hands and pulled him toward him.

"You've got a lot of nerve asking me that, boy."

Kell pulled Sonny from Tangent's grip. "Whoa, Tangent, let the temper cool. You'll not run roughshod over anyone in this house. Now tell us what got ya out on this snowy Christmas evenin'."

"That stupid boy is the reason. The present I got from my daughter this mornin' came from her mother. She told me Molly is with child. Molly has been taken advantage of by this half-witted son of Naomi Murphy. He has brought disgrace on her and our entire family."

"Sonny would never violate Molly. He knows the proper way to treat a young lady," Hannah said.

"Are you callin' my daughter a liar, madam? When I asked her point blank who was responsible for her...her problem, she told me. She said she loved Sonny Murphy, and he was the only boy she'd ever cared for."

"Mr. Tangent, I like Molly. We're good friends." Sonny sat in the chair near the window.

"Don't you lie to me, boy." Tangent's face was as red as the Christmas ribbons lying on the table near Sonny's chair.

"We talk all the time on Sunday. Sometimes, Molly wants me to hold her hand. Mollie and me even kissed each other three times.

Tangent went toward Sonny again, but Kell stepped between them.

"What else happened, boy?"

"I didn't ever hurt her. I promise ya that I'd never hurt Molly."

"You are a liar, Sonny Murphy. You're at fault."

Sonny's face was whiter than the snow outside the window. Naomi broke into tears. "Kell, what should I say?" Sonny looked toward his cousin.

"You don't have to say anything, Sonny. We'll work through this. Right now, go over to the settee and hold your mother. Tangent, you come with me. Hannah, I want you there, too."

Kell led the intruder and Hannah back to the dining room. He motioned for them both to sit down. "Tangent, why did ya decide to come here today with this story?"

"Look, Kincaid, I don't see this is your affair. My daughter is only sixteen. That older boy has taken advantage of her. I want to know what your family intends to do about this?"

"I am not sure we are obligated to do anything. As I see it, this is Molly's word against Sonny's. He said he didn't do anything more than kiss your daughter."

"I wonder if the sheriff will think so little of my complaint." Tangent spit his words back at Kell.

"Mr. Tangent, Sonny is only eighteen, not even two years older than Molly. That is not much of a difference in ages," Hannah said.

"Eighteen is considered adult in this state. Maybe Sonny could spend some time in an Arkansas prison."

"Mr. Tangent, that is a lame threat. Did Molly tell you that Sonny was the person who took advantage of her?"

"I told y'all what she said. She said Sonny Murphey was the only boy she'd been with."

"You didn't say that before. You said he was the only boy she cared for," Hannah corrected the ranting visitor. Tangent flew into a rage, stood, and took a step toward Hannah with an upraised fist. Kell grabbed his arm and jerked him back into the chair.

"Twill be a cold day in Hades when you lay a hand on a member of this family. I can see you're angry. I'd be upset if my daughter brought me news like that, too. I tell you true, Sonny Murphy is not responsible. I will talk to the lad, and I know he will tell me the truth. But before I even have that conversation, I know what he will tell me."

"I will leave it be for a week. If you don't come to me with some kind of proof or an honest proposal of marriage, I'll do what I need to do to protect my daughter." Tangent stalked out of the dining room and grabbed his hat from the table in the parlor.

"Boy, you best do the right thing by my girl. You can't shame her and walk away." He slammed the door. Shortly, horse hooves sounded on the snow-covered ground outside.

"Oh, Hannah, I can't believe that man came here today of all days with those awful lies. He can't harm my boy, can he?" Naomi spoke through her tears as she held Sonny as if it would be the last time.

"Mama, don't cry. I didn't do nothin' bad. Kell told me about how to treat a girl. I always treated Molly like he told me. Kell said it's okay to kiss once in a while. He told me that's not gonna cause anything bad to happen." At Sonny's words, Naomi cried even more.

"Hannah, please take Naomi to bed. I'll make a toddy to help her sleep." Kell took Sonny's arm and headed toward the kitchen. Kell dragged his hands through his hair. The last thing he wanted to do on what had been a fine Christmas day until the last hour was to talk to Sonny about the accusations that Tangent had made. Regardless, he had no choice. If he were to protect his house, he had to know the truth, even though he believed he already did.

"Kell, what did Mr. Tangent mean when he said I should do the right thing by his girl? I always treat Molly good. I like her. She always treats me like a grown-up, not like a kid the way the other boys and girls do sometimes. She's nice to me."

"Tangent is angry. Molly told him she's gonna have a baby."

"She never told me. When we walked last Sunday before Bible class, she didn't tell me anything bad." Sonny shook his head.

"Mr. Tangent said Molly told him that you are the baby's father. He wants you to marry Molly, so her baby won't be born without a father. Do you understand what I am tellin' ya, lad?"

"He said it was me? Kell, I didn't do what you said—you know about how babies are made. Can she be having a baby if I only kissed her three times?"

"No. I knew you weren't responsible because you promised me when we talked that you would not do that with Molly unless you were married. Mr. Tangent is wrong. If Molly is expecting a baby, you are not responsible."

"But Kell, I like Molly. I don't want nothin' bad to happen to her. I could marry her and take care of her like I take care of my mama."

"Lad, if the girl is with child, the baby isn't yours. Someone else is responsible."

"I don't care about that. Molly hates livin' at her papa's house. She told me that Mr. Tangent is mean to her and her mama. She said her papa is always mad at her. That wouldn't be a good place for a baby."

"Sonny, you're a good man. Before we make any decisions, we need time to think about everything. First, we'll need to make sure things are settled with your mother. Remember, lad, Hannah is the person who has the final say. She is still your legal guardian for three more years."

Chapter 26

When I was a child, I spake as a child, I understood as a child, I thought as a child: but when I became a man, I put away childish things. And now abideth faith, hope and charity, but the greatest of these is charity.
1 Corinthians 13:11,13

Breakfast at Sanctuary Hill the day after Christmas was a somber affair. Naomi came to the table in her robe and slippers, which she never did. Her red, swollen eyes told how she'd spent the night. Sonny was quiet, searching the faces of his family gathered at the table, but averting his eyes the second anyone looked toward him. Aaron had chosen not to eat with the family, picking up a biscuit and a cup of coffee with an excuse that he had to check on something in the barn. The pall in the room was uncomfortable for all.

Sonny broke the silence. "Excuse me, mama. I'm gonna go to the barn to feed and water Pal. I'll be back directly."

"Sonny, don't go." Hannah motioned for him to return to the table. "We need to talk about what happened last night. Aaron will see to Pal's feeding. Please sit down and at least finish your coffee."

"Hannah, what are we going to do? That man is a liar. My son didn't do that awful thing he said." Naomi once again burst into tears.

"Mama, don't cry. I'm sorry. Please don't be mad. I never, ever hurt Molly. I promise ya I never did."

"Sonny," Kell said, "none of us, not your mother, Hannah, or me think you'd lie about an important thing like this. We believe you."

"Kell, if I tell Mr. Tangent that I never hurt Molly, he'd believe me, don't ya think? Molly would tell him I never did. She would tell her papa if I asked her to."

"Sonny, Molly already told her papa that she loves you and none other. She made him think the baby she's going to have is yours," Hannah explained.

"But Kell told me that it can't be, didn't ya, Kell?"

"Yes, lad. If ya did nothin' more than kiss the girl, the baby isn't yours."

"Did someone else hurt Molly? I don't like anyone being mean to her. She's kinda my girl, I guess." Sonny turned and knelt in front of his mother. "I do like Molly, Mama. She's real nice to me."

Sonny's words only brought more tears. "Son, you don't understand. You can't raise some other man's child. It's not your place. You have enough to take care of here at Sanctuary Hill already."

"But, Mama, what if no one else will help Molly? Wouldn't that be bad for her?" Sonny looked toward Kell and Hannah with questioning eyes.

Hannah reached across the table and grasped Sonny's hand. "I am responsible for you until you are twenty-one. Your grandfather's will charged me to see that you have a good life. I don't want Narvel Tangent to put problems in your way. Sonny, taking on the responsibility of raising a child is something you will have to deal with for the rest of your life."

"Hannah, is it possible for Tangent to have Sonny arrested? Surely, he wouldn't want gossip about his daughter. That would be as bad for them as it would be for us. He wouldn't do that, would he, Kell?" Naomi waved her arms and clasped her throat. Her voice edged on hysteria.

"Naomi, settle down. You're upset, but comin' unglued will not solve anything. Tangent will cool down after he has a little time to consider. He won't want the talk any more than we do." Kell led Naomi to the parlor to the settee in front of the fire. Hannah and Sonny followed.

"Kell, I can't let anything bad happen to my baby. "

"Mama, I ain't no baby. Kell, I don't want no one to get hurt by Mr. Tangent. He's plain mean. Molly is afraid of her papa. If he's gonna hurt her, I want to bring her here to live. I can take care of her and Mama and Hannah."

"Whoa, Sonny. Let's slow down. Stop and think," Kell said. "If you try to bring her here, people will think Tangent is right to accuse you. Besides, he'd not let her leave."

"He would if I married her. She'd be my wife, and she'd have to live at my house." Sonny crossed his arms and jutted out his chin.

"No, Sonny! You don't know what you are saying." His mother sobbed, her shoulders jerking with emotion.

"Kell, isn't that what Mr. Tangent wanted when he told me to do the right thing?" Sonny asked.

"Yes, Sonny, but Narvel Tangent doesn't make decisions for this family. I told ya last night that Hannah will decide what needs to happen," Kell answered.

"All right. Hannah, I trust you to know the right thing to do. I'm goin' to work now down at the barn with Aaron. When y'all decide what I need to do, I'll listen." The back door slammed shut.

No sooner did the door close than Naomi rushed to Hannah who was standing in the doorway to the kitchen. She grasped her hands and pleaded, "Hannah, my boy isn't ready to marry. He's barely eighteen and not nearly as mature as most boys his age. You know he's never gotten over that dreadful disease that left him so childlike. Sonny can't see anything in that girl except her coy smile and sugary sweet talk. She flaunts herself around all the boys in the county. That little tart will ruin his life. You must forbid him to marry her. I demand you do so."

"Calm down, Mother Naomi. We'll work through this problem, just like every other hardship we've faced. Please have a hot cup of tea and then go lie down. I know you didn't sleep much last night. We aren't going to decide anything just this minute."

"Hannah, Sonny can't go to prison!"

Kell walked across the room and took his cousin in his arms. "Dear Cousin Naomi, Tangent was blusterin' like he always does. We will take care of this."

"All right, Kell. I trust the two of you to take care of Sonny. He's all I have left. Don't let anything happen to my boy."

With Naomi resting in her room, Kell took the opportunity to talk with Hannah alone. "Quite a mess Tangent left us. I am sorry he came and spoiled the holiday for ya, Hannah."

"He didn't. Except for that last ugly intrusion, this was the best Christmas I've ever had. I hardly had the chance to thank you for the lovely rosary you gave me."

"It was my pleasure. My mother will be happy when I tell her I gave it to ya. Still, we need to decide how to get Sonny out of this mess."

"Kell, I can't allow him to marry that saucy little girl. In so many ways, she is as much a child as Sonny is—maybe even more."

"You're right about that. Sonny has grown up considerably in the nine months you've been in Arkansas. He's made some minor business decisions with Marcus. He even set Molly in her place one day when she wanted to swim in the creek only in their underclothes. I watched that little episode myself. Sonny handled it verra well, and he didn't even hurt Molly's feelings."

"For goodness sake, Kell, a baby is on the way. It's not even his. Those two children aren't ready to be parents." Hannah pushed her chair back and paced back and forth across the room. "I can't in good conscience let Sonny be forced into a life he's not ready to handle."

"What do ya think Sonny wants to do? Ya know they are on about the same level—neither of them quite adult but both are far from children. She is pampered and never had a day of responsibility in her life."

"Surely you don't think I should let him marry that wayward girl!"

"Hannah, I'll not be tellin' ya how to decide this matter. It's not my place. I thought they may be a likely match. Molly has always treated Sonny as a young man—not like the other young folks that make him feel backward and childish." Kell rose and took Hannah by the shoulders. "Will ya stop pacin' the floor, lass? Frettin' won't solve anything."

"I'm sorry, Kell. I am so torn. I don't want Sonny to have problems with the law, but I am not convinced he understands what it will mean to take a wife and raise a child."

"Keep in mind what the lad told ya. He cares for Molly, and he wants to protect her. Will he have hard feelings against you if you refuse and things go bad with Molly?"

"I know he said that. I need to talk to Sonny I suppose. I guess I haven't been able to see him as anything more than the ten-year-old I've always known him to be, but you are right. He's grown beyond that point."

"My dear Hannah, you've a good head on those lovely shoulders. Ya have a good heart too. I know you'll make a good decision. Are ya goin' to the mercantile today?"

"No. Saturday will be soon enough. Since Christmas, there is little stock to sell anyway. Thank goodness, our next shipment from Memphis is due Tuesday."

"Well, I'm headed to Madison. I'll see ya at suppertime."

⚘

For the next two days, Hannah, Kell, and Naomi continued to talk about a solution to the problem they faced. In Kell's trip to Madison, he learned the sheriff had made little headway in finding evidence against any individual who may have started the fire at his barn. The sheriff told him that all the known night riders in the area seemed to have alibis for the night of the fire. He'd all but provided an alibi for Narvel Tangent himself. He did report that one of the known members of the group that rode a horse identified by both Sonny and Lijah Kincaid had left the state to return to Mississippi where he'd come from.

Kell also told them he'd run into Narvel Tangent at the post office when he stopped to send a letter home to Scotland. Kell told Hannah out of Naomi's earshot that Tangent had once again threatened to take the incident to the sheriff. "I don't know what charge Tangent could use to cause Sonny's arrest. Surely he's not so vile as to accuse the boy of rape."

"Kell, you don't think he would. Think of the problems he'd cause his own daughter. She would have to go to court and talk about the assault. How ugly it would get." Hannah wrapped her arms around herself and shuddered.

"Lass, I'm sure I've never met a worse scoundrel in my life."

"I think it's time we talked with Sonny. Then we will have to make a decision that will include Naomi. I simply don't know what the answer is. What I want to do is to protect Sonny, but I don't know how to do that. I don't know what will happen if I tell him that he can't marry Molly, and I have no idea what will happen if I tell him I will support any decision he makes."

"To tell the truth, Hannah, we may not be able to prevent it. The legal age for a male to marry in Arkansas is eighteen. Molly would have to have permission from her father, which wouldn't be a problem. I'll go with you. We'll talk to Naomi after we see what Sonny is thinking."

"Thank you, Kell. I've come to depend on you more than I like to admit."

On Saturday afternoon when Hannah returned from the mercantile, she and Kell decided they couldn't delay the talk with Sonny any longer. After a brief walk to the shed, they found Sonny knee-deep in wood shavings. He'd carved out the backs and arms of the five remaining chairs.

"Hey, Kell and Hannah. See what I've finished this week. I'll have these chairs finished for Mama in a couple of weeks."

"Looks like fine work. I know she'll be so happy to have the dining room furnished. Sonny, we came down here to talk about Molly and you."

"Did y'all decide what I need to do, Hannah?" Sonny wiped the sawdust off his face. "I've been wonderin' if you did."

"Sonny, I'm torn about what to tell you. I should have asked you before now what you think should happen."

"I ain't made a big decision like this Hannah. Mama or you always decided for me. Sometimes, Marcus asks me what I think about the crops, but we usually decide together."

"I know that, Sonny," Hannah said. "I want you to be a part of this decision because we are talking about your life. You aren't a kid that never has a say in what happens to you anymore."

"Kell, do you think I should tell Mr. Tangent I didn't hurt Molly?"

"Yes. I think that is what you should do. But ya know Mr. Tangent has threatened to get the law involved if you don't decide to marry Molly."

"But I didn't do nothin' bad to get in trouble," Sonny said.

"Lad, we know that, but sometimes people don't tell the truth. Mr. Tangent could cause you a lot of trouble."

"Sonny, we will stand behind you, regardless. You don't have to do anything you don't want to do." Hannah smiled to reassure the young man.

"How do you feel about that young lady?" Kell asked.

"I like Molly a lot. She's always nice to me. She talks to me about grown-up things. She never makes me feel stupid or like a little kid. She told me I was her beau. I liked that. I like it when she lets me kiss her."

"Sonny, has Molly said she loves you?" Hannah asked.

"She says it every Sunday when we take walks before Bible class. That makes me a little embarrassed 'cause I don't know what I'm supposed to say back to her."

"One time ya told us, lad, that ya wanted to bring Molly to Sanctuary Hill. Do you remember?"

"Yeah, that was the night Mr. Tangent came over and told me to do the right thing."

"Yes, it was," Kell replied. "Why would ya think that's a good idea?"

"Gee, Kell, you don't know how much Molly hates livin' at Fox Run with her papa. He's mean to Molly's mama and even to Molly.

Molly is scared of her papa. One time he hit her in the face when she sassed him."

"Is it that you feel sorry for her, Sonny? You can't help that Molly has to live with her parents. It's not your job to protect her." Hannah tried to explain.

"But Hannah, I like to know that Molly is all right. I never want her to have problems or anything bad to happen to her."

"She already has a problem," Kell said. "She is going to have a baby. We know the child is not your baby. People will talk and say unkind things about her if she doesn't have a husband. That is her problem and not yours."

"I don't want people saying bad things about Molly. Do you think if we get married everything will be fixed?" Sonny looked toward the ground. His cheeks reminded Hannah of an overly ripe watermelon— almost too red and very wet.

"Sonny, I need you to think about two things before you make up your mind. Do you understand when two people say their marriage vows, they are married for the rest of their lives?" The boy's mouth opened as if he were about to argue, but he shook his head instead. "Another thing…when Molly has the baby, she will be a parent for the rest of her life. As her husband, you will take that baby to raise along with her. You will be a Papa. That is a huge responsibility. Promise me you will think about these things seriously." Hannah laid her hand on his shoulder, but he flinched.

"Kell, what do you think I should decide? You always tell me what's the right thing to do."

"I can't make this decision. Just know whatever ya decide with Hannah, I'll be with you whenever you need me. We are Kincaids."

Hannah turned to leave the shed where Sonny had returned to his woodworking project. At the door, she paused. "Sonny, think about our talk and come tell me on Monday what you're thinking. Then Kell and I will go with you to explain our decision to your mother."

"All right, Hannah. I'm gonna think about this, but I'm still gonna work on Mama's chairs. She'll be real happy with them. Besides, I think fine when I'm workin' on wood."

❦

On Sunday, as soon as Brother Sam blessed the church, Sonny took Molly's hand, and they headed to the grove. He called back, "Mama, y'all wait for me at the mercantile. Molly and me gotta talk."

"Ya heard the lad, ladies," Kell said. "No need us standin' here in the cold." They stepped into the wagon and drove the short distance to the store.

Meanwhile, Sonny and Molly had settled on the carved bench in the grove.

"Sonny, we can't be kissin' out here in the daylight."

"Gee whiz, Molly, I didn't bring you out to kiss. Is it true that you are having a baby?"

Molly's coquettish smile vanished. She turned her back to Sonny and began to cry. "You're mad at me now. I knew you would be if Papa told you."

"Dang it, Molly, stop crying. I ain't mad at you. Just tell if what your Papa said is true."

"Well, my mama says I am. I don't know how she knows. She never told me anything about—well you know. Do you know about making babies?"

"Yes. And we ain't never done nothin' to cause a baby. You know that. I'd never hurt you, Molly."

"I didn't tell my papa you did. I just told him that I love you and you're the only person I want to be with. I promise, Sonny. I never lied about you to my mama or papa."

335

"Molly, did you let someone else…I mean did a boy…" Sonny could find no words to ask Molly what he wanted to know. "Oh, tarnation! Molly, how did this happen to you?"

"If I tell you, you won't like me anymore, and you won't want to be my beau."

"You gotta tell what happened. Molly, Hannah said trust is important. If I don't know important things, I can't make decisions so Hannah will be on our side."

Molly started to cry. Sonny hugged her and patted her head.

"I will try to tell you what I think happened." Molly sat, squared her shoulders, and wiped the tears from her face. "I went to a barn dance on my cousin's sixteenth birthday over in Cross County. I met a lot of new people there. One older girl was so nice to me. The barn was decorated with lanterns, paper streamers, pumpkins, and fall flowers. It was so pretty. Lacey's parents brought out lots of food and punch. The dance was so fun! About eleven o'clock a lot of the people started to leave. My cousin Lacey went somewhere. My new friend Laura and I stayed in the barn with three or four of the Cross County boys. We kept drinking the punch. It tasted funny, but it was still good. When Laura's parents began to put out the lights in the house, one of the boys asked if we wanted to play a grown-up game in the loft. So, we climbed up to the haystack. Laura said I'd like the game, and she always played it at parties. Jack, he was the boy sweet on Laura, said the game was called "Tumbling in the Hay." So, we started tumbling around in the hay. I was so dizzy that I don't remember much of what happened, but I did play the game with two of the boys.

"The next morning, Laura's mother found us asleep in the hay loft. We'd been covered over with some horse blankets. Our shoes, stockings, and some of our crinolines were laid in a neat pile on a hay bale. Lacey told her mother that we played the tumbling game. She got all red in the face. She said we couldn't ever tell anyone. I said I wouldn't tell. My aunt told my mother. Mama still won't hardly talk to me."

"Is there anything else you need to tell me?" Sonny asked.

"Laura wrote me a letter to invite me to a party at her house. She said that we would get to play the "Tumbling Game" again. I wrote to her and told her I couldn't come because my boyfriend wouldn't like it. You wouldn't like it, would you, Sonny?"

"Are you sure you are telling me the truth?"

"Sonny, I swear. I don't know if this is why I'm havin' a baby. Mama never told me about such things. I'd never heard anyone talk about the "Tumbling Game.""

"I believe you, Molly. If you are having a baby, you don't know who the father is, do you?"

"I want it to be you, Sonny. You're my best friend. And I love you an awful lot."

"Molly, I don't know what to say to you when you say things like that. I don't want to hurt you. I had to know before I decide what I'm gonna do. I'll take you back to your papa and mama now."

"Will you kiss me, in case it's the last time, please?"

"Not now. Got other things on my mind." He took her hand and walked her back to her father who was waiting on the church porch."

"Good day, Mr. Tangent. Goodbye, Molly." Sonny began to walk toward the mercantile.

"Wait a minute, boy. I want a word," Tangent bellowed.

"I'm sorry, sir. My family's waitin' for me."

When Sonny reached the store, his mother met him at the door. "Sonny, what happened with that girl?"

"Mama, I don't want to talk about anything until we get home." He opened the door to let Hannah, his mother, and Kell walk onto the porch. "And I don't want you to call me Sonny. I'm a man—eighteen years old. My name is Benjamin Murphy. I'd like to be called Ben."

Talk on the way home was trivial—how cold it had been since Christmas, what an excellent sermon Brother Sam preached, guessing of a date they could start plowing for next season's crop. They talked around 'family'. Then they stepped down and into the house to finalize preparations for the noon meal. Within an hour, the four members of the Murphy household were seated at the kitchen table, holding hands as Ben Murphy offered grace.

"Father, I thank you for this fine food we're gonna eat. I thank you for my good family that is always with me. Amen."

After the meal, Ben stood. "I think I know what the right thing is, but I need to talk to Kell."

"Sonny, please don't marry that girl," Naomi begged.

"Mama, I said I gotta talk to Kell. I need to have a man help me understand everything Molly told me. If he tells me what I think he will, I will know that I made the right decision. Please, let me make up my mind. I've been thinkin' and prayin' about this since Hannah and Kell talked to me. Kell, will you come with me down to the shop?"

"Let's go, lad. We'll talk as long as you need."

They spent more than two hours in Sonny's shop where Sonny retold Kell everything that Molly had told him. He asked questions that helped him understand parts of the story that he'd not fully understood. Then he asked Kell two very serious questions.

"Kell, Molly didn't really understand what those Cross County folks got her to do, did she?"

"Ben, I wasn't there, but I think perhaps Molly may have been drunk. She said the punch was funny tastin'. She said she got dizzy and didn't remember much of what happened. Perhaps she was taken advantage of by those older kids who were at the party. You also said her cousin left her with them. Molly shouldn't have stayed, but she may not have acted as she did if she were not left alone."

"Kell, do you think Molly will act bad if I decide to marry her and get into trouble again?"

"Lad, I'm no seer, but Molly seems to be a nice young lady. Ben, you will learn to make Molly happy. For the most part, she needs the opportunity to grow up like you have been doing since you came to Arkansas and have learned to make a living for yourself."

"Kell, I think I will marry Molly. She needs a better home, and maybe we can learn to be good parents."

"Ben, Hannah and I will support your decision."

When they returned, they found Hannah and Naomi in the parlor. When she saw her son, Naomi rushed to the doorway and clasped his hand.

"Mama, Hannah. I'm gonna tell ya what I think is the right thing to do. Kell helped me understand a couple of things, so I am sure I made the right decision. I am goin' to ask Molly to marry me and come here to Sanctuary Hill to live."

"Sonny, you can't marry that silly girl. I won't have it," Naomi cried out.

"Mama, I asked you to call me Ben. Sonny is a little boy's name. I'm a man."

"I am sorry, son. It will take a while to get used to calling you anything but Sonny, but why did you not listen to Kell? He surely didn't say it was right for you to wed that Tangent girl."

"He didn't tell me one way or the other. He said that he would stand behind me whatever I decided. I want you to do that, too. Mama, I love you. You always took care of me, but I am a man now. I want a man's name, and I want to marry Molly. This will be good for her. Maybe for me, too. I can't go on being a boy forever."

"No, Son—Ben. You are making a terrible mistake."

"Mama, I don't need your permission. Kell told me I can get married in Arkansas when I'm eighteen. But I do want you to bless me like you did Richard when he married Hannah."

"Ben, are you sure that this is what you want to do?" Hannah asked.

"Yes. I talked to Molly today. We will be okay here at Sanctuary Hill. I know you don't have to agree, but you asked me. This is what I think is right."

Naomi fled from the room, sobbing hysterically. Hannah knew her mother-in-law would need several days to come around to Ben's point of view. She would wait for a better time to talk with her.

"Kell, will you ride over to Fox Run with me tomorrow to tell Mr. Tangent I am going to do the right thing?"

"You know I will. If Hannah gives her permission, I will be happy to ride over there with you."

"Ben, I don't know if I am doing the right thing for you, but I will honor your decision. God bless you, dear brother." Hannah hugged the young man's neck, and he blushed.

♭

The trip to Fox Run was a short one and well-handled by Ben. He told Tangent that Molly's baby was not his. Then he asked the man to sign a letter giving his sixteen-year-old daughter permission to marry him. Finally, he asked to speak to Molly. In the presence of her mother and father, Ben Murphy asked Molly Tangent to be his wife.

"Oh, yes, Sonny. I will be so happy to be your wife."

"Molly, my name is Ben. Call me Ben from now on. And Mr. Tangent, we will get married this Friday at Sanctuary Hill. I'll ask Brother Sam to read our wedding sermon. Please come and bring your wife, Molly, and all her things. We will live at Sanctuary Hill." Kell smiled with pride as he watched the young man conduct the difficult meeting as well as any adult could.

"Wait a minute there, Sonny. I might have a say—"

"No, sir. My wife will live in our house on my land."

"Look here, Kincaid. Talk some sense in this boy. They need to live here with my missus and me so we can take care of Molly." Tangent's face was livid.

"Mr. Tangent, Ben is no boy. He wants to marry your daughter despite the questionable parentage of that child she carries. He farms his land, and he plans to live there." Hannah said.

"Good afternoon, Mrs. Tangent, y'all will always be welcome at our house. My mama will be happy to see you."

"Oh, Sonny!" Ben glowered at Molly. "I mean Ben. I'm so happy."

"I'm happy, too, Molly." Ben took her in his arms and gave her a chaste kiss. "I will see you on Friday."

Ben Murphy and Molly Tangent were married in a quiet ceremony in the parlor of Sanctuary Hill. Only family members were present. Aaron Pierce stood with Ben as his best man, and Molly's mother stood with her beautifully dressed daughter, who wore the formal white lace gown in which she had married Molly's father twenty years earlier. Ben slipped a wide gold band on Molly's hand and kissed her reverently when Brother Sam pronounced they were man and wife. The new year began with a new member added to the Sanctuary Hill family. Molly Tangent Murphy's name was written in the family Bible next to Ben's with the date January 1, 1867.

Chapter 27

For it is God, which worketh in you both to will
and to do of His good pleasure.
Philippians 2:13

January was bitterly cold in the Delta, but life at Sanctuary Hill was good. Sonny and Molly settled into a playful routine as a young married couple, constantly together. Molly spent hours watching her new husband craft items from wood. He made her a beautifully carved chest during the cold, isolating winter. Molly thrived under her young husband's constant attention. She didn't even object when he gave her chores to do around the house.

"Molly, everyone works at Sanctuary Hill. You and me need to do our share. I know your mama never made you do housework, but things are different here."

"I don't mind. Someday I'll have to be the lady of your home, so I need to know what I have to do."

"Well, my mama will teach you real good. For now, just take care of our room and help Mom Bec so you can learn to cook, but don't do anything to hurt the baby. Kell told me people have to be careful with ladies who are gonna be mothers."

"Sonny, you are so sweet to me."

"Molly, I already told you to stop callin' me, Sonny. We are grown-ups now. My name is Ben."

"I'm sorry, Ben. Sometimes I just forget." She stretched up and kissed him.

Molly's bouts with morning sickness became severe. Dr. Bolden came from Madison soon after the wedding to examine the girl for possible complications. Ben was beside himself to see Molly so sick almost every morning.

"I don't get it, Molly. How come you're sick to death in the mornin' but fine in the afternoon?"

"I don't know. My mama didn't tell me much about babies. I know my dresses are getting tight around my middle. Look. I bet you can't put your hands around my waist anymore."

"I don't care about that, Molly," Ben said. "I just want you to be well."

"Let's ask your mama about this, Ben."

"I can't talk to my mama about girl things. Let's ask Hannah."

"She ain't ever had a baby." Molly began to tear up.

"Don't cry. Hannah will go with you to talk to my mama." Ben put his hands on Molly's shoulders and led her to the kitchen where Hannah and Mom Bec had just put the cornbread in the oven.

"Gee, it's nice and warm in here," Molly said.

"That's the truth, Miss Molly. It's my favorite place in the winter, and my worst nightmare in the summer." Mom Bec laughed.

"Hannah, will you take a few minutes to talk to us?"

"Of course I will, Molly. What do you need?"

After supper that night, Hannah, Molly, and Naomi left the men sitting at the kitchen table. Hannah had said they would not be welcome in the parlor until they were called. Naomi balked at first when Hannah came to her. She had allowed the marriage to happen because Ben had been so determined to protect Molly. Yet, she felt little warmth toward the girl, whom she felt was unsuited to be a wife

343

to her son. Naomi hadn't mistreated Molly, but neither had she made any attempt to welcome Molly Tangent into the family.

Nevertheless, Hannah insisted Naomi was the only person who could answer the agonizing questions Molly had.

"Mother Naomi, Molly is scared. Her mother told her practically nothing about childbirth—precious little to help her understand why she was pregnant in the first place."

"Hannah, are you sure you can't answer her questions? I feel—well—uncomfortable talking to her about her condition."

"You would help her if the child belonged to Ben, wouldn't you?" Hannah pleaded her cause.

"I probably would if her mother wasn't around to do it."

"Well, then it's the right thing to do." Hannah settled the problem. "We'll talk together tonight after supper."

So, the moment had come.

"Molly, I wish your mother would explain things to you. Do you want to talk with your mother instead of me?"

"Oh, no, Mrs. Murphy! My mama would never let me ask her about boys or kissing or anything personal. She had Trudy, my girl servant before the war, tell me about a woman's monthly time."

"I see. I will try to answer any questions you have. Is something bothering you right now?" Naomi motioned for the girl to sit down.

"The doctor has told me it's called morning sickness. Does it last forever? I get so sick every morning. Ben doesn't understand because he said sick people don't get well in the afternoon and get sick again the next day. I didn't know what to tell him."

"I see that Ben has made you start using his name now," Naomi responded.

"Yes, ma'am. He told me we have to be grown-ups. I don't feel grown up," Molly answered.

Hannah sat next to Molly and laid her arm across the girl's shoulder. "You don't have to be totally grown up yet, Molly. You still have a little time to be young and enjoy each other."

"Molly, when did Dr. Bolden tell you this baby will be born?" Naomi asked.

"End of June or at least by Independence Day. That sounds like a long time."

"You've received a blessing. You will miss the hottest part of the summer," Naomi said. "The heat is so hard to deal with when you are with child."

"Mrs. Murphy, am I gonna be sick every day until July?"

"No, Molly, morning sickness usually goes away in about five weeks after it starts. You were already having nausea when you came to Sanctuary Hill. You should be better by the end of January."

"Thank goodness for that!"

"Do you want to ask me anything else?" Naomi asked.

"Am I gonna get really fat? My dress is already too tight."

"All mothers get big to make room for a baby, but it will go away after you have him. It doesn't matter. Sonny, I mean Ben, won't mind if you change for a while. He loves you, Molly. Anything else?"

"Not right now. I wish my mama had told me about the tumbling game. I wouldn't have been playing that game with those boys at that party. But Mrs. Murphy, if you will teach me, I will be a good wife to Ben. I love him."

A hint of a smile came to Naomi's face. Hannah noticed that the tension between them had lessened. When she spoke to Molly, her tone had changed to gentle and warm. "Molly, please stop calling me Mrs. Murphy. After all, we are both Mrs. Murphy, and Hannah makes three. I'd like you to call me Mother Naomi, just as Hannah does. We are family. You are welcome to ask me about anything bothering you."

"Thank you, Mother Naomi."

"May I call our menfolk in from the kitchen now?" Hannah asked.

"Yes, Hannah. You can spend the rest of the evening with Kell. We've all noticed it's become your favorite pastime." Hannah blushed. She knew it was true.

⨍

Kell and Hannah, too, had settled into a comfortable, affectionate courtship. Aaron moved to share a room with Kell. This allowed the family to make a pleasant room for the newlyweds. With a loss of his privacy, Kell spent much more time in the front parlor and at the kitchen table—anywhere Hannah was. They were never at a loss for things to talk about. Often in the late hours of the evening, ten or eleven o'clock on many days, they read and discussed a new portion of the Bible or debated some issue they'd read about in the latest edition of the Arkansas Gazette. They kept a careful watch for news concerning the growing number of vigilante raids in nearby counties.

Kell learned very little from the sheriff concerning the barn burning or the attacks on the Kincaids. He continued to post nightly security watches over the family and all the tenant farmers. He wasn't overly worried about an attack on Aaron Pierce's farm, but the Kincaids were as important to the success of Sanctuary Hill. He had promised Hannah he would do all in his power to keep the peace. Thankfully, there had been no attack since the barn burning.

Kell's dealings with Narvel Tangent had proved to him the man had not lost hope of getting a hold of Sanctuary Hill. He also doubted the marriage of his daughter to Ben Murphy caused any change of mind. Truly, the entire family was surprised that the man allowed Molly to come to Sanctuary Hill without a fuss.

⚘

In mid-February, Reuben Miller and his wife Rachel invited Kell and Hannah to Friday night dinner. Hannah looked forward to the event all week because she and Rachel had become good friends during ginning time. Since the Millers didn't attend the Community Church, they didn't get to talk except for brief visits at the mercantile. They shared a great love of reading, so they often swapped books and enjoyed talking about them. An evening at Rachel's table would be a real treat.

Kell said he'd take any excuse to have Hannah to himself for an evening. The cold weather that winter kept the family together nearly every night. Even though the night was cold, Kell had heated bricks for their feet and brought quilts to make the short trip as comfortable as fifteen-degree weather can be.

Rachel had prepared a fine meal with fried chicken and stewed potatoes cooked over a pot of green beans. She also baked light, buttery bread that Kell couldn't seem to get enough of. For dessert, she made an apple cake that made mouths water. She said the recipe had come over on the boat with her Irish grandmother.

"Hannah, ya must get that recipe. A man could live on that and die a happy fellow." Kell reached for a second slice.

Besides a great meal, Hannah and Kell enjoyed the feeling of a home that was built on devotion and love. Reuben and Rachel weren't outwardly affectionate, but to see them interact over the simplest thing spoke of a bond at the core of their marriage. True partners, they parented their two young children with love and attention—Reuben caring as much for their needs as Rachel. The three-year-old boy clearly adored his papa. When the tot threw his arms around Reuben's neck and said "Wuve voo, papa" Hannah thought she saw a tear on

Kell's lashes. But then the younger Miller said, "No. Go to bed!" Everyone laughed.

"See what you have to deal with when you have a little one around, Kell? Even though his speech isn't great yet, he's already a little manipulator. And when Susie gets old enough to try my will, I'm doomed. She's already got me wrapped around those baby fingers."

"You're a lucky man, Reuben. Ya have been blessed with a beautiful family."

"I agree. I couldn't have a better wife. We've got two healthy kids and another on the way. The Lord's been so good to us. I also have been blessed with wonderful friends and fair, honest business partners. The Lord's sending you our way to gin and bale your cotton saved our land this year."

"We hope to continue our business dealings with the Miller Gins for many years to come," Hannah said as she bent down and took the baby from her pallet. "Rachel, you didn't tell me about the new baby."

"I wasn't sure the last time I saw you at the mercantile. We expect this new Wilson in the early fall."

"I am so happy for you." Hannah rocked the baby in her arms as Kell looked on.

"Hannah, we should return to Sanctuary Hill. The later it gets, the colder it gets."

"Oh, come back to the table, Kell. Let's finish the coffee and eat the rest of that cake," Reuben said.

"Ya don't have to twist my arm at that invitation."

"Kell, do you need a third piece of cake?" Hannah asked.

"No, but need isn't want. Besides my host asked. Come sit with me while I polish off that ambrosia that Rachel made."

Within the half-hour, Kell and Hannah were bundled up, and Graystoke was headed home. The moon was full and brilliantly white

348

in the star-lit sky. The night was still—no wind or animal noises sounded over the crunch of the wheels on the icy road. The clopping of Graystoke's hooves on the road seemed amplified in the crisp cold air.

"Did ya enjoy the visit with the Millers as much as I did, Hannah?"

"I did. This was a wonderful night. They are such a lovely family."

"I'm wildly jealous of Reuben Miller."

"Kell! What a thing to say."

"Hannah, the life Reuben and Rachel have is the life I want. There is not one thing more in life that Reuben needs. He has a home."

"You have a home—not the same as the Millers, but you are loved in the household and very much needed. Since the barn burning, we have become a family."

"I knew I couldn't say what I wanted to say. Sometimes I am a blitherin' idiot!" Kell slapped the reins against Graystoke's haunches. "Gid up, boy."

At the crossroads, Kell pulled the great stallion to a halt. "Tarnation, Hannah, I'm just gonna say what's on my mind. I love you, lass. With every fiber of my bein', I want ya. I've never cared about any woman the way I love you. I want you to be my wife. Will you marry me, Hannah Ruth?"

"I don't know what to say. I didn't expect to have this conversation with you so soon. Kell, I care about you. As hard as I tried not to let myself get involved, I couldn't stop. I may even love you, but I'm not sure I know what that means."

"Hannah, did ya not see love in front of us tonight? Reuben and Rachel fit together like a hand fits a glove. We can share that kind of bond—an intimacy of knowin' and carin'. We will be a three-strand rope that canna be broken, you, me, and the Lord. Do ya not see we can have that life together?"

"I can't answer that question tonight. Will you let me have some time to consider what you've said?" Hannah brushed her hand through Kell's golden hair. "You've become my dearest friend. Maybe, I'm afraid to lose what I have now."

"Hannah, I'm a patient man, but I'm tellin' ya plainly, I know the Lord means us to be together. I love you, and I believe you love me. Please don't let the fear from your past hold ya from me. I'll not hurt ya, ever."

Kell drove into the lights of Sanctuary Hill and stopped the buggy at the porch. "I can't let this night end without a kiss. I hope you are not opposed."

"I welcome it. I always sleep better reliving the touch of your lips on mine."

"And, Hannah, I will not broach the subject again until ya are ready to talk about your decision. I love ya enough to give ya the time you need."

She cupped his face with her mittened hands. "You are too good to me, Kell Kincaid." He once again drew her into an embrace with all the passion that he'd spoken of. "Remember when you are thinkin' about my proposal, lass, that I love you. Regardless of what you decide, that will never change. Goodnight."

"Goodnight Kell. Thank you for another evening to remember."

∅

A restless night awaited Hannah. At first, she couldn't sleep at all. She ran her fingers across her lips more than once—reliving Kell's kisses. Lying alone in her four-poster bed, she missed the comfort of being held in his arms. Finally, when she slept, the most vivid dreams of a future life as Kell Kinkaid's wife danced in her unconscious.

Scenes of building a house on his land were followed by others where small children called her mama—smaller images of Kell with golden blonde hair and stormy blue eyes stirred her to wakefulness. In every scene she dreamt, Hannah belonged. She was safe and loved. She sensed these scenes of home were the things she'd craved all her life but had never found until Kell Kincaid loved her.

When she could no longer stand her restlessness, she sat upright and pulled her blanket to her shoulders. The same fears rushed back to hide the promise of her dreams. If she gave up her independence to another, she might find herself trapped as she had been with Richard. She might have to relinquish control of her life—the dread that scared her the most. She had sworn to herself she would never give that control to another person as long as she lived.

But the thought of living a life without Kell now was an even worse fear. In the short few months, she'd come to expect him to fill the role of confidant and beau. She'd enjoyed their courtship more than she wanted to admit. No, Hannah didn't want a world without Kell. *Do I have the courage to try once again where I failed so miserably before?"*

The raucous cry of the rooster brought Hannah to her feet. Saturday morning had come long before her need for rest had been sated. She had to open the mercantile at seven. She shuffled her way to the wardrobe, pulled out her clothes, and dressed for the day. She hoped for a slow day at the store so her lack of sleep wouldn't be a problem.

Ben was up and ready by the time Hannah dressed for work. He'd even made coffee. Hannah picked up a loaf of bread and sliced a couple of pieces to make toast. That was always an easy breakfast since the cook stove was hot. "How is Molly feeling this morning?"

"Don't know. She's still asleep. I don't wake her up when I have to leave. She won't get sick until she gets up."

"You've done a good job of takin' care of her. Does she like being here with us at Sanctuary Hill?" Hannah asked.

"Yeah, she loves our house. She helps Mama with the chores when she's not sick. I think she misses her mama some, but she's glad she doesn't have to be around her papa."

"Well, Ben, you will have to take Molly to visit her mother now and again. And you need to invite Mrs. Tangent to visit us here."

"I know, Hannah. Now you better get your coat on. We're gonna be late openin' the store."

The day was anything but slow. A constant stream of people came in to pick up an item or two. The weather was not as cold as the last few weeks, and people just wanted to get out. A quick trip to the mercantile was a perfect opportunity. Just before noon—closing time on Saturday—Hannah perched on a barrel of flour. "I'm worn out, Ben. I'm gonna let you close the store. I can't wait to get home, take off my shoes, and take a nap. It's been a long morning."

"Oh, Hannah, you're not old enough to be a draggin'." Ben walked toward the front door. Just as he was about to turn the sign to CLOSED, Kell walked through the door.

"Afternoon, Ben. You ready to close up?"

"Yep. It's high noon. Goin' home to see how Molly is feelin'. Watcha doin' in town on a Saturday?"

"Just came to see if my girl wanted to go on a buggy ride. The weather is nice, and I need to go over to my place and check on my herd."

"She ain't gonna want to go. She is too tired to do anything. She wants a nap."

"Is she now? Well, I'll ask anyway." Kell turned toward the back of the store.

"I heard every word of your conversation. The way the two of you were talking, I'll bet they heard y'all over at the livery stable."

"Sorry, lass, did we keep ya from noddin' off?" Kell teased.

"No. I would be happy to take a buggy ride with you since you came all this way. As long as I'm not on my feet, I'll be fine. Ben, tell your mama we'll be home for supper."

"All right, Hannah. See ya, Kell." Ben was off as quickly as he could hitch Pal to the wagon.

"Let's go, Hannah. The sunshine's glorious, and there is an almost spring-like breeze. A fine afternoon awaits us."

The drive to Kell's farm took less than fifteen minutes. The conversation they shared was small talk. Kell didn't mention any subject that would pressure Hannah concerning their talk the previous night. When they arrived at Kell's cabin, wisps of smoke hung above the chimney.

"Kell, someone's in your house."

"No, Hannah, I was here before I came to Linden. I know what a pitiful excuse for a lunch you take to eat while you're workin' so I made ya some."

"You didn't need to do that."

"I know. Come on in and let's eat. I've got some fresh bread that Mom Bec baked yesterday and some hot ham and beans simmerin' on the stove. I can probably even find us some sweets."

"Sounds wonderful."

Kell pulled Graystoke to a stop at his front porch and lifted Hannah to the ground. They spent the next hour eating a hearty meal and talking about Hannah's day at the store.

"Lass, come over here, and sit in the rockin' chair to rest a spell. Sonny, I mean Ben, told me you're exhausted."

"I am tired. I was busy all morning, and I didn't sleep very well. Too many dreams."

"I hope they were happy ones and not nightmares."

"No. No nightmares."

"Give me your foot, Hannah," Kell said.

"What do you want with my foot?"

"Just do it. I promise I'll not hurt ya." Kell unlaced Hannah's shoes and began to massage her foot. The tender sensation, the warm cozy room, and Kell's soft singing soon had Hannah nodding off. Kell covered her with a well-worn soft quilt and sat in his chair on the opposite side of the fireplace to read his Bible. Hannah slept for more than an hour before she startled awake.

"My goodness, I didn't mean to fall asleep. I've not been much company."

"My darlin' girl, I've enjoyed every moment. I truly enjoyed those little talks you have in your sleep," Kell said.

"I don't talk in my sleep! You're making that up to tease me."

"So help me, Moses, I heard ya singin' the words to a lullaby. I also heard ya ask me if I wanted bacon for breakfast…plain as day."

"I still don't believe you, but it could be. I was dreaming. I did last night—when I was finally able to sleep. I dreamed about a family, a son that looked very much like you, and I was so happy. I was where I belonged."

"Sounds like a fine dream to me," Kell said.

"Then I had ugly thoughts of how I failed miserably at marriage. I felt the fear I've told you about—so out of control and feeling trapped. I've always felt that way until I came to Sanctuary Hill."

"I know you're scared of the unknown, Hannah, but no one is ever really in control except the Lord. I want ya to know that. When ya learn it's not your responsibility, life is so free. You know that faith and God will handle the details."

"You have told me that before. Sam Naylor preaches it Sunday after Sunday. I can't figure out how to live that way. I don't understand how you just let go."

"It's no secret, Hannah. The story is laid out in scripture, so we don't have to guess or fear or work to find it. Just lay out your fear and humbly give it to Jesus. He will do the rest if you let Him."

"I'm trying Kell. I am. How do you know?"

"Faith is the only answer I know."

"You deserve a wife who understands and has that kind of faith. I wish I were that kind of woman because after last night—I can't live in a world without you in it. I'm scared. I've never had to make life-altering decisions like this before. People have always made them for me, or circumstances have forced me into roles that I didn't expect."

"I know."

"Kell, I want to be your wife, but I'm not sure that I'm the wife you need."

"Thank you, Lord! You have blessed me beyond words. Hannah, I promise you we will live together as true partners. I will always respect your need for some independence. Our love will be the bond that keeps us together. I love you so, lass. I hope you know how dear you are to me."

"I love you too, as much as I know about what that means. I hope I will grow to understand it more and be able to show you the devotion you deserve."

"When can I make you my wife, Hannah? Tomorrow, next weekend, at Easter?" Kell's words fell over themselves.

"Kell, I'd like to wait until after the harvest. Molly's baby will be born, I'll have another year to work on securing funds to keep Sanctuary Hill financially sound, and perhaps in the time we are waiting, I'll find that path to faith that is eluding me. Perhaps we can have a quiet wedding and go off to Memphis for a short wedding trip when we sell the cotton."

"If that is what you want, Hannah, so be it."

"And let's enjoy our engagement for a while, just the two of us. I don't want Naomi and the whole of Linden community making a big fuss over us just yet."

"That part will be a little harder. At this minute I'd like to shout from the rooftop that Hannah will be my wife. But I'll keep our promise to myself for a while."

Kell stood and pulled Hannah into his arms and swung her around his cabin as if she were a small child. They laughed and tumbled into a heap before the fireplace. Kell looked into Hannah's eyes. "Hannah Ruth, I've never been so at peace in my entire life. God is smilin' down at us this minute. I love you."

The kiss that followed stirred Hannah. She had made the right decision. Kell Kincaid was meant to be her husband.

Chapter 28

*And what will ye do in the day of reckoning and
desolation from afar? To whom will ye flee for help
and where will ye leave your glory?*
Isaiah 10:3

Hannah's request that Kell wait until harvest was probably a good decision. Spring arrived early in 1867. By the third week of March, the farmers at Sanctuary Hill were in fields behind mules and plows. Hannah had been told politely to stay out of the fields during the planting season. With five grown men, the two strapping sons of Lucas, and Lijah's son, none of the women were needed this year.

Now Hannah had the opportunity to keep the mercantile open every day except Sunday. She took Molly to help in the store once her bouts with morning sickness were behind her. Molly quickly learned the routine at the store. She was good to help the women who came in asking about fabric and clothing they usually had to order through catalogs.

Aaron decided to move into his cabin on his forty acres. He confided in Ben that he wanted to fix up his place and build two more rooms. He'd work in the evenings and any spare time he could find. He planned to use his money from the sale of his share of the crop the previous year to build what he called a real house.

"Gee, Aaron. I don't know why you wanna leave our house. I like havin' my best friend around." Ben frowned.

"We'll still see each other. We work this land together, don't we?"

"Sure, we do, but workin' ain't the same as talkin', whittlin', or just hangin' around together. You're gonna be lonesome down there all by yourself." Ben wiped the dirt from his face with his sleeve.

"Maybe not for long. You already found yourself a wife. I might find myself one pretty soon. I've been walkin' out with Nan Freeman sometimes on Sunday after church."

"That's why you've been skippin' out on Bible class, ain't it?"

"Yeah, I guess so."

"Aaron, are you sweet on Nan?" Ben asked his friend.

"We sure find lots to talk about. She's nice to look at, too—that copper hair and those green eyes. You know those green eyes of hers are the color of a ripe cucumber, dark and sparkly."

"Guess I never noticed."

"Good thing. Molly would have your hide if she thought you'd been lookin' at another girl."

"She knows I won't do that. We made our vows to Brother Sam. That's serious, Aaron."

"I know it is—that's why I'm holdin' back from courtin' Nan right out. I got no place for her yet. That is why I'm addin' on to my cabin to make us a nice place."

"I'll be your best man, like you was mine, Aaron. If you want me to."

"You know I do."

"Well, the workday's done. Guess I better head up the hill to see how Molly's doin'. So long, Aaron. See you tomorrow."

"Night, Ben. I think we'll finish the plowing' at Marcus's land tomorrow. That just leaves us three patches to go, Lijah's, mine, and yours. Have you decided how much you're gonna plant this year?"

"Hannah and me talked it over with Marcus. We decided to plant an extra twenty acres. If the price is good, we could make enough to save back next year's crop money without us having to pull it in from everyone's share."

"That would be a nice savings. Well, see ya in the mornin'." Aaron turned and walked toward his land, whistling as he sauntered down the road.

Aaron wasn't the only person at Sanctuary Hill who planned to build a house. Kell began dreaming of a home for Hannah and himself almost the moment she had told him she wanted to be his wife. Kell's vision for Hannah's house, though, was not his cabin with a couple of extra rooms. He wanted to give her a home comparable to the place she'd grown up.

She had told him about the large windows facing both the sunrise and sunset. She related stories of her playing on a spacious porch, even in the hottest of summers. Hannah told him her bedroom was attached to the governess's room because she frequently woke up afraid after a nightmare. That was not in Kell's plans. Hannah would never awaken from nightmares in his arms. The room he planned for Hannah and himself would be their private sanctuary, separate from other rooms in the house.

Before April had ended, Kell had hired a crew of workers and started to build the foundation for Hannah's cottage. By the time the cotton was planted, the rock foundation was complete. Before the first cotton bolls appeared, the framework for the walls of the first floor stood against a backdrop of Arkansas virgin forest, the place Kell had chosen for its beauty and the shade the trees would provide during the hottest days of summer.

Finally, Kell was ready to show the house to Hannah. One Saturday in early June, Kell came to the mercantile at noon—closing time—to take Hannah on an afternoon buggy ride.

"Kell, I can't go today. I told Rose and Shataka I'd help with the watering if we needed to. If not, I need to work in the garden."

"I'll get ya home in a short while, darlin'. I need to spend a little time with ya. I'm missin' ya. We've both been too busy lately." He turned the closed sign to the outside, picked Hannah up, and carried her out the back door where Graystoke waited.

"What's up? I know you have been gone a lot this spring. Are things all right with your herds?"

"Everything is fine as it can be. I've just been workin' on a little project. I need your input. That's all."

"All right, but I have to be home soon."

"Hannah, you work too much. I promise I'll get ya home in a while." Kell drove on to his cabin, and then he drove past it beyond his new barn, and he still didn't stop.

"Where are we going, Kell?"

"Just be patient, love…just beyond the grove of trees." As they reached the bend in the road, the sizable framework of a house came into view. Hannah sat, speechless. Kell drove toward the wide porch that stretched down the width and length of the house.

"Whoa, Graystoke. Well, Hannah, lass, do you not have something to say?"

"Kell, what are you doing? How can you…when did you…I don't know what to say."

"Hannah, this is your house. I started buildin' it about the time the cotton seeds went in the ground. And just like those green bushes all over Sanctuary Hill are growing to provide a future, so is this house."

"Kell, the money! It's too extravagant."

"Lass, I'm no poor man. I told ya my father gave me my portion when he sent me to take care of Naomi."

"You could have taken care of her! Then why did you let me think I had to…"

Cutting her off, Kell put his hand gently across her mouth. "Hannah, you told me from the minute we met that you were the guardian of that family, and you'd have no interference. I respected your right to do what you needed to do. You'd not take money from me anyway. If I'd tried, you'd have bolted. The last thing I wanted was for you to run from me."

"You're right, Kell. I treated you so badly in those first months, but you never turned away from me. Why didn't you?"

"I adore you, Hannah. I fell in love with that spirited lass dancin' in a field of clover and dandelions who then fell to her knees and wept as if her soul were dyin'. Since that moment ya have not been out of my thoughts."

"I love you. Thank you for not giving up on me."

"Hannah, the Lord never gave up on me. He never gives up on anyone. How can I be less than that when I love you?" Kell's passionate kiss stopped any further questions.

"Will ya walk with me through our house, Kell?"

"I thought you'd never ask."

As they walked through the skeleton of their future home, Hannah was awed by the details. Kell had included things she'd told him about her childhood home, things that she liked about Sanctuary Hill, and even conveniences she never had thought of. Kell had built closet space in all the bedrooms, something she'd never had before. He had put a pump in the kitchen, so she'd never have to carry water from the well. One luxury she'd mentioned from their Memphis excursion the previous year was a place to put a bathtub. Kell had designed a small room directly beside their bedroom that would have a copper bathtub that drained outside. The water would still have to be heated and brought to the room, but getting rid of the water would be so much easier. Hannah loved the full-length windows on the ground floor-- every room filled with light.

"Kell, this is all so wonderful."

"Lass, ya have made me the most blessed man in the state. I canna wait to carry ya across that threshold this fall."

"If it is God's will, we will share a long, happy life under this roof."

"I'll do all in my power to make sure we have that, too."

₲

Spring quickly turned into summer. Hannah and Kell had even less time to spend together. As soon as Hannah closed the mercantile at 3:00, she would hurry into the fields where she would join the five adult men, Shataka, Rose, Lijah's wife Dorrie, and all the children above the age of ten. They would chop until sun set. This was labor, but vital if the crop were to produce maximum yield. A couple of weeks they found themselves filling the irrigation ditches that Lijah and Marcus had dreamed up as a better way to keep the growing cotton watered. Thankfully, the rain returned before the third week, and they were spared that back-breaking chore.

At the end of July, cotton bolls were plentiful, and some of the first planted fields were nearly ready to be picked. However, before that first picking occurred, Molly's time came.

One Saturday morning, Hannah was dressed to go to the mercantile. She had planned to take Ben with her. She made breakfast, put the coffee on to brew, and called up to him.

He came down to the kitchen. "Hannah, something's wrong with Molly. She says her back is hurtin' somethin' terrible."

"Don't worry, Ben. I'm sure she is just uncomfortable. Women get that way when it's time to have their babies. I'll go up to see about her. You stay here and don't let the biscuits burn."

Hannah rushed up the stairs to the room Ben and Molly shared. When she saw the grimace on Molly's face, she knew it was more than an aching back. "Molly, when did the pain start in your back?"

"Hannah, please help me. It's not just my back. I've been hurtin' pretty much since midnight." The girl appeared so small in the rumple of bedclothes around her.

"Darling, you should have told someone. I think you are in labor, but I'm not sure there is time to get the doctor from Madison."

"But you can help me, can't you?"

"I'm not sure I know enough to help. I am going to get Rose and Mom Bec. They can help more than I can. I'm sending Ben to bring the doctor just in case we need him."

Mom Bec and Rose came to the house and shooed Hannah away. Hannah was relieved she didn't have to play the role of the midwife. She immediately dispatched her brother-in-law to bring the doctor back. She sent Aaron to bring Kell, and then she awakened Naomi. Having done all she knew to do, Hannah hurried into Linden to open the mercantile. She was more than an hour late, and several customers were waiting on the porch. Saturday was always their busiest day.

About 11:30, Kell sauntered into the store. "Ya did it, lass. Put everyone in the right place at the right time. Sanctuary Hill has a new resident—a beautiful little girl. Ben's as proud as any new father I've ever seen."

"Thank the Lord, the baby arrived safely. Is Molly all right?"

"I think so. Ben just got back with Dr. Bolden about half an hour ago. He made a lightning trip over those twelve miles. The doctor examined the baby and Molly. Said they're fine. He told us that Mom Bec and Rose had served as well as he could have."

"I can't wait to see the little one," Hannah said.

"You'll be glad to know they plan to name her Naomi Ruth Murphy." Kell smiled as Hannah wiped a tear from her lashes.

"Mother Naomi will be pleased with the name they chose."

"Let's close this store and go back to our family. We got celebratin' to do." Kell took Hannah's arm and escorted her to the door. "Flip that sign over to CLOSED."

φ

Having a new baby in the house didn't lighten the workload. Before July ended, Hannah had again closed the store except for Wednesday and Saturday mornings. Cotton harvest required all able-bodied workers to be in the field. Hannah picked cotton along with the entire Sanctuary Hill family, except Naomi, Mom Bec, and Molly. They kept the crew fed and cared for the small children who were of little use in the fields.

Once again, Reuben Miller was contracted to gin and bale the crop. One difference, this year their daily harvest was taken by wagon directly to the mill, which was guarded day and night. Only the weather was a problem this fall. Frequent rain showers hampered the crew from getting the crop out of the field.

By mid-September, the Sanctuary Hill yield was larger than their entire crop from the first year. At the end of the month, the crew still had three patches to pick—twenty acres at Aarons, twenty acres at Lijah's, and the fifty acres they'd planted for Ben. That weekend, Hannah and Kell planned a trip to Memphis the first week in November. By then, they would have a fair idea of their total yield. They would also have time to plan a quiet family wedding with Sam Naylor reading their vows for them.

On Sunday, October 10th, Kell came down to breakfast an hour earlier than usual. He slumped in a chair at the kitchen table. He was unshaven, his hair not tied back, and his clothes rumpled. He couldn't stay seated. Every few minutes he'd rise and pace, look out the window, and then return to his chair, his face in his hands. Groaning as would a wounded bear, Kell jumped up and slammed his fist into the stone wall behind the cookstove. Blood gushed from a large gash across his knuckles. He hardly felt the pain he'd inflicted on himself because of the pain he carried inside. He had to talk to Hannah. He started toward the stairs but halted at the foot of the staircase. Then he took the steps two at a time to reach the space outside her door. He knocked—something he'd never done before.

Hannah answered, "Come in." When Kell came into her room, she gasped and pulled her blanket over her nightdress. "Kell, what's wrong? You're bleeding. What have you done?"

"Hannah, I apologize for bustin' in on ya. I must talk to ya, now."

"Please wait in the hall a minute. Let me put on my robe."

"Please call me when ya can listen to me." Kell again dragged his hands through his hair, staining some of the golden tresses with blood.

Shortly, Hannah opened the door and asked Kell to come in. She offered him her only chair. "You didn't sleep last night, did you?

"No, love. I've been up all night. You were already in bed when I got home from Madison."

"Yes. We all were in bed by 8:30. Picking cotton is hard work."

"I wanted to talk to ya—I stopped myself twice from doin' what I just did—knock on your door."

"I know something is wrong. You have never come to my door in all the time we've lived together under the same roof."

Kell looked into Hannah's eyes. He stared at her, filling his memory with every nuance of her being. Then he stood up and walked to the window—not wanting Hannah to see the pain in his face.

"Kell, you're scaring me. What has happened? Has something happened to the crop?"

"No. No harm has come to the crop."

"Then tell me why this storm is settled in your face, my love."

Kell walked to Hannah and took her in his arms. His grasp was fierce and unyielding. He continued to crush her against his chest. Then he kissed her with a passion equal to his embrace. He pushed her an arm's length from him and continued to grasp her shoulders. He spoke then, never wavering his gaze. "Hannah, I must return to Scotland." Kell felt her stiffen, and he once more pulled her next to him. "Hannah, did ya hear what I said? I must go home—as soon as I can find passage."

"Yes, I heard what you said, Kell." Fear spread through him at the coldness he sensed in Hannah's words. This was the Hannah he'd worked so hard to displace with the woman he loved and who loved him.

"I never planned to leave your side, Hannah Ruth. I have no choice. Yesterday, I picked up the post in Madison. I received a letter from my father."

"I didn't know y'all kept in touch.'"

"He's written at least twice a year since I came to Arkansas. It's hard. The mail takes several weeks—sometimes even months to get here. This letter was sent on the first day of August. It's taken nearly two months to find its way here."

"Is there a problem with your family?"

"Yes. Hannah. My father wrote that Sean's deathly ill. The doctor's given no hope that he'll recover. My father asked me to return to secure the family lands. There have been some border raids by neighboring clans. Father's afraid some legal matters may arise if Sean passes, and I'm not there to safeguard our property.

"I'm sorry your brother isn't well. I suppose you must go—you are a Kincaid after all—pledged to protect your family above all else."

"Hannah, please come with me. We'll be wed in Memphis, just as we planned. Then we'll take a steamboat to New Orleans and get a schooner back to Scotland. Lass, I canna go without ya. Ya know I love ya more than life itself."

Hannah stepped away from Kell's embrace. Her cheeks were wet with tears. Kell reached to take her back into his arms, but she put her hand up to stop him.

"Kell, I love you. I tried for a very long time not to, but I couldn't prevent what my heart told me was good."

"Then come with me, lass. We'll find someone here to watch over Sanctuary Hill. We can come back now and again. I need ya, Hannah. Come with me and be my wife."

"I can no more leave Sanctuary Hill than you can stay. I promised Benjamin Murphy I'd safeguard his family until they don't need me. Neither Naomi nor Ben is ready to lead this family and take over the business of Sanctuary Hill."

"Hannah, we can....."

"No, Kell, we can't. There is no other solution. I understand you must go. You would not be the man I love if you made any other decision."

"Hannah, I have no life outside you."

"I hope that isn't the case. I want you to have a good life, children, and a home."

"Is there naught I can say to change your mind?"

"Would you expect me to do less than you are willing to do? My place is here."

"Hannah, can we talk about this again later?"

"No. Let's part as friends. I am grateful that you let me know what it is to be loved, though. I won't ever forget what you've taught me."

ϕ

Kell left Sanctuary Hill on Friday, October 5. Hannah rode to Madison with him as he planned to catch the train back to Hopefield. Kell had pleaded with Hannah to come with him, finally telling her that she must be present to sign some legal documents for him. She assumed he wanted to give her his proxy to see over his farm and the almost completed house he'd started for their future home.

They spent some time in the little office of Mr. Oldham, the attorney, signing document after document. Then Kell took Hannah to the little café near the train station for a noon meal. They spent a quiet hour, barely speaking and picking at the food in front of them. The small talk was painful but necessary to get them through this time until the train departed. Finally, they heard the whistle blare. Kell drove the few blocks to the station and lifted Hannah down from the wagon.

"Hannah Ruth, I love ya to the core of my being. I don't know if I can live without ya."

"Please don't make this any harder than it is. I love you. You have taught me how to love. I am proud you are a man who lives his convictions. I wish you well and your family, too."

"I have one more favor to ask. I want ya to take Graystoke as your own. He's the finest horse I've ever owned. I need to know he'll be well-kept and loved."

"I will see to his care. When your property is sold, how can I send you the funds?"

"The lawyer wrote it all out in those papers, he gave ya, lass. I'm not concerned." The whistle shattered the quiet once again. "Well, that's the last whistle. Will you let me kiss you one last time?"

Hannah nodded, and even though they were in a public place, Kell kissed Hannah, showing the depth of the love he had for her. When he pulled himself away, Hannah saw the tears flowing down his face. He walked to the open door of the passenger car and turned.

"God bless ya, lass. Never doubt I love ya. You'll forever remain in my thoughts, dreams, and prayers." Kell turned and he was gone.

Chapter 29

"No doubt about it: the Lord your God has blessed you
in all that you have done."
Deuteronomy 2:7

Hannah turned Graystoke toward Sanctuary Hill. In her lap lay all the deeds to Kell's property, a proxy to take care of any unfinished business, and a letter turning over ownership of his prized stallion to her. In her soul lay the dead weight of his leaving. Hannah had never known such loss—promised love now gone. She was relieved she'd refused Ben's and Naomi's offer to accompany her to the train station. She couldn't stem her constant flood of tears.

She knew that day-to-day life at Sanctuary Hill must go on. Harvest season was coming to a close. The rest of the cotton had to be harvested, baled, and sold. Yes, life would go on. Hannah knew the thing that had given her life joy the past few months and a vital hope that her future would not be a repeat of her past was gone. Her life would continue, but it would be her old life, the one she'd always known—only worse. She'd never known a hurt like the loss of Kell Kincaid.

On her isolated journey home, Hannah screamed. Nothing intruded on her desperation except the ancient pines, brambles, and briars, rutted, dirty roads, and a frightened squirrel who dashed up an old oak tree. "Kell Kincaid, why didn't you leave me alone? I told you to leave me be, more than once. I was able to deal with my life before.

How do you expect me to continue with this dead weight in my soul? I almost hate you for making me feel this loss."

Hannah pushed Graystoke into a quicker pace. "Get on, boy. Take me home so I can find something to get him out of my head."

Hannah did what she said. She found chore after chore to fill her time—working in the fields until it was too dark to see, constant cleaning, reshelving, and moving items at the store, and canning every edible thing she could find in the woods, from her late garden, or the mercantile. If that didn't fill every waking hour, she sewed clothes for the Kincaids in the quarters. She worked until she was exhausted so she could sleep.

Hannah didn't smile anymore. Laughter became an alien thing. Once again, the obligation of Sanctuary Hill was what she dealt with, not the joy and connection of family that she learned while Kell was a part of her life. She refused to go to the Community Church because Kell was so much a part of that place. Seeing Brother Sam only brought images of Kell—they had been best of friends. The only part of Kell's influence that she couldn't put away was her need to read scripture. She'd read the Bible every day for so long that it had become a habit. She couldn't sleep if she didn't spend some time in the Word. Most nights, she found comfort in what she read.

After she'd missed church for three Sundays in a row, Brother Sam came to the mercantile about noon on Wednesday. He took Hannah a bowl of soup that Mary Lee had made. Being the end of October, the weather was fit for a bowl of hot vegetable soup.

"Hello, Hannah. We've been missin' you at the church," Sam said.

"Oh, good afternoon. Can I help you?"

"No. I just came by to bring you some soup. Mary Lee made it this mornin', and it's good. You'll enjoy it on this nippy day."

"Thank you. That is very thoughtful."

"How have you been?" Sam didn't shift his gaze from her face.

"I'm fine. Been very busy. We've nearly got the crop out—probably by the end of next week. Then I can get back to the store more than just Wednesday and Saturday morning."

"That so? I was thinkin' you must be sick. You've missed church the last three Sundays."

"Just too much to do." Hannah picked up a bolt of fabric to return to its place on the shelf. Sam followed her down the aisle. "Hannah, why are you avoiding the church and your friends there?"

"I don't want to talk about it."

"I promised Kell I'd look after you. I know that you're hurt, Hannah, but goin' back behind that wall where Kell found the real Hannah isn't the answer to your hurt."

About that time, another customer came in. "Excuse me, Sam. I need to wait on Mrs. Tyer."

"Hannah, I want you to come to the church when you're done for the day."

"I can't. I'm needed at home. We're still pulling bolls."

"They'll be there tomorrow. I'm writing to Kell tonight. I don't want to share bad news with him."

"That's blackmail, Sam."

"Call it as you will. I'll see you about 5:00."

When Hannah closed the store at five o'clock, she grudgingly rode Graystoke the short distance to the church. She found Sam reading his Bible, sitting at a table near a lamp glowing in shades of red, orange, and blue. The sun was glinting pink through the church windows as it neared the horizon.

"I'm here. I can't stay long. It will be dark soon."

"I'll see you home. Hannah, Kell and I had a very long talk about you on the Wednesday before he left on Friday."

"Did you?"

"Kell talked to me about things that were on his heart. Lately, most of those conversations were about you."

"I don't know what you want me to say." She fidgeted with the strings of her reticule.

"Kell loves you."

"Yes. I know."

"He prayed that God would show him a way for you to be together. He knew that you would not leave Naomi and Sonny—I mean Ben. I don't know if I'll ever get used to calling him Ben."

"Prayers don't always get answered, I guess—not even for a true believer like Kell."

"Yes, Hannah, they do get answered. Some answers come immediately. Other times God allows us to wait, but sometimes the answer is 'I have something better for you'."

"I think sometimes the answer is you don't deserve any better. Be satisfied with what you have," Hannah snapped back.

"That's very cynical. Why would a loving Father ever say such a cruel thing?"

"What do I know about a loving father? My father was a domineering, angry selfish man who ignored me most of my life and used me for political and financial advantage when he gave me to Richard Murphy."

"Seems you've been hurt a great deal in your life. Kell knew that. He wanted nothing more than for you to know what love is and how it is to feel cherished."

"I knew for about three months. Now I know what it is to have my heart crushed. That never happened to me before because no one has ever loved me as Kell did. I have never felt such a loss, except perhaps when my mother died, but I was a little girl then."

"Kell hoped you could remember the good. Do you know that hasn't gone away?" Sam reached across the table and took her hand. "He showed you how it feels to be valued. He taught you to love in return. Hannah, those lessons remain."

"Sam, I need to go home. I've work to do. All this talk doesn't change one thing that I have to deal with every day."

"I'm not going to stop trying to reach you. Will you come talk to me again?"

"I really don't have time. Besides, I can talk until the world ends, and it won't bring Kell back into my life. Anyway, I've got to go to Memphis next week to sell the cotton. I dread that trip. We'd planned to make that our wedding trip."

"I'll still be here when you get back."

₲

Hannah made the trip to Memphis in the middle of the week. She hoped to avoid being pulled into any weekend social engagement the Levensteins would expect her to attend. She also insisted Ben go with her. She was determined that he learn something of the business end of cotton growing. Hannah booked two boarding house rooms for them. She didn't want to spend the money the Gayoso would cost, but if she admitted the truth, she didn't want to relive the memories of the previous year. Being in the city was enough.

The afternoon she and Ben arrived, Hannah visited Levenstein's cotton brokerage. She introduced Ben to Mr. Levenstein and his principal broker. Once again, they were glad to get the sample from Sanctuary Hill. They promised an offer first thing the following morning.

Ben was excited to be back in a large city. Having lived near Baltimore and in Washington, D.C., he knew this city would have stores, large houses, and entertainment places to visit, but he was most enthralled by the riverfront and the docks. He stood for some time watching the dockhands load enormous containers and scores of cotton bales on steamships—some going upstream and some going down the Mississippi.

"Hannah, look. Is that what they'll do with our cotton?" Ben continued staring at the muscular men hefting the bales onto their shoulders.

"That will depend on who buys it, Ben. We will never know really. After we finish baling the crop, y'all will deliver it to Mr. Levenstein's warehouse in Hopefield. He'll decide where and how it will be shipped."

"I can't wait to get home and tell Molly about this. Maybe I can bring her to Memphis to see all the sights."

"That would be fun, but you're going to have to wait until Nomie gets older." Nomie was the nickname Ben gave his five month old daughter "Right now, Molly still has to feed her."

"We can wait. Nomie is fun, too. We like taking care of her. Can't we go shoppin' so I can get a present for Molly and Nomie? They'd like it if I brought 'em home a present."

"All right, but then we need to return to the boarding house for supper."

The next morning at 9:00, Hannah and Ben returned to finalize the sale of their crop. Mr. Levenstein and his broker met them with paperwork ready to sign.

"Mr. Murphy and Mrs. Murphy. Again, you've brought us a quality crop. The lint is clean and white. Your lint length is among the best we've seen this harvest."

"Thank you, Mr. Levenstein," Ben said. "All the Kincaids work hard to make a good crop."

"Well, I hope you had a bumper crop. We'll take all you have if you can accept our offer. I'm afraid the price of cotton has fallen from last year, Mrs. Murphy. The goin' rate is about fourteen cents a pound this year," the broker said.

"Goodness, that is a significant price drop." Dismay was clear on Hannah's face—remembering all the labor it took to get the crop ready to sell.

"You can go to another broker and try to get a better price, Mrs. Murphy, but that seems to be the standard rate this year," Mr. Levenstein said. "The market has more cotton than last year. Farmers are getting back on their feet and are planting again, most using sharecroppers for labor," Mr. Levenstein explained.

"I see. We trust you to be fair with us, sir. It is because we don't use sharecroppers that I am disappointed. We are doing well with tenant farmers, who all have a stock in the profit. Admittedly, we are still rebuilding at Sanctuary Hill. Our home and many of the outbuildings received heavy damage during the war, and others were destroyed."

"Well, you are doing a fine job with your crops. Because of the quality, I am prepared to offer you fifteen and a half cents a pound. I know I can get a fair price for it at market."

"Thank you, Mr. Levenstein. We will deliver the crop to your warehouse before the first of December," Ben told the cotton brokers.

"Mr. Murphy, do you know how much cotton we can expect from Sanctuary Hill this year," Mr. Morris asked.

A huge grin popped onto Ben's face. "Yes, sir. We'll finish baling by the end of next week. We ain't having no fire this year, either. We've been posting guards ever since we baled the first load back in

August. We're countin' on deliverin' thirty-five bales of Sanctuary Hill cotton this year."

"That's excellent, young man. Your grandfather Hugh would be so proud of you for returning his land to producing so much fine cotton. You know, Hugh was a dear friend for many years. I am proud to do business with his grandson." Hannah stood back and watched Ben as he signed the contract and shook hands with both the men. His straight shoulders and wide smile told Hannah her pressing him to come was the right decision. With honest tradesmen and loyal friends, Ben could learn to handle routine business transactions. Hannah sighed with relief and gratitude for the successful transaction.

"Can I take y'all to dinner tonight, Mrs. Murphy? I'd like to celebrate our deal if you can accommodate an old man."

"Thank you, but not this time. We must return home on the afternoon train. My brother-in-law's family is waiting for him."

"And how is Mr. Kell Kincaid? I was hoping to see him again," Ira Levenstein asked.

"Mr. Kincaid has returned to Scotland on family business."

"Such a pity. I liked that young man."

"Good day, sir. We must catch the ferry, so we don't miss our train."

"I look forward to receiving your crop soon."

Even with the decreased price, Sanctuary Hill's cotton had sold for $2,712.50. Hannah had been planning for more, but she had been warned that prices vary with the size of the harvest and the quality of the cotton. Their cotton still earned top price, so everyone would receive a good return, even after they held back crop money for the next growing season and paid their taxes.

After paying the ginning bill of $525, Hannah had more than $2,000.00 to share with her tenant farmers. She knew that seemed a small return for the long hours of labor, but each family received nearly triple what they earned during their first season. She also gave Marcus the foreman's share.

"Miss Hannah, ya can't mean it. You gonna give me four hundred dollars?" Marcus trembled as she counted the money into his hand. "What am I gonna do with all that money?" Hannah had to laugh. Marcus's eyes were the size of guinea eggs. "Lord, be praised. I gotta be dreamin'."

"Marcus, you earned every cent. Not only did you work as hard as any other tenant, but you have also been a good manager and have taught Ben so much about cotton farming."

"I ain't gonna feel safe with so much money in my house. What if we get robbed or burned out by the night riders?" Shataka shook her head. "No sir, Marcus. Ain't keepin' that money in our house!"

"I know it's a lot. If you want me to, I'll put it in the old safe that Mr. Hugh had in his office. We still have it tucked away in the corner of the dining room."

"That would be better. I'll bet the folks won't want all their money neither. $332.25 is a hoard of money. Can we just come get what we need from time to time?" Shataka asked.

"Of course, you can. I'll keep a record of what you put away and what you take out."

"Miss Hannah, you been mighty kind to us Kincaids. We never 'spected to own our place or to have money to use for ourselves. We thank ya."

"Marcus, no thanks is needed. We have worked together, all of us, to survive. Without your willingness to work the land, Mother Naomi, Ben, and I would have nothing to live on. I am grateful for your hard work and that of all your family."

"Dear Lord, He's been mighty good to us all. How much should we put back for next season?"

"Marcus, you and Ben decide things for the farm. You did fine this year, so I trust you'll do as well next time. But remember, we still have to pay our taxes. I'll find out the amount next week. I'll make a trip to Madison."

"Imagine, Shataka, me a payin' my taxes. I must be a rich man."

"Hush up your silly face, Marcus. We ain't rich, but we sure are blessed. Let's get home and fix us a feast." Shataka pecked Marcus on the cheek.

The other tenants were as pleased as Marcus had been, and like him, they didn't want so much money in their cabins. Hannah had taken on another role...that of Sanctuary Hill banker.

Two days after Hannah returned from Memphis, Sam and Mary Lee Naylor drove to Sanctuary Hill for a visit. The day was pleasantly warm for mid-November, so Sam used the warm weather as an excuse to visit with Hannah.

After a short visit with the family in the parlor, Sam asked to speak to Hannah alone. "Hannah, will you drive with me to check on Kell's property? In his last letter, he asked me to get a bit of information from you."

Since Sam had asked in front of the family, she couldn't refuse without some kind of explanation. "Yes, I guess I can go."

As soon as they were seated in the buggy, Sam headed toward Kell's land. "Kell asked me to check on the progress of your house."

"My house? You mean Kell's house, don't you?"

"Haven't you read any of those documents he gave you before he left Madison?"

"No. I've had no need. He's not asked me to see about his farm or the herd."

"He turned his cattle and the horses over to Lucas, Aaron, and Lijah to watch for the time being. He struck a deal that they would own outright any calf or colt born to his herd for the next two years in exchange for their tending his livestock."

"I didn't know that."

Sam groaned. "You would have known, Hannah, if you'd cared to read the document. He left you all his land, the barn, the cabin, and the new house he was building for you. He told me in no uncertain terms that the house belongs to you."

"What if I don't want his property?" Hannah's voice had an edge that would cut leather. "I never asked him to build a house or to—to take care of me. I don't need the pity and charity of any man."

"Hannah, you are being unfair to Kell."

"I told him from the start I'd never be dependent on anyone again. Just because he's gone, I've not changed my mind. I don't need Kell Kincaid or anyone else. I can take care of myself and all my obligations."

"Pride is a mighty cold bedfellow, Hannah. Have you read any of the letters he has sent you?"

"No."

"Would you like to hear what Kell wrote in his last letter?"

"No, I wouldn't."

"Then he's right. You won't let your heart free to know the blessings you've been given."

"Did he say that?"

"Yes. He wanted to be your husband more than you'll ever know. I'm not sure he realized it or not, but your heart is not free to love. You've too many shackles from your past."

"That's pretty judgmental for a preacher, isn't it, Sam?"

"Hannah, Kell told me when we first became friends that he would never wed any woman who didn't know the Lord. He said he had seen what happened when couples were unevenly yoked. I asked him about this when he told me he'd proposed to you. He said the Lord had chosen you for him and that you would find your way when you had lived in His constant love for a while. Kell was willing to take that chance because he loved you that much. His faith was that strong. Could be I'm wrong, but I am almost glad Kell had to go back to Scotland. I couldn't stand to see him hurt again."

Hannah was stunned by Sam's attack on her. She had loved Kell. Sam had no right to deny that love. Yet this man who had been Kell's best friend believed her unworthy of Kell.

"Take me home. I've heard enough. Why did you bring me out here anyway?" The quivering sound of the words spoke of Hannah's anger.

"I told you, Hannah. Kell wants a report about your house. He won't finish the payment for it until he's sure it's finished."

"All right. Go in and inspect the house and make your report. That's good business, I guess."

"You're a good businesswoman, Hannah. You're thorough and methodical in evaluating what is good and right."

"I try to be. You can't manage things you ignore."

"Then I have a proposition for you. I don't believe I can ever reach you through your heart. Maybe I can show you the lesson Kell wanted you to learn through your head."

"I don't have the least notion of what you are talking about, Sam Naylor."

"Well, Hannah, your house is right around this bend. Let's look it over and then I'll tell you."

When Hannah saw the nearly completed house, she was in awe. The house wasn't as large as Sanctuary Hill, but it was spacious and grand. Across the front and south side ran a six-foot-wide porch with a roofline supported by massive columns. The façade of the house was centered by a double door and six floor-to-ceiling windows. The shutters were the dark hunter green of the Kincaid kilt. Over the door hung an etched shield with the Kincaid family emblem, and the motto, *This Will I Defend.*"

Each room of the house was large and filled with light. The formal parlor and the sitting room on the first floor had massive stone fireplaces. On each hearth sat a fire screen bearing the Kincaid family crest. One wall of the sitting room contained built-in bookshelves that could hold scores of books, as did the smaller, darker room on the other side of the fireplace. The kitchen was sunny and well laid out around a large cook stove and a sink with a pump.

She finished her tour of the house upstairs. Kell had built three spacious bedrooms on the west wing of the house and one large room on the other. This was the room Kell had claimed for himself. Adjacent to that bedroom was a small room with a copper bathtub, much like the one at the Gayoso Hotel.

Everywhere she looked, she saw Kell's influence—colors he liked, carved windowsills like those he'd admired at the Levensteins' home, and beautiful stained wood floors. Every room had a closet, a thing unheard of in the homes she'd lived in before.

This house also had all the elements she'd told Kell she loved and remembered from her childhood home in Maryland—sunlit rooms, a fireplace in her bedroom, and the beautiful woodwork stained a rich walnut color. He had even had a stained-glass transom installed over the front door with an image of a raven-haired girl dancing in wildflowers.

Hannah was speechless. Kell built this house for her. The design was perfect, so well planned. But did it matter? She would never live there. Every minute would torment her.

"Sam, if you are satisfied the job is complete, I'd like to go home."

"Do you not see in every inch of this house the love Kell Kincaid has for you, Hannah?"

"This is a beautiful house and well-built. Surely you don't think I could live here."

"I don't care whether you do or don't, Hannah. I just hoped you could feel the love you are denying. Kell didn't want to leave you any more than you wanted him to go. He did what he had to do."

"I know that. I'm not blaming Kell for meeting his obligation to his family. That is the same reason I couldn't go with him. I take responsibility for my hurt. I swore I'd never let another in, but I did."

"Prideful and stubborn...young woman, you are pushing me to my limits. After all the blessings God has heaped on you in the past two years, you still deny the greatest gift. Kell feared you might never know God's love. That was his greatest regret that he couldn't help you see it."

"Sam, please take me home. I don't want to talk about Kell anymore. I have a life to live alone. I don't need reminders of my foolishness."

"All right, Hannah, but there is something I want you to do for me. I want you to use your mind to look at your life since you came to Arkansas...just these past two years."

"What are you getting at, preacher?"

"Make a two-column list. Put the heading *My Life Since April 1866*. On one column write all the terrible things that have happened to you. On the other side write all the blessings God has placed in your path. Will you try? If you will, we'll talk in a couple of weeks, and then I'll leave you alone."

"Sam, this is ridiculous and time-consuming."

"Would it be worth it to get me off your back?"

"I suppose so."

"Well, humor an old preacher who likes you a lot, girl, and cherishes a dear friend who loves you."

"I don't see the point, but I will try."

"Just chalk it up to doin' a favor for your favorite preacher. Anyway, I'd like to see you back in church. You may not get anything from my sermons, but your friends are concerned about you."

Chapter 30

"Do not remember the former things or consider the things of
old. I am about to make a new thing."
Isaiah 43:18-19

Hannah did as Brother Sam asked her to do. She took her journal, which she'd neglected for several years, and wrote across one page 'My Life Since April 1866'. She then divided the linen-toned parchment into two columns, which she headed MY LOSS and MY BLESSINGS. Each night before she read scripture, she would sit and think of things to put under the two headings. At first, her negative thoughts were all that came to mind. Horrible, ugly things that she remembered over and over, but by Saturday of the second week, the day before Brother Sam wanted to see her list, she found her expectations were false. The number of good things far outnumbered the bad ones.

What I Lost

1. The house was a wreck.

2. Four confrontations with Night riders

3. Kell's barn was burned, destroying one-quarter of the crop.

4. Narvel Tangent's continuing threats toward Ben and the family.

5. Kell left me to return to Scotland.

6. My peachy complexion and smooth hands are no more

How I've Been Blessed

1. From the first day here, the house did provide shelter.
2. The Kincaids from the quarters had stayed at Sanctuary Hill.
3. The farm provided for us until the first crop was sold.
4. Lumber from our forest was bartered for material to repair the roof.
5. The lumber deal also provided much-needed cash.
6. Community Church helped rebuild the barn.
7. I made friends with women in the community.
8. Two years of taxes have been paid.
9. Good crops allowed us to buy work animals.
10. Cash remained for food and other needs.
11. Mr. Levenstein became a trusted friend and business connection.
12. The Millers have become good friends and valuable business partners.
13. Molly joined the family and is a true asset.
14. Everyone is blessed by baby Nomie.
15. Ben is maturing and taking responsibility at the farm.
16. Good crop in 1867.
17. The mercantile was profitable that year.
18. Naomi is happy to be back at Sanctuary Hill with old friends.
19. An excellent garden took away the fear of hunger.
20. Aaron Pierce settled as a tenant farmer with us.
21. Lijah Kincaid's family added to the workforce.
22. The tenant farming arrangement is working well. The families work to buy land.
23. Riding Graystoke around the property is a pleasure.

24. I've developed a sense of confidence and competence through working.

25. I've developed a backbone. No one will run over me again.

26. I enjoy reading scripture.

27. Kell loved me for a while.

When Hannah went to church that Sunday, she did so gladly. She realized Sam was right. She missed the family of believers at the Community Church. Even though she'd still not found the connection she knew many of them had made, she wanted to be a part of the congregation. After services, Sam sought her out. "Did ya do the little task I asked you to do, Hannah?"

"I tried, Sam." She took the folded parchment from her Bible.

"I am proud of you, young lady," the preacher said as he turned over the page to look at her lists. "You gave it a good effort."

"Well, the first day, my two columns were about the same length, but as I truly started to think about the past two and a half years, I began to see so many more blessings than losses, but Sam two of those losses are all but overwhelming."

"But you have survived regardless. Did ya learn anything special, even from the bad times?"

"Obviously, I've had many blessings since we came to Arkansas. I'm sure there are more that I didn't think of. I must admit Someone has been watching out for me. I have worked very hard, but I couldn't have accomplished all these things by myself."

Sam smiled in a way that always reminded Hannah of Kell. "That's a good lesson for you to learn. Hannah, none of us can thrive alone. We may try—work ourselves to death, but eventually, we all find that the Lord has been looking after us all the time."

"Kell told me that."

"He knows that lesson all too well."

"I miss him. I don't know if I'll ever get over his loss. I am so angry with him for making me care."

"I miss him, too. The loss is still raw. Kell's been gone barely two months. Give yourself some time to grieve."

∮

The cold winter came and passed with little to note. Christmas that year was not nearly as joyous or memorable as the last one. The highlight of the day was Nomie playing among her toys as she scooted across the parlor floor. She was an active little girl and loved toddling among her adoring family members.

The winter had been cold, but for the most part dry. Unlike the year before, only twice did Sanctuary Hill see snow enough to cover the cobbled drive. Marcus told Hannah and Ben that all the weather signs predicted an early spring. Toward the end of February, he and Ben had already made plans to start plowing by the first week in March.

"Miss Hannah, all the signs are good. Shataka came in yesterday with a ladybug on a leaf. That's good luck. Those ladybugs always mean spring's near."

"Yeah, and besides we saw a bluebird in a nest already and a robin digging for a worm in the garden. The surest sign was the woodpecker a'tappin' out his territory. Mom Bec said that's proof we can get an early start 'cause spring's sure comin','" Ben added.

"You two decide when and where you are going to grow your crops. I'll tend the store and help when needed." Hannah picked up her coat and started toward the door.

Ben caught her arm. "Hannah, wait. We got one other idea we been thinkin' about. Marcus and me think we need to add a couple more crops to our farm this year. People need other stuff besides cotton."

"That's true. What are you going to plant?" she asked.

"Seems to be a lot of call for corn and hay around the county. We been told the railroad camp a ways north of here will buy all they can get." Marcus stood, shifting his hat from hand to hand.

"Marcus, as I told you before, you and Ben are the managers of this farm. You decide what to plant, how much you plant, and when you need help." Hannah forced a smile in Ben's direction—proud of his initiative but irritated with being brought into the farm business.

Life changed little from day to day. Each day was a time to work, solve problems, and keep tabs on all the business conducted at the mercantile, the farm, the tenants, and the family under her care. All of those seemed to grow. The Sanctuary Hill family increased by two that spring. Aaron Pierce married Nan Freeman at Easter. He brought the shy young woman to live in his newly expanded, renovated cabin. Aaron's hard work and talent as a carpenter had transformed the small one-room cabin into a neat three-room house. The structure showed little resemblance to the cabin Aaron moved to his land. He had covered the exterior with clapboard and had put blue shutters at the newly installed glass-paned windows. He had also built a massive stone fireplace in the parlor and added a kitchen and bedroom. His industry had led the Kincaids to make improvements in their cabins.

The second person added to the Sanctuary Hill family was the little boy born to Shataka and Marcus. They named the baby Moses F. Kincaid. Marcus had told her, "Miss Hannah, when you write down our new young'un in the record book, please write out his whole name—Moses Freeman Kincaid."

When the postmaster died suddenly, the local post office was moved to the Kincaid Mercantile. The store became much busier as a result. Hannah became the new postmistress by default. She didn't mind much, though, because more people came to the store more frequently. She found that sales and profits both rose. By the end of the third month, she had been able to save the profit from the store as insurance against a bad crop year. By the stroke of fate, Hannah felt sure that adequate funds to pay the taxes were safely put away, offering some sense of security for Ben and Naomi.

And at the end of each day, Hannah returned to her mother-in-law's house, spent—exhausted from the endless work. She tried to put up a pleasant façade, but she knew her attempts failed miserably. Try as she could, she found nothing to look forward to, except another day of work just like the one she had finished.

Naomi had become once again the queen of the county's social life. She was always busy with one activity or another. Ben and Molly were a happy little family, playing with their precious little girl. In early May, they told the family they were expecting another addition to the family. Aaron teased that Ben had learned to play tumbling in the hay, too.

As much as Hannah tried to be happy for the blessings that were befalling her family, each new joy screamed out what she lacked in her own life. Since Kell left, the void he once filled was unbearable. Her greatest frustration was that she had no idea of how to make the loss go away. Coupled with the anger and disgust she bore toward herself for letting him become so important to her, her emptiness made every day as dark and meaningless as the day before. If it were not for the promise she'd made to Benjamin Murphy to safeguard his family, her life would have no purpose at all.

φ

Toward the end of October on a rainy Friday night, Ben burst into the kitchen. For a change, he wasn't moping about the cotton they had not been able to pick because of the rain last week. He could hardly stand still. His excitement tumbled out. "Hannah, I knew plantin' those new crops would be good for our farm. We got us a good order already."

"Slow down, Ben. Take a breath and tell me about what has happened." Hannah handed him a cloth to dry the rain from his face.

"That railroad camp needs hay and corn. They're paying good prices to have it delivered. All we gotta do is take 'em a hundred shocks of hay and seventy bushels of corn. They're gonna pay us $300.00."

"Ben, do we have that much to spare after we reserve enough to feed our animals and Kell's herd through the winter?"

"Aw, shucks. We even got more. We got Kell's barn full of hay already. We got corn set aside for our animals and us too. We could even feed a few hogs if we decide to buy some."

"All right, Ben. If you and Marcus decide it is a good business deal, you are in charge, but remember we still have bolls in the field and some ginning and baling to finish before I can go to Memphis in November."

"We won't stop getting our cotton ready for market. We'll do this on the side."

"I am happy for your successful venture, Ben. You are becoming quite the businessman." Hannah's words were meant to encourage, but somehow she dreaded the new venture. Perhaps she just didn't want Ben to become too independent. What would be her role when he proved a success without her advice?

Two weeks later at 6:00 a.m., Marcus, his son Abraham, and Ben drove two wagons loaded with hay and bushels of corn down the cobbled drive toward the main road, headed for the railroad camp. The delivery would take most of the day as the camp was nearly as far north as Madison was to the west. Ben yelled back to Hannah, who was standing on the porch, "Tell Molly I'll be home before too late. Tell her don't have our new baby 'til I get back." Then he laughed.

Naomi stood in the open doorway. "My son is proud of himself right now, isn't he?"

"Mother Naomi, I didn't know you were up already. Yes, he is becoming very confident, and he has a right. He has made some good decisions lately."

"I never thought to see him grow into a man. Now he's a good farmer, a husband, and a loving father. I guess I didn't have enough faith that God would heal him completely."

"Ben will probably always need someone to oversee—to encourage him, but he will live a much fuller life than either of us expected he would. Your bringing him back to the land was the right decision for him."

"Yes. He's a born farmer. I am so proud of him."

"I think you have also benefitted from coming back to Arkansas. You're the center of the social life here. I suppose that was how you lived when your father was the master of Sanctuary Hill."

"Yes, especially after my mother died. I do enjoy being with the ladies I've known most of my life. There is no stress or pretense that I felt in Washington. I'm only sorry that life for you hasn't been as good."

Hannah turned her back. The last thing she wanted was to become the center of Naomi's attempts to make her life better.

"And Hannah, I need to apologize to you. I have not been kind to you at times. I remember one time I accused you of being a bad wife to Richard…"

"No, Mother Naomi, I knew you were upset."

"Let me finish, daughter. I know Richard was not a good husband to you. You, dear, have been the saving grace for this family. You have helped Sonny—I mean Ben—learn his role, and you've taken the wreck of our house and made it back into a comfortable home. I know what you've sacrificed for us. I just wanted to tell you that I know."

"Things are fine with me. I'm doing what I expected to do. We are slowly but surely getting the family back on stable footing. But thank you for telling me. I love you and Ben. You're the only family I've known since my mother died."

When the wagons rolled in from the railroad camp near sunset, Marcus, Ben, and Abraham were not shouting celebration 'hellos' that should have come from their day's work. Abraham slumped over with his head in his father's lap. His knees were pulled close to his chest. He moaned in pain. Marcus's clenched jaw and dark staring eyes spoke of his concern.

Ben sat slumped in his seat, barely holding his head up, as he reined the mules to a halt.

"Hannah, please come help Abraham," Ben called out. "He's hurtin' somethin' fierce."

Hannah ran across the porch and climbed on the wheel to see about Abraham. His face was hot to the touch.

"What do you think is the matter, Marcus?" Hannah asked.

"I got no idea. He was fine when we got to the camp and was unloading the corn and hay before noon. Those fellas at the camp was nice to us. They asked us to eat the noon meal with 'em. We was glad to. They had some fresh bread and some mighty good stew. The cook said it was Irish stew, but it tasted fine. They had real coffee, too. I had me two cups. Ben and Abe just had cold water from the creek. We stayed about two hours and then started home. We was only on the

393

road about an hour when my boy started complaining about his belly crampin'."

"You are not well, Ben. Did those railroad men have some ailment?" Hannah asked.

"I gotta chill and my head hurts real bad. The boss did say a few of those Irishmen had been puny. I do feel kinda sick at my stomach."

Hannah walked over to the second wagon. She found Ben was also feverish, but not as hot as Abraham. "Marcus, take Abraham to Kell's cabin. I don't know why he's so sick, but we don't need to spread the sickness if it's bad. I'll get the doctor here somehow. I'll try to find Aaron."

"Yes, ma'am. You want me to take Mr. Ben there too?"

"I think that's best. We have little Nomie here and with Molly expecting another baby…Yes, take Ben and Abraham. Let me get you some more blankets. I'll come to help you as soon as I can get someone to go for Dr. Bolden."

"Hannah, what's wrong?" Naomi opened the door just as Marcus drove toward the creek road.

"Don't fret, Mother Naomi. I'm only taking precautions. I think they must have picked up some illness at the railroad camp. We don't need it to spread."

Hannah ran to the barn, fitted Graystoke's bit and rein, and jumped on his bareback to ride to Aaron's house. She hoped he was there. She needed a messenger, and she feared Aaron may have to search Madison to find the doctor.

Hannah rode back to Sanctuary Hill with Nan behind her in the wagon. She wanted Nan to keep Naomi occupied while she went to help Marcus. Unfortunately, they arrived too late. Naomi had already gone to Kell's cabin. She'd called Lijah and told him to drive her to take care of her son.

"Nan, will you stay here? I'm gonna ask Mom Bec to come up here and make some chicken broth to ease those stomach cramps. She may need some help."

"Of course, Hannah."

Hannah gathered some clean rags. She knew that cool water helped to lower fevers. She rushed back to Graystoke and rode to the cabin as quickly as the great stallion could carry her. When she arrived, Abraham was outside on the porch, retching and gagging. The liquid he expelled was vile green and putrid. At times, he would try to expel the horrid bile, and nothing came from his mouth. He writhed with pain in his lower torso. Marcus held him the best he could, but it was clear to Hannah that he felt helpless.

"Marcus, try to get him to lie down." The distraught father carried the seven-year-old into the bed and put him down.

Ben rolled into a ball on the floor. Naomi held his head in her lap. Tears streamed down her face, but she didn't make a sound. Her lips moved continually. Hannah knew she was praying.

"Mother Naomi, let me put a cool cloth on Ben's forehead. We need to keep the fever down." They spent the next three hours changing wet cloths, emptying the pots Ben and Abraham used to empty the vile liquid from their stomachs and helping them to the outhouse—over and over, until they could no longer walk the distance. Then Marcus and Lijah helped them with the chamber pot, that would be quickly emptied, rinsed, and returned to the bedside.

Finally, at 9:00 that night, Dr. Bolden arrived at Kell's cabin. He sent everyone away and examined Ben at once. Then he looked at Abraham. The doctor took very little time diagnosing the ailment. "Mrs. Murphy, these young men have cholera. The black boy seems to have worse symptoms than Mr. Murphy, but neither is goin' to be out of the woods for a couple of days."

"Cholera? They were both fine this morning when they left for the railroad camp. Now they are deathly ill," Hannah said.

"Will my son be all right, Doctor?" Naomi cried out.

"I will do what I can. The first thing is to keep that fever down. I'll give them some medicine that may help with the cramping. We need to get them to drink as much water as we can get down them. They lose too much fluid with all the retchin' and runnin'."

"Surely we can do something more!" Naomi ran up to the doctor and pulled at his collar.

"Naomi, you can pray, but you need to leave here and get some rest. Hannah will see to Ben."

"Yes, Doctor," Hannah said. "I will do what you said to do. Will you take Naomi back to the house?"

"No. No, I have to stay here to take care of my boy."

"No, Naomi. This is no place for you. You could get sick and then where would this family be?" The doctor took her arm and led her to his buggy. "Your boy will be taken care of. The last thing he needs is a sick mama to worry about."

Naomi continued to fuss, but Hannah directed her to the porch. She told her Ben and Abraham needed broth and tea, and it was Naomi's job to get them the liquid they needed.

When she sent Naomi home, she also sent Lijah back to bring Shataka down to help care for Abraham. "You stay with the families in the quarters. They will be afraid and need someone to take care of things until we can get past the crisis."

Hannah, Marcus, and Shataka became the nursemaids for the two sick boys. Constantly changing the wet cloths and forcing water into their mouths was an endless chore. By the morning of the second day, Ben began to show some improvement. His fever was not as high, and he was able to drink water, weakened tea, and broth, which he could keep down for a while. Abraham didn't seem to rally. Even small sips of broth caused him to vomit. Neither his mother nor his father could get him to swallow more than a tablespoon of water. At times, he kept the water down, but at other times, he would fall into another spasm of retching.

Dr. Bolden returned on Monday afternoon. He told Hannah that Ben had probably seen the worst of his bout with cholera. When she asked about Abraham, the doctor shook his head. "Mrs. Murphy, the worst thing that happens with this nasty disease is that all the retchin' and runnin' takes all the fluids out of the body. This causes havoc on the organs."

"Isn't there anything else we can try? He's only ten years old."

"Just do what you're doin' and pray for him. That's all the cure I know. Have any other of your folks started feelin' poorly? This disease can spread like a flood if it's not contained."

"No one has come to me, but we told them to stay away from the cabin. Will you stop at the big house and check on those folks for me?" Hannah asked.

"I will. If Ben doesn't have a fever in the next forty-eight hours, you can let him return to his family. He likely won't spread the cholera then. Burn all these clothes and the blankets and mattresses when the boys are well. We don't exactly know how cholera gets spread around."

When Dr. Bolden stopped at Sanctuary Hill, he discovered what he'd feared. Two of the members of the Murphy family had begun to show the early symptoms. Naomi and baby Nomie had fevers. Naomi complained of stomach cramps. Nomie cried continually. The doctor immediately sent for Hannah. "Hannah, you must get Molly out of the house. Being with child, Molly could get mighty sick—lose the baby. Maybe Mom Bec or Rose can see to the sick."

"Do you think Naomi and Nomie have cholera, too?"

"Appears so. Naomi was down with Ben, holding his head when he threw up. She might have come in contact with the disease. Molly said Naomi had rocked the little one to sleep last night. Naomi is in the same dress she was wearin' the last time I saw her. We know some people, especially little ones, are more prone to this sickness than others."

"What about the Kincaid's? Lijah went home to take care of the families so Shataka could help Marcus and me."

"I'll go down and see because I don't want this thing to spread any farther than it has." The doctor found Lijah with mild symptoms, but the baby Dorrie had given birth three months earlier had a very high fever. The doctor removed Lijah and Baby Ruthie and took them to Kell's cabin where Marcus and Shataka still tended their son.

When he returned to Sanctuary Hill, Dr. Bolden told Hannah about the two cases he'd found in Lijah's house. "No one else seems to be sick right now. If we can make it through two more days, I think we'll be past the danger that the cholera will spread further. You know what to do for these new cases, Hannah. And keep burnin' those contaminated clothes and blankets."

"I will do my best."

"And you need to get some rest, too. You don't need to come down with this sickness. I'll be back sometime tomorrow." The doctor picked up his satchel and left.

Hannah immediately sent Molly down to stay with Rose and Mom Bec. Molly tried to put up an argument, saying she should go down to nurse Ben. "Molly, think about the little one. Dr. Bolden said you could be in danger."

"Hannah, Nomie will cry if I'm not here to put her to bed."

"I'll rock her to sleep. You go down and get Mom Bec to make some more broth and weak tea. We must get Mother Naomi and Nomie to drink as much as we can."

About midnight of the third day, a very shaky Ben rode up to the porch of Sanctuary Hill. He stumbled his way into the parlor. "Hannah, Mama, is anyone up?" he called.

Hannah walked to the landing at the head of the staircase. "Ben, why are you up so late?"

"Abraham died a little while ago. He was shakin' so hard and jerkin' all over. Then he just stopped. Why didn't you come back to help us?"

"Ben, I didn't know any more to do. Your mama and Nomie are both sick. I have been taking care of them, just like Marcus, Shataka, and I were taking care of you early on."

"My Nomie is sick? Where is Molly?" Ben nearly fell in his agitation and weakness.

Hannah rushed down the stairs to help him to the settee. "Molly's not sick. I sent her away from the illness because of the new baby."

"Can I see my mama? It'll help if she knows I'm better."

"No, Ben. Not until her fever goes down. That's what the doctor said."

"I gotta do somethin'. My whole family is sick."

"Yes. You need to rest and get completely well. Why don't you ride Pal down to the quarters and let Molly know you're better. Then you two rest at Rose's house. I'll take care of things here."

Hannah felt a knot in her chest. How sad Marcus and Shataka must feel at the loss of their first born. She wanted to find some way to comfort them, but for now she had to focus on her mother-in-law and the sick toddler.

The next morning Rose came to help Hannah with the nursing. She insisted Hannah lie down for a nap, if only a short one.

"But Rose, your family needs you now. You've lost your grandson."

"Ain't nothing I can do to help Abraham now. Dorrie is takin' care of Lijah and Ruthie. Lijah don't seem so sick as I've seen. This ain't the first time I seen this ugly sickness. Cholera took my husband many years ago, but we didn't have no doctor then. I am scared for little Ruthie—her being so young."

"Thank you for coming to help me. I am exhausted, to tell the truth. I've slept little since last Friday night. What day is it today?"

"Miss Hannah, this is Wednesday. You best take care. We all know how important you are to this family. We can't let nothin' bad happen to you."

"Wake me if you need me. Nomie seems to be sleeping restfully, and she doesn't seem to have much fever now. If you can get her to drink some broth or water, let her have all she'll take."

Hannah got to sleep about two hours before Rose came to shake her. "Hurry, Miss Hannah. Miss Naomi is out of her head, cryin' out for her husband, Col. Ben and sayin' Richard is standing at her bed. Her face is terrible hot."

"All right, Rose. I'm coming."

"I gotta go back to the quarters. Glory came and told me little Ruthie is real bad."

Hannah ran down the stairs. Nomie screamed in fear at her grandmother's rantings. Hannah tried to put Naomi back in her bed, but the older woman fought as if deranged. When Hannah touched her forehead, she knew the fever was too high."

Hannah realized she was alone with Naomi and Nomie. She managed to calm her mother-in-law after several minutes. She led her back to her bed and placed cool, wet cloths on her face and chest. She fanned her with an old feather fan, hoping the fever would fall.

By noon, Naomi was delirious, calling out to her sons as she did when they were small. "Richie and Sonny dear, come over here and sit with your mama. Let me read you another story." At other times she carried on a conversation with her husband, telling him he must find more time to spend with his sons and chiding him for being away from home so much. Then she would revert to her childhood and talk to her mother and father, telling them of her new horse that she had named Scotty. The talking continued as did the fever. Hannah could not get her to take any liquid.

About sundown, Doctor Bolden returned. He managed to give Naomi enough laudanum to let her rest. He managed to get her to drink a couple of spoons of water. "Hannah Murphy, I told you to get some rest. You are going to be my next patient. I'll stay here with Naomi for a while. You go find a pillow and blanket and sleep. You have done all you can for your mother-in-law. She's in God's hands now."

Hannah awoke to the aroma of stew boiling on the stove and the scent of cinnamon in the air. Rose had prepared a late supper for her. Ben and Molly were in the kitchen, playing with Nomie who was still listless and cranky, but out of harm's way. Dr. Bolden sat at the table, eating the stew and fresh pone. He told her that Lijah was past the danger from the cholera, but beside himself at the loss of the baby. Little Ruthie had passed away just before the doctor had arrived at Sanctuary Hill, not that his presence would have made a difference.

After a quick supper, Hannah told the family she would care for Naomi through the night if they could take care of Nomie. Soon all had retired to the newly made beds. Outside, a large fire destroyed all the bed linens from the big house on which any cholera victim had slept. Hannah drew her chair near Naomi's bed and sat, watching the dear woman toss and turn in her drugged sleep. About midnight, Hannah heard a weak, trembling voice call out to her.

"Hannah, dear girl, come close. I'm…please promise…I need…."

"Mother Naomi, what is it you want?" Hannah leaned closer to hear the barely audible sound from her mother-in-law.

"Please take care of Sonny and my grandbaby. I will rest if I know you are watching over them."

"Mother, you don't need to worry. Ben and Nomie are both out of danger. You just rest and get your strength back."

"I have no strength left to fight with. And Benjamin is waiting for me. See he is there with his hand outstretched to me now."

"Mother Naomi, you are dreaming."

"No. Please promise me. You won't leave those children alone. They need you."

"You just rest now. I promise I will continue my guardianship as long as Ben needs me. Don't worry. Please rest."

A gentle smile touched Naomi's face. She closed her eyes and stopped her agitated movements for the first time in several hours. She reached out her hand in the direction of the door. She slept.

Hannah continued to apply the cool cloths to Naomi's face for some time. About three o'clock in the morning, Naomi whispered, "I'm coming, Benjamin." That Thursday morning, Mother Naomi found peace. Her outstretched hand lay atop the coverlet Hannah had so carefully placed around her. Her mother-in-law lacked the stamina to fight off the disease. However, the beautiful smile on her face told Hannah that Naomi had been right. Benjamin had taken his bride home with him.

Chapter 31

Pride goeth before destruction and a haughty spirit before a fall.
He that handleth a matter wisely shall find good;
and whosoever trusteth the Lord, happy is he.
Proverbs 16:18,20

Naomi Kincaid Murphy was laid to rest in the family cemetery next to her mother and father. The entire community turned out to honor one of their own. Brother Naylor read a beautiful eulogy, speaking of Naomi's generosity and kindness, mentioning several incidents Hannah had never heard of before. The Community Church pitched in to see that all the needs of the family were met during the entire week. They provided food, took care of the daily chores, and assumed nursing duties for members of the family who had contracted less serious bouts of cholera. Dr. Bolden remarked what a miracle had occurred because only three members of the family had succumbed to the deadly disease.

Hannah was numb to the loss. She believed she'd failed in her promise to Benjamin Murphy. Ben had nearly died, and Naomi's death was a shock. Now Hannah found herself walking through each day as if in a nightmare she couldn't awaken from. Ben's grief was overwhelming. While in many ways he'd become an adult in the last months, the person who mourned his mother was every bit the ten-year-old Hannah had met before her marriage to his older brother. Had it not been for Molly and Baby Nomie, Hannah doubted she could have saved Ben from following his mother to the grave.

"Hannah, what am I gonna do with my mama gone? She always took care of me," Ben said as they walked from the grave site.

"Ben, your mother knew you can take care of yourself now. Remember, you are the owner of Sanctuary Hill, and you've got your own family."

"I know that, but Mama has always been around to tell me when I did something right or wrong. She was teaching me and Molly how to be good parents to Nomie. And now we have another baby a'comin'."

"Ben, I will be here. I can't take your mother's place, but I will help whenever you need me."

"Please don't leave us alone, Hannah. Me and Mollie need you to show us things we don't know yet."

"I promise, Ben. I am going to be right here."

"That's good. I'm gonna check on Molly and Nomie. The baby still ain't feeling good."

"All right, Ben. I am so grateful that Nomie didn't get as sick as little Ruthie. It has been so sad to lose those two good children. Such a terrible loss for the Kincaids."

Christmas this year promised to be solemn because of the loss of loved ones and the weather had already turned extremely wet and bitterly cold. Hannah had no heart to celebrate. She made no plans to decorate, buy gifts for the tenant farmers, or even the members of the family. Making herself go to open the mercantile was almost beyond her. Only by dogged willpower did she drag herself to the store on the Monday after Naomi's funeral. She would not have gone then except Sam Naylor had come to the house the previous Saturday and reminded her in a not-too-gentle fashion that the community depended on her to order their Christmas needs this week if they were to be delivered by Christmas Day. That week was the last week she could send orders for catalog items and things that came from the warehouses in Memphis.

At seven o'clock on Monday, December 4, Hannah flipped the sign to OPEN. This was the first time in three weeks she had done so. She had come alone because Ben still lacked the energy to work for an entire day. Hannah realized he was recuperating, but this didn't change the situation. She did need some help. As soon as word got around that the mercantile was open, people began to flock to the store to place their Christmas orders.

She worked without pausing through the noon hour. Customers tried to be patient, but she sensed their frustration at the long wait for her to fill out their order sheets. Mary Lee Naylor came in and volunteered to help, but it took longer to tell her how to handle the sales and record the orders than if Hannah did it herself. Mary Lee only stayed about two hours.

"I am sorry, Hannah. I know I wasn't much help to you."

"Thank you for trying, Mary Lee."

About three that afternoon, Sam Naylor came to place his order for fruit and Christmas candy to give to the church members. "Hannah, I'm gonna do the church gifts this year. I know the past couple of months have been hard at Sanctuary Hill. Naomi always helped with this project, but I know you shouldered most of the work."

"That's true, Sam. I miss Naomi's help with some of our Christmas traditions. I haven't even gotten over to Memphis yet to sell our cotton. I don't see a light at the end of the tunnel. Ben is grieving so I don't know when I'm going to get any help from him. Some of the Kincaids are still weak from their bouts with cholera. Of course, two of those families lost someone, too."

"When's the last night you slept all night, Hannah?"

"I don't know. Things are still out of routine at Sanctuary Hill. Even when I go to bed, my mind continues to spin…trying to find solutions to all the problems that are still unresolved."

"Are you still reading your Bible?"

"When I have the time."

Sam Naylor opened his Bible and read. "Come unto me, all ye who labor and are heavily laden, and I will give you rest. Take My yoke upon you and learn of me, for I am meek and lowly in heart, and ye will find rest for your souls. For My yoke is easy, and my burden is light."

"Sam, I appreciate you're trying to help …" Before Hannah could finish her sentence, a stranger dressed in a black suit and black cravat walked through the front door. The gaunt features of the man sent shivers down Hannah's back. Even before he opened his mouth, she felt a sense of doom.

"I am looking for Mrs. Richard Murphy. I was told I would find her at this mercantile."

"I am Hannah Murphy."

"My name is Howard Floyd. I am from the circuit clerk's office in Madison."

"How do you do, Mr. Floyd? This is Brother Naylor, the pastor of the Community Church. Is there something I can do for you?" Hannah was angry with herself for failing to keep the tremors out of her voice.

"I need you to sign this affidavit that says I delivered this subpoena to you. Please sign it Mrs. Richard Murphy and put today's date below your signature." Mr. Floyd handed a fist full of papers to Hannah.

"A subpoena? Why are you serving me with a subpoena?" She looked down at the papers in her hand.

"The documents will explain the cause and set the date for you to appear in court with your attorney, if you choose to have one," Floyd answered.

Hannah took the folded document and opened it. The first words that caught her attention were PLAINTIVE: NARVEL TANGENT. She saw her name beside the word RESPONDANT. When she read the following paragraph, her dread was validated. Tangent was contesting Hannah's guardianship of Ben. She had been given one month to find an attorney.

Hannah handed the gaunt man his signed affidavit and walked him out. She closed the door and locked it as she turned the sign to CLOSED. It was only 3:30, but Hannah was done for the day.

"Are you all right, Hannah?" Sam asked her.

"I'm finished. I can't do this anymore. No matter how hard I work, how many things I accomplish or the hours I toil from one task to another, it's never enough. I'm tired of carrying the load and fighting a battle I can't win. Everything I've done has been for nothing."

"Hannah, that's not true."

"I don't want a sermon or a handful of false promises. Just leave me alone."

Hannah left the store. She didn't take the money from the till or any of the order forms to prepare for the freighters. She locked the door, jumped atop Graystoke, and headed toward the creek where she had first cried her anguish when she arrived in Arkansas nearly three years earlier. Even in the miserable cold, it was a better place for her than Sanctuary Hill where she had failed once again.

The sun edged below the horizon. The north wind whipped the limbs of the ancient trees that lined the creek. Hannah shivered and realized her hands and cheeks burned from the cold. She had stayed at the creek far too long. The clear night sky was moon bright, spangled with thousands of crystal specks—made sharper by the sharp, frigid wind. Nature mocked her defeat and failure. "Get me home, boy."

Hannah rode up to the porch, dismounted, and walked up to the door, and called out, "Ben, take Graystoke to the barn. Feed him well and bed him down for the night."

"I will. Hannah, where have you been? It's way past suppertime."

"Ben, surely you and Molly can have supper without me."

"Well, we did, but I was wonderin' where ya were. When I get back, I need to talk to you before I go to bed."

"Not tonight, Ben. I'm too tired. Put that horse away. I'm going to bed. I will talk to you in the morning." Hannah ran up the stairs where she ran into Molly who had just put Nomie to bed.

"Hannah, I'm glad you're home. We were so worried about you— being so late."

"Molly, you are a grown woman. You don't need me here to tell you when to eat supper or go to bed. You did fine without me."

"But you know Ben and I depend on you." Molly reached over to help Hannah with her coat, but Hannah moved a step away and removed it by herself.

"Perhaps it's time to learn to depend on each other. I'm tired. I'm going to bed."

"I saved your supper, Hannah. It's all warm in the oven."

"I don't want anything to eat. Good night."

The next week passed. Hannah went to the mercantile every day to handle the increased business that came with the upcoming Christmas holiday. On Friday, the freighter brought the next to last shipment for the year. Hannah, in turn, handed him the finished Christmas orders that the store had received that week.

When she returned to Sanctuary Hill that Friday night, Ben stopped her before she went to her room. "Hannah, will you come over here and talk to me and Molly?' He pulled out a chair at the table for her to sit. He then sat at the head of the table. "Will you tell me why you're mad at us? What did we do wrong?"

"Ben, I'm not mad at you or Molly. I'm just very tired."

"But you said you was gonna be here to help Molly and me with my mama gone. I'm kinda scared right now."

"I don't know why. Everything is all right. We've got the cotton ginned and baled. The taxes are paid already this year, even before we sold the crops."

"But you don't listen when I need to ask you questions. I don't know what to do for our Kincaid families for Christmas. I don't know if we should grow corn and hay again."

"Sonny—I'm sorry, Ben. You aren't a little boy anymore. You make those decisions. You don't need me to tell you what to do."

"All right. You order those things we need for our Kincaids this Christmas, and I'll take care of the rest."

"I can't. I sent the order off last Friday. The freighters only come back one more time before the end of the year." Hannah pulled off her hat and set it on the table. "I should have asked you already."

"What can I do now?" Ben dragged his hand through his hair and began to pace across the kitchen floor.

"I think you can figure something out. You are responsible for the farm." Hannah stood and started for the door.

"Hannah, I don't know what to do. Won't you help me?" Ben pleaded with his sister-in-law.

"You and Molly talk about it. I'm tired. I need to go to bed." She left the young couple standing arm in arm with stunned looks on their faces. She ran up the stairs before they could raise another question she didn't want to answer.

That Sunday, Hannah didn't get up for church. When Molly knocked on the door, she pretended to be asleep. Truthfully, she'd not slept at all. Molly and Ben didn't return directly from morning worship. With them and little Nomie gone, the house felt like a tomb. Hannah had prepared Sunday dinner the best she could, being a poor cook. She sat down to eat alone. The silence weighed on her, pushing her into a darkness she'd not known before. She bit into the bland stew and spat it back into the pewter bowl. She reached for the cup she'd filled with coffee, sipped, and gagged at the cold, grainy concoction she'd produced. In her frustration, she rose and swiped her arm across the table, sending the pewter dishes across the room—clanking and dinging on the stone wall behind the stove, the kneading cabinet across the room, and even above the wainscoting on the newly cleaned wallpaper.

Hannah dropped to the floor, screaming. She didn't know how long she cried out. Finally, she said, "I am not doing this anymore. God, do you hear me? I'm done. I am beaten! Is that what you want me to say?" She raised her fist and continued to rant. "What else do you want from me? I look at all the people who seem at peace with you. Am I so much worse than any of them? Why don't you leave me be? I am so tired."

Hannah's rage left her spent. She was unable to push herself up and away from the mess. She lay her face against the old cypress plank floor and fell asleep. It was there that Sam Naylor found her at six that evening when he'd accompanied Ben and Molly home from Bible class.

"Hannah, are you hurt?" Sam gently shook her shoulder.

She was startled and sat upright. "What are you doin' here? What time is it?"

"Hannah, the sun has set. It's past six. What happened here?"

410

Hannah looked across the mess she'd made and remembered what she'd done that afternoon. Color rose in her face. "I'm afraid I had a tantrum this afternoon, Sam. I'll clean it up now."

"Wait, Hannah. I need to talk to you before Ben and Molly return from the barn. That young man stopped me after Bible class and asked me to talk to you. He told me you are mad at Molly and him. He's worried about you, young woman. He said you've never been mean to him until this month. He doesn't think he could live at Sanctuary Hill alone with Molly and Nomie if you go away."

"I never said I was going away."

"You didn't have to. Ben is maturing, it's true. But he's just lost his mother, and you are the stable adult in his world now. And he thinks you are mad at him."

"I didn't mean to frighten Ben. I'm not leaving Sanctuary Hill."

"Is the woman he depends on still here for him?" When Hannah heard that question, she turned to walk away. "Don't run away from me Hannah. This is serious."

"Sam, quit pushing me. I'm doing the best I can. I'm exhausted. I don't have anything else to give. I cried out to God, and I didn't hear an answer. What do you expect me to do? I can't give something that I don't have to give."

"Hannah, you have worked very hard to do all you've done. I've seen you. You believe that you've done all that has been accomplished here through your strength, will, and determination. You—you of all the people on this earth need no one. You will do everything alone."

"I never said that either."

"That's exactly what I've heard and seen in the time we've known each other. Hannah Murphy needs no one to make Sanctuary Hill productive, run a mercantile, and keep a family safe and cared for. That is the height of arrogance!"

"You aren't being fair."

"Am I being truthful? Your pride has been a stumbling block between you and the community. Your obstinance was a barrier between you and Kell for months. Worst of all, your haughty arrogance has prevented you from seeing the grace and love that the Lord has been offering you your entire life." Sam slammed his Bible down on the kitchen table.

"But Sam, I asked God what He wanted from me, and He didn't answer."

"Hannah, he just got tired of telling you what He's already shown you so many times—in the scripture, in Bible class discussions, in the lives of friends who care about you, and in the love of a faithful man who cherishes you beyond your knowing."

"What don't I know, Sam?'

"Not one of us makes our way in this life alone, Hannah. When we surrender our will, the Lord becomes the life force living in us and all we do."

"I want to know that but…"

"There is no but. When you put your pride aside and look at your life, you will see God in every step. You will then serve with joy and love, not because of an obligation to a dead man."

Tears welled up from the depth of Hannah's losses. She ran from the room, sobbing uncontrollably, to seek the asylum of her bedroom. She could find no truthful response to the accusations Brother Sam had made. He had told her the truth. Her attempt to deal with life on her own terms had been a farce. She had built barriers between herself and all the people in her life. The biggest lie she told herself was that she didn't need anyone. She knew she was neither self-sufficient nor invulnerable. She had played a role for years and lost again and again.

Hannah sank to the floor beside her tall four-poster bed and began to pray. At first, her thoughts were garbled and senseless, like the sound of a person trying to speak through uncontrolled tears, but after a while, she spoke her prayer aloud. "Father in Heaven, I'm not worthy, but please hear me. I want to know the love and peace Kell and Brother Sam have told me about. I am tired of living alone and being disconnected from the people around me. Please forgive my arrogance and misplaced pride. I have so many faults. Forgive me for hurting Ben and Molly. I was unkind. Please forgive me and help me be a better sister to them. I want to belong to your family—and mine. Lord, please show me the way."

Hannah continued to cry out to God. She cried until she was spent. She lay her head on the side of the bed. Then she felt safe—the way she felt when she was in Kell's arms. This new sensation was the sense of belonging she'd searched for all her life. She rose, changed into her warm winter night dress, climbed into her bed, and laid her head on the goose-down pillow. She slept.

Chapter 32

Speak ye everyman the truth to his neighbor, execute judgment
of truth and peace at your gates: and let none of you imagine evil in
your hearts against his neighbor, and love no false oath
for all these I hate, saith the Lord.
Zechariah 8:16-17

The following Sunday, Hannah stood before the members of the Community Church and asked to become a member of the church family. As she spoke, she remembered Brother Sam's reaction when she had told him earlier in the week of her night with the Lord when she'd admitted her pride and stubbornness and asked Him to forgive her.

Sam grabbed her up and hugged her. "Hannah, Kell will be so happy when I write to him. He's been praying for you ever since he went home."

"I am happy he has."

"Better yet, why don't you write to him? He'd love to hear this news from you."

"I can't do that, Sam. I told Kell to make a life for himself in Scotland. He may have a wife by now. He's been gone for more than a year."

"He's not looked for a wife, Hannah. You'd know that if you had read his letters."

"Sam, I didn't come to talk about things beyond my reach. I want to join the church and be a real member of the congregation."

"We can certainly make that happen next Sunday." And he did. As they had arranged, Sam poured the consecrated water from an antique pottery bowl he'd been given when he took up his charge as pastor.

As the water ran down her face and onto her shoulders, Hannah whispered, "Thank you, Father. I never knew how wonderful it felt to truly belong." With that act, Hannah became a member of the Community Church. The congregation welcomed her as one of their own. This was a happy day.

The week before Christmas, Hannah made her third trip to Memphis to sell their cotton crop. She insisted Ben accompany her. While they made their way to Hopefield on the train, she told him that she was going to support him, but he would make the deal with the Levenstein Company. "Ben, selling the crop is part of the farm business. You need to take responsibility for getting the business done to its end."

And Ben did just that. He presented their sample box, offered their forty bales to the cotton factor who worked with Ira Levenstein and bargained for a half-cent increase in their offer. When they accepted the price Ben had asked for, the young farmer accepted the deal and scheduled their cotton delivery for the first week in January.

"Mr. Murphy, it has been a pleasure doing business with you and Sanctuary Hill again this year. I look forward to many more years of association with the Sanctuary Hill growers," Ira Levenstein said.

"My grandpa Hugh said you were always fair and honest with him. Hannah found where he wrote it in his journals. We will keep doing business with your company." Ben reached out his hand to seal the deal.

415

"Mrs. Murphy, it's good to see you again. We were afraid you'd sold to another firm this year since we usually see you in the fall," the broker said.

"The fall was a difficult time. We had several of our farmers and family members contract cholera. We finished our baling about two weeks ago."

"Hannah took good care of us, but some of our people were very sick. We lost my mama and two children from our tenant farms," Ben replied.

"May God console you as you mourn. I know your mother was well-loved in St. Francis County."

"Thank you, Mr. Levenstein."

"Will you let me take you and Miss Hannah to dinner tonight at the new hotel dining room? The Peabody has just opened, and it's quite a sight to behold."

"Mr. Levenstein, it will be our pleasure to dine with you. What time would you like to meet?" Hannah responded.

"My wife and I will meet you here at 6:00. We'll walk. It is only in the next block."

With the successful sale of the cotton, the new year seemed promising. Ben and Molly now had a son, and Nomie doted on her little brother, trying to help her mother with his care even though she was not yet three. Aaron and Nan were expecting their first baby in late spring. Hannah felt a sense of relief after Ben had handled the cotton sale as well as he did. She found herself smiling often and enjoying her role as Aunt Hannah.

The Kincaids not only received larger shares this year due to the increased profit from the cotton, but they also gained cattle and colts from Kell's herds. Of course, the family didn't broadcast much about their good fortune because the farm had not been visited by the night riders since they burned Kell's barn. The supreme hope at Sanctuary Hill was that they would never return. The families could have paid off their farms with their saved profits, but they remained loyal to their original bargains—six years of labor for the cost of the farms.

One shadow loomed over Sanctuary Hill. In January, Hannah had to face Narvel Tangent to protect her guardianship of Ben until he was twenty-one. Ben turned twenty in September. He was becoming more competent every year, but Hannah knew how much Tangent wanted the land. He would make a case if he had to bribe and lie to win. He also was a local male—in with the political powers that be. Hannah had one undeniable flaw. She was a woman.

She knew with the right kind of support and advice that Ben would be able to manage the estate and take care of his family. Her greatest fear was that Tangent would be awarded guardianship and that Ben and his family would live under the thumb of that loathsome man for the rest of Tangent's life.

With the hearing set in front of the circuit judge in two weeks, Hannah went to Madison to seek Mr. Oldham's help with the lawsuit. He had represented Hugh Kincaid for many years. When Hannah went to the attorney's office, she didn't expect the reception she got.

"Well, Mrs. Murphy, it is nice to see you again. Have you come to talk about selling Hugh Kincaid's land?"

"Whatever gave you that idea?"

"I just thought that after nearly three years, you'd had enough hard work to last you a lifetime. Surely, you know by now that living on that property is impossible."

"I came here today to ask you to help us uphold the wishes Hugh Kincaid laid out in his will."

"Have you run into a problem? I suppose you've not been able to meet the expenses at Sanctuary Hill."

"Not at all. We've shown a profit every year. We have paid all our taxes and begun to repair the house and have enlarged the crop every year. Narvel Tangent is contesting my guardianship of Ben Murphy."

"Oh, yes. Seems I heard something about that. I'm sorry, Mrs. Murphy. I can't represent you in this case. I am also Mr. Tangent's lawyer—conflict of interest. You understand?"

Hannah jumped to her feet. "You can't be representing him. He's trying to break a will that you wrote."

My obligation to Mr. Kincaid ended when he died, I'm afraid."

"Is there another lawyer in this county?" Hannah's anger rose with each word the man spoke. "Is anyone here man enough to stand up to that bully?"

"Mrs. Murphy, I'd advise you to settle on a price and sell the land to Mr. Tangent. Your decision to give land to the freed slaves hasn't made you a popular person in some important circles in our county."

"Are you saying that because we found a way to make our land profitable, we don't deserve to keep what's rightfully ours?" Hannah raised her fists and took two steps toward Oldham. He quickly retreated behind his desk.

"I'm only stating facts. You have no ownership. You are a woman. Ben Murphy is a half-witted boy incapable of handling an estate of that size. The landowners here about don't want neighbors like the ones you are populating the land with. You have no hope of maintaining that property."

"Are you threatening me?" Hannah's steely posture was reflected in her voice. "Tangent is not offering a price that will support Ben and his family for the rest of their days. He now has children to support."

"You can go to court if you like, but I believe the law and the feelings of the people here about will be against a single woman running such a large estate. Not even using that idiot boy as a front will sway a Southern judge."

Oldham removed his glasses and rubbed his nose. "I may be able to negotiate a better price for you if you'll be sensible."

"You cannot get a price that will support that family for the rest of their lives. I can see you've already decided to end this suit. I'll trouble you no longer." Hannah left slamming the door.

She walked two blocks to the building that served as the county courthouse. She hoped to find the name of another attorney she might hire. The task was indeed as futile as Oldham had painted it. She did learn that the case would be heard before a judge named John E. Bennet. A ray of hope had arisen. This judge had the reputation of being a fair and honest man.

When she returned home, Hannah spoke to Ben and Molly about the upcoming trial. She knew that both would be called to testify and might become agitated when asked demanding questions. Molly was afraid of her father so she might say things to placate Narvel Tangent.

"Ben, you know that Mr. Tangent wants to take over managing your farm, don't you?" Hannah asked him.

"You told me once he tried to buy us out, but you said no."

"That's true, Ben, but do you remember before we went to Memphis I told you about the lawsuit?"

"I remember, Hannah." Molly stood up and took Ben's arm. "We just got home from visiting the Millers."

"Oh, yeah. I remember. I thought that would just go away," Ben replied.

"No, Ben. It didn't go away. I am going to have to prove to a judge that we are doing well here at Sanctuary Hill. They will ask you questions, and you can't let them make you say bad things about how we manage the farm or the store. You must tell them the truth, but don't answer anything they don't ask you."

"Will they ask me things, too, Hannah?" Molly's voice trembled. "I'd rather not talk to them, especially my papa. He's so mean."

"I'm sure they will ask you things. Molly, it's important to tell how Ben takes care of you. Talk about how Ben works on the farm and makes furniture from the lumber in our forest. You need to tell them how Ben helps take care of your babies. Can you do that?"

"I will try." Molly had tears in her eyes.

"Good. Remember to tell the truth and just answer what they ask and don't add anything else." Hannah stressed.

"Molly, remember to tell the truth." Ben nodded.

That night, Hannah prayed for guidance. She had to present a positive picture of the life they had created at Sanctuary Hill. *Lord, I believe we are doing what Hugh Kincaid hoped for.*

The next morning, she knew what she had to do. She set about collecting every piece of information that would show the improvement in the estate their family had made in the three years they had worked the land. At the end of the week, she had a large crate filled with receipts, invoices, contracts, order forms, work orders, and payment agreements for work done to the house and the outbuildings. She added legal documents, ledgers, and crop reports to the top of the stack. She also had letters supporting her and Ben from Brother Sam, Reuben Miller, and Ira Levenstein. She'd done all she knew to do to support the claim that they were succeeding as Hugh Kincaid had wanted.

The day court convened on a bitterly cold, wet January day in the Delta. Hannah, Ben, Molly, Aaron Pierce, and Marcus Kincaid made the ten-mile trip to Madison, all fearing what a negative outcome would mean to them and their families. Hannah had her crate filled with documents and held it close in her lap.

At nine o'clock, the judge of the first judicial district, John E. Bennet, slammed his gavel down, calling the start to the hearing. On the plaintiff's side sat Narvel Tangent with Mr. Oldham, acting as his lawyer. Hannah wasn't surprised. She would act as her own attorney.

Hannah sat at her table alone, a fact the judge noticed immediately. "Young woman, are you not represented by an attorney?"

"No, sir. When I approached the only lawyer in town who knew our situation, he told me he couldn't help me due to a conflict of interest. I guess that conflict is here with him today." Laughter broke out around the room.

"Do you want to delay this suit until you can find an attorney?"

"No sir. I don't have time to go north and find an unbiased one. I need to get this problem over before planting season. I will try to present our side of this suit." Hannah sat back down and began to unpack her evidence.

The judge leaned back in his tall chair and adjusted his glasses. "Folks, I don't want to make this a long, drawn-out affair. Let's approach this informally and orderly. I see no need for pomp. Mr. Oldham, will you state the reason your client wants to contest this will?"

"Yes, Your Honor. The matter is simple. My client, Mr. Narvel Tangent, is asking for legal guardianship over his half-witted son-in-law so he can protect the interests of his daughter Molly Tangent Murphy. We will show that Mrs. Hannah Murphy's charge of this boy has been inadequate and at times perilous to this family." Oldham pointed toward Hannah with his remark.

"And Mrs. Murphy, what do you say to this charge?" The judge leaned across the desk where he sat.

"First, I resent Mr. Oldham referring to Mr. Ben Murphy, my brother-in-law, as half-witted. That term is demeaning and untrue. Mr. Hugh Kincaid left all his property to Ben, who at the time of his grandfather's passing was only seventeen years old. Together, we have put our land to use, have produced three crops of quality cotton, and covered all expenses. We have money in reserve for next year's crop."

"Very well, I will hear your case. Mr. Oldham, you may call your first person to present evidence." The judge motioned to a vacant chair at the end of his desk. Narvel Tangent rose and walked forward.

"Mr. Tangent, can you explain your concerns about this present situation at Sanctuary Hill?" Oldham asked.

"Certainly can. My daughter Molly is married to Ben Murphy. Since the marriage, my wife and I rarely see our daughter, but on the few occasions, she has told us things that are worrisome to both of us."

"What might those things be, Mr. Tangent?"

"Mrs. Hannah Murphy runs the household like a tyrant. She makes all the decisions about the farm, the general store in Linden, and how the family can interact with other folks."

"How has Mrs. Murphy's treatment of this family caused problems for Ben and Molly Murphy?" Oldham once again pointed a finger in Hannah's direction.

"That woman has total control of the money. Molly can't buy a new dress or shoes for her babies without begging for money from Mrs. Hannah Murphy." Tangent spit out his venomous words.

"You don't have reason to believe that she is keeping money that is rightfully theirs, do you?" Oldham's smirk was directed at Hannah. At the sarcasm, Ben jumped to his feet, but Hannah waved him down before he spoke.

"Of course she is. She don't know how to run a farm. She divides crop money among those sharecroppers that have infested the Kincaid land. That money belongs to Ben and Molly to take care of their children. If I was in charge, they'd get what is rightfully theirs."

"You mentioned she had put them in peril under her care. When did this happen?" Oldham paced across the room and stood in front of Hannah.

"Three times her coddling of the black sharecroppers has brought the night riders to Sanctuary Hill. One night Ben Murphy was bludgeoned by one of those vigilantes. He could have been killed instead of just getting a good knock on his head. Another night the entire family could have died. The night riders burned a barn and were headed for the house when I and some men from the sheriff's office scared them off."

"How have you offered to intervene to help this family?"

"You know yourself, Oldham, I offered Naomi Murphy a handsome price for the land so she could return to Washington. That was her fondest hope, to return to her home. She'd agreed to the sale, but Hannah Murphy refused to sell."

"What reason did she give?" Oldham asked.

"She wanted more money. I offered her five dollars an acre, even said they could keep the house and the immediate grounds for a yard and gardens. Judge the goin' price for land hereabouts is about $2.50 an acre if it's got good water."

"Have you tried to help since the marriage of your daughter?"

"I asked Ben to come and live with us at Fox Run. I could have helped the boy in running his farm. My wife would have been close to see to Molly and the babies."

"Why did they not accept your generous offer?"

423

"Hannah Murphy told Ben he had to do what she told him because she was his guardian. I heard it with my own ears."

"Do you have other concerns, sir?"

"You and the law makers of this state know a woman ain't got a head for business. I was more than surprised when my dear friend Hugh Kincaid left so much valuable property in the control of a woman. Of course, he was not well those last couple of years before he passed. I didn't worry as much when Kell Kincaid was here. Kincaid would have stepped in to take control when it became obvious that woman couldn't make a go of the place. Unfortunately, Mr. Kincaid was called back to Scotland to deal with some family problems. That left the void."

"Mr. Tangent, Ben Murphy's guardianship is scheduled to end at his twenty-first birthday, which will be in about eight months. What would you do with the property when he reaches his majority?"

Well, if I considered him capable of taking care of the estate and my daughter, I'd not be worried. I doubt the boy will ever be a man. His family has always treated him like a boy. Since he was struck with Scarlet Fever at the age of ten, he's always acted like a boy. His mama babied him too much. His brother would have inherited the estate if he'd survived the war…God rest his soul. I will continue to oversee the property as long as the need remains, of course."

"Your Honor, I don't have any more questions for Mr. Tangent." Oldham returned to his chair.

"Mrs. Murphy, would you like to ask Mr. Tangent any questions?" the judge asked.

"No, sir. I wouldn't know how to even begin unravelling the lies he just spoke before you." Hannah sat back down.

"I object to Mrs. Murphy's besmirching my client's honesty." The lawyer's face turned the color of beets. "She obviously knows nothing about the legal system and how it works."

Rising to her feet, Hannah spoke to the man across from her. "That may be so, Mr. Oldham, but I do know what is true." The people in the courtroom began to cheer and clap at Hannah's words.

"Order in this courtroom. Mrs. Murphy, you may have your say in turn. Please don't comment on the testimony presented by Mr. Oldham's client. I believe that is my job to evaluate what is presented to me."

"Yes, sir. I apologize."

"Mr. Oldham, have you other witnesses to bring forth?"

The rest of the day was filled with a string of people, many of whom Hannah didn't know. The local sheriff said that the Murphys had filed a complaint about the night riders, but no one in particular had been found that participated in the barn burning. Most of the suspected vigilantes in the area had alibis for the night Kell Kincaid's barn was burned. One man told of being cheated at the mercantile in a barter. Hannah had no record of the transaction he spoke of. Two of Tangent's workers testified that the farm buildings were in disrepair and the fences for the herds were down more than they were up.

Mrs. Tangent wept on the stand, telling the judge that she rarely saw her daughter and grandchildren because Hannah refused to let her visit. She reported that Nomie had contracted cholera from the unsanitary servants at Sanctuary Hill and had nearly died. "Judge, please rule so I can bring my daughter home where she will be safe. I will take care of her and her babies. I am her mother."

Hannah sat through the entire day and did not ask questions of any witness. She couldn't discount their half-truths, insinuations about her character, and the total fiction sworn to in front of the judge. She knew her only hope was that she could show the judge the truth of all their hard work and progress made since they had come to Sanctuary Hill. Perhaps the Lord would grant the wisdom of Solomon to Judge Bennet.

"I am going to recess this case until tomorrow. It's near four, and I've got a great deal to consider. We will begin tomorrow at 9:00. Please be on time."

Before the court was called into session the next morning, Hannah was surprised when Ira Levenstein came into the room. "Good morning, Hannah, dear."

"I am so happy to see you. How did you know I'd be here?" she asked.

"I had a message from a friend. I hope I might be of some help."

"Thank God for you, my friend. You are such a blessing." Hannah hugged the tall cotton broker who sat behind her.

Mr. Oldham called his last two witnesses, Molly and Ben Murphy. When Ben was called up, the sheriff swore him in and asked if he would tell the whole truth. Ben said, "I always tell the truth."

Oldham stood very near Ben. "Mr. Murphy, what is your relationship with Mrs. Hannah Murphy?"

"You know that, Mr. Oldham. You read it to us from my grandpa's will." Ben looked at Hannah. She smiled and nodded to him.

"No. I don't mean that. Sonny, how do you get along with Mrs. Hannah Murphy?"

"My name is Ben. I'm not a little boy anymore."

"Excuse my error, Ben. Can you answer my question?"

"I get along real good with Hannah."

Oldham pouted. "Doesn't she tell you everything to do at Sanctuary Hill?

"Nope. Just me and Marcus Kincaid run our farm. Marcus is our foreman." Ben pointed him out to the judge.

"One of your sharecroppers runs the farm?" Oldham shouted at Ben.

"We ain't got no sharecroppers," Ben replied.

"Doesn't Marcus Kincaid work your land?"

"Yes."

"Is he a black man?"

"Yes."

"Do you think it is right to have a black overseer?"

"Yes. He's our foreman. I think it's good for all of us."

"Mr. Murphy, who makes all the decisions about how the farm is run?"

"Me and Marcus."

"Do you handle the money at the farm?"

"No. Hannah keeps the books."

"You have no idea if your farm is making a profit." Oldham had his *ah-hah* moment finally.

"Yes, we all know. We paid our taxes, got plenty to eat, and have money to fix our house. The money had to come from somewhere."

"Do you have any responsibility for the overall operation of your grandfather's property?"

"Yes, I told you. I take care of the farm."

"Does Mrs. Murphy make your wife do the housework?'

"This is our house, mine and Molly's. Hannah said since my mama died, Molly is the lady of the house. Yes, Molly works in our house. Everyone works at Sanctuary Hill."

"Who is Mom Bec, Mr. Murphy?"

"She is one of the Kincaids who lives at Sanctuary Hill."

"Is she your servant?"

"I don't think so. She's just part of the Kincaid family."

"Is she a paid cook?"

"I don't know about that. You'd better ask Hannah."

"Mr. Murphy, without your sister-in-law telling you what to do, could you manage your property and family at Sanctuary Hill?" Oldham's leaning in toward Ben caused the young man to pull himself back in his chair.

"I think I could. I am a good farmer." Ben smiled and nodded his head.

"Is there any more you can tell us, boy?"

"No. Hannah said to tell the truth and not be saying anything else. I did that."

The judge put his hand to his face to hide a smile.

"Your Honor, I am through with this boy. It seems plain he's been coached on what to say."

"Mrs. Murphy, do you have any questions?

"Yes, sir, just a couple." Hannah stood before the desk where the judge and Ben sat. She smiled at Ben. "Will you tell the judge about our trip to Memphis just before Christmas and what we did there?"

"We did lots of things, Hannah. We ate at that fancy restaurant at the Peabody Hotel and walked by the Mississippi, watching those big men loadin' steamboats. We shopped at fancy stores and bought Christmas presents for everyone at Sanctuary Hill. We had a good time."

"Yes, we did. Ben, tell the judge why we went and how that all worked out."

"Well, Mr. Judge, we had to go late this year because we had cholera at our farm. My mama got real sick and passed away. So did Marcus's son Abraham and baby Ruthie that belonged to Lijah Kincaid and Dorrie."

"I am sorry to hear about your losing people at your place, Mr. Murphy," Judge Bennet said.

"More of us got sick, but Doctor Bolden and Hannah took good care of us, and most of us got well."

"That's a miracle. Cholera is a bad disease." Ben nodded at the judge.

"Anyway, Hannah and me went to Memphis. I sold our crop. Best one we had in the three years. We sold forty bales. Just like the past two years, we got top dollar. I got to haggle with the broker for a half-cent better offer. We grow good cotton, and Mr. Miller does a fine job ginnin' and balin' for us."

Oldham jumped to his feet. "I object. What does this have to do with the case you're considering?"

"Mrs. Murphy, do you have a reason for this information?"

"Yes, sir. I will make it clear when I have my turn to present our story."

"Mr. Murphy, you can step down. Mr. Oldham, do you have any other witnesses?"

"Only one, Your Honor. I'd like Molly Tangent Murphy to come forward."

Molly stood up slowly. She looked at Ben as he returned to the bench. Her eyes showed her fear. Ben gave her a quick hug and whispered, "It's gonna be fine, Molly. Just do what Hannah told us."

Hannah sensed the terror Molly was feeling. She took slow deliberate steps as she approached the chair. Her feet made no sound on the old wood floor. She turned her face to avoid looking at her father.

"Mrs. Murphy, may I call you Molly? Too many Mrs. Murphys in the room can be confusing." Oldham crooned his first question to Molly.

"Yes." A whisper so quiet the judge asked her to speak up.

"Yes," Molly repeated.

"Molly, do you like living at Sanctuary Hill away from your parents?"

Molly turned pleading eyes toward Hannah. "I guess I do."

"You guess you do? Don't you know how you feel?" Oldham growled at the girl.

"I love Ben and our babies. Sometimes I miss my mama. I wish she would come and visit me."

"Does your husband force you to do servant's work at Sanctuary Hill…you know, things that you never did when you lived at home with your parents?"

"I take care of our babies and help keep the house."

"Does Hannah Murphy expect you to work at the mercantile, too?"

"Sometimes I do, but not much since our babies came. We all have to work to keep our home going."

"Did you have to pick cotton, like a field hand, last year?"

"I did. Everyone did, especially after the rain stopped. We had to get our crop out." Molly lowered her eyes.

"Does your husband ever buy you nice things, like your parents did?" Oldham sneered.

"We watch our money. We have to plant a crop next year, so we save money back."

"Has your father offered you a better life to come home to Fox Run?"

"Yes, but I don't want to leave Sanctuary Hill. I am the mistress of the house since Mother Naomi died. I love Ben and our two little ones."

"Isn't it true that you told your father that Ben Murphy has been mean to you and threatened to beat you if you went back home?"

Molly stuttered, "I don't think...no... maybe I said I'd be hurt...No. Ben's never treated me bad. He's good to me, and he's a good daddy to our babies." She turned to face her father. "Papa, please don't make trouble for us." She began to cry. Her mother rose to comfort her, but Tangent pulled his wife back into her seat beside him.

"Molly. I only have one more question. Would you be better off back at home with your loving parents than slaving away at Sanctuary Hill?"

Again, Molly mustered the courage to look at her father. "I need to be with my husband and children at our home."

"Did Hannah Murphy tell you how to testify here today?" Oldham asked.

"No...yes. She said to tell the truth and answer the questions. I tried to do that."

Oldham pushed his thumbs into his vest pockets and addressed the judge. "Again, I have no more questions. This witness has been told what to say. I think I've made my case, Judge Bennet.

"We will adjourn for the noon meal. I will hear from Mrs. Murphy beginning at 1:00." The judge left the room, and the members of the Sanctuary Hill family approached Hannah.

"Miss Hannah, this judge seems serious. Do ya think he will listen to us when we ain't got no lawyer to talk for us?" Marcus's drawn face told Hannah he was doubtful.

"All we can do is to tell the truth, show the judge what we have accomplished together, and rely on the grace of the good Lord to take our side," she replied.

When Hannah had the chance to tell her side of the story, she asked the judge if she could just talk to him instead of asking questions as Mr. Oldham had done.

"Yes, Mrs. Murphy. I said we'd keep things informal today."

"Thank you." Hannah picked up her crate of ledgers and documents and brought them before the judge. "Sir, these are the ledgers where I've kept a record of all expenses and income, both at the farm and at the mercantile. Because this property belongs to Ben and not me, I've tried to keep accurate accounts. See, here was our total worth in April of 1866. We arrived at Sanctuary Hill with one twenty-dollar gold piece and $33.00 in cash. That was all we had the day we left Madison where we had purchased one horse, a small wagon, and enough food to last two weeks. We needed those things to get started that spring of '66." Hannah pointed to each expense.

"Things were hard at first because our house was damaged, and we had very little food. We'd have starved had the Kincaids not stepped up to help us. These were Mr. Hugh's people who had stayed on the land during the war. Two families remained, and they worked the land to provide for themselves after Mr. Hugh had gone to Marianna during his illness.

"We opened the store in Linden, bartered with a logging crew, and worked our land with those two families to produce our first crop that fall." Hannah showed the judge the first contract she'd made with Mr. Levenstein's firm. He nodded at what he saw.

"That was a pretty small crop for such a large amount of land, wasn't it?" Judge Bennet peered at Hannah over the rim of his glasses.

"We lost more than three bales of cotton when the barn we stored it in was burned by night riders."

Oldham jumped from his chair. "I object. This woman has no proof the barn was torched. Did the sheriff find any culprits you claim burned the barn?"

"Sit down, sir. You told your story. Let Mrs. Murphy tell hers."

"Judge...I..." The judge raised his gavel, and Oldham returned to his chair.

"We know it was torched, Your Honor. Elijah Kincaid saw the masked riders throw the tar brands into the loft full of hay."

"Is this man here to testify today?" the judge asked.

"No, sir. He is at Sanctuary Hill, but we can bring him if you need to hear from him. He is still recuperating from the cholera that struck our farm. He also lost his infant daughter."

"I'll bring 'Lijah if you want him, judge." Marcus stood to support Hannah.

"We'll see. Go on, Mrs. Murphy."

"The next year, we had a much larger crop and made a fair profit, even though cotton prices had fallen." Hannah showed the judge a second contract. Then she handed him the third Levenstein contract with an even larger amount showing. "Judge, we also had enough profit from the mercantile to pay our taxes this year before we sold our cotton. Besides that, our house has been repaired, and it's comfortable and warm now."

"Young woman, what do you say to the charge that you are keeping money due Ben Murphy?"

Ben jumped up and called out, "Shucks, Judge, Hannah keeps everybody's money. It's all safe and locked up in my grandpa's old safe built into a stone wall at our house." The people in the courtroom broke into a gale of laughter.

Judge Bennet slammed the gavel on his desk. "Sit down, Mr. Murphy. I'll talk to you when Mrs. Murphy asks for you."

"What was said is true, Judge. I'm the banker at Sanctuary Hill. I keep the profits of any of our tenant farmers who want me to. I have the Kincaids' and Aaron Pierce's account with Ben's money in the vault. See the amounts are noted in the red ledger." She turned several pages showing the judge what each household had put back and when they had withdrawn money."

"This seems to work well. This still doesn't show that Ben Murphy can manage that large property left by his grandfather."

"Judge Bennet, I believe Mr. Levenstein may help with that matter." Ira Levenstein stood before the judge's desk. He was sworn in. In a short time, he explained how Ben Murphy had presented the Sanctuary Hill crop sample before his broker, demonstrated both the lint quality and the excellent color of the clean crop, and negotiated the top price for the entire crop during a visit to Memphis in December.

Levenstein took out copies of his records from his vest pocket. "Judge, this fine young man knows the cotton business. They not only grow the best cotton we buy, but he scheduled an immediate delivery, which was well-ginned and baled. We will continue to do business with the Murphys for as long as they want to grow cotton."

"Did Mr. Ben Murphy conduct the business, or did Mrs. Hannah Murphy act in his stead?" the judge questioned.

"Your Honor, I have been a cotton broker for nigh on to thirty years. Mr. Murphy handled his business as well as any planter I've known, including his grandfather Hugh Kincaid."

Oldham rose and asked, "Isn't it true that Hannah Murphy was there telling him what to do every minute, Mr. Levenstein?"

"She was in the room. The only question she answered that afternoon was to say yes to my dinner invitation, sir. We had a lovely meal at the Peabody dining room, Hannah, Ben, my wife, and I."

Again, Oldham returned to his chair. A snarling Narvel Tangent grabbed his arm and whispered something. Oldham gasped aloud.

"Thank you, Mr. Levenstein. Do you have any other pertinent information to add to this hearing?" Judge Bennet asked.

"Only this. Ben Murphy and Marcus Kincaid could teach the local planters a lesson or two about producing quality cotton. My coffers would be so much richer if all my planters produced as good a product." Levenstein rose and offered his hand to the judge. "I am sorry to have to leave before you make your decision, sir, but I must catch the train back to Hopefield this afternoon." He shook hands with Ben and left the courtroom.

"Mrs. Murphy, do you have more I need to hear?"

"Yes, Judge Bennet. I would like you to hear what Reuben Miller has to say about our work at Sanctuary Hill."

Reuben took the stand. "Judge, I work steady now because of the folks at Sanctuary Hill. They helped me save my farm, too, back in '66. They hired me to gin and bale their first crop. They even got me the parts I needed to repair my gin so I could do the job right. That year the money I earned ginning the Kincaid land crop let me catch up my taxes and have enough left over to put in my crop the next spring."

"Mr. Oldham, do you have any questions for Mr. Miller?"

"No, sir. I don't see this man added anything to this case."

"You're excused, Mr. Miller. Mrs. Murphy, continue."

"Judge. I'd like you to hear from, our foreman, Marcus Kincaid."

" Mr. Kincaid, raise your hand and be sworn in."

Marcus walked up from his place in the back of the room and stood beside Hannah. "What you want me to say, Miss Hannah?"

"Marcus, I want you to tell the judge how you work alongside Mr. Ben at Sanctuary Hill."

"Well, sir, we all work together. Me and Mr. Ben talk about what needs to be done, when to plant the crops, if we want to get more mules, how many acres we can handle with our crew, and anything else that comes up at the farm. Mr. Ben asks me about somethin' he can't figure out for himself. After we talk, he decides, and that's what we do."

"Isn't that unusual for a sharecropper?" Oldham shouted.

"Ain't no sharecroppers at Sanctuary Hill. We're all farmers. We work together so all of us can live. Miss Hannah, here, she pick cotton, just like my wife Shataka. We grow most of our food, and we take care of our own. This last year we all grieved together. I lost my boy, Abraham, to cholera. Lijah, he lost his new baby girl, Ruthie. Even the Murphys lost Miss Naomi. We all grieved together. Now we stand together to keep our home. Mr. Ben owns Sanctuary Hill due to his grandfather left it for him. My family worked for Mr. Hugh, and now we work with Mr. Ben and Miss Hannah. We's makin' the best lives we ever had."

The judge dismissed Marcus. As he returned to his place in the back, Hannah addressed the judge.

"Your Honor, we have told you the story of our three years at Sanctuary Hill. Ben has grown up a great deal. He manages the farm very well, as our earnings show. He is married, and he and Molly are good parents to their two babies. Ben is more than capable of doing what his grandfather wanted him to do. I hope you see that we don't need Mr. Tangent's interference at Sanctuary Hill."

"Thank you, Mrs. Murphy. You have given me a great deal to think about. I want to mull it over tonight. I will convene court tomorrow at 9:00 a.m. I will have a decision then. I need to look at a couple of points of law and one precedent that I am aware of. Court adjourned."

436

Hannah felt an overbearing sense of foreboding. She knew being a woman would be the biggest obstacle. If she hadn't convinced Judge Bennet that Ben could deal with the business end of the farm, the judge might very well rule in Tangent's favor.

Hannah turned around to pack up all the ledgers, contracts, and other documents she'd displayed for the judge. A shadow passed between her and the window flooded with gold from the evening sun.

"Am I too late to help, lass?"

Hannah looked up and shaded her eyes with her hand. Before her stood Kell Kincaid

.

Chapter 33

And we know that all things work together for good to them
that love God, to them called according to His purpose.
Romans 8:28

Hannah rushed into Kell's waiting arms. "Thank you, Lord. My darling, I never thought I'd see you again."

"My bonnie lass, I wished every minute we were apart I could be exactly where I am right this minute. I'm home." Kell brushed her lips with a gentle kiss.

"We aren't home yet. After tomorrow, there may be no home at all."

"The Lord will take care of us all, Hannah. But if I had to live with you, Ben, Molly, and both of those babies in my wee cabin, I'd be home because you are home to me." Kell's second, more passionate kiss confirmed to Hannah his words were true.

"I'm so happy to see you. I convinced myself you'd found a wife and settled in Scotland. Sam told me you hadn't, but we've been apart so long."

"Hannah, did ya not believe what I wrote to you over and over?"

"I've never been able to work up the courage to read your letters, Kell. Every time I looked at your script on the envelopes, I knew my loss. I didn't believe I could stand to see the words that you would never return. I'm an awful coward."

"Well, whether you be or not, I care not. Let's go back to Sanctuary Hill."

"All right. Graystoke is in the livery stable. I'll ask Ben and Marcus to go back in the wagon."

"We can ride my fine stallion together—a fortunate excuse to hold ya in my arms all the way home. I can hardly wait to have some time alone, my love. This courtroom wasn't the meetin' place I'd dreamed of." Kell's smile lifted the gloom Hannah had felt since Monday at the start of the hearing.

Their conversation never lagged the entire trip back. Hannah sat in Kell's comfortable embrace, in awe that what she was experiencing was real. She told him of the good yield and successful year at the mercantile. She also told Kell of Benjy, Ben and Molly's new son, who was born in late November. Then she spoke of the hard times.

"Kell, I'm sure that Sam wrote to you about Naomi's passing. We had a very bad couple of months. Ben and Abraham contracted cholera, probably at the railroad camp just west of Linden. Several of our people were very sick. Besides Naomi, Shataka and Marcus's son Abraham died, as did little Ruthie, Elijah and Dorrie's baby daughter.

"Were you ill, Hannah?"

"No. I didn't seem prone to the sickness. Rose, Mom Bec, and I did most of the nursing. Thank goodness, Doctor Bolden was here to help with the treatment. We could have lost more, but for the grace of God. Almost everyone else had the disease to some degree. Ben was ill for more than two weeks. He's still weak."

"I'm sorry I wasn't here to help ya. The trip across the ocean seemed to last forever. That was the longest fifteen days of my life. Did my cousin Naomi suffer a great deal?"

"I don't think she was aware of things most of the time. She was delusional with a high fever. She often talked to her husband and called out to her sons as if they were children. Only at the very end when the convulsions began was she in the worst pain. By God's grace, they only lasted a few hours."

"Do ya fear the judge's decision tomorrow, Hannah?"

"No, not really. According to Arkansas law and male dominance in the world we live in, I'm prepared for the worst."

"I watched you handle the judge's questions verra well. I was late because the train didn't leave Hopefield on time. I watched from the back."

"It's in God's hands, Kell. Regardless of what the judge says, I know we'll be provided for. You told me that right after we met...Romans 8:28."

"Lass, you've changed since I've been gone."

"You're surprised? A girl changes when Godly people pray for her."

"Praise be. Sam wrote to me about your joining the church. I guess I wanted to see for myself. God has answered my every prayer."

"We'd better get a move on, Kell. We won't get any supper if we lollygag around much longer. Besides it's getting cold out here."

"Giddyap, Gray, ole boy. Our lady seeks a fire." Kell kicked Graystoke into a somewhat quicker pace.

At the dinner table that evening, Molly played hostess to Kell, Hannah, Aaron, Nan, and her husband. Along with Mom Bec, she'd prepared a feast of roast chicken, dressing, creamy potatoes, a huge pot of beans and ham, fresh baked rolls, and a peach cobbler. She said, "I was planning for this to be a celebration supper, but since we don't know how this is gonna play out, we'll just make this a welcome home supper for Kell."

"Molly, my dear, ya have made us a feast. Thank you for the welcome." Kell stood up, kissed her hand, and pulled out her chair.

"Kell, you know that Mom Bec made the hard dishes. I am learning, though. I peeled the potatoes, mashed 'em, and whipped in the butter and cream. I also made the ham and beans."

"Well, wife, you did real good. This is fine eatin'," Ben said. The dinner conversation went on and on. Kell told about his trip across the ocean and about the hustle and bustle in New York City. He told them about his several days on the railroad to reach Memphis. The family extended the talk longer with scores of questions.

At 7:30, Nomie toddled up to her father. She laid her curly head on his knee and looked up at Ben with her beautiful brown eyes. "Sleep, Papa."

"Well, folks, I guess that's the end of the party for me. My princess wants to be put to bed."

"Goodnight, everyone. It's past our babies' bedtime. We'll see y'all tomorrow." Molly rose, took her infant son from the cradle near her and followed Ben from the dining room.

Aaron took his cue from Ben. "We're gonna head home, too. Nan needs all her rest. We're gonna have our own little one in less than a month." He took his wife's arm and helped her to her feet.

"It's nice you're home, Kell. I know your family is happy to have you back," Nan said.

Hannah brought their coats from the bedroom. "Goodnight, you two."

"Aaron, I'm happy to see you settle here. I know Ben's glad ya stayed."

"It's home, Kell. We feel like family." Kell closed the door as they started their short walk to their house.

"Well, I guess I need to clean up these dishes. You want to help me, Kell?"

"That's not what I had in mind, lass." He drew her into his arms and kissed her with all the longing and passion he'd held inside for the last eighteen months. Hannah's response matched his. "I've yearned to do that since the minute I set my foot on that train deck when I left Madison all those months ago. I was barely able to check my need since the minute I saw you in that courthouse, telling that judge about cotton bales, tenant farmers, and profits. I couldn't make out a word. This was all I could think about. Hannah, I love you. My partin' from ya only intensified that longin' to make you mine forever."

"Let's go sit by the fire in the parlor. The dishes will wait." Hannah took Kell's hand and led him to the settee in front of the fireplace. The flames leapt from the dried hickory logs. The snapping from the pinecones and the crackle of the fire as it devoured the wood was the only sound in the room.

Again, Kell pulled Hannah into an embrace. They sat—not speaking, only reveling in the feeling of completeness and belonging. A solitary tear slipped from Hannah's lashes.

Kell raised her palm to his lips. With the gentlest kiss, he laid his heart in her hand. "Hannah Ruth, I love you. I want ya to be my wife. I thought of nothin' else all the way across the ocean. I don't want to wait ages. Will ya marry me this Sunday?"

"I want nothing more than to be your wife. I do love you, more than I ever knew I could love. I know that is because of the grace of God. I have learned that people can't love until they know love. You and Brother Sam and so many friends at the Community Church have shown me the grace of God. You are the one who began this learning in me—all love is a gift from above."

"Will you marry me this Sunday, lass?"

"Kell, I can't tell you that yet. I need to see what is going to happen to Ben and Molly first. I couldn't save Naomi. I tried, but I couldn't. She made me promise to take care of Ben."

"When will ya know he is all right, Hannah?"

"Let's see what the judge says tomorrow. Then I will know what I have to do to make sure Ben and his family are taken care of."

"If the judge gives guardianship to Tangent, what do you expect will happen?"

"First, I think he will try to void my arrangement with the tenant farmers. He will replace them with sharecroppers so the land will remain under his control. He isn't even working his land, so I expect he plans to sell the property."

"Could he void those contracts you signed with the Kincaids, Hannah?"

"I'm only a woman. He'd say I had no right to give away Ben's property." Hannah turned and looked into Kell's face. "But it will be all right, won't it Kell?"

"Darlin', we're gonna make sure Ben and Molly are taken care of. If all else fails, we'll give them our house, and I'll build another."

"Let tomorrow come soon! My good Lord, how I adore you, my Scottish beau. I count you among my greatest blessings."

They settled back into the settee and watched the logs crumble into chunks of glowing red and orange. Unwilling to part, they sat, embracing, until the glow turned to ash. Even the short distance between their bedrooms upstairs was too far apart. They fell asleep entwined in each other's arms. Hannah didn't stir until the rooster called out the dawning of a new day.

At 9:00, Judge Bennet called the court to order. Before him lay several documents. He said, "Does either side have any further comment before I provide my decision to this case?"

Mr. Oldham stood with a smirk on his face. "No, Your Honor. I am sure your review of Arkansas law has made this case an easy one to decide."

"No, sir," Hannah said. "I have shown you all we've done at Sanctuary Hill. I believe Ben and I have met the expectations of his grandfather, as he outlined it in his will."

"Very well…"

Kell rose. "Excuse me, Judge Bennet. My name is Kell Kincaid. I am the nephew of the late Hugh Kincaid. I have a letter here…"

"Mr. Kincaid, I don't think I need any more evidence. If you disagree with my decision, you may file your own claim after this one is settled."

"Yes sir. I meant no disrespect." Kell returned to his seat behind Hannah. She looked at him with a hundred questions in her eyes.

"Mr. Ben Murphy, who is the owner of Sanctuary Hill?" the judge peered over his glasses directly at Ben. The young man flinched and looked toward Hannah. She smiled at him and nodded.

"Well, sir, my grandpa Hugh Kincaid left it in his will to me when I am twenty-one. I will be twenty-one in a few months."

"Who makes the decision about the day-to-day operations of your farm?" Judge Bennet continued to stare at Ben.

"Marcus and me. We talk about things, but I have the final say. Ain't that right, Marcus?" Ben looked to the back of the room where Marcus stood.

"Yes, sir, Mr. Ben. You always make the final call."

"I see. Mr. Murphy, does Hannah Murphy tell you how to run Sanctuary Hill?" Another stern question from the judge.

"She always listens to me when I tell her about the farm, but she says I have to decide. I like havin' her there as my guardian because she knows a lot and she takes care of all our family—even when my mama got so sick, Hannah was with her all the time. She took care of my little girl, so my wife didn't get sick with the cholera. Molly was gonna have our new baby then."

"I see. Do you believe Mrs. Murphy has taken money that belongs to you and your wife?"

"All our money is safe at Sanctuary Hill. It ain't gone nowhere. Hannah works real hard at the mercantile and even helps pickin' and choppin' cotton. She don't even take a share."

"Thank you, Mr. Murphy. I have all the information I need. I'll give you my decision now."

"I thank you, Judge, for listenin' to me. I know Hannah is still my guardian, but she says I am a man now. I believe I am. I can take care of Molly and our two babies. Hannah can live with us as long as she wants."

Judge Bennet rose, removed his glasses, and picked up Hugh Kincaid's will. "Mr. Tangent, this case should never have been brought to court. After reading this will several times in the past two days, I am convinced the intent of Hugh Kincaid has been fully met. He asked his grandson to take care of his mother and to rely on Mrs. Hannah Murphy for advice when he needed it." Narvel Tangent jumped from his chair with his fist clenched and raised. "Sit down, sir, before I call for the sheriff," the judge warned.

He slumped back into the chair. "But she's just a woman. She has no legal standing in this state."

"Mr. Tangent, I don't want anything else from you. You heard yourself that Mr. Ben Kincaid made the sale of his crop and delivered it to Mr. Levenstein."

"You know the contract wasn't legal. The boy's a minor," Tangent replied.

"Mr. Ben Murphy is no boy. You said he is married to your daughter, and they are the parents of two children—your grandchildren." Tangent broke eye contact with the judge. "And you, Oldham, I'm surprised you could represent Mr. Tangent. Your name is in Mr. Hugh Kincaid's will as the attorney who prepared the document. Did you do such a poor job that you thought the will could be overturned?"

"Judge, I...well...no..."

"Enough. You'd be better off to honor your work."

Oldham averted his eyes and slumped in his chair.

"My ruling is that this will is valid and will stand as written with one exception. As of today, Mr. Ben Murphy, you have reached your majority. Although Mrs. Hannah Murphy has been a good guardian, I see no further need for her services. You are able to manage your estate. This court is adjourned." Judge Bennet slammed his gavel to close the case.

"Did ya hear, Hannah. The judge says I'm grown now."

"Yes, Ben. I'm happy he sees how capable you are. I hope you will still feel that you can talk to me whenever you want to."

"I will always need you, Hannah. I meant what I told the judge. You can stay with us as long as you want. You're my sister."

"Thank you, Ben. Let's all go home." Hannah looked back and saw Kell grinning at the scene he'd just witnessed.

By noon, the entire family, the Murphys, the Kincaids, and the Pierces were gathered in the kitchen. The heat from the cookstove was wonderful on that cold January day. Mom Bec sat in a tall ladder-back chair, holding Benjy, the newest member of the clan.

Ben cleared his throat. "Folks, I want to tell ya the great news we got today. The judge says Sanctuary Hill belongs to us. He told Mr. Tangent we'd done exactly what my grandpa Hugh expected. We ain't gotta worry no more. We're gonna keep workin' together as long as y'all want to stay."

Rose Kincaid clapped her hands, dancing in joy. "Praise the Lord. I wanted us to stay. This land has always been our home, and now we got our own farms. We've been blessed more'n we ever thought we could be. Thank you, Lord, and thank you, Mr. Ben and Miss Hannah."

"Rose, Mom Bec, all of you...We couldn't have done what we've done without each of you." Hannah's voice broke with emotion. "We've all lost dear ones, but we've also now assured a home for us all. Thank you for making it possible."

Kell slipped his arm around her. He whispered, "Life has been good to us all."

Chapter 34

Delight thyself in the Lord,
and He shall give thee the desires of thy heart.

As soon as the family finished their midday meal, Kell took Hannah's hand and led her to the back door. "Lass, they'll be no work today. The mercantile can stay closed until tomorrow. I know Saturday is a busy day at the store, so I'll let ya out of my sight for five hours."

"Kell, where are we going? It's cold out here."

"So 'tis. I'll get our coats and scarves. We're goin' to your house."

"Kell…"

"No arguments, Hannah. The rest of this day belongs to me." They drove in silence for a few minutes.

Hannah fidgeted beside Kell. "I'm very happy you've come back to Sanctuary Hill."

"No more than I. To be home again is a prayer answered."

"How did you arrange to return, Kell? I thought your father expected you to become head of the clan," Hannah said.

"We'll talk about me later, lass. Tell me why ya did not move into your house, Hannah?"

"For many reasons, I guess." She evaded the truth.

"Did ya not like the cottage, Hannah?"

"The one time I came after it was finished, I thought it was beautiful—so well-planned out for a family."

"When did ya come here?" Kell asked.

"The week before the family came down with cholera. Sam insisted I come and point out things that the carpenters needed to finish."

"You know I built this place for you."

"I felt you built it for us. With you gone, there was no us to live in this house."

"I wanted you to have your home, Hannah. I tried to build into it things you love and deserve, even though I knew you'd never ask for them." Kell pulled Graystoke to a halt at the wide veranda of the completed house. "Let's go in and I'll build us a fire."

He stepped down and lifted Hannah to the porch. Taking her arm, he escorted her into the wide entry hall that ran the entire width of the house. A gleaming walnut banister lined the stairway to the second floor, and beautifully finished but empty rooms flanked either side of the entry hall. On the left side, Hannah pushed open the doors to a parlor—not overly large but filled with light from the ceiling to floor windows. Adjacent was a smaller room with not yet filled bookcases along two walls.

"This is my space, Hannah. Ya see the double-faced fireplace here will heat both rooms. Being mistress of this house, the decision of what other rooms will be is yours. I've only claimed two for myself."

"I see. You chose this cozy little nook for your own sanctuary. Am I not allowed here?" she teased.

"You, my dearest, are allowed everywhere I am. I never intend to leave ya again as long as I'm breathin'."

"Show me more, sir, if you please." Kell took Hannah's hand and led her to the kitchen. The room had been partially furnished. A cookstove sat against a stone wall on the brick floor. Kell had taken that idea from Sanctuary Hill.

"Verra safe, lass. No wood exposed to the fire."

"I see that, and I love the convenience of a pump right here at the dry sink." Hannah also delighted in the large windows on the east wall of the house. Every morning, she could watch the sunrise. "This is a wonderful kitchen, Kell…but you know that I'm not much of a cook."

"Ya don't mean it! I thought all southern ladies knew how to cook, tat lace, and play coy with their beaus," Kell laughed.

"I am afraid, I don't do any of those things very well."

"Hannah, it makes no difference to me. You do the one thing I need. You make me whole. Together we will build a good life here. The Lord has given you to me, as surely as he has given me air to breathe." Kell enveloped Hannah in his arms. "Lass, can we be wed on Sunday?"

"That's only two days from now. You haven't talked to Brother Sam, and our house is bare except for a cook stove and a pump. How can I be ready to leave Ben and Molly without a bit of preparation?"

"All right, Hannah. How long do you need to make this commitment? I told ya I'm a patient Scot, but I've about used all that I have." Kell crossed his arms and jutted his chin out in a pose that reminded Hannah of a little boy who just had his favorite toy taken from him. Her heart melted.

"If you can talk to Brother Sam and somewhat furnish the kitchen, the day room next to your office, and get us some place to sleep, I will happily marry you one week from Sunday."

"Praise the Lord. I feared you'd say one year."

"My darling Scot. I want to be your wife as much as you want me."

Kell pulled her into his arms and kissed her once again, "I'm a happy man, Hannah Kennedy."

"Why did you call me Kennedy?"

"Because you've never really been married. Richard was no husband to ya."

"That's one of many things I want to talk to you about. If you will meet me at the mercantile at noon tomorrow when I close the store, we'll go somewhere so we can talk."

"I will be there, my love."

"Kell, I think we'd better finish our tour and return to Sanctuary Hill. You never built that fire, and it's still January."

Kell led Hannah to each room, and she told him what purpose she'd have for each space. The large room on the right side of the entry hall would be their formal parlor, and she would use the smaller, cozy room next to Kell's office as her day room. The large room at the back of the house would be their formal dining room, but Hannah told Kell she wanted a smaller table in the kitchen for their daily meals.

Upstairs, Kell showed Hannah three nearly identical rooms she'd remembered from the trip with Brother Sam. She commented on the wonderful idea of having a storage area in each room. The entire area on the opposite side of the house was only one room. "Hannah, you can decide what to do with all those rooms over there. This room is my second space."

"All right, Kell. I can make very nice bedrooms on that side of the house. There is plenty of room."

"As you will, my darlin'. This is the master bedroom. Here we will share our marriage bed. In time, Lord willin', ya may bring our bairns into this world right here. We will spend the rest of our lives sharing our dreams in this room," he told her.

The room was twice the size of any other upstairs room. Light flooded into the room from windows on both the south and west walls. At the back of the room was a small bathing room. In that space was a deep copper tub. Just like the one she'd bathed in at the Gayoso Hotel in Memphis. "Kell, a bathing tub. How perfect! How did you get it here?"

"It's amazing what can happen if you have friends."

Hannah ran her hand down the side of the gleaming copper. "How blessed I am."

♍

The next day at noon, Kell met Hannah as he promised. She had a busy day, so she was happy. Saturday was always a short workday and passed quickly because she was busy. Kell brought a basket with a simple lunch and came for her just as she locked the door.

"Hannah, I spoke with Sam today. He said he'd be glad to perform our marriage service next Sunday. He suggested we do it directly after mornin' worship so all our church family will be there with us."

"I like that idea. Was he surprised?" Hannah asked.

"I'd say he was. He told me he thought I'd want to wed ya tomorrow. Sam broke into laughter when I told him I did, but ya said no."

"Oh, you!

"He also said we could use the church this afternoon so we could be alone. I told him you'd made it clear we had to lay out all our doubts, expectations, and fears before we make eternal vows."

"What did he say to that?" Hannah asked.

"He said he knew he'd always liked ya for some reason. Said he wished more women were as level-headed and direct as you."

"That was a nice compliment."

"I told him not to be makin' eyes at my lady!"

"You didn't!"

"Assuredly, I did." Kell closed and locked the door to the store.

"Let's go eat the lunch you brought and make us a comfortable place to sit at the church. It's real cold out here."

"At your service, my lady." Kell turned Graystoke in the direction of the church and shortly tied his horse on the sheltered side. When they got inside, they found the sanctuary warm and welcoming. Sam had built a fire in the woodstove, and the aroma of coffee filled the room.

"Sam is such a thoughtful man. We are lucky to have him as our pastor," Hannah said.

"I'm blessed to have him as my best friend. Let me bless our lunch, and we'll eat." Kell prayed.

"Hannah, what things do you think we have to lay in the open before you will wed?"

"I want...no I need to tell you about my fears...I told you I am a coward. I have so many fears that I've used as walls my entire life. Probably it's only one thing...I am terrified to let anyone get close to me...the way I was before you swept me off my feet. I want to know what happened to you in Scotland that let you come back to me. I also believe that we need to lay open all our expectations for a life together. If we can get past those things, I will be free to make my vows with no regret. What things do you want to share with me so that everything is open between us? Kell, I hope we never have secrets from each other."

"Darlin', I'd love to hear you tell me how you came to the Lord. I so wish I had been here when you realized the Lord loves you more than anyone—even me. I need to tell you a few things about my family, mostly because they are important in the makin' of the man I am now. Maybe we should talk about havin' a family. And a weddin' trip. Ya wanna go away for a while on a weddin' trip, lass?"

"That's a lot to talk about in one day. We may have to spend two or three days to talk about so much."

"Let's start on an easy one then, and we'll get it out of the way. Where would you like me to take you on a weddin' trip, sweet Hannah?"

"Maybe a few days in Memphis. There are places there I'd like to visit and perhaps go to a concert or to the theater. There is even a new hotel called the Peabody. They have a fine restaurant that Mr. Levenstein took Ben and me to when we sold our crop last year."

"Memphis it is. When do ya want to go? Now or in the spring?"

"We can't go after planting season starts. Next month would be better or the very beginning of March."

"I'll look into it, but need to talk about this work thing, too."

"It's on my list. Here, have some apple butter. Mom Bec made it, and it's delicious." Hannah licked her finger. They ate for a few minutes. The room was warm. They sat shoulder to shoulder on the blanket Sam had left for their 'picnic.' After Kell had polished off every spoonful of apple butter. Hannah took her napkin and wiped a dab from Kell's neatly trimmed beard.

He took her hand and raised it to his lips. "Thank you, lass."

"Yesterday you asked me why I hadn't moved into the house you built for me. I evaded answering you."

"I was aware of that."

"When you left me, I was so angry with you—with God—with everyone. I felt betrayed. In my mind, I knew you had to go. Family is at the core of what I love about you."

"I know I hurt ya, Hannah Ruth. For me, it was the deepest wound I ever had to bear. I felt I was leavin' my soul here in Arkansas."

"I told myself I hated you—that you had left me—like every other person in my life who was supposed to love me. Just like my mother, who died when I was nine. Like my father, stern and distant after mother died, gave me away to a man I hardly knew—really never knew."

"I am sorry I added to your hurt. Please forgive me. I had no choice, but I should have taken ya with me."

"You know I couldn't go."

"And that is one of the things I love about you. You are loyal to your family."

"That's another thing, Kell. I'm not sure I can even tell you this. This is one of my worst sins." She paused, thinking he would say something to help her. He remained quiet.

When the quiet became too much, Hannah said, "Before I understood unconditional love when I was accepted into God's family, I only served Naomi and Ben as an obligation—not because I felt family bonds with them." Hannah searched Kell's face, expecting to see disappointment from what she'd just told him. She saw only his love looking back at her. Tears ran down her cheeks. Kell wiped them away.

"What a gift ya have just given me, lass. To open your heart to me as ya have."

"Because you showed me, I can let the Lord love me. Before my redemption, I never felt that I belonged anywhere or to anyone."

"Will ya tell me how you came to that point, Hannah?" Kell's stormy blue eyes were locked with Hannah's brown ones.

"Most of it is not pretty, I'm afraid. We had a good crop the year you left. Cotton prices were down, but we raised more cotton. The night riders didn't bother us at all that fall. We turned a good profit that year. The next year was harder. The weather was rainy in the late summer and early fall, so we had a hard time getting the crop out of the field. Of course, I was a stoic, cranky businesswoman, not nice to family or friends. Ben told Sam I was just mean."

"Then we had the cholera outbreak. That was a horrible month. We lost Naomi, Abraham, and baby Ruthie. More than two-thirds of our crew and family came down with the disease to a lesser degree. Mom Bec, Rose, and I tried our best to nurse our sick folks, but we couldn't help much. Dr. Bolden said it was a miracle that we didn't lose more than we did. Then, the day we buried Naomi, I was served with papers from the court, scheduling the hearing for Tangent to contest my guardianship of Ben. That was my breaking point."

"Lord, what strength ya had to last that long. Did ya talk to Sam?"

"Kell, I couldn't talk to anyone. I had told myself I was sufficient. I didn't need anyone. Besides, seeing Sam was just another reminder that you were gone." Hannah turned her face from Kell, remembering her shame.

"What did you do when you got the court order?"

"I closed myself off more and became meaner to everyone who crossed my path. I had an angry confrontation with Sam at the store the next day. I wouldn't listen to Ben or Molly when they needed to talk. But that Sunday, I broke. I flung dishes across the kitchen and screamed out at God. I was ranting, I believe. Finally, my rage ended, and I fell asleep on the floor. That's where Sam found me. He told me bluntly I'd hurt Ben—making him think I was deserting him. Sam said I was arrogant, and I used my pride as a barricade to keep the world away from me."

"My dear Hannah, Sam must have hurt you with those words."

"No. I ran to my room, but immediately, I realized he had told me the truth and how ugly I'd allowed my life to become. That was when I surrendered to God's love and acceptance. The next day, I awoke to light for the first time since you had gone."

"Thank you, Lord, for providing my mate to me. Hannah, that's what I prayed for since the day I saw you dancing and crying out in the field of clover. The thing I couldn't give you."

"I know what unconditional love is now. I never would have if you hadn't loved me. You showed me the thing I sought all my life. I know now how to live within His love because you live within His love and protection every day."

"I love you, Hannah, and you are the woman I've waited for. I canna wait to be your husband."

The following day, Sam Naylor announced to the Community Church that Kell and Hannah would marry the following Sunday after the morning service. He also told the congregation that all were invited to share the day with the happy couple. When the service was dismissed, the ladies of the community flocked to give Hannah their best wishes for her future. Hannah reached out to take Mary Lee Naylor's hand. "Will you be my Matron of Honor? You've been a dear friend since I've known you."

"Thank you, Hannah. What an honor you have given me. I'd love to stand with you."

Pelting snow clinked on the windows of the church. Brother Naylor looked outside at the dense clouds and canceled afternoon Bible study. "Folks, we may be in for an ice storm. I know the Lord will forgive us if we go hurriedly to seek the shelter of home."

They made a quick trip back to Sanctuary Hill. The sleet had turned to freezing rain about the time they turned down the cobbled drive. Within a few minutes, the family was safe and warm inside their home. Kell and Ben quickly returned from sheltering the animals in the barn, both soaked to the skin and shivering from their exceedingly cold showers.

"It would be a great day for a hearty stew and some pone. Let's cook our Sunday dinner," Kell said.

"First, you need to go upstairs and put on dry clothes. You're not getting out of our wedding after letting Sam invite the whole town today."

"Yes, ma'am, Hannah, but you can stoke up that stove so we can cook together when I come down."

The afternoon continued in a playful, comfortable fashion until well past dark. Even though the freezing rain continued to fall, the spirits in the great house were joyous. When Ben and Molly said good night and went upstairs to put their little ones to bed, Kell pulled Hannah next to him in front of the blazing fire.

"Finally, we're alone." He kissed her. "I've been waitin' to do that all day."

"I wanted you to kiss me, too."

"'Tis normal. I've kissed ya before I left for Scotland—more than once. Ya seemed to find my kisses pleasant enough,"

"I did, I wondered about more...." Hannah shrugged off Kell's embrace and walked toward the fireplace. Staring into the glowing embers and leaping tongues of fire, she spoke, "Kell, I..." she faltered. "Before you marry me, I must tell you...I..." Again, the words refused to come.

Kell rose from the settee and attempted to pull Hannah into an embrace. She stepped away. "Please don't look at me right now. Let me say what I must." She straightened her shoulders, wrapped her arms around herself, and began to choke out the words. "Kell, I may be a disappointment to you as a wife."

"Hannah, stop..."

"No. Let me finish. I don't like the physical side of marriage. You know what I am trying to tell you?"

"Hannah, you nearly scared me to death. I thought you were goin' to tell me you'd not wed next week."

"But you deserve a wife who will…ah…who wants you …." He turned her to face him.

"My dearest lass, that is not a matter for you to fret. I've no fear I'll find ya a cold woman. I told you on Saturday that you are Hannah Kennedy, a maid never married. You've never known the joy of marriage. No man has made love to you. You have no idea what pleasure God has planned for two people who love each other. Let me worry about that, lass." Once again, he kissed her, a tender, gentle kiss that led to a passion Hannah hadn't expected. She freely returned his kiss.

"Come back to the settee and let me tell ya about my time back in Scotland." Nestled together, Kell began to explain how his brother Sean had been brutally attacked by the outlaws on their northern border. The band had been rustling small numbers of their beef cows and sheep for several months.

"The first thing I had to do was rout out those villains. I took a few of our clan, and we got into a nasty brawl, but in the end we caught or killed all of them. We then made a pact with the neighbors to set up a watch system to guard all the estates in the shire."

"You could have been killed, Kell."

"No. The Lord had other plans for me. I didn't feel at home in Scotland. I wanted to be back here in Arkansas, living on my own land with you. So, I went to my parents and told them I would not be stayin'. I told 'em about you, Hannah. When I knew Sean would live and return as head of the clan, I made plans to come home. I told my father that if Sean could not continue as the clan leader, our younger brother, Ryan, was of age and could lead with some support."

"Are you sure that giving up your place as head of the Kincaid clan is what is best for you and your family?" Hannah asked.

"As long as Sean lives, I'll always be his second. I wanted to make amends with him, but the old barriers still exist. Not about Claire. I feel naught for her except as a sister, perhaps. But Sean and I still have issues to bury. I will need to pray to overcome that shortcoming. Besides, you are my family. We will start our own clan here with Ben and Molly. We will join my lands with Sanctuary Hill and build a secure life together."

"I'm so blessed to be loved by you, my dearest Kell."

"Is there anything else we need to lay in the open? Are ya ready to speak those vows with me yet?"

"Well, Kell, I guess the last thing is whether I will continue to work."

"Am I surprised you don't want to just stay at home and be my wife? No. I never thought you would. Darlin', I told ya before I left Arkansas that we would walk together as equals. I know you are an independent, capable woman. If you want to stay at the mercantile and continue to be Ben's advisor, you will do that."

"I'm glad you understand. I promised Benjamin Murphy I'd protect his family. I can't go back on my commitment, even though Naomi is gone."

"But Hannah, I won't have you workin' as a field hand. We can hire some men for that. And we'll renegotiate this work thing when our own little ones decide to join our clan."

"Do you want to have a large family?" Hannah asked him.

"We'll add as many Kincaids to the clan as the Lord sees fit to bless us with. With a mother like you, they'll be blessings to us, our state, and our country."

"I'll pray they will be strong like their father...strong in their faith, strong in their love of family, and strong in character. If they are children with those traits, we can have a dozen—if the Lord wills it." Hannah folded herself into Kell's embrace. "I love you."

"And I love you. I wish this week would just vanish. I want you that badly."

Chapter 35

Wives, be subject to your husbands as you are to the Lord.
Husbands, love your wives, just as Christ loved the church and
gave himself up for her.
Ephesians 5:22, 25

Sunday, February 7, 1869, dawned crisp and cold, yet the sun sent brilliant streams through the bare trees. This day would be a perfect day for a wedding. Hannah was up before the rooster broke the morning with his raucous song. It wasn't wedding jitters that woke her, though. She was calm and excited by the anticipation of her marriage to Kell Kincaid. Not one second of regret or doubt plagued her that beautiful winter day. She knew marrying Kell was God's will. She felt nothing but love and joy.

Hannah had seen very little of Kell since the previous Sunday. Every day he'd find some excuse to drop by the mercantile for a quick peck on the cheek or a more proper kiss if no audience was around. But as quickly as he dropped in, he was gone again with an excuse of someplace he had to be or someone he had to meet. He even made two fast trips to Madison causing him to miss supper twice that week. On Thursday, when Kell got home particularly late, Hannah waited up for him.

"Kell, where have you been this week? You've only had supper at home once since Sunday," Hannah said.

"Just some things I had to take care of, lass. Don't ya fret. I'll be home all the time after we're wed. You'll be telling me to go find something to do."

"I'm not complaining. I guess I was concerned about you missing meals."

"You are the only thing I'm hungry for, lass." Kell planted a quick kiss on her lips. "I'm kinda beat tonight, though, so I'm gonna say good night."

On Saturday, Hannah didn't see Kell at all. He sent a message by Aaron Pierce that he had a last-minute problem to deal with and that he would meet her at the Community Church the next morning.

That beautiful Sunday morning, Hannah took special pains to fix her hair the way Kell liked it. She pulled her raven mane back and then freed little wisps of curls to frame her face. Shataka helped her coil her raven tresses into a perfect chignon interwoven with blue ribbon. "Shataka, thank you for getting up so early to help me. You've been such a good friend to me. I wish you and your family would be with us today. We are all family, bonded by all the work, hardships, and loss we've shared. After today, I'll even be a Kincaid."

"Maybe in Heaven it be so, but you know that can't be, Miss Hannah. We's all happy for you and Mr. Kell, but we ain't had no trouble with those night riders in more'n a year. We plan on keepin' it that way."

Shataka lifted the blue ballgown over Hannah's head. This was the dress she'd worn to the first Community dance she'd gone to after moving to Arkansas. Kell had told her how beautiful she looked that night as they danced their first waltz together. She looked into the mirror at her vanity and smiled. She knew her groom would be pleased.

When Hannah came down, Mom Bec stood by the stove, smiling at her. "Lookee here at this beautiful bride. Many blessin's, Miss Hannah. Set yourself down and eat your weddin' breakfast."

"Mom Bec, you didn't have to go to so much trouble."

"Now ya jest hesh up, Missy. Every bride oughta be pampered on her weddin' day!" The bent, smiling woman pulled a tray of hot cinnamon buns from the oven and drenched them in sweet icing. Ben poured the coffee, and Molly dished up hot oatmeal for her little ones.

"Ben pulled out Hannah's chair and sat at the head of the table. "Lord, thank you for all blessings. And we ask ya to give Hannah and Kell a special blessin' today. We ask ya to bless this good food Mom Bec made for us and always make us grateful. Amen."

Ben said, "Hannah, sure ain't gonna be the same here with you and Kell gone."

"We aren't going far, Ben. All of us will be the family at Sanctuary Hill. You will help us, and we will help you."

"Hannah, I'm gonna miss you, too. You've taught me a lot about running a house. I'm glad that we are sisters, so I can always talk to you."

"Thank you, Molly. That's a lovely compliment. I never had a brother or sister before you and Ben."

"Well, let's finish this breakfast. We gotta get headed to church. We don't wanna be late today," Ben said. "Before we go though, Kell asked me to give ya these two coins. He told me they're sixpence, and you are supposed to put 'em in your weddin' shoes."

"Oh, he did? Why did he want me to do that?" Hannah asked.

"He said it's an omen…so y'all will always have all ya need and never be hungry or without a home. You can save 'em up to pay your taxes." Hannah took the coins and slipped them into her shoes.

When the Murphys arrived at the Community Church, the tiny sanctuary was filled beyond capacity. Several men were standing along the back wall. Even the Millers, who didn't normally attend the Community Church, were in the pew behind Mary Lee Naylor. The room had been decorated with ribbons and candles set in brass candlesticks, which had been nestled in evergreen boughs. In the corner of the raised area behind the pulpit sat a tall upright piano. Seated at the piano was Millie Garland, the wife of the Indiana man who had bought the plantation just to the north of Kell's land. They had become friends through their dealings at the mercantile.

In his place across the aisle from Hannah sat Kell, dressed in his family's tartan kilt. He looked every bit the Scottish Laird he could have been—regal, courageous, and honorable. When he saw Hannah, a smile reassured her this day would be everything she would have it be.

Brother Sam's sermon that Sunday dealt with the concept of the covenant. "A covenant, my brothers and sisters, is the agreement between God and his people. These are the most sacred of promises. True marriage is a covenant—between a man and a woman who speak their sacred oaths before God. That covenant makes a three-strand cord, which is not easily broken. We see this proven in stories from scripture, but also in the lives of believing brothers and sisters who make this sacred commitment to live their lives as one." When Sam finished his sermon, Mrs. Garland began to play the hymn "Blest Be the Tie that Binds."

At the close of the service, Sam walked to the pulpit again and said, "Dear friends, we ask ya to stay for a while longer. Our brother and sister in the Lord, Kell Kincaid and Hannah Murphy, would like ya to witness their marriage."

Mrs. Garland began to play an unfamiliar piece of music that reminded Hannah of a tune Kell sometimes played on his violin. She continued to play until Brother Sam had brought the couple and their witnesses to the altar. Hannah carried her Bible in lieu of flowers. In the depth of winter, few flowers were available. When she and Kell stood side by side in front of the dais, he handed her a small, dried bouquet of white heather and thistle tied with the tartan plaid of his clan.

"Hannah, my mother sent these to ya. If we'd wed in June, they'd be fresh and beautiful, but my mum said no bride should wed without this blessin', so she asked me to give these to ya. It's a wee bunch of posies, but the meaning is large—the white heather and thistles are the omen for blessings in marriage."

"They are very pretty, Kell. I'll write to thank her for thinking of me." Hannah replied.

Brother Sam Naylor conducted the traditional wedding ceremony. He solemnly asked Kell and Hannah to speak their vows to each other, stressing the nature of the covenant once more. Kell placed a wide gold band on Hannah's hand, another gift from his mother to his bride. Strangely, though, Sam did not complete the ceremony at this time.

"Will a member of the Kincaid family bring forth the tartan plaid of the Kincaid clan?" Ben rose from his seat and carried a three-foot length scarf of hunter green, black, and red plaid to Kell, who wrapped the scarf around his own wrist and then around Hannah's. Sam Naylor tied the scarf in a knot.

Then Sam asked a representative of the Kennedy Family to bring her family tartan to the altar. Mary Lee Naylor picked up a scarf of a lighter shade of green, red, and white plaid, and she carried it to the altar and handed the cloth to Hannah.

"Kell, where did that come from? I've never seen the tartan of the Kennedys. I didn't know my family had a tartan."

"The Lord provides, my dear," Kell said.

Hannah repeated the act she'd seen Kell perform.

"Now that you have accepted the bond of each other's family in the Hand Fastening, Kell, I ask you to pin the tartans with your family crest," Sam said.

Kell removed the gold crest from his shoulder and placed it to connect the two tied tartans that bound their wrists. "Hannah Ruth Kennedy, I vow to you, our family, and all who are in our home, 'This I Will Defend'."

Hannah gazed into Kell's eyes. The depth of his love was so clear. For the first time in her life Hannah belonged with another person. A profound sense of security brought tears to her eyes.

Sam Naylor then turned to the piano and picked up a pewter cup with a handle on each side. He handed it to Ben.

"Hannah, we welcome you to the Kincaid clan." Ben handed her the cup. Kell nodded that she was to drink from the cup. She sipped the dark liquid. She then offered the cup to Kell, who drank from the opposite side of the cup.

Sam Naylor then stood before them once again. "As you have spoken covenant vows, accepted each other into the families from which you hailed, and have shared the Quiach, I will complete the marriage ceremony.

"May joy and peace surround you. Contentment latch your doors. And Happiness be with you now and blessings evermore. In the presence of these witnesses and in the name of our blessed Savior, I pronounce that you are man and wife. What God has joined, let no man put asunder."

Ben approached them once again. He handed Hannah a well-worn sword. "Hannah, a gift from Kell's father to your first son. We give it to you to present on his tenth birthday." He laid it at her feet.

Kell and Hannah stood holding hands, still tied with their tartan colors. Neither seemed able to move.

After a minute, Sam said, "Well, Kell, it's customary to kiss your bride." And he did. They stepped across the sword, and thunderous applause broke out. People rushed forward to congratulate the newlyweds. At the same time, others converted the church into a party site. The community came together to provide a celebration. Within minutes, tables were laden with food of all kinds. Hot cider, cocoa, and coffee steamed on the wood stove. At the center of the table stood a beautiful two-tiered cake with the top layer being much smaller than the bottom. Rachel Miller had baked a traditional Scottish wedding cake with a smidge of brandy from the recipe sent by Kell's mother. The bottom layer would be shared with their guests, but the smaller one would go home with them for their wedding supper.

The feasting and dancing lasted for more than three hours. Kell danced every waltz with Hannah. Finally, the little band and Mrs. Garland played the music for the Lang Reel. All the couples lined up down the center of the floor. Kell and Hannah were pushed to the end of the line. Each round, a couple in the line left the floor, and the music became faster and faster. The couples seemed to disappear in a flash until Kell and Hannah were the only two remaining in the center of the sanctuary.

Brother Sam called the group to prayer, asking a special blessing on the marriage of Hannah and Kell. He ended with a benediction, "May the road rise up to meet you. May the wind be always at your back. May the sun shine warm upon your face, and the rain fall soft upon your field. And until we meet again, May God hold you in the palm of His hand."

The congregation replied, "Amen."

"Now, Kell Kincaid, take your pretty bride out of here. It's getting' nigh on time for Sunday evenin' Bible class. Of course, if ya want to stay…" The last words were spoken as Kell and Hannah hurried to their buggy.

φ

The three-mile ride home was a perfect ending to the beautiful wedding Kell had planned and carried out with the help of Sam Naylor and Ben. Even the cold proved no drawback. Kell had arranged with Aaron Pierce to have Graystoke ready to pull the buggy where he had placed warm blankets and heated bricks for their feet.

Kell lifted his new bride into the seat, nestled her in the quilt, and jumped into the other side and immediately pulled her into an embrace. He then flipped the reins across the great gray stallion's back. "Take us home, boy." Kell pulled Hannah to him for a quick kiss. "My darlin', I can't believe you are mine—for all time, you are my wife."

They hardly got out of Linden before lacy snowflakes gracefully swirled in front of them.

"It's so beautiful out here tonight. Did you arrange the dancing snowflakes, too?" Hannah asked.

"Surely did, my love. I asked my Lord to give us the perfect weddin' day. He threw in this night as a bonus."

"The day has been perfect. Having Sam combine our traditional wedding vows with the customs of your homeland has made our day so very special. I've never seen a wedding ceremony with so much meaning. I doubt we could ever undo all those 'knots' if we tried."

"You're a beautiful bride, Hannah. Ya need never worry. I'll never want to untie even one of those vows. Thank you for returning

469

the memories of our courtship. I love ya dressed in that blue gown. That was the image I carried with me the entire time we were parted."

"I never considered anything else. I remember so well that first time we danced together. Even then, when I was trying to push you away, I felt drawn to you. You always made me feel that I belonged when I was in your arms."

"Ya do. And that's where you'll be for the rest of our days."

"I love you, Kell."

"Those are precious words, lass…to be loved by the one who owns your heart. God can grant only one greater favor."

The drive was over before Hannah realized they'd reached home. Soft light glowed from all the windows. As they reached the porch, Lijah Kincaid met them.

"Welcome home, Mrs. Kincaid. Blessin's to you and Mr. Kell." Elijah took the reins from Kell. "I'll take Graystoke to the barn and bed him down. I don't 'spect you'll be needin' him any more tonight."

"Thank you, Elijah. So good of you to meet us tonight."

"All us Kincaids wish the best for this new Kincaid family." He took the stallion and buggy as Kell lifted Hannah to the porch as she carried the top tier of their wedding cake, which they would share with their supper.

"Kell, what else have you planned?" Obviously, nothing had been left to chance on this day.

"People wanted to show us their love, so I let them."

As they entered Hannah's day room, a blazing fire in the fireplace greeted them. The room was toasty warm and lit with many candles along with three low-glowing lanterns. The room had been outfitted with a small sofa, a beautiful rocking chair, and an elegantly carved walnut lady's secretary that stood beside two floor-to-ceiling bookcases filled with scores of books. Side tables holding opalescent hobnail lanterns completed the furnishings of Hannah's room.

"I know now why I've seen so little of you this past week. You've made this space a wonderful place to rest and read..."

"And sit nestled next to the fire."

"It's all too wonderful." Hannah moved from one point in the room to the next, looking at everything. An aroma from the kitchen filled the room. "Do you smell that?"

Kell answered, "Something tells me our wedding supper awaits us, milady." He took her arm. As they opened the door, they saw a table set for two. On the stove, they found ham, green beans, and steaming baked potatoes. Warming on the back of the stove, they found creamy gravy to smother the meat and potatoes. In the warming oven, a freshly baked loaf of bread waited to be slathered with butter. Hannah placed the top tier of their wedding cake in the center of the table, poured piping hot cups of coffee, and sat next to Kell.

"Father, thank you for answering my every prayer today. This has been a perfect wedding day. Father, keep our covenant vows always before us. And bless our friends who helped make our day so fine. Please bless this meal. We ask it all in Jesus' name. Amen."

Easy, comfortable conversation took them through their wedding cake dessert at the end of the excellent meal. Shortly, they found themselves nestled together on the new sofa before the roaring fire. "Well, Mrs. Kincaid, tell me about your favorite part of this magnificent day."

"How could one thing be more special than another?" Hannah said.

"I did notice one thing during our vows that worried me. I saw tears on your lashes. Did something unpleasant cross your mind?"

"No, Kell. That was probably the most meaningful part of the Scottish rites. That part with the 'Hand Fastening' did surprise me because we hadn't talked about it."

"Did you find it unpleasant, lass?"

"No. Where did you find my family tartan? I'd never seen it."

"I'll tell ya about the Kennedy clan sometime, but it's not a tale for our weddin' day. Will ya tell me what brought on the tears? I wanted this day to be full of joy and happiness for ya, but when I saw the tears…"

"Darling, that was the most memorable part. When we finished the 'Hand Fastening', I sensed a belonging that I'd searched for my entire life. At that moment, I belonged with you—I was part of a family. I've never known that sense of security before in my life. At that moment, I knew I was loved."

"Hannah, you knew I loved ya before we parted."

"I knew, Kell, in my head, I knew. Now my heart knows, and my soul knows—like surrendering to the Lord and knowing you belong to God's family. To feel love is so much more than just knowing. I thank you for both…your love has not only provided me with a husband I love in return, but your love helped me find my way to faith."

Kell didn't respond to Hannah immediately. His storm-blue eyes searched hers. After a time, he pulled her closer. "I am the most blessed of men, Hannah Ruth. It is my prayer that from this night forward, we will always share our souls. What a gift ya have given me tonight."

"Let this be our covenant, Kell. We will always bear our hearts to each other so we will truly be one."

With tears on his cheek, Kell kissed Hannah with a passion neither of them had known before.

"Now I want you to take me to our marriage bed and make love to me." Hannah did not look away as she spoke the words to Kell.

"Hannah, are ya certain?"

"You told me once no man had ever made love to me. I believe you. I want you to be that man."

"Hannah, we became one this mornin'. I've no greater need or want than to make love with you."

Kell pulled her into a passionate kiss once again. Then he lifted Hannah into his arms and carried her up the broad stairway to the room he'd claimed as his own—their master bedroom.

"Lass, I dinna carry ya across the threshold downstairs because this is your house. But this room as mine. I claim that privilege now." He kissed Hannah, pushed the door open, and carried his bride across the threshold into the new life they would build together.

Patricia Clark Blake
Christian, Arkansan, Author, Educator

Patricia Clark Blake is a lifelong educator. Now retired from the Arkansas public school system, she spends her time writing and reading in her favorite genre, historical fiction. She holds degrees from Arkansas State University in English, Reading Education, and Counseling Psychology. During her career, she

taught students from seventh grade to master-level college students.

Known as Pat to her friends, Blake has published in juried psychological journals, but the Shiloh Saga novels are her first attempts at writing fiction. Her proposal for 'Til Shiloh Come won an award from the Blue Ridge Christian Novel Competition in 2016. This proposal eventually became The Shiloh Saga: In Search of Shiloh, The Dream of Shiloh, Beyond Shiloh, Shadows Over Shiloh, and 'Til Shiloh Come. These books are the story of a frontier family carving out a life in the new state of Arkansas, beginning in 1857 with an arranged marriage and ending with the close of the Civil War. In 2022, 'Til Shiloh Come took second place in a national readers competition, **The Angel Awards**. The same novel was awarded second place in the **Blue Lake Writers** Competition in 2022.

The new novel, <u>No Man's Chattel</u> is the sixth book by Blake. Unlike the Shiloh Saga, this book, recounting the struggle through reconstruction, is a single volume. Like her other works, this new book contains a great deal of history and a positive picture of Arkansas people.

Pat is passionate about genealogy and loves being an Arkansan. Both have been wonderful resources for her writing. She resides near the Greensboro community, a town frequently mentioned in the Shiloh Saga. Greensboro, no longer a town, is adjacent to Jonesboro, Arkansas.

Her best gift to the world is her daughter, Tara, to whom she has dedicated this book. Tara and her family, Kennedy, Noah, and Kinley are her greatest treasures. Her career in education, her writing, and her family have been blessings from God.